Leo

Also by Deon Meyer

Dead Before Dying
Dead at Daybreak
Heart of the Hunter
Devil's Peak
Blood Safari
Thirteen Hours
Trackers
7 Days
Cobra
Icarus
Fever
The Woman in the Blue Cloak
The Last Hunt
The Dark Flood

Leo

Deon Meyer

*Translated from Afrikaans
by K. L. Seegers*

HODDER &
STOUGHTON

First published in Great Britain in 2024 by Hodder & Stoughton Limited
An Hachette UK company

1

Copyright © Deon Meyer 2024

A CIP catalogue record for this title is available from the British Library

Hardback ISBN 978 1 529 37558 9
Trade Paperback ISBN 978 1 529 37559 6
ebook ISBN 978 1 529 37560 2

Typeset in Plantin Light by Manipal Technologies Limited

Printed and bound in Great Britain by Clays Ltd, Elcograf S.p.A.

Hodder & Stoughton policy is to use papers that are natural, renewable
and recyclable products and made from wood grown in sustainable forests.
The logging and manufacturing processes are expected to conform
to the environmental regulations of the country of origin.

Hodder & Stoughton Limited
Carmelite House
50 Victoria Embankment
London EC4Y 0DZ

www.hodder.co.uk

For Marianne
With love

Leos tend to be full of primal, creative energy. This is a sign that embodies the fire that lives within us all.
www.mindbodygreen.com

The desire of gold is not for gold. It is for the means of freedom and benefit.
Ralph Waldo Emerson

The desire for gold is the most universal and deeply rooted commercial instinct of the human race.
Gerald M. Loeb

Rooikat
(Caracal caracal)
Benny & Vaughn

I

Anjané van Tonder sat in the charge office of the Stellenbosch police station. Her right hand was gripping a large iPhone as if her life depended on it.

On the other side of the weathered government-issue wooden table, two detectives were seated on equally battered government-issue wooden chairs. They had introduced themselves as Warrant Officers Benny Griessel and Vaughn Cupido. Together they bent their heads to study the statement she had just painstakingly completed. In meticulously neat handwriting. Grammatically correct. Factual. They were frowning.

She was twenty years old, she had written. In her second year of a bachelor's degree in Arts and Literature majoring in Afrikaans and Dutch, and General Linguistics. She lived at Minerva Residence for Women.

She had been robbed.

Anjané was an attractive young woman, with long straight blond hair, big hazel eyes and a flawless complexion. The pursed rosy lips hinted at her frustration. Because these two – and this stark, sterile space – made her uncomfortable.

Firstly: why were they shaking their heads, as if they didn't understand her statement? It was all clearly laid out.

Secondly: the Griessel detective looked . . . unreliable. Strange eyes. Almond-shaped and dark. And melancholy. Not heartsore-sad. Just melancholy. His hair was dishevelled. Too long for a man of his age. A face with some mileage to it. Rough mileage, booze mileage. His crumpled shirt and jacket screamed *Pick n Pay Clothing* over the middle-aged *dad bod*.

Thirdly: the Cupido guy looked like a much better proposition. Strong and athletic and good-looking, even if the snow-white shirt stretched tightly over his midriff. Smartly dressed, hair short and precisely shaven. But the man had an attitude. Faintly superior.

She'd noticed, when they entered, the look he threw his colleague. One that said: Here we go again.

She had rights. She was the victim of a devious crime.

The Griessel dude looked up from the complaint form. 'Miss,' he said, 'what exactly did they steal from you?'

'Not "they". Kayla Venter. She stole my IP.'

'Your eye pee?' Cupido asked, puzzled.

She raised her eyes heavenward, as if seeking help from above. 'My I. P.' She repeated the letters slowly and clearly. 'It stands for intellectual property.'

They stared at her blankly.

Her heart sank. How unlucky could a girl be? The two dimmest light bulbs in the police chandelier, and she was the one to get them.

The Griessel guy said: 'Okay. Miss, can you tell us the story from the start? In your own words.' A touch of exaggerated patience in his voice, which she did *not* need.

'My statement is literally in my own words,' she said.

'We're just not feeling it, miss,' said Cupido. 'Please. Just take it from the top.'

She drew a slow deep breath to calm down. 'I posted an Insta story,' she said. 'Yesterday. And Kayla Venter stole my intellectual property.'

'An Insta story?' said Griessel.

'Instagram?' she said. 'You *do* know about Instagram?' She clicked on her phone.

'Yes, we know Instagram,' said Cupido.

'Great. So, I posted this story on Instagram . . .' She swiped her phone screen with her thumbs, and turned it to face the detectives, letting the Insta story play.

Victoria Street, the road that runs through the heart of the university campus. The camera following a young woman walking. Long red hair, a short dress, athletic legs. Music too, ominous and threatening. As the redhead walked on unawares, words appeared on the screen, one after the other, in dramatic cursive:

Rooikat.
Ear.
Rooikat.

Hear.
Rooikat.
Disappear.

The image faded to black.

She looked at them expectantly.

'That's your Insta story . . .?' the Griessel one asked.

'That's right. And then . . .'

'But what does that mean?' Cupido asked, pointing at her phone.

'It's a poem,' she said.

'I get that. But what does it mean?'

'It's an allegory.'

'Still not with you.'

She sighed. She should have known. 'An allegory is a poem that says one thing, but it also has a deeper meaning. A rooikat is a sly creature. It steals sheep and it has very big ears, there's something like sixteen tiny muscles just to make the ears move. So, the poem just talks about a rooikat that can hear very well, but that won't save it. It can still disappear. And the deeper meaning is, Kayla Venter can try spreading gossip about me – which isn't true – but she will lose.'

'The girl in the video is Kayla Venter?'

'She is.'

'And then she stole your IP?'

'She did. And I have the proof,' said Anjané. 'Look . . .' She tapped on the phone again, showed them the screen. 'She took my story and she changed it and she posted it . . .'

The same video. The same music. The same words. Until just before the end. Before the word 'Disappear', 'NEVER' appeared in blood-red letters.

'How can you steal a video that you are in yourself?' asked Cupido.

'The poem,' said Anjané. 'She stole my poem. My IP.'

They stared at her again. Like a pair of village idiots.

The Griessel fellow's phone rang. He took it out, then said to her, 'Excuse me, I have to take this.' And answered: 'Colonel?'

'What are you going to do about this?' Anjané asked Cupido.

'We'll come right away, Colonel,' Griessel said on the phone, and rang off.

'Miss,' Cupido said in a serious tone, 'intellectual property cases are way above our pay grade.'

She'd thought as much. 'Now who can help me?'

'Vaughn, the colonel wants to see us in his office,' said Griessel. They both stood up.

'Miss,' he said, 'our best advice is to rather consult a lawyer. One specialising in copyright. This thing is more of a civil affair.'

'Then you can sue Kayla Venter,' said the Cupido one. 'For a lot of money. That should teach her a lesson.'

'But will you excuse us,' said the Griessel one. 'Our commander wants to see us.'

'Good luck, miss,' said Cupido.

'Goodbye,' said Griessel.

They walked out.

She could swear she heard the Cupido guy laugh, but she wasn't absolutely sure.

★   ★   ★

In the car Cupido said: 'What have we done wrong now, Benna?'

'Nothing,' said Griessel, 'so far as I know.'

'How did he sound?'

'You know Witkop. He always sounds the *moer in.*'

'Was he regular the *moer in,* or extra special?'

'Sounded like regular.'

'And he said "you must come *now*"?'

'He just said he wants to see us as soon as possible.'

'Benna, I think this is it . . .'

'What?'

'The Hawks want us back, partner. That's what I scheme. No more IP theft, stolen bicycles and lost cell phones. Back to the big time, *pappie.* At last.'

'I don't know, Vaughn . . .'

'Trust my instincts, Benna. Trust my instincts.'

★   ★   ★

Griessel and Cupido jogged down the corridor of the first floor of the South African Police Services' Stellenbosch detective offices, three kilometres west of the Eikestad charge office.

Cupido knocked.

'Yes,' said the voice from inside.

They went in.

Lieutenant Colonel Waldemar 'Witkop' Jansen was the detective branch's commanding officer. He was close to retirement age, a small and grumpy grey-haired terrier with a snow-white Chaplin moustache. He scowled from behind his desk, but they knew it wasn't necessarily a reflection of his mood.

'Morning. Sit,' said Jansen.

They greeted him and sat down.

'When you transferred here, from the Hawks, I thought you were two arrogant *windgatte*,' said the colonel.

They waited.

'I was wrong. Your work is good. Your dockets are by the book. Now, receive me clearly, I can't promote you yet. You stay warrant officers. But I'm going to move you. To S and V.' Serious and Violent Crimes was the only specialist team at the Stellenbosch Detective Unit.

'Thank you, Colonel,' said Griessel.

Cupido was disappointed. He said nothing.

'*Ja*, don't be too grateful. It's twenty-four hours on call, seven days a week. No more of only every fourth week on standby. Our S and V team is still understaffed, you will have to carry a heavy load. You receiving me?'

'*Ja*, Colonel.'

'You up for it?'

Cupido stood to attention. 'Colonel, that is how we roll. That is how we worked at the Hawks too,' he said. 'Day and night. And they are going to take us back any day now, and we will be working like that in any case.'

'Chances are not good,' said Jansen.

'Colonel?'

'Sounds like you haven't heard yet . . .'

'Heard what, Colonel?' Griessel asked.

'Brigadier Manie. Top dogs have pushed him out. Probably because he's an honest policeman.'

Brigadier Musad Manie was the commander of the DPCI – the Directorate of Priority Crime Investigations, generally known as the Hawks – in the Western Cape while Griessel and Cupido were attached to that elite unit.

'*Jissis*,' said Vaughn Cupido.

'The service has become a swamp,' said Jansen, 'and the *skarminkels* in Pretoria are pulling us deeper into it. We thought state capture[1] was over. But they are still sitting there. The corrupt ones. Behind the scenes. Never thought I would be so glad to retire.'

It was the first time that they had heard Witkop Jansen say a negative word about the police. They sat in silence, shocked.

'So?' asked Jansen eventually. 'Are you ready for S and V?'

---

[1] State capture is the illicit control of the state for personal gain by corporations, the military, politicians, etc, through the corruption of public officials.

Brown Hyena
(Parahyaena brunnea)
Christina Jaeger

2

What do you do if a lion charges you?

It was one of the women who asked, in her Texan accent.

Nine Americans, late at night around the campfire deep in the Okavango. Four middle-aged couples and a sprightly widow in her late sixties. Above them the Milky Way hung suspended, the dome of the night-sky cathedral. But the tourists' attention was not on the breathtaking firmament. Their eyes were fixed on Christina, their field guide. They called her 'Chris'. Or 'Chrissie'. A lovely young woman in the fire's soft light, highlighting her honeyed complexion, long plait of black hair down her back, her elegant neck and cheekbones.

Chrissie smiled. Foreigners always asked that question. Casually, the tone hinting that they weren't scared. Merely curious.

She said, 'If you run, you'll only die tired.' She waited for the ripple of nervous laughter to subside. Then she explained to them that Usain Bolt could run at forty-four kilometres per hour. Forty-three point nine nine to be exact. A lion could reach eighty kilometres per hour.

Chrissie was a seasoned and skilful storyteller. She knew the value of the pause in a story. So she waited until only the crackle of the fire and the frogs' hearty chorus could be heard.

She said a lion's charge was mostly for show. A test. His roar was deafening, very intimidating. He wanted to terrify you, put you to flight. And if you fled, you were cat food.

'What you do is confront him.' She stood up from the camp chair. Planted her hiking boots wide, lifted both arms high, opened her palms. 'You become the biggest version of yourself that you can possibly be. You roar back at him. As loud as you can. Clap your hands. Show no fear. He'll stop charging. They always do. When he stops, you start moving backwards. Very, very slowly. Always facing the animal. If he moves, you freeze. If he stops, you withdraw.'

They were hanging on her every word.

She slowly lowered her arms. Sat down. 'The trick,' she said, 'is to allow them to retreat with dignity. You know, like men in general.'

They laughed again, as they always did. At the joke and the release of lion-fuelled tension. She knew what the next question would be: 'How many times have you been charged by a lion?' About four or five times, she would answer. Then, as was her way, she would reach for the hunting rifle, the Ruger Hawkeye. And say she had been working at Letsatsi Lodge for four years. She had never needed to fire the weapon. But she always carried it with her. And she knew how to use it. Tomorrow morning they could relax and enjoy their walking safari. They would be completely safe.

Before the question had been asked, Chrissie became aware of movement, a presence on the edge of the fire-lit circle. A vaguely remembered silhouette, a half-familiar tread. She turned her focus towards it. And recognised the face from her past.

Her heart began to beat a little faster.

The man in the half-light nodded at her. A subtle signal, a gesture that said: I am here to see you. Then he disappeared behind the *lapa*'s pole fence, in the direction of the bush pub.

★　★　★

Rousseau. Ian or Ivan. Something like that. He used to work for Ehrlichmann in Zimbabwe back in the day. Seven, eight years ago. Ex-soldier. Tall, big shoulders and hands, quiet and kept to himself. She'd liked him.

She pondered on this as she finished her campfire chat with the Americans. Then she excused herself and went to find him.

He was sitting with half a beer remaining, stood up when she entered. She recognised the same pale blue eyes, short reddish-brown beard. 'Hello, Flea,' he said with a polite smile.

It was odd to hear that name again. She let it pass for now. 'Rousseau,' she said. 'What are you doing here?'

He waited until she sat down beside him: 'Do you want something to drink?'

'No, thank you.'

He nodded, slowly picked up his beer and took a sip. Looked at her. 'I have a job offer.'

She raised her eyebrows.

Rousseau checked to see if the barman was within earshot. 'We want to steal twenty million dollars,' he said, quietly, so only she could hear. 'And we need you.'

She looked intently at him, scanning for any sign that he was joking. Until she felt the slight shock of adrenaline. He was serious.

'Who is "we"?' she asked.

'Me and Brenner and two others. With you we will be five.'

Brenner. She remembered Brenner. She'd been wary of him. 'Why me?'

'We're going to need a honey trap. And a cool head. And we hope you still have contacts to exchange the dollars.'

'I don't know . . . They are very old contacts.'

'We have a Plan B. Bit risky, so it will be great if you can try . . .'

'Whose dollars are they?'

'That's what makes it so good. There are no victims. It's part of the Chandas' stolen state capture money. They couldn't get it out of the country.'

She knew about the three Indian businessman brothers who'd allegedly helped to loot her birth country, in cahoots with the former president. It was the hottest topic of conversation for all the South Africans who came here nowadays.

'Where is the money?'

'You'll have to say first if you're in,' he said with an apologetic smile.

His eyes were sadder than she remembered. There was a scattering of pepper and salt in his beard.

'How long do I have to think about it?'

'What time does the hopper arrive tomorrow?' He was referring to the Cessna Caravan that flew tourists and supplies in and out daily.

'Ten o'clock.'

He nodded. That was how long she had to decide.

She suddenly recalled his first name.

'Igen,' she said. 'My name is Christina now. Chrissie.'

'And your surname?'

'Jaeger.'

He ruminated on it. 'Chrissie. Jaeger.' Then: 'I like it.'

'Is Ehrlichmann still alive?' she asked.

3

She lay on her bed with her earphones on, listening to Nigel Kennedy playing Beethoven's violin concerto. She was deep in thought.

After midnight she picked up the rifle, walked down to the water. She took one of the *mokoro*s and began poling it eastwards. The moon was a crescent just above the horizon.

She thought about Ehrlichmann.

Igen Rousseau said he'd been shot by ivory poachers. More than a year ago, just south of Kariba.

So their numbers dwindled. The generation of conservationists who had grown up in a more pristine Africa. Whose love for this continent and its wildlife was a consuming fire. Who believed that they could still save it all.

Like her father.

Ehrlichmann had sat down beside her during the WWF elephant census. They drank coffee together, watched the sun rise, listened to the birds waking up. Then he said quietly, full of compassion: 'I knew your father. I thought Louis van Jaarsveld was the most brilliant tracker I ever encountered.'

She didn't answer.

'And I think you will be even better than him.'

That was before she tried to smuggle the diamonds.[2]

She had wondered what Ehrlichmann would think of her then. Because eventually they would all have found out about it – him and his companions. That was why they wanted to recruit her now for The Big Robbery.

She heard a hippo snort, blowing air out as it surfaced in the next channel. She wasn't worried about them. It was the giant crocodiles that bothered her.

---

[2] See the novel *Trackers* (2011) for complete details.

It took her another twenty minutes to reach the sandy beach where they had eaten her father.

She dragged the *mokoro* out, turned it over. She sat down on it, rifle across her knees.

'I've come to say goodbye, Pa,' she said.

4

The first meeting with her co-conspirators felt surreal, like an out-of-body experience.

A middle-class house in Rooihuiskraal, Pretoria. She rang the front doorbell, heard children in the yard next door laughing and kicking a ball around. She hadn't left the Okavango for four years, so to be back in a city again felt strange and pleasant and disconcerting all at the same time.

Brenner opened the door. Wearing a white T-shirt and rugby shorts. Barefoot. He looked pretty much the same in her eyes. The wrinkles on his face perhaps a bit deeper, but he was still lean and fit. The short-cropped hair, stubble beard. Intense eyes. The alpha male. He was an ex-Special Forces soldier, and he still kept that aloofness. The aura.

His smile was thin, just as she remembered. But still a faint hint of warmth, a controlled concession to nostalgia. 'Christina Jaeger,' he said as if he wanted to memorise the name. He had known her as Cornél van Jaarsveld, in those days. She couldn't remember whether he had ever called her 'Flea'.

'Brenner,' she greeted him.

'Glad you're here. Come through, we're in the back.'

He looked at the rucksack she was carrying. 'You can leave that here,' he said, pointing at the couch. 'No, it's okay,' she said and followed him through the lounge and the kitchen. A man's house. Practical. Painfully tidy. Painfully suburban.

Out through the back door. The other three were sitting in the yard on garden chairs. She smiled inwardly. How very South African – planning a robbery around the altar of the *braai*. The fire crackled and smoke trailed lazily skywards, an offering of atonement to the gods of malfeasance. Beside the fire was a wire garden table laden with meat and *braai* sandwiches in iconic oval Hart aluminium roasting pans. She wondered who had made the sandwiches.

The three men stood up in unison. Igen Rousseau greeted her warmly. She didn't know the other two – a muscleman and a strange wiry figure. They looked at her with open curiosity.

She wondered what had been said about her before she arrived.

'This is Christina Jaeger,' Brenner said. 'She knows Ig. This,' he said, pointing at the muscular one, 'is Themba Jola. Themba was a Parabat, but I don't hold that against him.' The Xhosa man was wearing a sleeveless shirt, as bodybuilders always did, to best display the fruits of their labours in the gym. But she liked the way he shook her hand, with a broad and easy smile.

Beside Jola stood the peculiar figure. He had strongly East Asian features, but there were other genes in the mix. Long hair down to his shoulders, jet black and straight. From under the edge of the short sleeve of his shirt a dragon tattoo trailed down his arm. Physically smaller than the rest, yet he still had an intensity about him. 'Jericho Yon,' Brenner introduced him. 'Best bush pilot in Africa. We just call him "Jer".'

Yon nodded, his hair bouncing. Shook her hand with a soft grip. He has clever eyes, she thought.

Inside the house the doorbell rang. 'That'll be Nicky,' Brenner said. 'Sit down, I'll fetch him.' He walked towards the back door, then turned to say: 'No names while he's here.'

She took her rucksack off and put it next to the vacant chair beside Igen Rousseau, and sat down. 'Nicky?' she asked him. 'You said we were five.'

He smiled. 'Nicky is . . . Wait, don't let me spoil the surprise.'

* * *

Nicky was fat, thirty-something. He was wearing military boots, khaki camo trousers and a green T-shirt that stretched across his rather significant belly. He held a cigarette between his fingers. 'Howzit,' he said and fist-bumped each in turn.

'This is Nick Berry,' Brenner said. 'Nicky, you understand if I don't introduce anybody?'

'Better that way, better that way,' said Nicky. He reached Christina, drew deeply on his cigarette. '*Jissis*, you will do for a honey trap,' he said suggestively, his eyes on her breasts.

While Nicky found a seat, she gave Brenner a look that said: What's this idiot doing here?

'Nicky won't be taking part in the execution of the operation,' he said.

'I could be,' said Nicky. 'Any time, any place, I'm ready.'

Brenner was at the fire, stirring the coals. 'Tell them, Nicky. Tell them why you're here.'

5

As if he'd been waiting for his big moment, Nicky launched in: 'I saw the money. I was this far from the fucking money.' He gestured with his thumb and index finger less than a centimetre apart. Then he took a final drag on his cigarette and flicked it towards the fire.

He missed completely.

'Nicky works for Ace Security,' Brenner said. 'They guard the depot where the money is.'

'It's more of an old warehouse,' said Nicky, eager for the limelight. 'It was a large retailer's, back in the day. Then they made it into this, like, fortress. They divided it into these strongrooms, sort of mini-vaults, separated with helluva thick walls and *moerse* doors. There's other stuff in those vaults, not just the dollars . . .'

'Other stuff?' asked Jericho Yon with a frown. He sounded annoyed and his accent held slight Cape undertones. 'What other stuff?'

'I don't know, dude, we never saw the inside of the other vaults.'

'So how do you know there are dollars?'

'We're getting to that,' said Brenner.

Yon gave a slight nod. His hair barely stirred this time.

'Tell the story, Nicky,' said Brenner.

Fat Nicky's self-esteem was slightly dented. He took out a fresh cigarette, not looking at Yon while he spoke. 'So, we were four guys on a shift. Every shift is eight hours. And it's eight hours of doing fuck all, because nobody ever comes there, you just sit there talking shit with the animals and watching the camera and walking up and down the aisle.'

He snapped his Zippo open and lit the cigarette, snapped the lighter shut again. Deftly but deliberately, as though he'd practised.

'The aisle is a long passage between the vaults, and you wonder what's in them, 'cause nobody's breathed a word to you. But you know it's something, because the place is a fucking fortress. So one day we were on second shift, four o'clock to midnight, and at six o'clock HQ phoned to say a dude was coming to drop off a key at half past six. And another dude was coming at eight to get the key and check something in a strongroom. HQ gave us code names for them, then they had to come and give us the right code name. Romeo and Foxtrot. Romeo was not allowed in, he could just drop off the key. Foxtrot was the main mac, he was allowed in. He would go into the vaults, but we were not allowed to escort him, we had to stay in the control room. Cameras to be switched off. The control room is in front by the door. Helluva door, bulletproof one-way glass with a view of the parking lot. Beside the control room there's a kitchen and the bog. Anyway, half past six dude number one, Romeo, arrives and hands in a key. A big special key, with these holes in it. And we knew, the key would fit one of the strong-room doors, we just looked at it, we didn't do anything. And we waited for the eight o'clock Foxtrot dude, and the other guys on the shift went to make coffee, and one went to piss, and left me alone with the key, and I got an idea. I took pictures with my phone. Of the key, not the guy who was pissing,' Nicky said and waited for them to laugh.

Only Igen Rousseau smiled. Just to be polite, Chrissie thought.

Nicky sucked on his cigarette, blew out the smoke. 'Anyway, about a week later I took the photies to a pal of mine. He used to be a lock-smith, but now he installs motorised garage doors. But he still knows about it. He said no, that's a Z-Tech Chromium, it's heavy duty, high security, but check here, this is the serial number, clearly on the photo. You can order those keys online. But there's one, like, catch. If you just want to order the key, you have to have proof of purchase. For the whole lock. So I schemed, let me try. And I ordered two locks, *moer* expensive, nearly four thousand rand for the two. The proof of purchase was a fucking PDF file, and if you know what you're doing, it's fuck all to change a PDF. I faked it with the photie's serial number and waited a month and then I ordered the key.'

He crushed the cigarette under his heavy boot.

'And then I walked the aisle, every shift, and I would try another vault door. Every shift I tried one door. When I knew the other dudes were playing cards or making coffee or whatever. 'Cause you can't take the chance that the other dudes would see what you're doing on the CCTV. And so it was the fifth one. The fifth strongroom.

And I checked what was inside, and there was this fucking huge pile of dollars, all wrapped in plastic.'

'How do you know it's twenty million?' asked Yon, tossing his long black hair over his shoulder, his voice devoid of respect.

Chrissie shared that sentiment. She knew men like Nicky Berry. Too lazy or too dumb to be a policeman or a soldier, but seeing themselves as action men too – in uniform, often with a firearm on the hip, bragging about how brave they would be if they only had the chance.

'Dude, I did the math,' Nicky said. 'I measured the stack like this. It's a mix of hundreds and fifties and twenties. If it was just twenties, in that size, then that's already seven, eight million. But with the mix . . . I'm not saying it's exactly twenty million. It might be eighteen, or twenty-five. But it's still a shithouse full of money. Think of the exchange rate, dude. Just fifteen million dollars, times fifteen, that's two hundred and twenty million rand.'

She suppressed the impulse to shake her head. Nicky thought they would get the full exchange rate for the stolen dollars. They would be lucky to get five rand on the dollar. But that still came to seventy-five million rand. Divided by five people meant fifteen million each. More than enough.

She wondered what Nicky was going to get out of the whole business.

'Okay,' said Brenner. 'Thanks, Nicky. We'll excuse you now. You understand.'

Nicky stood up, very reluctantly. 'Okay. Cool.' He looked at Chrissie. 'Cheers,' he said. 'See you again.'

She didn't react, waited along with the others in the uneasy silence that settled as Nicky walked to the back door. Igen Rousseau and Themba Jola raised their hands to wave.

When the back door closed, Yon said: 'Ten per cent for that fat fuck. *Jissis.*'

6

Brenner spread the meat out on the folding *braai* grid. Chops and sausage. 'That's the price we're paying to keep him out of the operation,' he said.

'Where did you find him?' asked Christina.

Brenner smiled his thin smile. 'I was married to his sister.'

She hadn't known he'd been married.

'Even Recces fuck up some of the time,' said Themba Jola.

Brenner nodded. 'Doesn't work if you're never home. She's a sweet girl. Not like Nicky at all . . . He's the black sheep of her family.' He settled the *braai* grid over the coals, turned to Christina. 'He heard from my ex that I was back from Zim. He came to see me. With this proposition.'

'Probably wanted to lead this Op too,' said Jericho Yon.

Christina felt uneasy about Nicky's involvement. 'If the Chandas hear their money's been stolen . . . They'll look at the security guys first. They'll know it's an inside job.'

'Good point,' said Igen Rousseau. 'But firstly, "they" . . .' he said, making air quotes with his fingers, '. . . aren't going to report it to the police. It's stolen government money. Secondly, Ace Security rotates their people. Nicky hasn't been working at the depot for four months. There would be no reason to suspect him.'

'He's the sort of idiot who would take his ten per cent and splash it on flashy cars and girls,' said Yon. 'I know his vibe. He's a weak link.'

Brenner turned the grid over. 'Jer, there are risks. There always are.'

'It's how we manage it,' said Themba Jola.

'And if he begins blowing his money conspicuously . . . *I'll* manage it,' said Brenner.

'Four months since he was at the warehouse. How do we know the money is still there?' Christina asked.

'Because his Ace colleagues are still guarding the place.'

'How do we know it's the Chandas' money?' she asked.

'Remember Nicky telling us about the second man who came? Foxtrot? The one who picked up the key, the one who could go into the safe?'

'Yes.'

'Nicky said two weeks after that he was watching the news on TV. About the Zamisa Commission, the judge who investigated state capture and corruption. Next thing they were showing Foxtrot's photo, and they said his name is Ishan Babbar.'

She didn't recognise the name. 'Who?'

'Ishan Babbar,' said Brenner. 'He's . . .'

'A piece of work,' said Themba Jola.

'He worked for State Security,' said Brenner. 'Under the former president, Joe Zaca. Did all the dirty work. And the Zamisa Commission lawyers say he's the one who introduced Zaca to the Chandas. Middleman, and everyone's enforcer.'

'How certain is Nicky that it was him?'

'Dead certain.'

'An enforcer?' she asked.

'If you don't do what the Chandas want, they send Babbar to encourage you,' Rousseau said.

'Or eliminate you,' said Brenner.

'Is he the one who will investigate the robbery?' Chrissie asked.

'Yip. But there's no way he will find us.'

'Unless Fatty fucks us over,' said Jericho Yon.

'I'll handle it,' said Brenner.

7

They ate inside, around the table.

The men talked sport. Rugby and soccer.

She still questioned herself: What am I doing here? Between these men and the chutney and tomato sauce and white paper serviettes.

She trusted Rousseau and Brenner because Ehrlichmann had trusted them.

And she had trusted Ehrlichmann because of what her father had said about him. That he had integrity. That he wanted to conserve and protect Africa's natural world for all the right reasons. Not for money or fame or a TV series on *National Geographic*. But because he loved it all so passionately.

She also trusted Ehrlichmann because, in the few months she had spent with him, she had seen that it was true.

Brenner pushed his empty plate aside. He placed his knife and fork precisely and looked around at the group. 'Okay, let's get to work. There are a few rules. Number one: cell phones. We – Ig and I – recruited each one of you personally; we never used your cell phone numbers. We will keep it that way. I'm going to give you each a new cell phone in a minute. You must never phone from it, use Telegram only. It's already installed on your phone. If you aren't familiar with it, it's a messaging app, encrypted, it's safe. Never send a message to anyone except one of us. Number two: no alcohol, no drugs. You can drink all you like when this is over, but until then, not a drop. Number three: no set routines. We will never meet twice at the same location. But try to vary your own routine too. Never the same coffee shop or restaurant or supermarket twice. And number four, I'm sure I don't really need to tell you: you don't talk to anybody about the operation. Any questions about the rules?'

Nobody had any questions.

Brenner nodded at Igen.

Rousseau said: 'D-Day is Saturday, April third. Why April third? It's Easter weekend. The security guys are going to be unhappy, not in the mood for work. If they sound the alarm, we hope the response will be slower than usual. We are aiming at eighteen hundred, when the shift has been on for two hours, with another four before the next shift arrives. Four hours to get as far away as possible. And April third means we have twenty-eight days from now. We think it's enough time to plan, rehearse, and get the vehicles. But the big question is . . .' He looked at her. 'Can you line up the dollar dealers in that time?'

'I'll have to go to Cape Town.'

Brenner and Rousseau exchanged a look.

'What?' Christina asked.

'We thought your contacts were in Zim,' Rousseau said.

'Or further north,' said Brenner.

She just shook her head, secretly grateful they knew so little about that time.

'Can you go tomorrow?' Brenner asked.

'Yes.'

'How quickly do you think you can tie it down?'

'I don't know. They are old contacts . . .'

'More than a week?'

'I hope not.'

'Okay,' said Rousseau. 'Let's clear the table. It's time to show you what we're dealing with.'

8

Rousseau had a file, blue as the African sky. He opened it, took out a few photographs.

They were of an unobtrusive single-storey building, somewhat dilapidated, in what appeared to be an industrial area. A broad tarred space in front of the building.

'This is the depot,' Rousseau said. 'In Spartan. Near Kempton Park.'

'Looks like a dump,' said Jola.

'I think that's exactly why they chose it,' said Jericho Yon.

'They also chose it because of the distance from the road,' said Rousseau. 'This section of tar was the parking lot, when it was still a warehouse. Look, there's the camera that covers the parking area. The security guards can see you coming a long way off. Towards the only entrance. They bricked up all the others. The entrance is a double door of steel and concrete. Beside the door – you can't see it very well from here, it's in the shade – is a window, about three metres wide, one metre above the ground. Double-glazed bullet-proof glass, one-way vision outwards. They can see you, but you can't see them. There's an intercom box below the window, so they can hear what you have to say while you are outside. The building is perfect for its purpose. There are no weak points . . .'

'What about the roof?' Themba Jola asked.

'Flat roof, reinforced concrete.'

'Okay.'

'The weakest link is the people,' said Brenner.

'The security men,' said Rousseau.

'Nicky says they are unmotivated, underpaid and over-confident. Bored. Nothing ever happens. Now and then a salesman will ring the intercom, they ignore it and wait until he leaves,' said Brenner. 'There are no deliveries, the stuff in the safes was there from the beginning. Nothing is ever removed, nothing is ever brought in.'

'They play poker, watch YouTube and porno on their phones, they make coffee or tea, eat and complain,' said Rousseau.

'And they talk about sex,' said Brenner.

'Apparently a lot,' said Rousseau.

'And that's what we are going to use.'

★   ★   ★

She wanted to call an Uber, but Rousseau said he would drop her off.

He drove a single-cab Toyota Hilux, ten years old or so, unflashy, inconspicuous. On the N1 past Doringkloof he asked: 'Why did you agree to this?'

She looked out the window at the slow-moving traffic. 'I trust you. You and Brenner.'

'No. I mean, why did you give up your Letsatsi job? You . . . It's your passion.'

'To take rich tourists with hangovers on walking safaris?'

'No, I mean, the bush. Africa . . . Sorry, probably none of my business.'

'I know what you mean,' she said. 'And it's okay.' She pointed outside, at the mass of crawling cars, the grimly staring people. 'Look. It's either this . . . This meaningless existence, this soul-destroying life of nine to five in a job you don't really like. And every year you owe the bank more, and it's load-shedding and roads with more potholes every day, and more broken traffic lights, you are literally watching your country and your world slowly imploding in front of you . . . Or you are a field guide in an African illusion. An illusion that only exists in pockets of reserves and in the minds of Americans and Europeans. The Africa of my father and Ehrlich-mann is dead. The pockets are shrinking. I want to leave before . . .'

'Before your heart breaks.'

'Yes. Before my heart breaks.'

9

On the plane she listened to Rossini's sonatas for strings and thought about Rousseau's question again.

Her answer was just the ear-tips of the truth-hippopotamus. Enough to divert him from the topic.

What if she told him the whole truth?

Would she have said: 'Igen, when you knew me seven years ago, my philosophy of life was "Fuck the world". That is what the world deserved. This world, that broke everything that was good and right and beautiful. Such as what? Like my father. This world betrayed and rejected and mocked my father. Because he was different. This world, breaking the planet. Destroying ecosystems. Devastating communities. I think about my father's stories a lot, about the time he was living with the Bushmen. The harmony, their compassion, respect for each other and the environment they survived in. It's gone, Igen, all gone. Not only the environment, the values too. Shattered. Gone.

'It was my "Fuck the world" that drove me to do stuff. No, that's not an excuse, it's just an exposition of what happened. And then when everything went pear-shaped, I had to go into hiding. Two years in Europe. Then four years in the Okavango, it became my refuge. Away from the wider world, nearer to what I knew and loved, and closer to my father.

'And so slowly I came to my senses. I processed the anger and pain. Regained my balance. Became comfortable. And bored, I have to confess. And then, a few months ago I read about the elephant cow, the last one of her kind remaining in the Knysna forest. The others had all been murdered. They started seeing the old cow again. The game warden photographed her. And he said it was if she was walking the forest trails searching. For her herd. It touched me deeply, in a strange way, Igen. Because she held out hope that she would find them. Can you imagine, the loneliness, the longing, how she grieved and still hoped. And you know, elephants do grieve. You were with Ehrlichmann long enough to see that with your own eyes.

'Then I wondered, why did I feel it so strongly, why did it make me so deeply sad? That's when I realised, Igen, that I am like her. I was there, in the Okavango, because I hoped, in one way or another, that I would find my herd. And then I realised I would not. My herd are dead. And I had to get out. But how? And then you came with your offer and I knew.

'That's why I said yes.'

She wondered what would Igen say to that?

It was part of the truth. But she would not tell him that, nor the full truth. Keep your weaknesses hidden. Because people are like the giggling spotted hyena. They search out your weakness. And unlike lions, where you can stand your ground and yell at them to go away, there was no escape if spotted hyenas hunted you in the dark.

★ ★ ★

It was six years since she had set foot in the Cape. The city had changed, and lost something in the process. A piece of its character, she thought. Some of the texture.

Altman's offices were on the corner of Loop and Riebeek, on the first floor of a pretty old Victorian double-storey. She knew he wouldn't willingly grant her an appointment, so she waited on the pavement at a coffee shop. Until lunchtime. Altman would not have changed. He was a lunchtime man, he had said expansively. He worked from early morning until one, and then enjoyed good food and good wine in a good restaurant. 'You've got to earn it, *ketzele*. And I earn it every day.' His words as she sat opposite him at the table and watched him slice through the bloody beef fillet.

She waited for one o'clock. She ordered decaf. And sipped it slowly.

She remembered seeing him the first time, and she thought: I was so fucked up, back then. Sore, hurting. So angry. So reckless and fearless.

It was synchronicity, back then. She hadn't known how she was going to sell the uncut diamonds. Until she by chance picked up the newspaper, a *Cape Argus* that someone had left at the Chizarira Airport in Zimbabwe. On the front page was a picture of the white lawyer and Coloured gang boss in front of the High Court in Cape Town. The caption read: *Lawyer David Altman and Restless Ravens leader Willem 'Tweetybird' de la Cruz, after their victory in the Cape High Court yesterday.*

Eight days later she was sitting in Altman's office with a proposition.

'Take off your clothes, *ketzele,*' he'd said to her.

'Fuck you.'

'I want to make sure you're not wearing a wire. Either you take off your clothes, or you get out of my office.'

So she undressed. Totally. His twirled his finger to show her to turn around. And then she saw the sly smile as her looked her up and down.

'Nice,' he'd said.

'Fuck you.'

Then she dressed again and they came to an agreement.

Angry, fucked up, reckless and fearless.

She'd asked him over lunch what *ketzele* meant. 'It's a Yiddish term of endearment. It means "kitten".'

The diamond affair was a mess.

She sipped her decaf and wondered what he would say when he saw her again.

IO

She walked along the sidewalk, trailing him.

He'd aged. The stride wasn't as self-assured, his curly hair had gone entirely grey. But the suit was still tailored, cufflinks shiny. She spoke his name and he turned around. For a second his face lit up at the sight of a pretty young woman, and then recognition slowly dawned. His bushy eyebrows rose and dropped, his mouth opened, eyes flashing with rage and dismay.

Eventually he said: '*Kusemeq,*' taking a step back.

'I have a proposition,' she said.

'Go away.' He turned and began walking up Loop Street, away from her. Not looking back.

She caught up and fell in step beside him. He was a head taller than her, but he looked shorter than she recalled. 'Twenty million dollars, in hundreds, fifties and twenties. I need someone who can trade. An electronic transfer in exchange for the cash.'

His pace slowed momentarily.

That was encouraging. 'I'll take eleven rand to the dollar,' she said.

He kept on walking. At the junction with Strand Street they had to wait for the traffic light. Other people around them. He didn't look at her.

The light turned green. He walked on. She walked with him. She gave him a chance to gather his thoughts.

Past Mad Macs Motorcycles, he paused. 'You almost got me killed. If they didn't shoot Tweetybird, they would have come for me.'

He was twisting the truth, but she let it pass. 'Ten rand to the dollar.'

He stared at her. 'You're something, *ketzele.* You're really something.'

She didn't react, just waited.

The look in Altman's eyes began to change, slowly. From rage to admiration. Till it was the same gaze as the day she'd stood naked in front of him. 'Want some lunch?' he asked.

★ ★ ★

The restaurant in Parliament Street was called FYN. The high ceiling and the lighting took her breath away.

The manager greeted Altman by name. Their table was next to the window. She looked through the menu.

'It's a big number,' he said. 'Twenty million.'

'But you're a big operator, David.'

'Is the money hot?'

'That's the beauty of it. Cold cash. There won't be any media headlines, no law enforcement attention.'

'My, my, you're not the little babe-in-the-woods *ketzele* any more, are you? How old are the notes?'

'Recent. Three to four years.'

He nodded. It was good news. 'I'll have to shop around. Split it up. It's too big for just one transaction.'

'I need one transfer. I show the cash, you make the transfer. Right there.'

'You won't get ten rand to the dollar. You'll be lucky if I get you four.'

'I can get eight-fifty,' she lied.

'Five.'

'No.' But she would take it if he refused to budge. It was fair, under the circumstances. And it meant they would get a hundred million rand. Eighteen million each, even after Nicky Berry got his ten per cent.

'Then I suggest you take your eight-fifty.'

'Okay.' She stood up.

'The food here is fantastic,' he said.

'Goodbye, David.'

'Six. Take it or leave it.'

She sat down again.

He smiled, pleased with himself. 'Have the gamefish sashimi. It's sublime.'

*   *   *

When they had finished eating, he wiped his mouth on the linen serviette, leaned back and looked at her. 'You remember that day at my office, when I told you to undress?'

She stared back at him.

'There is one thing I will never forget about that moment. Your eyes, *ketzele*. Now, don't get me wrong, the rest of you was spectacular. But your eyes . . . I had never seen such intensity. Such pure fury. That, I'll take that to my grave.'

II

Every fourth day she moved to a new Airbnb flat in Pretoria – Moreleta Park and Waverley, Lynnwood and Faerie Glen. Just herself and her rucksack and duffel bag. She used Uber, DiDi and Bolt.

The rucksack was ready to grab and run. Her survival pack. In the bottom, in a concealed, sewn-up bag, were three passports and enough foreign currency – euros and dollars – to live on for six months. On top of that, compactly and neatly folded, were two pairs of socks, a tightly rolled pair of tracksuit pants, two T-shirts, a bra, two pairs of panties and a thin windbreaker folded into its own bag. Then a cosmetics bag, toilet bag, sunglasses in a case, regular spectacles in a case, a box of tampons, her purse, a box with spare earphones and cables and a phone charger. And the phone. Mostly for music.

The duffel bag held the rest of her clothes.

In each new flat, in each new neighbourhood, she was aware of how strange it was to be here. She had never stayed longer than a few months in a city or town. The first two years of her life – with her mother – didn't count. She couldn't remember any of it. The two years at Alldays, before her mother died. While her father was tracking for hunting outfits in Botswana and Zimbabwe.

She couldn't remember a thing about her mother. And her father never wanted to talk about her.

It didn't matter.

Her father, Louis, came to fetch her. She grew up in the bush with him. The city was foreign to her, she didn't like it. People hid behind walls and electric fences, the streets deserted at night, lonely dogs barking, barking, barking.

Her first priority with each flat was to find a Woollies Food store. She got everything there. Then she sought out the closest gym, and went running on the treadmill, earphones playing Shostakovich or Tchaikovsky.

At night she would read. With Vivaldi or Corelli or Bach playing very quietly in the earphones, until sleep overcame her.

Occasionally she would think about the woman who introduced her to this music. Professor Inès Fournier, the French woman who studied brown hyenas in the Kalahari, and hired Louis van Jaarsveld as tracker for seven months.

Chrissie was eleven years old. Her real name was Cornél Johanna van Jaarsveld. Her father just called her Flea, because she was so small. Long skinny legs, with knobbly knees that mortified her. In the mornings she went out to the veld with him, in the afternoons she was home-schooled, despite her protestations, in the big tent. In the evening she had her books beside the fire, while Fournier's music played. The professor was wise. She didn't force herself and the music on Flea. But waited until Flea began to trust her and grow familiar with the notes. And when Flea began to ask questions about the music, the composers and the style, the eras from which it all came, Fournier answered her with stories. She told her how Edvard Grieg always carried a small cloth frog doll in his pocket for luck. How Mozart composed the breathtaking overture for *Don Giovanni* in a mere three hours – on the morning of the opera's debut, and while suffering a horrible hangover. Chopin was buried with a small flask of Polish soil. Beethoven would count out exactly sixty coffee beans every time he brewed himself a cup. Handel ordered enough food for three men every time, and would eat all of it. Dvořák loved trains. Her favourite was the story of Mozart and Beethoven meeting, when Ludwig was still young. The professor said that if ever they could travel back in time, that was where she wanted to go. To eavesdrop.

It was the closest Chrissie ever came to having a mother. She inherited both her love of music and an admiration for brown hyenas from Inès Fournier.

★ ★ ★

She went to Menlyn Park shopping centre to look for a dress, shoes and a handbag for the robbery. She saw young people constantly on their phones, and women dressed up to the nines, laden with shopping bags, mincing from shop to shop. Businessmen eating and drinking and looking her up and down with unwelcome interest.

People wandering, as if in a maze. Surrounded by canned music and canned air-conditioning and artificial light. I don't want to live like this, she thought.

She completed her purchases.

On the way out she popped into Exclusive Books to see if there was a new Azille Coetzee. There wasn't. She bought Sally Rooney's *Beautiful World, Where Are You* and Marida Fitzpatrick's *Mara*. She settled down at the Seattle Coffee Company with Rooney's book and a decaf cappuccino. She became aware of someone watching her. The woman was sitting at another table facing her. Attractive, late forties. Elegant, in a dress and high heels. Wedding ring on her finger. Chrissie looked up, and straight into her eyes. There was an undercurrent of desire. A gentle invitation. For a split second she considered it. To be held. Hands on her body. Skin touching skin. Mouth on mouth. An hour or two or three of slow, all-encompassing pleasure. It had been eleven months since she had had any kind of loving contact.

Not now.

She smiled, shook her head slightly. A little wry smile of regret in return.

Chrissie got up and left.

She wondered about the woman and her loneliness.

★ ★ ★

She found the wig in Struben Street in the city centre. The streets were busy, dirty, loud.

With a flood of relief she ordered an Uber and escaped to her flat.

12

Two weeks to D-Day.

They met at Jericho Yon's temporary flat in Lynnwood, eating rusks with instant coffee.

She felt less remote, more present.

Brenner said: 'Right, let's say Phase One was successful. Now we're in the building. Phase Two is loading the cargo. The biggest factor is the weight. Bank notes are heavier than you think. If all the money was in twenty-dollar bills, twenty million would weigh about one and a quarter tons. That's a helluva load for four people to shift . . .'

'Four people?' Themba Jola asked.

'Remember, Jer is in the Hino outside. He's the lookout, and he's monitoring the radio,' said Rousseau.

'Right,' said Jola. 'Makes sense.'

'Okay,' said Brenner. 'So, we take four trolleys along with us in the Hino, one for each. Just keep focus, do what you can do. Load up, push out, chuck in. As far back into the truck as you can. Don't worry about being tidy, speed is everything. Take your trolley, don't leave it behind, we load the trolleys in the back of the Hino too. Themba and I get in the back with the money, Ig and Chrissie take her Atos.'

He pulled the blue file closer and opened it, took out a Google Maps printout and pointed: 'Here is the warehouse.' He drew his finger along the route. 'We drive down Albatross Street to here, take the R21. Casually, some distance apart, there won't be much traffic. The Hino always in front so we have Ig and Chrissie as backup. We stay on the freeways, R21, then the N1, then the N4 here at Doornpoort, take the R511 through Brits. The airfield is here. It's about an hour and a half's drive. Wish it was otherwise, but that's where the plane is. There's nothing we can do. Our biggest risk is roadblocks, traffic cops wanting to test for alcohol. Chances are low on the freeways, only the last section on the R511 where that might happen, but we don't think it's likely. The Brits municipal speed cops won't want to work that time Saturday of the Easter weekend. But make sure you have your driver's licences with you, and the vehicles' rental paperwork. At worst they stop us and want to take a look in the back of the Hino. Plan A is for Chrissie to jump out of the Atos and create a scene. Call Ig a swine and say he's tried stuff with her, et cetera. If that doesn't work . . . We take ten thousand in cash with us. If bribery doesn't work, we take out our weapons. And then it's a question of handling things as they unfold.'

'A snafu there will be,' said Themba Jola with a sigh. 'There always is.'

'Not going to happen,' said Jericho Yon. 'I've been working at the Brits Aerodrome for more than a year now. Never seen a speed cop on a weekend.'

'The airfield has a gate with a lock. Jer has a key, Ig will have a spare in his pocket. The PC-12 is in the hangar there, the one furthest south.' He pressed a finger to the map. 'Themba and I open the hangar, you drive in, both vehicles, and you close the doors. We offload the money, we take the photo . . .'

'What photo?' asked Chrissie.

She saw Yon and Rousseau exchange a glance.

'We'll get to that,' said Brenner. 'We pack the money in boxes. The boxes all have a MedVet logo on them. It's a real pharmaceutical company. Each box has a label saying it's Horse Sickness vaccine. Then we weigh the boxes. Jer, tell them why.'

'The Pilatus PC-12,' Yon said, 'is a single-engine turboprop. Great plane. It belongs to the mine, the company I work for. With any plane it's a question of the heavier the load, the shorter the distance you can fly. That's why I'm alone in the plane, so we can transport the maximum amount of dollars. We weigh them, because we know we can take one thousand three hundred kilograms and fly to the Cape without refuelling. We don't want to stop, because each stop is a risk. Inquisitive people, paperwork, all that jazz.'

Brenner nodded, satisfied.

'So, we weigh the money, and we pack it in the boxes. And we load the boxes in the plane. If Jer has to land because of bad weather, or if we have to offload the money in the Cape for Chrissie's contacts, there will be at least one layer of camouflage, just in case anyone comes to look. The story is that it's an emergency flight to get the vaccines to Cape Town. That's what Jer is going to tell the mine. They like that sort of PR, especially if they don't have to pay for the fuel. When the plane is fully loaded, Jer stays behind, he's going to spend the night in the hangar. I drive the Hino back to the rental agency, Chrissie takes the Atos back. Chrissie and Igen get on the late-night FlySafair flight to Cape Town. Themba and I stay nearby; we fly early the following morning. Jer brings the PC-12 and the money Sunday morning, and we join him at Fisantekraal Airfield . . .'

'Winelands,' said Yon. 'It's called Winelands Airport now.'

'Okay, Winelands Airport, where we will exchange the money. They do an electronic transfer to my account and I do the transfer to all of you. Right there. And from then on everyone is on their own. Any questions?'

'So we're leaving Jericho Yon alone with twenty million dollars,' Chrissie said. 'And an aeroplane?'

The men laughed. Jericho Yon took out his wallet and handed Rousseau a hundred-rand note.

'What?' asked Chrissie.

'I bet him you would have something to say,' Rousseau said.

'Of course I would have something to say.'

'I just hoped you'd trust me,' said Yon.

'I don't even trust myself with twenty million dollars,' she said.

Yon grinned. 'Me neither.'

'The photo,' said Brenner.

'We take a picture of Jer with the money and the plane, before we pack the dollars in the boxes,' said Rousseau.

'And if Jer doesn't arrive with the money, we send the photo to Ishan Babbar,' said Brenner.

'With the address of Mrs Yon and their two daughters,' said Rousseau.

'And just to make sure Mrs Yon and the kids don't get on a plane to Dubai: Vern Abrahams was with me in 5SFR, way back. He's got his own security business in the Cape now . . .'

'What is 5SFR?' Chrissie asked.

'Five Special Forces Regiment,' said Brenner.

'Recces,' said Themba Jola. 'Just below the Parabats in the food chain.'

'Vern is going to sleep over at Jer's house that night,' said Brenner. 'To keep an eye on the family. He's doing me a favour. And don't worry; I'm paying him out of my share.'

'And you're okay with that?' Chrissie asked Yon.

He shrugged. 'I understand the set-up. Honour among thieves is a myth.'

'Everyone happy?' asked Igen Rousseau.

She just nodded.

'Right, Themba,' said Brenner, 'time to distribute the firearms.'

13

She listened and observed closely, noting all the men's interactions. Occasionally she asked Igen and Themba questions. They were the two she felt most at ease with.

Gradually, systematically, she learned about the team.

She was reasonably certain that Rousseau was the real brains behind the operation. The one who had done most of the research, who'd worked out the strategy – about her role too. He was the one who'd originally identified her as a suitable candidate. She didn't think he wanted to be the leader. He liked working out the logistics, identifying problems and solving them, the cerebral part of the project.

Her perception of Brenner hadn't changed. Formerly she'd been wary of him, the closed book, the enigma, the strong, silent one. No visible show of emotion. All business. Almost robotic. She kept her guard up with him. But he was a good leader, naturally commanding authority. And he inspired confidence in everyone about the task that lay ahead. Perhaps the coolest head if things were to go awry.

She wondered about Brenner's marriage. What was his wife like? Chrissie had to force herself not to create a female version of Nicky Berry in her mind's eye. Siblings could be very different. But how was Brenner with his wife? Had he shown emotion with her? Was he sometimes loving and romantic? Or was the lack of that one of the cracks which had led to the eventual break-up?

Themba Jola was the phlegmatic one, solid, jovial. Not a leader, but an excellent follower. Fitness fanatic. Firearm genius. From the conversations and references and jokes, she gathered that he and Igen had been in the same military unit overseas, where they had met. There was a camaraderie between the two, which they underplayed so as not to let anyone in the group feel excluded.

From Jericho Yon's answers to Jola's carefully probing questions she learned something about the pilot's background. Yon's father was a married senior manager at a Taiwanese bicycle manufacturing company. During a business trip to Cape Town he'd had a short-lived but passionate affair with the Coloured receptionist of a five-star hotel. Jericho was the unintended consequence. The father had met his responsibilities regarding maintenance for the child, eventually helping the boy to realise his dream of becoming a pilot.

Yon was the only one of the team who was married. His wife and two daughters lived in the Cape and he saw them two week-ends a month. He had a permanent position with a mining company, and they had to schedule their planning sessions around his work timetable.

Everything that she saw and experienced gave her confidence in them as a team.

14

Chrissie and Rousseau trained together at a shooting range at Zwartkops. She wanted to thoroughly familiarise herself with the 9 mm Smith & Wesson M&P Compact.

He was done before she was. He stood behind her; she got the feeling that he was watching her.

Afterwards they ate Woollies sandwiches under the blue gum trees. Igen produced a stick of beef biltong and a large jackknife. He carved off a piece, handed it to her.

'Who taught you to shoot?' asked Rousseau.

'My father.'

'He did a good job.'

'Against his will.'

'Oh?'

'He said that's what killed Africa. Guns. But he also knew that if you wanted to live in the bush, you had to know how to shoot. When it was life and death.'

'The Ehrlichmann philosophy.'

'Yes. And now they're both gone.'

They ate in silence. Then Rousseau ventured carefully: 'Can I ask you something personal?'

She looked at him, countered with her own question: 'Igen, you were a soldier before you went to work for Ehrlichmann?'

'Yes.'

'What sort of soldier were you?'

'In my last four years I was a Pathfinder in the British 16 Air Assault Brigade.'

'Scary guys.'

'You could say so.'

'Then why are you so wary of me?'

He laughed. 'We're all a little scared of you. Even Brenner.'

'What for?'

'You were scary. Back in the day.'

'I'm better now.'

'Okay.'

'What did you want to ask me?'

'You have a tattoo on your back . . .?'

'I thought you were watching my shooting technique.'

'Your T-shirt . . . Every time you took aim, part of the pattern showed. I didn't mean to . . .'

She laughed, pulled her T-shirt up at the back and turned it to him.

He looked. 'Brown hyena,' he said.

She nodded.

'Because they're alpha females.'

'And solitary,' she said.

He thought about that for a while. 'Of all the names you could choose . . .'

'Why Christina Jaeger?'

'Yes.'

'Google,' she said and smiled again.

'Google?'

'I searched for the most popular name in my birth year. I didn't like Jessica or Ashley or Nicole. Christina was number twelve on the list. And Jaeger . . . I like the feel of it.'

'You know it means "hunter"?' He handed her the last piece of biltong, wiped the blade of the penknife carefully on his trouser leg and folded it.

'I know.'

'It suits you.' He pushed the knife into his trouser pocket.

He is a good man, she thought. And handsome. Perhaps, if circumstances were different . . .

★ ★ ★

One day before the robbery, she bought an electric clipper at Clicks. And Renew Cinnamon Red hair dye.

That night she first used a pair of scissors to cut her hair in the bathroom. Three years' growth. Long dark locks fell like black snow.

Then she pulled the clippers through her hair leaving just a centimetre's growth.

She put on the gloves, mixed the two bottles of dye, shook well and carefully applied it.

When the dyeing was done, she fetched the large fashionable glasses from the case in her rucksack. She went to the mirror and inspected herself. Her long, slender neck was emphasised by the short hair, the high cheekbones even stronger. She knew there were flaws in her beauty. The creases around her mouth made her look a bit mean, her jawline could be firmer. There was that tiny mark below her left eye. A scar from her childhood, a tiny notch in the lower lid, like a teardrop. She believed it softened the imperfections, with a hint of melancholy.

Tomorrow she would hide it with some skilful make-up.

She put the glasses away again.

Then she tried on the blond wig.

15

Phase One was a visual, sensual assault on the four guards inside. The honey trap.

If it didn't work, they were fucked.

Phase One was her responsibility.

Ten minutes to six in the afternoon, on Easter Saturday. In Spartan, that soulless industrial area beside OR Tambo Airport. The streets were deserted. She parked in front of the big dingy warehouse. Thirty metres from the building. Determined. She opened the door of the white Hyundai Atos. Swung her feet out.

Her pulse began to accelerate.

Here we go.

She hesitated a second in front of the security cameras. Tight white mini dress revealing her bare athletic legs, that lovely muscle definition. Blood-red stiletto heels, blood-red lips. Plunging neckline. Push-up bra. Long blond wig, very expensive, very convincing. She stepped across the hot paved surface towards the building entrance, white handbag slung over her shoulder.

She'd been practising walking in the heels: it had been years since she'd worn anything like them. She still needed to concentrate.

'There was a young maid from Madras,' Rousseau said over the tiny radio receiver in her ear. 'Who had a magnificent ass.'

He tried keeping her calm, his voice light and soothing.

She took a deep breath, in, out, in, out.

'Not rounded and pink.'

She kept on walking. Deep breath.

'As you probably think.'

The large double door was to the left of her, the long bullet-proof window was straight ahead. She had no idea if they had seen her approach. 'It was grey, had long ears, and ate grass.'

Jericho Yon giggled in the earpiece, nervously.

She stood still in front of the glass, pressed the intercom button and propped her hand on her tilted hip. 'Well?' she said and stared provocatively at the glass.

No response.

Shit.

She had visualised this moment. Tried to think what the most credible action would be.

She frowned, pressed the intercom button again, spoke in an irritable tone: 'I don't have all day.'

Her heart was pounding. This was the first moment of truth. So much speculation over their reaction, mostly based on Nicky Berry's insights. And he was an idiot.

Total silence.

She did what she thought was natural. Looked angry, turned away.

'What do you want?' a voice over the intercom.

'This is fifty-one Derrick Street,' she said and pointed at the bleached sign on the wall above the door.

'Yes.'

She turned back. 'So. You called. And here I am.'

'Called who?' the voice asked.

'Naughty Nights. The escort agency.'

'You've got the wrong address, *bokkie*.' And inside she heard at least two others laughing.

She stared at the window. It wasn't going to work. All the planning, all the preparation, and it wasn't going to work.

She looked angry. 'Fuck,' she said and spun around and flounced furiously away.

'Shit,' she heard Themba Jola in the earpiece.

'Hang on,' said Brenner. 'Give it time to come to the boil.'

Twenty metres away from the Atos. Swinging her hips.

Fifteen metres.

'Hey!' the voice shouted over the intercom.

She stopped.

'*Bokkie*, wait. Come here.'

She turned around, but didn't approach. Her voice was angry: 'What?'

'How much?'

She had researched fees. 'What the website says. Two thousand for an hour.'

Silence.

'Hang on,' Brenner repeated.

'There are four of us,' the intercom said.

'No,' said another voice inside. 'I'm out.'

'Okay, three. There are three of us.'

'I only do one at a time.' She put her hand on her cocked hip. She knew they were debating inside. The seconds ticked past.

'Okay,' said the voice. 'It's a deal.'

'Thank God,' said Themba Jola in her ear.

Her heart pounded.

16

They had rehearsed the sequence over and over in Brenner's sitting room. Tried out every possible scenario. Now she felt as though she had forgotten everything, adrenaline made her feel faint, plunged back into a surreal space.

The huge double door opened. A big man with a wide moustache, a bit of a beer belly under the Ace Security uniform, stood there. Forty something. Ogling her bare legs.

When that door shut behind her there would be no turning back.

'Show me the money,' she said and stepped inside.

He shut the heavy door behind her. Locked it.

The aisle to the strongrooms led away from her. To her right was the entrance to the security control room, where they could look out the window. There were three more waiting. A painfully thin man, his grin exposing strange teeth, like a shark. A bespectacled fat man, and a young blond man, blushing furiously.

Each one had a firearm on his hip.

Moustache Man put a hand on her back and steered her into the control room.

'Hands off until I've seen the money,' she said. To her own ears, her voice sounded shrill and panicky.

He took his hand away. She walked into the control room. CCTV monitors, radios, the intercom, the view of the parking outside.

Her cell phone began to ring. 'That's my manager. He'll want to know if I'm okay.'

They stared at her. She put her hand in her bag, reached past the pistol and took out her phone. She answered.

'You okay?' Themba Jola asked.

'I'm okay. But they haven't shown me the money.'

Moustache Man put his hand in his pocket and took out the notes. He put them on the counter.

All four were in front of her now.

'Okay, they've shown me the money.'

'Easy now,' said Themba.

It was no use. Because she knew the moment had arrived.

She didn't switch off the phone, kept the connection open, put it back in her bag. She gripped the pistol and pulled it out. She screamed as loudly as she could. 'Hands on your heads!' She swung and shot the radio, the sound was deafening, sparks flew, all four jumped in shock. 'Now! Hands on your heads, or I'll kneecap you!'

That was the signal for the Hino to pull up to the door, and for Brenner, Rousseau and Themba to jump out. She had to control the guards until then, when she unlocked the door. This was the riskiest part of Phase One, where everything could go wrong.

They stood transfixed, lust changing to something else. Dumb-struck. She fired another bullet into the nearest CCTV monitor. 'Now!' she screamed. The smell of the propellant was in her nostrils along with the stink of burning plastic.

'*Fokkit*,' said the blond man. 'I told you . . .' It was the voice of the one who'd said 'I'm out'.

Moustache Man's hand moved towards his holster. She aimed at the man's leg. 'Three, two, one . . .' she shrieked, adrenaline fizzing through her veins, a cocktail of rage and fear.

He lifted his hands to his head.

She heard the Hino stop outside.

The others all held up their hands.

With her left hand she pulled the high heels off her feet and threw them into the passage. Edged backwards, step by step.

Brenner banged loudly on the big door outside.

She swapped the pistol to her left hand, keeping it pointed at Moustache Man. Walking backwards into the passage. She could still see all four of them.

With her right hand she felt for the lock on the big door. She turned it. The door clicked open.

'Fuck,' said Shark Tooth. 'Fuck, fuck, fuck.'

Then Brenner and Rousseau and Themba were inside, balaclavas over their faces, pistols ready.

Rousseau touched her hand, a gesture of admiration.

It made everything feel real for the first time.

She picked up the high heels and shoved them into her handbag.

17

They struck the four security guards with controlled violence. Themba was in front, shouting orders and forcing them face down on the floor, while Brenner grabbed their firearms. Rousseau made sure they stayed on their bellies, securing their wrists and ankles with cable ties.

'You're fucking stupid,' Moustache Man said. 'Everything's locked in the safes.'

Brenner went to the CCTV system to delete the footage of her approach and entry. Then he shut the control room door behind him. The three men pulled off their balaclavas. Chrissie, Themba and Igen walked out and fetched the trolleys from the back of the Hino.

'Okay?' Jericho Yon yelled from the front.

'Okay!' Rousseau yelled back. Then Brenner joined them and all four ran down the corridor with the trolleys to the fifth strongroom.

Brenner fished the key out of his pocket. Inserted it in the door. Turned.

The door swung open.

'Thank God,' said Themba.

They walked in.

The money was there on a large wooden pallet. Neatly packed. Dollar bills.

'This is much more than twenty million,' said Igen Rousseau.

Brenner whistled through his teeth.

★ ★ ★

They worked as though possessed. Themba shifted the most, he was like a machine, strong as an ox.

Seventeen minutes passed until Chrissie pushed the last trolley with the final load up to the Hino and said: 'Done.' They helped her, tossing the packets of bills in, and then the trolley.

Brenner emerged from the building, pulled the big door shut.

He and Themba jumped into the Hino, Rousseau closed the back.

The Hino drove away.

In her bare feet Chrissie ran with Rousseau to the Atos, feeling the rough tarmac under her soles. She got into the driver's seat, drove after the truck.

At the end of Albatross Street, at the stop sign, she stopped and pulled off the wig. Tossed it over her shoulder onto the back seat.

'You are fucking incredible,' said Rousseau, with a mixture of relief and euphoria.

She grabbed his face with both her hands and kissed him. Open mouth.

18

They drove in silence as far as the R21.

Igen took two cans of Coke out of the glove compartment. Opened one and passed it to her. The sugar for the adrenaline, the fluid for her parched mouth.

He cracked open his own can, and they drank deeply.

Her hand holding the can was trembling on the steering wheel. Her body was as taut as a wire.

'What are you going to do with sixty million rand?' he asked her.

She burst out laughing. She knew it was tension looking for release, and she let it.

He laughed with her.

'I'm serious,' he said at last. 'Do you have plans?'

It was the insane circumstances that made her lift the veil a little, just for a moment. Sharing her small secrets with him.

'The Berlin Philharmonic. The Concertgebouw Orchestra in Amsterdam. Opera La Scala. The Vienna State Opera. The Royal Opera House in London.'

'Fuck me,' he said in genuine admiration.

'Antico Caffè Greco,' she said. 'Every Wednesday. Torta della Nonna. And their perfect coffee.'

'Greece?' he asked.

'No,' she said. 'In the Via dei Condotti in Rome. It's the oldest coffee house in Europe.'

'Every Wednesday? Do you want to live in Rome?'

'No. I want to buy a little house in the Sabine Hills. In the country, between the streams and olive orchards. And a cute little Fiat Panda, so I can go to Rome whenever I like.'

He looked at her for a long time.

'What?' she asked.

'Hell, I wish I knew you. Really. I wish I could get into that mind of yours, just for a few minutes, to know what makes you tick.'

She laughed.

⋆ ⋆ ⋆

They drove west down the N4. The last glow of sunlight faded, night descended. Traffic was light, the roads were quiet.

After the road sign to Brits/Sandton, they took the R511 following the Hino. Rousseau took out his pistol, put it down to the right of his seat. This was the final risk, from here, through the town and out the other side.

Past Brits KFC. Rousseau said: 'Hell, now I'm hungry.'

'Me too,' she said.

There were no road blocks. They turned left into Van Deventer, towards the airfield.

'What are you going to do with the money?' she asked.

'Nothing exciting,' he said.

'Oh?'

'There's a farm for sale between Van Wyksdorp and Herbertsdale. A few thousand hectares, some mountain, some plain, two springs . . .'

'You want to farm?'

'No. I want to . . . just let everything grow wild.'

'Why there?'

He shrugged. 'It's my Sabine Hills. The place talks to me.'

She liked that.

'And that's all you're going to do?'

'Maybe, if I find the right woman, have seven or eight little Rousseaus.'

That made her laugh again.

19

The airfield was in darkness. Cloaking the menace.

At the gate Brenner jumped out of the Hino to unlock it. They drove through. Chrissie stopped. Igen jumped out and locked it behind them.

They drove in convoy up to the hangar, the headlights lighting up the huge doors.

They climbed out, all a bit stiff from sitting so long. None of them had a weapon in hand or even on the hip. All five gathered together, fist-bumping and congratulating each other in muted tones. Post-adrenaline weary, all letting go. Even Brenner's smile was wide now.

The men patted her on the back, praising her courage, her coolness, her calm. She protested briefly, saying she had never been so stressed.

Themba called her amazing. Yon said she was spectacular.

She said nothing, but relished the moment. Then she went to fetch her duffel bag so that she could change out of the skin-tight mini dress.

Yon opened the lock of the hangar, rattled the chain off. He and Themba Jola pushed the doors apart.

The PC-12 was inside, slender and beautiful, lit up by the headlights. The cartons with the MedVet logos were neatly stacked.

Yon clicked a switch. Neon lights flickered against the roof. He walked out. 'I'll turn the truck around,' he said.

Rousseau pulled the big wool scale closer, so they could weigh the cash.

Chrissie carried her handbag and duffel bag to the small bathroom at the back of the hangar.

She switched on the light, closed the door and wiggled out of the dress and bra. She heard the rumble of the Hino's engine as it pulled in parallel with the plane.

She took out her jeans, T-shirt and socks and running shoes from the duffel bag. She put them on.

She could hear the calm voices of the men inside. She squatted on her haunches to fasten the laces.

Three, four, five, six shots boomed out; shock jolted her. Voices, men screaming.

More shots.

She grabbed the pistol from her handbag. Switched off the light. Opened the door.

The scene before her was seared into her memory forever:

At the Hino, beside the plane, she saw Brenner on the ground. On his back, a chest wound bleeding. Over him Nicky Berry was standing with an automatic rifle aimed at Brenner. He screamed, voice filled with rage and hatred: 'You're not so fucking smart now, fucking Recce cunt!'

Themba, bleeding from a hip wound, was wrestling two other men dressed like Berry in military camo and bullet-proof vests. Fists, feet, jerking motions, Jola grimaced in desperation. One man was on his back, arm around Jola's neck, the other was pounding him from the front.

Igen Rousseau lay stretched out under the wing of the PC-12. The side of his head one massive wound.

Jericho Yon was in the cab of the Hino, slumped over the steering wheel. Blood dripped down the front windscreen.

She aimed at Nicky Berry's head, hit him in the neck.

He jerked, looked at her in surprise. She shot again. She missed.

He didn't turn the rifle on her. His awful intensity was focused on Brenner, he shot him in the chest, two lightning shots before Chrissie shot him in the temple. Berry crashed down.

A fourth man came around the Hino, spotted her, raised his rifle. She shot first, hit him in the shoulder, jerking him sideways. His automatic clattered, bullets tearing through the side and wing of the plane, until the magazine was empty. Fuel sprayed and splashed. She aimed at his unprotected thighs, fired four rounds. He screamed, crawled backwards to use the Hino as cover. The blood from his legs left a trail. She made her way towards Themba Jola and his two attackers. They had the upper hand.

Christina stepped closer, screamed at them, a wild jungle cry, raw with rage and fear. One looked at her. She shot him between the eyes.

The other one, on Themba's back, tried to use the Xhosa man as a shield. Themba fell backwards, on top of him.

The wounded one behind the Hino dived around the truck, pistol in hand. He shot at Christina, hit the wing a glancing shot. A spark, and fuel ignited with a low whump.

She shot him, four shots; she didn't know how much ammunition she had left. Flames everywhere. She must get Igen out of the fire, she didn't know if he was dead or not.

Through the fire and smoke she saw Themba on top of his attacker, fist like a hammer. She ran to Igen, grabbed his collar, dragged him towards the big hangar doors. He was so heavy, the heat of the fire overwhelming.

Themba pulled Jericho Yon out of the cab, shouted something at her.

She roared, used all her strength, dragged Igen outside.

He was lifeless.

Themba Jola approached, weak now, carrying Yon on his shoulders. He reached the outside air. Themba gasped, looked at her. 'Thank you,' he said.

The PC-12's wing exploded with a dull boom. The cab of the Hino was in flames.

Christina grabbed a pack of dollars out of the Hino's cargo space, threw it, far, outside.

Another one and another, then the fire ripped through the truck and she leaped back.

'Get the fuck out of here,' Themba said.

She stood still.

'Take the car. Go. They'll be coming.'

Leopard
(Panthera pardus pardus)
Benny & Vaughn

20

Benny Griessel didn't take in the captivating view over the town. All his attention was on the body of the young woman in the hip-high fynbos shrubbery.

He was standing on the near side of the wide sandy firebreak path, high up on the slope of Stellenbosch Mountain. At a quarter to nine on a bright and clear autumn morning in May. She was lying semi-concealed beneath the silvery green flora, nine metres away from him, on the far side of the yellow crime tape that the uniforms had set up. The only visible wounds were to her legs: they looked like scratch marks. The foliage around her was undisturbed. Her mountain bike was lying on the ground beside her.

He didn't want to go any closer. He knew it would upset him. It always did.

Besides he wasn't wearing his PPE suit – the Personal Protective Equipment that SAPS detectives had to wear at crime scenes. It was still in the boot of his car. He would suit up when Cupido arrived.

He couldn't understand why Vaughn was so late this morning. It was their first investigation as newly promoted members of the Serious and Violent Crimes team.

Behind Benny and the small, graffiti-daubed ruin that had once been a fire lookout post, were two paramedics beside an ambulance, eight uniformed SAPS amidst three police vans. And the youngster who had discovered the body, still distressed, leaning against Griessel's white Toyota Corolla.

They were all staring at Griessel in silence. At his dishevelled hair, one or two haircuts behind, his slightly creased jacket, the dark blue Edgars chinos.

Griessel shifted his attention to the fire path. He examined the footprints that led to her body – the marks of the youngster's running shoes, and the boots of the two paramedics.

Something didn't add up.

He walked a few metres to the left, then a few metres to the right, his head bowed, careful not to tread on the footprints.

The drone of Cupido's Volkswagen Golf coming up the mountain broke his concentration. Benny walked backwards, and then towards to the uniforms. To ask them if they had summoned Forensics. And if they would extend the yellow crime tape a few metres further from the fire path and the body. Then he called the crime office of the Stellenbosch police station to ask them if there had been a Form 55 for a young woman in the past twenty-four hours. The form they filled in whenever someone was reported missing.

★ ★ ★

'Morning, Benna.'

They had been working together for more than a decade. Griessel could clearly tell from his partner's voice that he was not in a good mood. And Vaughn hadn't shaved that morning.

'Morning. You okay?' Benny asked, while he pulled on his PPE.

Cupido shook his head. 'Don't ask.' He snapped his murder case open and removed his own PPE. 'What have we here?'

'Female victim. Cycling apparel, the bicycle is on the ground beside her. No visible mortal wounds. The paramedics say it looks like she broke her neck.'

'Crashed with the bike?' Cupido asked hopefully, stepping into the overalls.

'Something doesn't look right to me.'

'Shit,' said Cupido, with deepening gloom.

Griessel nodded. He understood. She was young and white, most probably a student. It might not be an accident. When that news went public, social media would go berserk. Especially targeting the SAPS. Front page reports in the mainstream media would follow and pressure start mounting – from the top down. A world of trouble.

Cupido inspected the large graffiti letters on the back of the ruin. GOD'S DICE FALL DIFFERENTLY it read. He just nodded in agreement. He had no witticism to offer. Another indication, Griessel thought, that something was wrong.

The pair of detectives walked side by side towards the youngster who had found her here on the mountain. Cupido was a head taller than Griessel, broad in the shoulders, nearing forty, nine years younger than his colleague.

'Are you struggling with the diet again?' Griessel asked. Cupido was determined to shed fifteen kilograms. The first four kilos had melted away, but since then it had been an uphill battle. What he'd mostly lost was his usual joie de vivre.

'No, partner. Relationship complications,' and he sighed deeply.

★   ★   ★

The youngster's name was Werner Kilian. He was lean, like a marathon runner, and still very pale after his distressing discovery. He gave them his address and telephone number, which Griessel wrote down in his notebook. He told them he ran this route four times a week, in the morning, before his university classes commenced. It was by pure chance that he'd spotted her, it was barely light then.

'What time?' Cupido asked.

'It was about seven o'clock, *Oom.*'

'Come,' said Griessel. 'Show us exactly where you were.'

They went closer to the yellow tape. 'I was running here, *Oom*, I wanted to go up there on the path to the beacon. Then I saw something, and I stopped. I saw it was a girl lying there. I ran straight to her. Through there. To help her, I thought she had fallen. But then I saw that she's . . . I tried to feel for a pulse, *Oom*. But she was ice cold. And stiff, *Oom*. And I phoned the police.'

'Where were you standing when you phoned?' Griessel asked.

'Right beside her.'

'And then?'

'Then I came here and waited at the ruin. Then the ambulance arrived . . .'

'Are these the footprints of the paramedics?'

'Yes, *Oom*, they went to check her.'

Griessel waited for Vaughn to inspect the greyish-brown soil surface of the fire path.

In the silence Werner said: 'I think it was a leopard, *Oom*.'

'A leopard?' Cupido asked.

'Yes, *Oom*. The marks on her legs. Looks like bite marks. And scratches.'

Werner could tell the detectives were sceptical. '*Oom*, there are leopards in these mountains. Some of my mates even saw one, other side in Jonkershoek.'

* * *

They asked Werner to go and wait at the ambulance.

Cupido stared at the fire path.

'Something's not *lekker* here, Benna,' he said at last. 'Something's not right.'

'Amen,' said Griessel.

'There are no tracks for her bicycle,' said Cupido. 'Look. It's like someone has swept here. With a branch or something. Killing the tracks.'

They silently took out their cell phones and began to take photos and videos of the ground surface, as Forensics and the videographer were still on their way and they didn't want to wait any longer.

Then they carefully made their way to the body while pulling on their latex gloves.

Griessel saw a beautiful young woman. Clearly physically fit. A blond ponytail lay across her shoulder. Mercifully, her eyes were shut. He was grateful for that. His habitual involuntary response was to visualise a victim's final moments. And when that carried a freight of enormous pain and fear, it caused him severe distress. One of the things that drove him to drink.

Cupido raised the woman's arm, and lowered it down again respectfully. 'She's been lying here since yesterday evening.'

'The station says there's been no fifty-five over the last three days,' Griessel said.

'Student? Who lives alone?' Cupido lifted her helmeted head carefully. He felt the back of her head and neck.

'That's what I think.'

'No head trauma,' said Cupido. 'But the helmet has a *moerse* dent here. She definitely hit her head helluva hard. Paramedics might be right about the broken neck.'

'No strangulation marks,' said Griessel. 'But look here.' He pointed to her orange cycling jersey. There were three little tears, equidistant from each other, four centimetres long, from top down to the lower hem.

Griessel lifted the bottom of the jersey. There were no corresponding marks on her skin. He took photos, and then lifted her hands one by one.

'No defensive wounds,' he said.

'Check here,' said Cupido, and studied the marks on her legs. He pointed at her ankles and calves. 'Bite marks. Three, four, five of them. Animal, definitely.'

Griessel examined them. There were clear half-moon bite marks. And on three places, higher up her leg, straight lines that looked like an animal's claw marks. He shook his head. 'It doesn't make sense.'

'What?'

'Remember the woman-in-the-blue docket?'

'*Yebo*,' said Cupido. Three years ago, when they were still in the Hawks' Serious and Violent Crimes team, they had to unravel the murder of an American art expert.[3] There was a painting involved known as *The Woman in the Blue Cloak*.

'Remember the guy from the Cape Leopard Trust? The one who set the cameras in the mountains to photograph the leopards? His name was . . . Willie, I think.'

'Yip.'

'He told me that your Cape Leopard doesn't attack people. Because it's much smaller than the northern type. There has never been an attack recorded.'

'Partner, I'm not buying this leopard theory either,' said Cupido, still studying the bite marks.

'Why?'

''Cause why, I scheme this is a dog bite.'

'Are you certain? What about the tear in the shirt? And the scratch marks? Dogs don't do that.'

Cupido hesitated before answering. 'That is a bit of a mystery. But I scheme it's a dog. Eighty per cent sure. Eighty-five. Big dog too.'

Griessel's gaze turned up to the mountains, his mind working.

'What do you think?' Cupido asked. He knew that faraway look.

'Come on,' said Griessel. 'I want to show you something.'

---

[3]   See the novella *The Woman in the Blue Cloak* (2017)

21

They drove in Vaughn's Golf. Griessel wanted to head for the Park Street entrance to the mountain grounds, the way he'd come in.

As they drove down the slope Griessel asked: 'Relationship complications?' He could tell that Cupido badly wanted to offload.

Vaughn sighed deeply. 'Spare room, *pappie*. That was my sentence, last night, and I still don't understand what my crime was.'

'What happened?'

'Benna, you tell me how this works: here I sit, a soon to be reinstated member of the Hawks elite. Ace detective, reader of people, solver of the most puzzling cases in the Cape Peninsula, and I haven't a clue when it comes to female logic.'

Cupido lived with the gorgeous Desiree Coetzee. Inspired by Griessel's marriage plans, he hoped to ask her to marry him soon. Her twelve-year-old son, Donovan, had also begun making positive hints in that direction. Benny was under the impression that everything was moonshine and roses.

'What happened?'

'Miscarriage of justice, *pappie*. That's what happened. Yesterday. At home. Entertaining Danville Arendse and his cherry, Merle. *Lekker braai*, enjoying a beer, sitting on the patio, shooting the breeze. Talking about celebs and stuff, you know, about how there are people who are famous just because they're famous. Great looks, no substance, influence of social media, that kinda thing. And Danville said, he must admit, that Kim Kardashian was really gorgeous, despite the absence of real accomplishments. And he asked, so innocently, Benna, very innocently and hypothetically, as men do: "Vaughn, let's say Desiree didn't like you, and you could choose any woman in the world. Who would it be?" Now, Benna, I mean, the core of the question is, "let's say Desiree didn't like you". So, in the spirit of conversation and the question, and in all honesty, I said "Diana Krall". You know how much I like that woman. Pianist supreme, best jazz singer ever, that sexy voice, fantastic aura. Style. Looks *and* substance. She's far away in America and I'm here, I reckoned it was a diplomatic choice. Honest, but safe . . .'

'*Ai*,' said Griessel; he knew the outcome.

'*Ja*, Benna. No diplomatic deed goes unpunished. But Desiree sat there and didn't say a word. Just a little smile that said "duly noted". And I thought, Vaughn, that was a smart move. Conflict averted, everything A for Away. But, *pappie*, as soon as Danville and Merle left, the bomb burst. She tore a strip off me. I should have told Danville that "a world in which Desiree does not love me is unthinkable. Can't happen, never will." I should not even have contemplated that game with Danville. 'Cause it's a "betrayal of our trust". And the more I said, Lovey, it was hypothetical, Diana Krall is fifty-something, she doesn't even know I exist and she's far away, the more I have to hear that it's not Diana, it's the principle. And I have to apologise, and I said, I've got nothing to apologise for, and then it was banishment, Benna. Spare room blues. Now you tell me, what was my crime?'

'Honesty.'

'That's a virtue in my book.'

'Tell that to the spare-bedroom ceiling.'

Cupido sighed.

They parked at the Park Street entrance to the university experimental farm. 'Do you know a good florist?' Griessel asked as he got out.

Vaughn followed him. 'Flowers in the Foyer.'

'Call them.'

'Benna, this doesn't sit right with me. I still scheme it's because I should actually have said something like: Danville, if Desiree didn't like me, I would have dedicated my life to getting her to like me, she's the only woman in the universe for me.'

'And so we learn.'

'*Ja*, partner. So we learn.'

Griessel walked up to the tall wire gates. There was a big sign on the smaller pedestrian gate. He examined it. Pointed a finger.

Cupido read: IMPORTANT NOTICE: *All dogs must be kept on a leash while on the university's property. Please respect our farm animals and other users of the university's property. Offenders will be prosecuted and can forfeit their rights to access Stellenbosch University's experimental farm and mountain.*

'I see where you're going with this,' said Vaughn. 'And that means there could be another crime scene somewhere out there.'

'We'll have to seal off the whole area,' said Griessel. 'All the gates.'

'Needle in a haystack. On this mountain.'

While they walked back to the car, Cupido said. 'Now that's my point, Benna. Ace sleuths, deductive geniuses, but we just don't get female logic. Maybe it's all true, that thing about female logic and military intelligence. Contradiction in terms.'

'The golden rule is: you have to know when to shut your mouth.'

'That's not my strong point.'

'You're too young. You'll learn.'

Griessel's phone rang.

Cupido sighed. 'Okay, grandpa . . .'

Benny saw that it was Captain Rowan Geneke calling, this week's senior detective at the Stellenbosch station charge office. He answered.

'Benny, we've just got a fifty-five. For Le-Lanie Leibrandt, twenty years old, blond hair, green eyes, approximately one-comma-six-five metres tall. She's a mountain biker and her bike is also missing . . .'

'Who reported it?' asked Griessel.

'Her brother. They live together in a flat in Soeteweide Street. He said he'd gone to the farm, their parents' farm at Merweville. He only came back this morning.'

Griessel sighed; he knew what lay ahead. The brother would have to identify her. Then they would have to notify the parents. 'The description, Captain, it's her. And we don't think it was an accident.'

'Shit,' said Rowan Geneke.

'We'll have to get more uniforms. All the gates to the mountain must be closed.'

'Okay, I'll organise it. But there's another thing. The brother said he and his sister are on Find My, on their iPhones. And his sister's phone shows she is at seventeen Park Street. He tried there, but there's no one home.'

'We are in Park Street now. At the experimental farm gate.'

'Can I send him to you?'

★ ★ ★

While they waited for the brother to arrive, they walked the twenty metres west to 17 Park Street. The house was behind a small park, on a long panhandle plot. A dense mass of shrubbery beside the high fence of the house. There was an intercom at the gate. Griessel pressed the button. Four, five times. There was no answer. They walked slowly back to Vaughn's Golf.

'*Jissis*, Benna, I don't take direct contact with the bereaved so well any more,' said Cupido. 'It's time The Flower took us back. I mean, we have a new president, things have changed.'

Colonel Mbali Kaleni had been their commander at the Hawks. Six months ago they had been suspended and posted to Stellenbosch after an incident with the corrupt State Security Agency.[4] Kaleni – her first name meant 'flower' in Zulu – had promised to bring them back once the political dust had settled.

Griessel nodded. This face-to-face exposure to grief and trauma was just as hard for him. He always felt somehow responsible. As if he should have prevented it all. His psychologist said this was the other reason he was driven to drink. But perhaps he was less eager to return to the Hawks than his colleague. He had begun to enjoy Stellenbosch and this work environment. Less stress and exposure to serious and violent crimes, and the hours were more predictable. He liked this pretty town, filled with students, street cafés, oak trees, historical architecture.

'Talking of flowers,' he said. 'Call the florist.'

'Benna, you know that feeling, that weird sensation, the moment you fall in love?' Another sigh. But he took out his cell phone and looked up the number.

'Yes?' said Griessel.

'That's the moment common sense leaves your body.' He made the call.

★ ★ ★

Le-Lanie Leibrandt's brother was built like a rugby player. He drove up in a Ford Bantam *bakkie*, got out. He walked quickly over to them, glancing twice at number seventeen, a look of deep concern on his face.

'*Oom*, where is she?'

---

[4] Read the novel *The Last Hunt* (2019) for this story.

22

He introduced himself. His name was Arno. They would later learn that he was studying for an agricultural degree. He was a final-year student.

Griessel told him there was a woman on the mountainside who matched his sister's description. Apparently she'd had a fall from her bicycle.

Cupido said the woman was fatally injured.

Arno Leibrandt shook his head. It wasn't what he wanted to hear.

They knew all the stages of grief he was yet to experience. They had to navigate the first two: denial and rage.

'We're trying to find out exactly what happened,' said Cupido.

'We know it's very hard, but it would help us a lot: are you prepared to identify her?' Griessel asked.

'Yes, *Oom*. It's not Lanie. There's no way she would fall on the mountain. She can ride.'

'Captain Geneke said you believe her phone is at number seventeen?'

Leibrandt nodded. 'That's what my app shows.' He took out his phone, activated it and started the Find My app.

'*Oom*, what bicycle does the girl up there have?'

Griessel knew mountain bikes. In the summertime before work he would ride his old Giant up the slopes of Table Mountain. One of his dreams was to be able to afford a new top-class mountain bike one day. Like the one lying up there. 'Red Specialized,' he said. 'It looks like a Stumpjumper.'

'God, *Oom*.'

'So sorry,' said Cupido.

'Very, very sorry,' said Griessel.

They gave him time. He stood with his head bowed. Gulping for breath. Eventually he remembered the phone in his hand. He showed them the screen. The app displayed a small round photo of Le-Lanie Leibrandt on a map of Stellenbosch.

'When did you first check the app to see where she was?' asked Cupido.

'When I arrived home this morning. Probably just before seven. Lanie . . .' He paused, to bring his emotions under control. 'Lanie . . . She sleeps, *Oom*, she struggles to wake up, she swots till late, then . . . When she wasn't there, and her bicycle wasn't either, I started to worry, *Oom*. She doesn't ride in the morning. Never. So . . . *Oom*, it can't be her. Wait, I have lots of pictures of her . . .'

They waited patiently while he brought up a photo on the phone and turned the screen towards them.

'Look,' said Arno.

It was the girl on the mountain. Laughing. Full of life.

All Griessel could do was put a hand on his shoulder.

'Oh, God, *Oom*. My ma and pa . . .' Then he began to cry.

* * *

They had close on fifty years of police experience between them, and the detectives knew there were no words that would make this better. They just repeated that they were very sorry for his loss.

He wanted to phone his parents. Griessel asked him to wait. The protocol required a positive identification of the victim first.

Arno just nodded. They gave him time, then asked if they could search for Le-Lanie's phone. It was Cupido who clambered over number seventeen's high fence and after a while located it in the dense foliage of the hedge. Griessel brought him gloves, he picked it up and climbed back over.

The phone was still on, but the locked screen was cracked.

'It wasn't like this,' said Arno.

'Must have been the fall,' said Griessel.

'But how did it get here?' Arno asked.

'We'll find out,' said Griessel. And then he realised they might be able to track her movements: he tracked his own mountain bike routes and times with a phone app. 'Did your sister use Strava?'

'Yes, *Oom*.'

'Do you know her phone's PIN code?'

'Yes, *Oom*.'

They unlocked the phone and found that Strava was still active on Le-Lanie Leibrandt's phone, her ride session had not been terminated. Griessel did that now, so they could see the entire route.

The program showed that she started the 18.7-kilometre route yesterday afternoon at 16:27, from the flat in Soeteweide Street. She rode down the tar road to Paradyskloof first, then through the Eden plantation along the mountain track. Down the G-Spot speed track, up the slope again to the Coetzenburg mountain bike trail. Finally, up to the ruins of the fire watch house. Then it moved down the contour path off the mountain, back to here, at number seventeen.

Griessel studied the graphs below the route map. The one that interested him most was the speed. For the final leg – from the ruin to here – the pace was consistently slower, a mere six kilometres per hour. Walking pace.

'The phone was picked up,' said Griessel. 'He was walking, and then threw the phone away here.'

'Who are you talking about, *Oom*?' asked Arno.

'We don't know yet,' said Griessel.

'But we're going to find out,' said Cupido.

'That means she rode up to the ruins. And that's where . . .' Griessel chose his words carefully in Arno Leibrandt's presence. '. . . she fell.'

*   *   *

Up on the mountain Forensics and the videographer had arrived. In dead silence, along with the uniforms, the paramedics and the detectives, they were standing and watching Arno identify his sister's body. Then kneel down beside her and pray for a long time, his shoulders heaving.

Griessel and Cupido offered to arrange psychological support for him, as protocol required. He said he didn't want it. He was going to phone the *dominee* at Merweville first, so that the minister could drive out to the farm. Then he would call his parents. And he had friends here in town who could support him.

Arno walked to a SAPS vehicle with two uniforms, so that they could take him back to his *bakkie*. Then he stopped in his tracks and walked back to the detectives. '*Oom*, Lanie was big on Instagram.

She took photos of where she rode. Almost every time. Maybe that could help.'

They said they would have a look, and let him go. Then they asked the uniforms and paramedics to drive down to the gate, because the area directly around the ruin was a crime scene now. Although they had faint hope of finding anything after all the trampling around the old building.

Griessel made a note in his book to phone Professor Phil Pagel, the chief state pathologist, later. He wanted to find out if it would be possible to collect saliva samples around the bite marks for DNA analysis.

One of the forensics team tested Le-Lanie Leibrandt's phone for fingerprints. 'Someone tried to wipe it off,' he said. Then he found a partial palm print on the left side of the phone cover.

'Enough for an ID?' Cupido asked.

The technician merely shrugged.

When he was finished, Griessel and Cupido looked at the photos on her phone.

The very last two that she would ever take were both selfies. Here, at the ruin. She was standing looking at the mountain, so that the little house, the town far below, and the setting sun were behind her. She was wearing dark glasses, and her helmet. She was smiling, full of self-confidence and the joys of life.

They checked the time stamp on the photos. It was yesterday at 17:28.

Neither had been posted on Instagram.

The forensic technician called them. He had found blood spatters, just single drops, on the raw bricks of the fire lookout building's front wall.

They couldn't find the dark glasses anywhere.

23

The Eikestad detective offices were in the Onder-Papegaaiberg
suburb's old Stellenbosch Commando headquarters. A gate, ornate,
but with peeling white paint, led off the road. Beyond that a road
sign displayed in elegant sans serif capital letters, in three of the
country's eleven official languages:

STELLENBOSCH
MISDAADONDERSOEKEENHEID
CRIME INVESTIGATION DEPARTMENT
ELEZOPHANDO NGOLWAPHULO MTHETHO

A hundred metres past the gate was the double-storey complex,
about sixty years old, stately in the middle of the large expanse of
grass and trees. On the first floor's eastern corner, in Lieutenant
Colonel Witkop Jansen's office, the commander was listening to
Benny and Vaughn with a scowl.

'Those are dog's teeth, Colonel,' said Cupido. '*Hond se tanne,*' he
repeated, for good measure.

'And the scratches and tears in the clothes . . .' said Griessel.

'Fabricated,' said Vaughn.

'How do you know?' Jansen asked.

'Colonel, we have a contact at the Cape Leopard Trust. Willie
Bruwer. He researches them, over at Betty's Bay. I phoned him just
now. Then I sent him the photos of the scratch marks. He said a
leopard's claws would leave very deep wounds. And the bite marks
. . . He said the canines are way too shallow. And there has never
been a case of a Cape Leopard attacking a person.'

'He said the scratches look fake to him. But the bite marks look
genuine. I scheme they are dog bites.'

'I'm not receiving you,' said Witkop Jansen with a frown.

'Our theory is, she rode her route, and then she wanted to take her
selfies up at the ruin. Just before half past five.'

'Sunset was ten to six yesterday afternoon, so maybe she was in a hurry to get down the mountain,' said Griessel. 'When she mounted the bike to ride off, the man with the dog turned up.'

'What man with a dog?' asked the colonel.

The lights suddenly blacked out, the load-shedding power cut starting. Jansen's office was momentarily in twilight. Then the building's diesel generator kicked in and the lights came back on.

'We don't know yet, Colonel,' said Griessel. 'It could also be a woman, but I don't think so. To carry Le-Lanie from the house into the bushes . . . In any case, there is a very clear notice at all the gates that people have to keep their dogs on leads. We think the dog was off the leash, and it attacked her up there. When she was just back on the bicycle. There are a lot of bites on her right ankle and calf. It must have happened at the ruins. There are blood spatters on the wall.'

'And there are no big rocks around there, so we scheme she fell with her head against the house. There by the low brick wall. That's what broke her neck, and made the ding in the helmet,' said Cupido.

'Then the man panicked,' said Griessel. 'And he dragged her and the bicycle into the bushes. Trying to make it look like something other than a dog attack. The scratches . . . We think he tried to make them with something sharp. Like a leopard's claws would make. But he either didn't know how deep they had to be, or he didn't have something with him to make them deeper.'

'Which really pisses me off. 'Cause he schemed the SAPS are idiots, Colonel, like we are going to fall for *that* ruse,' said Cupido.

'I'm receiving you,' said the colonel.

'The area,' said Vaughn, 'between the house and the fynbos is all loose sand, and lower down there are tracks of Nikes and bikes, but there between her and the house everything is smooth and clean. We scheme he saw the tracks of his dog and her bicycle and he knew that told a story. So he fetched a branch and swept the ground clean. Covering his tracks.'

'And coming down, he threw her phone over the fence the other side of the experimental farm gate.'

'Now why would he do that?' asked Jansen, his frown deeper.

'We can only speculate, Colonel.'

'Maybe he had the phone in his pocket when he moved her,' said Griessel. 'And her dark glasses too. We can't find them up there.'

'And, halfway down, it struck him that the phone was still in his pocket. Then maybe he panicked. And he threw it there.'

Witkop Jansen's dense, snowy eyebrows lifted and dropped. He leaned back in his chair. 'I don't like "maybe's",' he said.

'Neither do we, Colonel. That's why we . . .'

Griessel's phone rang. He quickly checked the screen. It was Alexa Barnard, his fiancée. She would understand if he couldn't answer. He rejected the call. 'Sorry, Colonel. That's why we want to look for video footage.'

'You're going to struggle,' said the colonel. 'The municipal system doesn't cover the experimental farm and the mountain.'

'We know that, Colonel. But they and ADT have cameras in Van Rheede Street and in Piet Retief, and the thing is, there's a guest-house on the corner of Park and Piet Retief with a camera that points towards the entrance. Looks like a quality cam. We want to look at everything. Door-to-door, if we have to.'

'Park Street isn't the only entrance to the mountain,' said Witkop Jansen.

'That is a problem, Colonel. But he threw the phone away in Park Street. So he must have exited there.'

Jansen just nodded.

'Colonel, we want to keep the bite wounds out of the media,' said Griessel.

'Keep the dog dude in the dark as to what we know,' said Cupido.

'If we can just say that it looks like she fell, for now,' said Griessel.

Jansen leaned forward again. 'Okay. But you have to move. It will come out. Are you receiving me?'

'Yes, Colonel.' They stood up.

'*Manne*,' said Witkop Jansen. 'Good work.'

* * *

They drove to the municipal control room in the middle of town.

Griessel said: 'Ninety per cent? Why weren't you a hundred per cent sure up there on the mountain that it was a dog bite? Something bothering you?'

'*Ja*, Benna, there's something . . . Something was just a little bit off. And I just can't nail it down. Which is weird, 'cause why, you could say I'm an expert dog-bite witness, *pappie*.'

'Oh?'

'My *komvandaan*, partner. My heritage. I come from Mitchell's Plain. Hell, I used to hate them. There were all sorts of dogs. Uncle on the corner had this *moerse* Alsatian. On a chain in the yard. Demon dog, total psycho, this white fur around his mouth from pure *moerigheid*. I was just a *laaitie*, five or six, and Granny would send me to the café. That Alsatian had a way, when you walked past, he would ambush you. Lie and wait till you were next to the fence, then leap up barking and it's all just fucking razor teeth and saliva dripping, damn dog drooling for your flesh. Scared the shit out of me, every time, even though I knew the chain would stop him. But the dogs that really scared me shitless, who actually bit me, were the pavement specials. These tall, skinny, vicious things roaming around on the loose. Three or four together. No barking, bloody silent assassins, by the time you see them, they're already on you. And if Granny didn't pour the Dettol on, those incisor wounds, especially, they would fester, and that meant weeks of suffering. Fever too. That's how I know what a dog bite looks like, Benna.'

'Okay,' said Griessel.

'Those pavement specials, someone threw them out, Benna. So-called animal lovers, but only as long as the puppy is small and cute. Once they grow up, then it's just abandonment. That's why there's one thing I dislike more than dogs, and that's dog owners.'

Griessel could hear his partner gathering steam.

'Special fucking breed, always holier than thou. Such kind and gentle animal lovers, St Francis pendant around the neck, darling dog's mug tattooed here on the arm. And if you dare say a thing, then it's "dog's a man's best friend, noble creatures, blah blah blah", and they quote all the bladdy Lassie movies. But they never treat the dogs like their actual best friends, partner. Leave the thing alone at home, and they go to work while Wagter or Rover or Fido barks all fucking day long, driving the neighbours crazy, ripping up the garden. And then they scheme, oh, I'll make it up to the dog, 'cause why, I really care, 'cause now I'm taking my dog for a stroll up the mountain. And fuck the regulations, what the hell, I'm just gonna let the dogs loose. And all that pent-up animal aggression and frustration from being locked up all day comes roaring out. Then things happen like what happened now. That's why I'm going to nail this dude, Benna. Nail the bastard, and then let him think we're bladdy

idiots. Multiple counts. Throw the fucking book at him: Animal
Matters Amendment Act, interfering with a crime scene. Obstruct-
ing the course of justice. The works.'

'I can tell you didn't sleep well in the spare room.'

'True, that. But still . . .'

Which reminded Griessel of the phone call while they were with
Witkop Jansen. He took out his phone. 'I have to phone Alexa back.'

She answered immediately, the phone barely rang.

'I've booked Lize Beekman, Benny,' she said, excitement in her
voice.

He didn't understand, his mind was still on dogs and as Alexa
owned a music production company she was always booking artists.
Why was she telling him this?

'For recordings?' he asked.

'No, Benny. For the wedding. June twelfth. Zorgvliet let me know
they had a cancellation, so our date is June twelfth. Otherwise we'll
have to wait more than a year, they are so incredibly popular as a
venue. And Lize said yes. She's available, she's going to sing at the
ceremony. And she's bringing Mareli.'

A flood of anxiety engulfed him. Twelfth of June. A month away.
It was so soon. Fucking soon.

'*Jissis*,' said Griessel before he could stop himself.

Alexa was quiet for a long time before she said: 'I thought you
would be glad. About the date, and Lize.'

He could hear the disappointment in her voice.

'Alexa, I am,' he said. 'It's from happiness that I . . .' Then he
realised she had rung off. His shoulders sagged.

'What's wrong, Benna?' asked Cupido.

Griessel sighed.

'All okay with Alexa?' asked Cupido.

'Give me the number.'

'What number?'

'Flowers in the Foyer.'

'What happened?'

Griessel just sighed.

Cupido parked in front of the municipal control room. 'Where's
that advice now, grandpa? About knowing when to keep your mouth
shut?'

24

They had never been big fans of municipal law enforcement, thanks to years of bumping up against uniformed tinpot dictators, insufficient training and petty corruption. So they had been sceptical about Stellenbosch's new 'security initiative' announced to the media a year ago, with all the usual political fanfare. Up until they put the CCTV control room to the test for the first time. They had to reluctantly admit that the system was impressive. And effective.

The centre's entire front wall was a massive panel of high-resolution monitors. On the floor were twelve work stations arranged in three rows, from where the operators could determine which of the multiple camera feeds should be displayed. The network covered the entire municipal area, from Raithby to Klapmuts, from Khayamandi to Franschhoek.

They asked the operator on duty to show them the material for Piet Retief Street, the previous afternoon between four and half past six – especially the cameras facing the Park Street corner.

They counted fifty-seven people walking in the direction of the experimental farm from four the previous afternoon. Eighteen had dogs on leads. They eliminated seventeen, since their dogs were small and harmless, or the time slot of animals and owners returning was too early.

The one strong candidate was a man in a red baseball cap and dark glasses, with two massive Rottweilers straining at their leads. He ran around the Park Street corner in the direction of the farm at 16:32 and returned hastily in the dark at 18:13 – much later than any of the other walkers. He was tall and athletic, somewhere in his late thirties or early forties.

The trouble was that twelve cars also turned off Park Street between 16:00 and 18:30, and exited again before sundown. They were people who either parked outside the gate, got out – with or without dogs – and went walking, or residents who lived in the street. The control room's video feed didn't cover the gate to the mountain grounds itself. The only camera that would shed light on it was the one at the big guest house on the corner. Provided it was in working order.

They asked the operator to do screen captures of Rottweiler Man, both times when he and the dogs were closest to the camera – at the intersection of Piet Retief and Park.

They let the video roll as he returned. They saw him turn south, and jogtrot up the slope of Piet Retief. And they could just make out in the glow of the streetlights that he turned right in Welgevallen Street. Then he disappeared from view.

* * *

At three o' clock, in the car on the way to the guesthouse, Griessel studied the screen-capture prints.

The first photo was time-stamped 16:32. Rottweiler Man was holding the dogs' leads firmly in his left hand. He was carrying something in his right hand.

'It's a water bottle,' he said. 'I think it's a water bottle.'

'Okay,' said Cupido.

The second picture was Rottweiler Man returning, at 18:13. The cap was pulled down lower over the eyes. Water bottle still in his hand.

'It's a quarter of an hour after sunset,' said Griessel. 'But the dark glasses are still on?'

'Partner,' said Cupido, 'that water bottle . . .'

'Yes?'

'The whole time I was trying to figure out what was wrong with those bite marks. Why I was not completely convinced. And I think I've got it . . .'

'What?'

'Blood, *pappie*. Big dog bite, those incisors draw blood. Like, right away. On your hands, on your ankles. There was blood against the wall. But there was no blood on her. Just the marks.'

'And?'

'The water bottle. I think he washed her wounds, partner. To get rid of the DNA.'

* * *

The good news was that the people at the guesthouse were co-operative, and the camera resolution was good. It was installed on the front wall and set to cover all of Park Street in the direction of the experimental farm. Reasonably quickly they ascertained that there were no dogs in any of the twelve cars that parked on this side of the gate the previous afternoon.

The bad news was the lack of light when Rottweiler Man hurried back. It was already dark, and the streetlights cast deep shadows from the row of trees on the north side of Park Street. They couldn't make out whether he threw a cell phone into the garden of number seventeen or not. He did seem to hesitate for a moment. His arm may have swung for a second, but they knew that was not enough to serve as evidence in court.

Griessel showed the screen grab pictures to the guesthouse manageress. 'Do you perhaps know this man?'

She shook her head. 'I don't live in Stellenbosch,' she said.

* * *

They sat down at De Vrije Burger in Drostdy Street, because it was after four and they still hadn't eaten and Griessel was addicted to their new bacon jam burger. They also had to plan their footwork. That was all that remained, going door-to-door with their photos in the hope that someone would recognise Rottweiler Man.

They used Cupido's phone to examine the area on Google Maps.

'One of two possibilities,' said Cupido. 'He was on the way home, or he deliberately chose another route, to throw us off the scent.'

'Going home,' said Griessel.

'Why?'

'She's lying up there on the mountain. Nobody is chasing him. He wants to get home, or his wife will ask him where he's been so late. He wants to wash his hands and feet, bath the dogs . . .'

'I concur, your honour. If he turned in here in Welgevallen, then that means he lives somewhere around here. Binnekring, Buitekring, maybe Brandwacht or Barry Road.'

'We'll have to wait until people come home from work. Around six o'clock.'

Griessel realised that he would have to let Alexa know he would be very late getting home. If she answered the phone. Maybe he should just leave a voice note on WhatsApp. And say he was sorry about his reaction. Because the flowers wouldn't reach her till tomorrow.

He sighed. 'Alexa wants to get married on the twelfth of June,' he said.

Cupido put two and two together: 'I see. And then you said "*jissis*".'

'Yes.'

'Hence the flowers.'

'Yes.'

'And the reaction was because you're scared. That is . . .' He counted on his fingers. '. . . just over a month away.'

'Yes. What if Doc is right, Vaughn?' Doc Barkhuizen, retired doctor and Griessel's sponsor at Alcoholics Anonymous, had warned him many times that a marriage between two alcohol-dependents held dangers for both.

'It's going to be okay, Benna.'

'I don't know. I've made a fuck-up of so many things in my life already. I don't want to do that to the children, and I don't want to do that to Alexa. She's been through enough.' Griessel had a son and a daughter – Fritz and Carla – with his first wife, Anna. Both were now adults and he worked very hard on his relationship with them. Especially with Fritz, it wasn't easy, but in recent months there had been a gradual improvement that he was desperate to maintain.

'Partner, that love that you and Alexa have is true love. It's a match made in heaven. And you see the shrink every month, you're a changed man. Two years now you've been on the wagon . . .'

'Only four hundred and eleven days.'

'Same thing. Alexa is four years clean, 'cause you aren't a shit like her late ex. She's a good, strong woman, smart and caring, all that jazz. A ring and a licence aren't going to change that. You're worried for nothing.'

★ ★ ★

In Brandwacht Street, just before seven that night, the woman looked at the photo of Rottweiler Man and said: 'Oh yes, that's Basie.'

'Basie who?' Cupido asked.

'Basie Small. My neighbour. I knew he was a crook.'

They waited for her to explain.

'He's a lawyer,' she said.

25

They parked in front of the house. It was behind a high, plastered wall. Inside, the lights were on.

Fixed to the white metal security gate at the front door was another sign: *Warning. This property is guarded by attack dogs. Not responsible for injury or death.* With an image of a Rottweiler's barking profile, sharp canines prominent.

'Your kind of people,' said Griessel.

'Potential new bestie,' said Cupido.

'What do you think? Are we going in?'

'It's dicey, Benna. A lawyer knows the law.'

'A lawyer would know to wash off the DNA,' said Griessel.

'And he won't let us near the dogs without a warrant.'

'We don't have enough for a warrant.'

'That is the conundrum.' It was Cupido's new favourite word. Griessel wasn't sure where he had heard it.

'It is.'

'All we can hope for is that we can find an eyewitness, tomorrow, when the news breaks.'

That sat a moment in silence.

'Let's go in, partner,' said Cupido. 'I want to see what the bugger looks like. And maybe he'll panic a bit.'

Griessel nodded. They got out and approached the front gate. They took out their identification cards.

Cupido pressed the button on the intercom.

The dogs barked inside the house.

A gruff, impatient voice over the intercom: 'Yes?' With the dogs still barking in the background.

'Warrant Officers Cupido and Griessel, SAPS,' said Cupido.

'Yes?'

'We would like to talk to you, Mr Small. Can you open up, please?'

'What is the problem?'

'We are not going to talk over the intercom.'

No reply, just the barking.

Then the outside lights came on. The front door opened. Small pushed the dogs back into the house, closed the door again and came outside.

He was a big man, mid-forties, athletic. Head smooth-shaven, two or three days' stubble, but manicured. He was wearing tracksuit pants, running shoes and an Adidas golf shirt. He came up to the gate. Didn't greet them, just scowled.

Griessel held out their identification cards.

Small took the cards and studied them carefully. 'What's the problem?' he asked, before handing back the cards.

'You have two Rottweilers, Mr Small,' said Cupido.

'Not a crime.' With a little smile.

'Yesterday between half past four and six o'clock you were on the mountain with your dogs.'

'Not a crime.'

'You let your dogs run loose up there on the mountain, Mr Small,' said Griessel. He hoped Small would think they had an eyewitness, so he made it a statement rather than a question.

'I would never do that.'

'You're a lawyer?' Cupido asked.

Griessel's cell phone rang. He took it out quickly, glanced at it. Colonel Mbali Kaleni calling. He declined the call.

Cupido repeated the question.

'What has that to do with my dogs?'

'If you are a lawyer, then you will know Article One of the Animal Matters Amendment Act?'

'What is your point, Officer?'

'My point, Mr Small, is that that article states that any person whose animal causes injury to another person, as a result of the owner's negligence, shall be guilty of an offence and be liable for conviction, receiving a fine or a sentence of imprisonment for a period not exceeding two years.'

Small's smile widened. 'You're barking up the wrong tree, if you'll pardon the pun. My dogs wouldn't hurt a fly.'

'Then would you let us take jaw imprints and saliva samples from them?' Cupido asked.

'Of course. Just show me the warrant.'

'But you have nothing to hide, Mr Small. They wouldn't hurt a fly.'

'But I have rights, Officer. This is the new South Africa now.'

That's when they knew they had lost.

'We will have the warrant tomorrow,' said Cupido. 'Where will we find you?'

'Right here, Officer. Right here.' He turned and walked away.

Inside the house the dogs were still barking.

* * *

In the car Cupido said: 'Benna, phone the prof.'

Griessel nodded. He understood what Vaughn was after. He looked up the number of the legendary state pathologist Professor Phil Pagel in his contacts and called him.

It was seven rings before he answered with 'Nikita, this is a surprise.' For twenty years he had been calling Griessel 'Nikita', because back then he was convinced that Benny looked like a youthful Nikita Sergeyevich Khrushchev. The former Soviet leader, 'but with much more hair'. It had been over a year since they had last had contact.

'Prof, sorry to bother you at this time of night . . .'

'No rest for the wicked, Nikita, how can I help you?'

'Dog bites, Prof . . .'

'Yes?'

'Do you have imprint profiles that can identify specific types of dogs?'

'We do, Nikita, but odontological identification of specific breeds is not without its challenges.'

'Why, Prof?'

'Your biggest problem is mongrels. Let's say you have an Alsatian-Labrador cross, with the Labrador genes dominating the bite profile. I can connect the specific wound pattern to the specific dog, but to say that there is only one breed with a bite like that is not a scientifically correct statement. You understand?'

Griessel's heart sank, because this was not good news for a possible warrant. 'I understand, Prof. There's a victim who was sent to you today. Le-Lanie Leibrandt, twenty years old, blond hair, green eyes, approximately one-comma-six-five metres tall. Cause of death is most likely a broken neck . . .'

'What we would call a cervical fracture.'

'Right. She had bite marks on her leg. Could Prof take a look tomorrow? And point us in the right direction?'

Pagel was in his late sixties, he'd seen it all: 'Ah, you want to get a warrant.'

'Yes, Prof.'

'I will see what I can do, Nikita.'

★ ★ ★

They drove back to the station in silence. Eventually Griessel said: 'Her dark glasses, Vaughn. All the time I've been wondering what he could have used to make the scratches on her legs. You don't normally carry anything sharp with you when you go running with your dogs.'

'Yes?'

'Her dark glasses. I think he broke them against the brick wall. Or perhaps they broke when she fell. And he used a piece . . .'

'Clever, Benna. Clever. We'll have to have a look tomorrow. For splinters, at the ruins. And he's a sly bastard, he would have taken the pieces with him. Maybe he threw them away with the phone. We must go and look there again. But it's him, *pappie*. That body language. It's abso-fucking-lutely him.'

'We'll have to use the media. Maybe someone saw something.'

'Long shot. But worth a try.'

They stopped in front of the office. 'Mbali phoned,' Griessel said.

Cupido's face brightened, for the first time that day. 'Here it comes. We're going back to the Hawks, *pappie*. Phone The Flower.'

Griessel took out his phone and made the call.

'Hello, Benny,' said Kaleni. 'Thanks for returning my call. How are you?'

'We're okay, thank you, Colonel. Working a tough case.'

'Well, they have their best detectives on it. Benny, I'm calling for both you and Vaughn. I owe it to you not to hear the news from someone else.'

'What news, Colonel?'

'I'm leaving the Hawks. So, I won't be able to bring you back.'

'Where are you going?'

'I'm not at liberty to say.'

'What did she say?' Cupido asked when Griessel ended the call. 'When do we start?'

Cat
(Felis catus)
Christina Jaeger

26

She was dreaming.

Igen Rousseau lay stretched full length under the wing of the PC-12. The side of his head was a gaping wound. The fire, billowing, threatened to engulf her. She had to reach Igen, her legs felt like lead, her movements sluggish, she was going to be too late. He was on fire, he was burning, flames all around him. She saw blood in his hair, heard the roaring of the fire, smelled paint burning. And footsteps, thunderous, a hammering on the hangar door, more intruders, more of them.

And then she woke, on the thin mattress on the floor of her little flat. The knocking was on her door, loud and urgent. She sprang up, befuddled, unsteady on her feet. She had to find a weapon. The small tool chest near the door – she staggered, stumbled, jerked it open, tools clattering out onto the floor. She grabbed the hammer, hefted it, pulled the door open, ready to attack.

The man standing in front of her was sturdy, angry and scowling. He spotted the weapon and stepped back, startled, hands raised defensively.

'*Mi scusi, mi scusi, signora.*'

She took in his overalls, the gloves. Behind him, on the other side of her little porch Christina could see a small truck, and she understood. He was the garbage man. She lowered the hammer, the adrenaline still coursing. '*Non parlo Italiano,*' she said.

He stood transfixed, eyes wide.

'*Parla Inglese?*' she asked, her tone apologetic.

'*Un po.* A little. *Mi scusi, signora.* You must put *organico* in bag. Please.' He gestured at the green rubbish bin that she had placed outside in the small inner courtyard. 'In bag. *Organico.* In *un sacchetto.*'

She understood. She ought to have put the organic waste in a bag in the rubbish bin. 'Okay,' she said. '*Scusi.*'

He nodded, attempted a tentative smile. '*Mi chiamo Giovanni,*' he said. 'My name. Giovanni. Please to meet you.' He held out his hand, realised it was in a garbage-soiled glove, and withdrew it sheepishly.

She put the hammer down on the ground and combed her dishevelled hair with her fingers. 'Christina,' she said and worked hard on her smile.

'*Benvenuto a Poggio Nativo,*' he said. 'Welcome in Poggio.' He looked her up and down curiously. Then he turned and left.

She called '*grazie*' after him. Closed the door. Realised she was wearing paint-spattered shorts and T-shirt.

She pictured herself facing him with the raised hammer and a crazed look in her eyes.

That was a mistake. She wanted to keep a low profile here. Now he would go off and talk about her. They were already gossiping, after her altercations with the grumpy middle-aged plumber. She'd contracted him to install the new water heater and replace the ancient piping. It was an explosive relationship: he found it hard to take orders from a woman, didn't understand English, and constantly adjusted the price upwards. They had not parted as best friends.

After that she could feel inquisitive eyes following her on her occasional walks up the steep, narrow alleys as she tried to get to know the village.

How could she put that right?

★ ★ ★

The flat consisted of just two long rooms. The one that she'd already renovated comprised the kitchen and bathroom. A week with the plumber, thereafter three weeks watching YouTube videos to learn skills, long days of sweat and sawing, measuring and fitting, sanding and painting. But she was pleased with the result.

She switched on the little electric mocha pot for coffee, then came back to the bed- and living room. A stack of equipment and materials – paint and varnish tins, brushes and sealant for the tile floor – occupied the middle of the room, and on the far side, under the window, was her thin camping mattress. She began to pick up the tools and return them to the chest. She had worked until midnight yesterday. All she'd wanted was a nap before showering, but she'd fallen asleep. Dead tired. The manual labour, mental exertion, on-the-go-ness of it all was meant to help her process those terrible events at the aircraft hangar. But the dream was more evidence: the trauma and loss were still there.

The room smelled of paint, so she opened the windows wide. For a moment she looked out over the valley down below, the dirt road winding away along the babbling brook, olive trees covering the slopes of the hills on either side.

It was the right choice. This place.

She turned back to the room. She needed to finish today. Tomorrow she was going to Rome, to buy a bed at Ikea, a porch table and chairs at Leroy Merlin. Then second-hand armchairs and a chest of drawers and carpet at the Mercatino in the Via Matteo Bandello.

Later she would tile the narrow porch and have a metal railing made.

Tonight she would have to sit down and work out her finances.

She had arrived in Cape Town with only $220,000, after the night of the fire. Altman was not happy. He called her accident-prone, and said she was ruining his reputation. And still gave her six rand on the dollar. R1.32 million. And now she had to think in euros. She had just under €50,000 left, after buying the flat and her Fiat Panda, and the renovations to date.

It would last three years. Four, if she was careful.

Enough time to make plans.

$\star$　$\star$　$\star$

She heard the cat while she was pairing her phone with the small Bluetooth speaker so she could play music while she painted.

She looked out of the open front door. It was a skinny grey tortoiseshell, at the bottom of the porch steps. Chrissie walked outside. The cat trotted away, semi-feral. She could see its teats were swollen, but she was skinny. Somewhere she had little ones.

Chrissie knelt and spoke to the cat. She didn't approach, but mewed, briefly and plaintively.

Chrissie fetched some of last night's prosciutto, broke it in small pieces and placed them on the steps. Then she went inside and began painting again.

When she took a glass of fruit juice to drink in the sun on the porch at ten, the meat was gone.

★　★　★

Late afternoon she cooked an omelette. The phone played through the speaker. *Rigoletto*. Quietly, so as not to disturb the neighbours.

She paused, thinking about the dream this morning.

About the violence, the fear, Nicky Berry's all-consuming hatred. Brenner: expert, fit, relentless Brenner – dead. In a horrendous blink of an eye. And she couldn't save him. Igen probably dead as well. Jericho Yon?

Through the open window she heard a voice outside. A male voice, deep and gruff. She ignored it, sprinkling grated pecorino over the omelette, it was nearly ready.

The voice again, more urgent. She heard him calling her. '*Signora.*' Summoning her.

She walked to the living room and out of the front door. He was standing just below her porch with a walking stick in his hand. Short and stout, long grey hair down to his shoulders, a full, grey beard. Late sixties. She had seen him in passing a number of times.

'*Non capisco,*' she said.

'That makes sense,' he said in fluent English. 'Are you an American?'

She shook her head. What did he want?

He pointed the walking stick at the kitchen window. 'That is the Viennese Philharmonic recording. With Cotrubaş and Domingo,' he said. 'And Giulini.'

She realised he was referring to her music. 'Yes?'

'Don't you know the Pavarotti and Sutherland version?'

'I know it.'

'It's sublime. The quartet, "*Bella figlia*", it's perfect.'

'It is.'

'Then why are you listening to this one? Domingo is not even in the same league as the king of the high C's.'

'I . . .' She didn't owe him an explanation. 'Because I want to.' She smelled the omelette burning. 'Excuse me,' she said and ran inside.

'Maybe you should come for cooking lessons too,' he shouted after her.

When she had rescued her omelette and came outside again, he was gone. But the cat was back. With a kitten, an exact replica of its mother. They were sitting just below the wall of the fountain.

When she had eaten, she scraped some of the egg onto the bottom step, but the pair of them fled.

Well done, she thought. Neither the residents nor the cats like me.

★ ★ ★

That evening she drove the Panda to Toffia, the picturesque neighbouring town. She sat down at the café in the square, drank a cold drink, ate a cornetto and switched on the cell phone. The one Brenner had given her, the one the team used to send each other Telegram messages. She only activated it on rare occasions, when she was away from her new home town. A safety measure.

Now, as always, she felt a tingle of suspense, and hope.

But there was nothing. Just the same as every time since that night.

She switched the phone off.

27

Her three porch steps led down to a small inner courtyard, just inside the gate in the town's southern wall. There was a fountain, and the neighbours' plant pots of herbs and flowers. Early in the morning she sat on the top step with her coffee, listening to the bird-song from the valley below.

It was this prettiest of piazzas that had convinced her to buy the flat. That – and the gate – were over a thousand years old, the agent had said. And when you stood beside the fountain, the view stretched out over the valley in the middle of the *tre valli* to the stately Monte Soratte.

Suddenly the cat jumped up onto the wall behind the fountain. She sat there watching Chrissie. In the soft light the grey of her coat took on a golden glow. Almost like an African wildcat.

They stared at each other.

'Katse,' Chrissie said to her.

The cat blinked her eyes.

'That's the Tswana word for cat,' she said in Afrikaans.

No reaction.

Chrissie thought: This is the first time in more than seven weeks that I am speaking my mother tongue out loud.

The kitten appeared behind his mother. He danced around her, and lay down, wanting to suckle.

'Sebini,' said Chrissie. 'That means dancer. In Tswana. Sebini from Sabina.'

Katse jumped off the wall and came and sat in the middle of the courtyard, curling her tail neatly around herself, as if waiting. The kitten hung back.

Chrissie stood up and went to fetch a saucer of milk. 'Just because you have a little one. That's all. I'm not looking for a pet.'

Katse began to groom herself.

Chrissie placed the saucer a metre away from the cat and sat down on her step again.

Katse approached warily, her eyes on Chrissie. And then she lowered her head and lapped.

★   ★   ★

Wednesday. Her furniture would be delivered in the late afternoon.

She drove to Rome in her grey Panda, eight years old, fifty thousand kilometres on the clock, well maintained.

She parked close to the Villa Borghese and first walked down the Spanish Steps to the Anglo American Book Co. to find something to read. She bought Robin Lane Fox's *The Classical World* and *SPQR: A History of Ancient Rome* by Mary Beard. Then she went to Caffè Greco for Torta della Nonna and coffee.

In the restaurant she took the Brenner phone out of her pocket. Switched it on.

Her heart leaped. There was a small red '1' beside the Telegram app logo. She activated the app.

It was from Themba. *Be careful, wherever you are. They have footage of you at the warehouse. Babbar hunting us. Stay strong.*

She quickly switched the phone off. Her hand trembled.

★   ★   ★

In the days since the robbery she constantly wondered what happened after Themba persuaded her to leave. The consequences of it all.

For example: Nicky Berry's body at the plane hangar. If they could identify the charred body, they could easily follow the dots from there to the warehouse and the dollars. But even if Berry was unrecognisable, he and his henchmen would have had vehicles nearby. Could Themba have got rid of them? With a badly wounded Jericho Yon with him? And the body of Igen Rousseau?

If he couldn't, the connection between the vehicle and Berry was relatively easy to make. And from there it would eventually lead to Brenner, the former brother-in-law, the ex-Recce, a man capable of carrying out a robbery with military precision.

In addition: Jericho Yon was connected to the plane. He was the primary pilot, he had submitted a flight plan for the following day, and had official permission to use the PC-12. For someone investigating it all, it would be a small step to see the link.

And Yon was the one with a family. A soft target.

Had Jericho survived?

They have footage of you at the warehouse.

Surely Brenner had deleted the CCTV video? Did they have backups? Had Brenner made a mistake?

She'd been wearing a wig. And heavy make-up. She should have worn the dark glasses, but Brenner and Rousseau thought it detracted from her appearance, diluting the honey trap.

Babbar hunting us.

Who was 'us'? Only her and Themba?

She paid for the coffee and cake, and left, heading back to her car, anxious now.

On the night of the robbery she had flown from Johannesburg to Cape Town to exchange the money. Two days later from Cape Town to Doha, Doha to Paris. Using her other passport, under another name. There were cameras at all the airports. Her passport photo was there somewhere, on the system.

Did they have facial recognition software? You feed in a photo, and it searches the data bases and cyberspace for a connection. She didn't use social media. But there were photos of her on the Internet. The tourists at Letsatsi Lodge in the Okavango often asked to take selfies with her. And they would post them on Instagram and Facebook. With her name.

Would they be able to identify her? If they had the technology? She'd travelled with short, red hair and the big, fashionable glasses. And no make-up.

What if they could identify her? What if they could follow her to Paris? From there she'd left no trace. She'd paid cash for train tickets, first to Torino, where she'd dyed her hair black again, and taken off the glasses. Then by train to Rome.

The flat and the car were in Christina Jaeger's name, but they would not have access to Italian databases, Babbar would not be able to involve Interpol, he was working for swindlers.

Babbar hunting us.

Why? Most of the money had gone up in smoke.

But she knew why.

He'd want to make an example of them. He would want to show that you don't steal from the Chandas.

★ ★ ★

She took the Via Salaria back to Poggio Nativo, the slower route, so that she could think.

At an Esso petrol station she filled up the Panda and then sent Themba a Telegram message: *Thanks for the heads-up. I'm lying low. Please keep sending news. Will check for messages every few days.*

She waited twenty minutes. He didn't reply.

She switched off the phone and drove home, to be in time for the furniture delivery.

Now, for the first time, she kept an eye on the rear-view mirror.

★ ★ ★

The front door open, she was busy making up her new bed when she heard someone on the porch.

It was the man with the long grey hair and walking stick.

'*Salve*,' he said. And then, in English: 'I was a real old *scorbutico anziano* yesterday. A grumpy old man. I've come to offer my apology.'

She went to the front door. 'Okay,' she said. Warily.

'My name is Luca Marchesi. I am a new incomer, like you.' He held out his hand.

'Christina,' she said. 'Christina Jaeger.'

'Ah,' he said. 'German? I have a few words, mostly from *Die Zauberflöte*: "*Der Vogelfänger bin ich ja*" . . .'

She smiled: 'No. I'm from Botswana.'

'Africa. How exotic. Will you tell me more? I want to invite you to dinner. As a penance. Tomorrow night?'

Her first instinct was to say no thank you. But she realised it was an opportunity. To script a fiction about herself. So that the garbage removal man and the plumber were not the only ones telling stories about her.

'Thank you,' she said. 'That would be lovely. What time?'

'Eight o'clock? I live up there in the town, but I will fetch you, because these alleys are like a maze.'

'Good,' she said.

He looked at the flat behind her. 'It's looking good,' he said. 'But you will have to put in mosquito screens, before next summer. In the windows and doors.'

'Oh?'

'People imagine the Italians in the Middle Ages built the towns so high up the hills for defence against the Saracens. It was actually for the mosquitoes. Unlike the Saracens, they are still with us.'

★   ★   ★

Her duffel bag was finally emptied and the contents packed in the new, second-hand chest of drawers, every item of furniture in its place. She made herself a Caprese salad with fresh tomatoes, basil and mozzarella. She took a beer out of the fridge and carried it all to the small table on the porch.

Katse and Sebini sat in the last rays of the sun and washed, on the wall behind the fountain.

'Cheers,' said Chrissie and raised the beer glass in their direction.

The mother cat stood up and approached slowly, just as far as the first step.

28

In the morning she went to buy fresh bread at the bakery in Castel-nuovo di Farfa. She took the Brenner cell phone along, anxious for news from Themba

On the way back she drove to the abbey in Farfa, and switched on the phone there. No messages.

She sent another one to Themba, the question that had been keeping her awake last night: *How did you hear that they have footage of me?*

* * *

Luca Marchesi came to fetch her just before eight that night. The two cats were on her porch, at a food bowl. They skedaddled when he came to the steps. He said: 'One of these days they'll be moving in with you.'

'No good deed goes unpunished,' she replied.

Luca laughed. His grey hair was tied back in a ponytail, his beard neatly trimmed. He looked at her appreciatively. 'You look lovely,' he said.

She had gone to some trouble. She'd put on make-up for the first time in weeks, and was wearing her rust-and-white checked tweed dress with bell sleeves and high-heeled espadrilles that she had bought in Rome. 'Thanks. It feels good not to be covered in paint for a change.'

She locked her flat and they walked up the steep narrow alley be-tween age-old houses. 'Why Poggio Nativo?' he asked. 'Foreigners usually aim for Tuscany.'

She knew he would ask questions. She had decided to turn that to her advantage. An opportunity to create a narrative, an image for the townspeople, so they could put her in context, put a damper on the rampant speculation, dull the curiosity.

'Foreigners are the best reason to avoid Tuscany,' she said. 'That, and the prices.'

He laughed. 'That's true. But Poggio . . .?'

He could tell she was having difficulty with the high heels on the cobblestones. He offered her his arm and she tucked hers into it. 'Seven years ago I crossed Italy with a backpack and a guide book. The area I loved most of all was the Sabine Hills,' she said. It was close to the truth. 'I don't really know why. The landscape is one reason. It's my kind of beauty, these hills and valleys. And the simplicity . . . It still feels authentic here. Like the real Italy. And I wanted to be near Rome. The only reason I chose Poggio to live was because I liked this flat. And the cost. It was affordable for an African. And you?'

His deep voice echoed off the walls. He led her to his flat in the eastern town wall. He said it was necessity that brought him here. 'I had a little restaurant in England. Ship Street in Brighton, a block from the sea. La Tavola Italiana. Only seven tables, small menu, but authentic Italian food. Seventeen years . . .'

'Now I understand the fluent English,' she said.

'Indeed,' he said. 'The British summers were profitable, the winters not always, but I did well enough. Built up a nest egg. I knew I could sell the place one day to give my pension one last boost. Then Covid happened, and everything went with it. I could rescue the nest egg at least, but it's not a lot of money. This flat belonged to my late brother. He retired here, I could never really understand why Poggio exactly, it seemed a backward place to me. But Covid took him, and he left me the flat in his will. It saved me.'

'How long have you been here?'

'Thirteen months.'

'And?'

'Maybe I'm getting used to the quiet. I might open a little restaurant beside the town square, if I can borrow the money. I'm still thinking about it. Not that I have many choices.'

* * *

His flat was considerably bigger than Christina's.

The living room boasted an entire wall of books. She stood and stared. Only a quarter were recipe and food books. There were many works on history, art and music and a sizeable quantity of fiction as well. And more than half of the collection was in English.

'You like reading?' he asked.

'Very much,' she said.

'*La mia biblioteca è la tua biblioteca,*' he said.

'*Grazie,*' she replied.

He led the way to the kitchen, which was spacious and well equipped. He poured wine for her and played Verdi's *Otello*, with Pavarotti, Te Kanawa and Nucci, on a superb sound system. He said he was a fanatic and a somewhat over-the-top patriotic fan of the late Italian tenor. She must forgive him for his outburst the other day. He was easily offended when people equated Domingo with the maestro Pavarotti, but he knew he could be too snobbish and outspoken when it came to music and food.

He asked about her reading preferences, and told her about his. He gave her a flamboyant culinary demonstration: carbonara with guanciale – prepared pork cheeks – freshly ground black pepper, egg yolks, pecorino and bucatini pasta. He railed against his former restaurant rivals in England, who used bacon and cream. 'Even the famous Gordon Ramsay, he's a barbarian, I'll have you know.'

She laughed. For the first time in months.

He explained how Italian cooking was all about the magic of simplicity. And the best, freshest ingredients. Always seasonal. He said there was a saying in his language: *A tavola non si invecchia.* Around a table, with friends and family, you never grew old. That was still what he enjoyed the most. To be a chef, bringing people together around a table, breaking bread, sharing happiness with them.

It was the noblest profession of all.

Luca spoke with his hands, his voice climbed musical scales of passion and enthusiasm, he was constantly in motion. He said he would teach her to cook the perfect ragu, to make amatriciana and puttanesca, ziti pasta with fontina cheese and prosciutto in the oven, all easy, cheap and delicious.

He drew out a chair for her at the table, served the food, and sat down opposite her. He watched expectantly while she ate. He asked her how the carbonara was. It was divine. He laughed with his eyes squeezed shut and said it was his mother's recipe. He kept her wine glass topped up, so that she forgot how much she was drinking.

He regaled her with stories from his youth, his personal journey to chefdom. Her tension melted away in the face of his easy charm and the effect of the alcohol. Luca was intelligent, funny and warm, and, she thought, probably very lonely.

For dessert he served panna cotta with a strawberry syrup. He poured her sweet Tuscan Vin Santo and said: 'I had to flee from bankruptcy and creditors. What are you hiding from?'

The question took her by surprise. 'What makes you think I'm hiding?'

'*Cara*, you are a beautiful young woman in the flower of your life. You belong in the light, somewhere, where young men line up to court you. But you are here. Poggio! It makes no sense. And besides, there's a . . . It's none of my business, you don't have to say a word, but there's sadness in your eyes.'

She shook her head to disguise the strange way his words had touched her.

'Forgive me,' he said. 'I didn't mean to pry.'

His empathy, his genuine honesty, the tranquilising effect of the wine and warm companionship all conspired together. It brought a pressing of emotion. It allowed her to feel the great weight of her burden, and suddenly the overwhelming desire to find release.

She heard her own voice speaking: 'Do you want to hear my sad story, Luca? The soap opera of my life? I wonder if you would even believe it. It's odd, Luca. It's a conspiracy, a satirical tragedy . . .'

'*Cara*,' he said, 'I shouldn't have . . .'

'No, it's okay,' she said. 'It's okay.' She held out her glass for a refill, sipped it. She took a deep breath. And said: 'I came to hide away from my past.'

And then she told him.

★　★　★

Her father's name was Louis, she said.

Soft-spoken, soft-hearted, so very sensitive. And perhaps never entirely stable.

He was the son of a struggler, a widower, piece-worker drifting from farm to farm in the Kalahari offering his limited services for hire. He often left Louis as a small child with the San people, the Bushmen, when he felt the need to quench his great thirst. That's where her father grew up, half wild, semi-schooled, but grounded in the culture, the beliefs and the bush lore of the San.

At seventeen Louis was an orphan: his father's alcohol abuse eventually overtook him.

Louis dreamed of working with animals in the open spaces of the African bush. Of becoming a nature conservationist in the Kalahari Gemsbok Park, or Kruger Park. His complete lack of any formal qualification – and the financial resources to earn them – soon dashed those hopes. Out of desperation and sheer need he began tracking for hunting groups. First in the Northern Cape and Botswana. The news of his extraordinary skill and encyclopaedic knowledge of nature spread like wildfire. Within two years he had more work than he could handle, and a reputation as the best in the business.

He was nineteen when he got the call from a very rich farmer in the Lowveld. It was a turning point that would change the course of his life forever.

29

As she spoke to Luca, it felt as though she was outside her own body. The music had stopped; there was a sense of almost-sacred silence in the flat. She heard her own voice, quiet, faintly amused, as though she were recounting someone else's history. He sat still, listening intently, stirring only when she held out her glass for more Vin Santo.

She wondered, as the words flowed out of her, why now, why here? Why hadn't she told anyone so honestly about her past before? It wasn't just the wine. It was the place and time and all that had just happened. And fatherly Luca here with her.

She said the man who phoned from the Lowveld was Big Frik Redelinghuys. He had seven farms, producing citrus, nuts, bananas, and game. He hired Louis to act as tracker for groups of foreign trophy hunters. Frik had three daughters, as seemed fitting for such a tale. The youngest and the prettiest one was Drika. Nineteen, rebellious, sensuous, and thoroughly spoilt.

'I wish I could have been a fly on the wall that day,' said Chrissie. 'Watching their meeting. My father was a very handsome young man. I've seen the photos. Wiry and fit, with long blond hair, such a shy, vulnerable boy's face. And my mother so sultry, with her pitch-black hair, very sexy, and not scared to show it. I believe it was an explosion of nineteen-year-old hormones, pure lust, nothing more. They were so very different, you see, different origin, person-alities . . . absolutely everything. Within weeks my mother was pregnant. With me.'

Oupa Frik Redelinghuys, an old stalwart, staunchly, painfully con-servative, reacted to this scandalous stain on the family name by disowning his daughter immediately. He denied her very existence, and nine months later the existence of his little granddaughter too, despite the fact that Louis and Drika had married in haste in the magistrate's court before she was born.

The marriage, built on passion's fickle foundation, was doomed from the outset. Louis had to put food on the table. Drika was too young and restless to sit at home with a baby. Soon she began to blame her husband and child for her captivity, the drudgery, the dull routine, the unwanted responsibility.

Instinctively Chrissie withheld from Luca that she had been christened Cornél van Jaarsveld. That her father nicknamed her 'Flea' early on. Later she would wonder if it was her way of trying to protect the child in her. Or was it just her habit to keep certain secrets?

'And here,' she said, 'is where the soapie truly begins. After a year my mother started leaving me more and more in the care of a Venda nanny so that she could go out, on Friday and Saturday nights when my father was in the bush. In the Lowveld there are bush pubs, in the middle of nowhere. Where the four-by-fours park in long rows on weekends, and the drinking is done in earnest. Young people, especially, because that's all there is to do. They became my mother's hangouts. Her drinking increased, she stayed out later and later. When I was two she met this hippie singer. A man who played his guitar and sang in one of the bush bars on weekends. Older than she was, from a coastal town in the Eastern Cape. My mother began an affair with him. Some of the people who were sympathetic to my father tried to send him a message, telling him he should come home. By the time the message reached him, it was too late. My mother and the singer heard my father was on his way back, so she ran off with her lover. That night, boozed-up, they drove off a bridge. My mother died.'

There must have been something in her voice, a hint of emotion breaking through, because Luca reached his hand across the table and touched hers, his face filled with sympathy. She shook her head, no interruptions now.

'My father came to fetch me, and he raised me to the best of his ability as a maverick, an eccentric outsider. It was only his incredible skill that kept him and his child alive. Until I was thirteen I was with him every single day. And then he found permanent employment as a guide and game ranger at Moremi, in the Okavango Delta. For less pay, but because he wanted me to be educated. There were people to look after me, a little school for the employees' children. Then my father began disappearing. Sometimes for a day or two, sometimes longer than two weeks. When I asked him where he'd been, he said: with his people. The Bushmen. In the Kalahari. And I mustn't worry, he would always come back. But I saw that he . . . it was as if he was slowly but surely losing his balance. His grip on reality. Maybe he was grieving for my mother, maybe the responsibility of raising a child was too much for him to bear, after his own parentless youth. He gave me a dog, a Jack Russell with the name of Khutlô, so that I wouldn't be alone when he was away. I was devoted to that dog, the best thing in my life, the one bit of normality and stability. In the winter when I was sixteen, my father went away again. It was a very dry year, the animals in the Delta were struggling. Khutlô and I went walking in the morning alone, beside the river. And then the baboons came, a starving troop, and they wanted to catch Khutlô, and when I tried to save him they attacked me too. See this mark, under my eye? It's from that day. There are scars on my back too. I couldn't save my dog. I loved him. But he's dead. Like my father . . .'

This time her voice cracked. For the first time, she felt the tears, fought them.

'*Cara*,' said Luca Marchesi, his emotions were threatening to overwhelm him too. He reached for her hand, comforting.

She pulled her hand away. She didn't want comfort now, she wanted to finish.

'And then my father came back, and he saw my wounds and said it was all his fault. The attack, the injuries, Khutlô's death, my mother running off, my mother's death. All his fault. It was the gods punishing him, because he had done wrong. I cried and said no, no, he mustn't talk like that. And he said I don't understand these things. When he was a child, he stole honey. He was terribly hungry. From a beehive that was marked by someone. It's a big crime in Bushman culture, it is like stealing someone's water, or cutting down a shade tree. If he was a Bushman he would have been given the death penalty. But the shaman said they couldn't kill him, because he was a white boy.

But they could curse him. And they did. That was why he kept going back, to beg them to remove the curse. For my sake. And my father said there was only one way to end the curse. I didn't know what he meant, I just said it's all silly stories, but my father . . . His obsession . . . His . . .'

She was there again, in the dusty camp, with her father. She remembered her keening, her pleading, because she could see the mania in his eyes, his fear, his paranoia. She clung to him, she screamed that it was all just superstition, foolish, stupid, mad.

Then he became calm and held her tight and said she was right. Everything would be okay.

And that night he went and sat beside the water and waited for the crocodiles.

All that was left behind was the letter to her, placed neatly on a pile of clothes.

30

'*Dio mio*,' Luca said, after a long silence.

She came slowly back to reality. She felt stripped, calm. Lighter.

'What did you do?' he asked.

She wrapped her arms around herself. She said the people at Moremi wanted to place her in foster care. So she ran away. To her grandfather, in Nelspruit. She knocked on the door of the rich farmer, Big Frik Redelinghuys and said: 'I'm your granddaughter. Drika's child. Pleased to meet you.'

Frik just said, 'I don't know you.' And shut the door in her face.

Reliving that moment, her rage and humiliation, made her get up from Luca's table. 'It's such a cheesy story, such a melodrama.'

'I'm so sorry,' Luca said. 'What did you do?'

She stood behind her chair, gripping the backrest. She smiled and said: 'I hear so many people say things like "I went to Bali, or Thailand or where-the-fuck-ever to find myself". Or "I wanted to discover the real me". Or "I want to be the best version of myself". It makes my head explode, Luca, because I can't do that. I haven't got the faintest idea who I am. Half of me is from my mother, I look like her, I'm sly and reckless like her. Half of me is from my father, I can feel and read the African bush as if I'm bound to it by my umbilical cord. I'm a loner, like him, restless like him, and I'm waiting for that crazy streak to surface sometime. I can see and feel the genetic influences, bits and pieces, but I can't see myself as a whole. I don't know who I am. Maybe it's because . . . You know what Ubuntu is, Luca? It's an African philosophy. Ubuntu says, I am a person through other people. I am a real, genuine, individual person because I am part of a greater and more meaningful social and spiritual world. Maybe that's true, but the trouble is, I never was part of anything. Nobody wants me. Not my mother or my father or my grandpa or my grandma wanted me. And when Pa died, nobody knew what to do with me. So I ran away. And I lied about my age and looked for work in the

Lowveld. I cleaned rooms in a guesthouse, I was a waitress at a bush pub, cashier at a mini-market. I packed avocados on a farm, cleaned cages at an animal rehab centre. For two years and three months. Just to survive, to eat and sleep in tiny soulless rooms. All my worldly goods in a backpack. I was abused, exploited, harassed, twice I was nearly raped. Ubuntu was for other people, never for me.

'But I learned. I saw how the world worked. And somewhere in that time I realised, if I didn't want to be a victim, I would have to make a decision. I would have to use what I inherited from my oh-so-very-admirable parents. So I took my mother's cunning and father's history and I committed an act of petty fraud. At the animal rehab centre I shared a room with a guy who had enough money to study for the field guide qualification. When he graduated, I stole his certificate and forged my own. A victimless crime, the guy thought he had lost his diploma and he requested a duplicate. The irony is, I was far better qualified than he was. I paid with my entire youth for that expertise.

'And then my life changed, Luca. Just one little misdeed, and suddenly I was no longer one of the outcasts, the marginalised, the mavericks. Suddenly I was one of them, part of a greater, more meaningful social and spiritual world. Viva, Ubuntu, viva! I found work as a guide for a small start-up outfit offering walking tours in the Kruger Park. And I was good at it. Increasingly I was given the foreign tourists, and their tips were generous. I could start *living*. I could pretend that I was normal. Respectable. I created a front, a fiction of who and what I was. And then doors began to open, and later I was able to resign and do just freelance tracking, for hunting groups and for the WWF and the Parks Board.

'You ask me why didn't I just keep on doing that? It wasn't a bad life. I could buy a car, I could rent a decent flat, I had money in the bank. Why not stick to that?

'The thing is, Luca, you don't forget. You don't forget the rejection and desperation and poverty and mockery. You're constantly afraid you'll end up back there, always worried that something might happen that could take away what you have. But above all you can't forget that your victimless crime made such a huge difference to your life. That you could cheat and get away with it. That it was fun to pull one over the establishment. A little titbit of revenge. I felt no remorse, Luca. Nothing. I wondered what that said about me? Did I also inherit that from my mother, a kind of sociopathy? I still wonder. But then I console myself: I can feel the pain of animals, I have empathy for them, so I can't be all bad.

'Then something came across my path, something that could make the barricades against my old life so much bigger and sturdier. It wasn't legal, it was exciting, it was another morsel of revenge. And I thought, why not?

'I'm not going to tell you about my other wrongdoings. They were all supposed to be victimless. But the problem is that they were not without damage and loss. If you want to know who I'm hiding from, it's not really from the people I harmed, I don't think they will find me here. I'm hiding from myself. I'm hiding from that part inside of me that feels no remorse, that thought, why not? I don't want to find out how exactly my mother and father's genes are embodied in me. I really *don't* want to find myself. I'm afraid the truth might be too much to take.'

★ ★ ★

In the morning she had a hangover. Remorse too. What on earth had she been thinking?

She lay in bed hoping the nausea would pass, finally got up to make a cup of coffee and came back to bed to drink it, downing two headache pills. Read the news from South Africa on her phone. Corruption, 'load-shedding' power cuts, violence and death. Nothing new there.

She took a shower, wanting to get out, to sweat out the poison.

The cats were waiting on the porch. She called them 'vultures', put milk out for them and went for a walk, past the small San Rocco church, down the stony footpath, to the bottom of the valley.

It was the first morning that she hadn't immediately thought of Rousseau and Brenner and Themba and Yon. A milestone. Despite the headache and nausea, she felt lighter today, as though there had been some point to her revelations. Her instincts told her she could trust Luca. Last night he had escorted her back to her flat. She was tipsy, unsteady on her high heels and had to cling to his arm. He said to her: 'You are a good human being. I know people. You are good. You must believe me.'

She walked beside the silver stream, past the ruins of forgotten farmhouses, past tractors chugging in olive orchards, listening to dogs barking somewhere on the hillsides, the birds singing. She felt the early summer on her skin, saw trees in blossom, darting lizards and a small black grass snake.

She could smell the wine in her sweat.

What had come over her? The first time in five years that she'd got drunk.

Perhaps it was what she needed. To loosen the reins, held tight so long, just a bit.

She walked the seven kilometres to Toffia, ate just half a cornetto, drank more coffee.

She hadn't brought the Brenner phone with her. She wanted one day without the suspense.

She walked back slowly, the headache pills wearing off. A faint new worry in the back of her mind: how was she going to fill her days? In all her planning and anticipation she had just focused on the big things. To get away, leave no trace, to buy a flat, a car, to renovate the home and equip it, to establish herself. And now she was almost there and the days stretched ahead, empty and lifeless.

She knew it was the lack of sleep and the toxins in her body that made her feel this way. She would have to find something to keep her busy.

Perhaps she should take another look at her finances. And find out if there was a small piece of land for sale in the valley. She could tend it herself. Olives and vegetables and fruit. Flowers. Get her fingers in the soil. An earthy, simple life. Grow for her own use, maybe sell to the market in Osteria Nuova. Learn from Luca how to cook, she had never really tried.

Maybe she should look at other available flats and houses in town. There were a few. She had some good experience, she knew now how to sand and paint, hammer and saw. She could buy, renovate, sell at a profit. But farming or speculating would make a big dent in her finances.

She didn't have enough.

Up the hill again, past the little church.

Babbar hunting us.

The tension was back.

Late in the afternoon she slid a thank you note under Luca's door.

31

On Saturday they installed the metal railing on her porch. The noise and activity scared Katse and Sebini away.

She drove to Castel di Tora, ate at L'Angoletto and stared out over the lake. She switched the Brenner phone on.

No messages.

In Osteria Nuova she bought tins of cat food, three planter pots to hang on her new porch rails, soil and compost, flowers and herbs. In the late afternoon she worked on the pots and plants. When she watered them from the fountain's hose, the cats jumped up on the wall. Katse came closer, and rubbed against her ankles. She fed them in front of her porch.

Sunday morning she knocked on Luca's door, a bit concerned that he hadn't come round again. He wasn't home, or he wasn't opening the door. Had she scared him off? Had she ruined her one chance to have a positive local interaction?

Late in the afternoon she drove to Rome for a concert at the Teatro di Marcello. The Bach and Beethoven sonatas were beautiful, Schoenberg's *Phantasy for Violin and Piano* disturbed her, left her with a feeling of impending doom that she couldn't shake.

After the concert she walked down the Tiber, stood on the Ponte Fabricio and switched on the Brenner phone.

Nothing.

Why no response? Why would Themba send her that one single message and then not respond?

Had Babbar found him?

Did Babbar have Themba's phone?

Then they would be able to track her. They would know at least that she was in Italy.

★   ★   ★

On Monday morning, when she opened the door, Sebini came in cautiously, curious. Katse sat on the threshold and watched her son. The little one sniffed at and scrutinised everything, until Chrissie went to open a can of cat food in the kitchen. Then he bounced out playfully and waited beside his mother.

She fed them on the porch, then sat down outside with her own breakfast and notebook in front of her, the one she used to write down all her expenses, set against what remained of her money.

On a local estate agent's website she had seen there were eight hectares on the hill up the valley for sale for €19,000, including a dilapidated shed and established olive, plum and fig trees. Here in the village there was a reasonably spacious one-bedroom flat for €20,000. She had to weigh up the two options against each other – the income from the agricultural land against the profit from reselling a renovated flat. The problem was that she knew nothing about farming or what demand was like in the local property market. She could do the research, but both possibilities seemed too risky and too expensive.

Then Luca strode purposefully around the corner. His face brightened when he saw her. '*Cara*, good morning, thank you for your note. I was away, I wanted to let you know, but I don't have your telephone number, how are you?'

* * *

They drank coffee outside. He said he'd had an urgent call from an old colleague in Siena who had a restaurant near the Piazza del Campo. Two of his chefs were in hospital with Covid – 'When is this plague going to leave us alone, Christina?' – and Luca had to go and help. 'I earned a few euros at least, and, *cara*, I realised just how much pleasure it brings me. Do you think I should open a restaurant here? The little place on the town square, the old bar. It's been empty for two years. If I could find an investor, a financier. What do you think?'

She said she would eat Luca's food any day. She'd been thinking of asking him for cooking lessons.

'Wonderful, *cara*, wonderful. We can start tomorrow.'

* * *

Tuesday. He taught her how to make crudo.

'Pesce crudo, that literally means "raw fish". The easiest thing in the world, *cara*. But there are three big secrets: the fish must be very fresh and the olive oil must be of the highest quality. But the most important ingredient is self-control. Nothing more than the fish, oil, fresh lemon and coarse salt. Nothing. Today we are working with sarago, because it's very fresh, but tuna is also suitable. Good, step one is how you cut the fish.'

★　★　★

Wednesday.

The joy and companionship of her interaction with Luca was gone. She felt that nagging anxiety again, the feeling of impending doom.

She drove to Rome, to buy a decent set of chef's knives. Luca said that was the foundation stone of good cuisine – a quality knife that you always kept sharp.

In the Via Mario de' Fiori she bought a set of Wüsthof in c.u.c.i.n.a.

It was only five minutes' walk to the Caffè Greco for Torta della Nonna and coffee.

Usually the Greco delighted her – the maze of rooms, the deep red walls, cabinets of books and an endless array of beautiful paintings, the astounding history: Charles Dickens came here, as did John Keats and Henry James, Lady Di, Sophia Loren and Audrey Hepburn. But this afternoon she felt she should be looking over her shoulder. *Babbar hunting us.*

She went up to the bar counter for an espresso because it was cheaper that way. She ordered custard tart, and suddenly she felt the hairs on the back of her neck rise. The overwhelming feeling: someone was watching her. Ever since she'd come in. She didn't want to turn her head, she wanted to keep calm, nothing could happen inside here.

She waited for someone to stand up so that her eyes could follow him naturally. She looked.

There was no one.

She took a deep breath. She couldn't go on like this. Her reason said that they could not track her down here. She had been careful enough. They didn't have Themba's phone. He was smart, he would have sent the message and then disposed of the phone. To protect himself *and* her.

It was time for her to move on, to shake this constant anxiety.

She took out the Brenner phone. She would switch it on one last time. Make sure. Then chuck it.

She switched on the phone.

No message from Themba Jola.

She took a bite of her tart.

The phone vibrated.

Her heart leaped.

She touched the screen and a Telegram message appeared. From an unknown contact. She opened it.

> *There's a Roman with something to say*
> *About living your life the right way*
> *The credo of Horace*
> *Is meant to implore us*
> *And lead us to seize every day.*

It was as if her world stood still. The possibilities flooded her mind, engulfed her.

The phone vibrated.

Turn around, the message said.

She turned around.

Igen Rousseau was sitting there, blue bandana around his head, the long, raking scar across his cheekbone and temple half concealed.

'Hey,' he said with a wry smile.

32

She uttered a sound of joy *and* fury.

Heads swivelled towards her.

She stood up, went over to him, thumped him on the shoulder with her fist.

'You bastard, you bastard, you could have let me know. I thought you were dead.' She punched him again.

All eyes in the room were on them.

He stood up, smile unwavering. 'Lord, it's good to see you.'

Only then did she embrace him.

★ ★ ★

They sat in the corner of the big room, at the back of the café. Questions poured from her: Was Themba okay? Jericho Yon? Why didn't he let her know he was okay? How did they get away that night? What about Babbar, who was hunting them? How did Nicky Berry know?

He gently touched her hand, he said wait, let him tell it properly.

'You should have let me know.'

'I couldn't.'

She pulled her hand away from his. 'You sent me a Telegram now.'

'Chrissie, are you going to let me tell the whole story?'

'You're a bastard.'

'I am.'

'Okay. Tell.'

'Remember the first time we got together? At Brenner's house?'

'The *braai*.'

'We think that Nicky planted GPS trackers on some of our cars that night.'

'We? Who is we?'

'Me and Themba and Jer.'

'So they are okay?'

'They are reasonably okay.'

'Reasonably?'

'They are okay.'

'It took you long enough to tell me that.'

'I'm a bastard.'

'You are. Go on.'

He said that according to Nicky's screaming that night at the plane hangar, Berry must have hated Brenner intensely. Jealousy over his Special Forces background perhaps, maybe something that happened between Brenner and Berry's sister, but they suspect Berry decided right from the start to manipulate Brenner to take on the robbery and then to steal the dollars from him.

'We think they followed us. That's the one thing that didn't worry us, and we weren't on the alert for it. Brenner and Jer went to the airfield together twice during planning. And once Nicky found out who Jer was and where he worked, it couldn't have been too hard to figure out the plan. Nicky gave Brenner the idea of an Easter week-end robbery; it was he who said it was the best time. So he and his mates knew when, and they more-or-less knew where we would take the dollars. So they waited for us . . .'

'Did nobody find their cars?'

'Car. They all came in a fucking Toyota Quantum. That's the first thing that saved our asses. The other one was Themba. He was unbelievable . . .'

'I thought you were dead, Igen. How . . .? You and Jer?'

'They hit me with something,' and he pulled off his blue bandana so that she could see the long scar clearly. 'I don't know what it was. A gigantic spanner perhaps. I was just outside the hangar, they probably didn't want to start shooting and alert you too soon. So they hit me. Broke my cheekbone, cracked my skull, knocked me out, serious concussion, a lot of blood. Jer and I still get helluva headaches. He was lucky. They shot him from behind while he was sitting in the Hino. Something in the truck must have deflected the bullet. Or maybe his head was more than ninety degrees turned, because it went through the tip of his temporal skull bone. A lot of blood, out like a light, but no permanent damage. And Themba saved our asses.'

He said the Xhosa had been a Pathfinder with him for four years
in the British 16 Air Assault Brigade. Part of their training was field
first aid. The first thing Themba did was to bind his own hip
wound to stop the bleeding. The second was to stabilise Igen and
Yon. When he realised neither of the two was going to bleed to
death, he summed up the situation, and knew he was working
against the clock. Themba had to get them all away before the fire
brigade and police arrived. By that time everything was being
consumed by the fire.

'He remembered that Nicky and Co. must have a vehicle somewhere, and he ran limping through the hangars. He found the Toyota
Quantum, maybe fifteen years old, a real vintage banger, but it
started first go. And he raced back and dragged us into the Quantum
and drove off. But he also knew that he had to get Jer on his feet the
next morning. Because Jer is connected to the plane. And the mine
guys would phone him to say their hangar and the plane were burned.
So he drove to the Airbnb where he and Brenner were meant to stay
that night, at Hartebeespoort. And he carried us inside, and did
everything he could to bring Jer back to consciousness. At five in the
morning Jer was awake. Very confused, couldn't remember a thing.
But Themba kept his cool and explained everything, gave him a lot
of Energade. And pills. And when the mine people called, just before
seven, he took an Uber, he arrived at the hangar with a hoody to hide
the wound, and so full of painkillers that he couldn't talk very well.
He said he'd partied a bit too much the previous night, he only
meant to fly to the Cape in the afternoon, it was such a big loss, the
PC-12, all the horse vaccine gone. Who would have wanted to damage a plane like that? Or steal it? Was there any bad feeling with
workers? A rival company? They must catch the fuckers, it was out-
rageous. Then the mine people said that the police had found dollar
notes. They suspected it was drug smugglers. Cocaine maybe, that
was the big thing in the country now. A drug deal gone wrong. They
were just relieved that Yon wasn't in the aeroplane, the plane at least
was well-insured. And then Jericho Ubered back, but he passed out
in the car. The Uber sat in front of the Airbnb for twenty minutes
waiting for Jer to regain consciousness.'

'And you?'

'Two days.'

'You were out for two days?'

Igen nodded. 'But when I woke up I saw the dollars beside the bed. Themba saved just under three hundred thousand. Nearly six million rand. That man is incredible, I'm telling you.'

★　★　★

She had so many questions she wanted to ask, but Rousseau smiled and held up his hand, not now. 'I really want to tell you everything, but first there are a few things you have to understand. The first point is, those weren't the Chandas' dollars.'

She stared at him.

'The story,' he said, 'is much more interesting.'

'What about Babbar? Themba sent me a message. He's hunting us . . .'

'That's true. Babbar is after us, but not for the Chandas. They are sitting in Dubai. And our new president is tightening the screws, they might well be extradited to South Africa. Ishan Babbar has been back with his old bosses for over a year already.'

'Who?'

'I'll get to that, Chrissie. The second thing you need to understand, is that I can only tell you the rest if you're in.'

'In what?'

'In the next job.'

'What next job?'

'We're going to steal four thousand kilograms of gold.'

'Whose gold?'

'The same guys that the dollars belonged to. Are you in?'

33

That Thursday morning she knocked on Luca Marchesi's door.

He was delighted to see her, said nothing about her hair, cut very short again. '*Cara*, come in, come in.'

'I came to ask you a favour,' she said.

'Of course. Anything.'

'I'm going to be away for two or three weeks . . .'

'Where?'

'I can't tell you now. But could you please feed the cats? I will buy enough food and I'll give you my key.'

He looked at her in concern. 'I will do that with pleasure. But . . . Is everything okay?'

'I hope to collect an investment. For your restaurant,' she said.

'*Cara*. You're not serious.'

'I am,' she said.

'That's wonderful. Are you going far?'

'Yes.'

'*Mio Dio*,' he said. And then: '*Cara*, you will need something to read on the long journey. Come, let's have a look.'

Hyena
(Crocuta crocuta)
Benny & Vaughn

34

Monday, 24 May.

Nineteen days before the wedding.

Eleven minutes to four in the afternoon. In a townhouse in Stellenbosch's Welgevonden complex, Warrant Officer Vaughn Cupido walked out of the bedroom looking smug. He ran his hand over his belly and the smart light-blue striped shirt.

'Check this out, Donnie,' said Cupido. 'I can fit into your ma's favourite shirt again, five kilos down, baby, just ten more to go.'

Donovan, Desiree Coetzee's son, was in the sitting room, gaze fixed on his cell phone. Interrupted, he looked up. 'Uncle V, with all due respect, that shirt is still *lekker* tight,' he said and focused on the phone again.

'Maybe, baby, but not so *kwaai* that I can't close the buttons . . . What's up with all that staring at the phone? Expecting a call?'

'No. I'm wooing.'

'You're *wooing*?'

'Damn straight.'

'Who do you woo?'

'Esmerelda Daniels. Prettiest girl in Grade 6. I scheme she *smaak*s me. But relationships . . . That is complicated business.'

'Out of the mouths of babes . . .'

'I'm *twelve*, Uncle V.' Indignant.

'Fair enough, Donnie. Fair enough. But the cavalry has arrived. Your Uncle V is the greatest wooer of all time. How can I be of service to solve this conundrum?'

'Okay, cool. So, I Whatsapp her, and I ask: "M&M's, Bar One, Tex or Smarties?" 'Cause why, I want to bring her a chocolate tomorrow, just to take the relationship to the next level.'

'The next level? With a chocolate?'

'That's how it works, in my world.'

'So what's the problem?'

'Problem is, I don't know if I must include an orange or a yellow heart emoji.'

'What's wrong with a red heart, that's what I always send your ma.'

'Uncle V, that is why you can't be my woo advisor. You are a dinosaur. You don't get the subtleties of modern love. A red heart expresses love or romance, but that's like a bit premature in our relationship. An orange heart is for love that can exist between two friends, and a yellow is for pure and sincere love linked to friendship. That's where we are now. Orange. Or yellow.'

'Well, I never . . .'

'There's still green, blue, purple, black and brown hearts too, but none of those are relevant to this.'

Cupido was still trying to absorb all this before venturing an opinion, but his phone began to ring. He went to pick it up from the kitchen counter. The screen showed the name of Sergeant Erin Riddles, one of his detective colleagues.

He answered: 'Sarge?'

'I know it's your and Benny's day off, Warrant, but the colonel said you must come in for this one.'

★ ★ ★

In the Sew Elegant shop in Plein Street, Stellenbosch, the woman was feeling very high up Benny Griessel's inner thigh. He stood stock still, obviously uncomfortable and extremely unhappy.

'Pa, relax. It's going to look fantastic,' his daughter Carla said, chirpy as ever. She was twenty-five years old, a publicist at a wine estate, an attractive young woman who had inherited the best of her father's facial features.

'I am relaxing,' Griessel said, but he knew it wasn't true. It was the touching in strange places that made him so tense. And the time he was wasting to go through this. First he had to spend hours looking at designs with Carla on her Pinterest app. When all the while he really had no say in the final choice, because his 'dress sense is shaky'. Then it was a whole morning at a fabric shop in Somerset West, and now the entire afternoon to take his measurements. He'd wanted to just buy a suit off the rack at Woolworths or Markhams, but Alexa and Carla were having none of it. The only bit of good news was that the tailored garments wouldn't cost more than a Woollies suit did.

And the source of the biggest influence on his stress levels, was the wedding itself. It was barrelling towards him like a bullet train. Unstoppable. Utterly beyond his control.

He heard his phone ring. Carla had put it in her handbag while he stood for the measurements. She took it out quickly and checked the screen. 'It's Uncle Vaughn.' She answered: 'Hello, Uncle Vaughn, can Pa call you back, they are measuring him for his wedding suit.'

She listened for a long time, gave Cupido the address of Sew Elegant, and said goodbye. She said to Griessel: 'He said good luck with the wedding suit, listen to your daughter, she's a genius. And they want you at Basie Small's house. I have to tell Pa that it's urgent, the colonel's orders, Uncle Vaughn will pick you up, and karma is a bitch. What does that mean?'

★ ★ ★

'It means Basie Small is *muertos, moer toe*, dead as a doornail,' said Cupido when he picked up Griessel with the Golf. 'That's all I know, partner. Karma. I'm telling you. Karma.'

He had to weave his way through the parked SAPS vehicles and curious bystanders to stop in front of Small's Brandwacht Street house. Sergeant Erin Riddles hurried over. When they got out, she said: 'It's bad. Him and his dogs. I have never seen something like this. The whole house is a crime scene, you'll have to suit up.'

'Give us the headlines,' said Cupido while he and Griessel took out the PPE suits and pulled them on.

'Neighbour there . . .' She pointed at the house across the street. '. . . came home from work, two o'clock to change for golf, and he saw Small's gate standing open. Very unusual, because Small always made sure that his dogs never got out. So he came over to check, and saw the front door was open too. When he saw Small lying there, he called the station . . .'

'Cause of death?' Cupido asked.

'Suffocation, if you ask me. But it's weird. Dogs were shot, two shots each. Head shots, close range. This Small, he was a lawyer, *nè*?'

Griessel shrugged. 'The woman next door said that's what he told everyone, but when we looked for him on the roll, he wasn't registered. Never had been. Clean as a whistle, innocent as the day he was born. No record, no outstanding fines, nothing.'

'This isn't a home invasion and robbery,' said Riddles. 'Expensive watch still on his arm, laptop and cell phone undisturbed in the room. This is gang-related, this,' said Riddles. 'Professional hit. With a strong message.'

'And that is?'

'Hold your tongue. That's what I'm getting.'

★   ★   ★

Basie Small lay in the space between the open-plan kitchen and sitting room, on his back. He was dressed in shorts and a T-shirt. A big Garmin watch on his arm. His eyes were stretched wide, mouth gaping, and filled with a white clotted mass that looked like it had erupted from his innards.

'*Jissis*,' said Benny Griessel.

'That what I said too,' said Erin Riddles.

'He put up a *moer* of a fight,' said Cupido. From the kitchen counter to the sitting area chairs were overturned, cushions strewn about, a Persian carpet rucked up. There were multiple bruises and cuts on his hands, arms and legs, defensive wounds. Blood on the limbs, blood spatters and smears on the floor. Vaughn counted the small, dark red twin burn marks of an electroshock weapon. 'Tasered. Four times, at least.'

He realised Griessel wasn't responding, and saw his colleague's expression as Benny stared vacantly into Small's eyes.

He went over to Benny, laid a hand on his arm. 'Benna,' he said gently. 'Don't go there.'

Griessel slowly drew back from the vision of death, looked at Cupido. 'It's filler foam,' he said. 'Down his throat.'

'Filler foam?'

'It's for . . . I used it, back we were suspended, when I painted the house.'

'I remember. The job you loved to hate.'

Griessel nodded. 'The stuff dries quickly, Vaughn. A minute, and it's hard. You spray it with a long pipe into the holes . . .'

'That's what suffocated him,' said Riddles. 'There must have been four at least. He's a big man. Strong. Fit. It would take a lot to push him down and force that stuff down his throat.'

'Where are the dogs?' Cupido asked.

She gestured with her head towards the outside and walked out the big sliding door that led to the swimming pool. There was a starburst of cracks on the glass. 'This door was open when we arrived. Those cracks – I think he or one of the attackers fell against the door; it's not made by a firearm.'

They followed her outside. The Kreepy Krauly was on, running across the bottom of the pool unaffected, making tiny ripples on the water. She pointed a finger. Both Rottweilers lay between the swimming pool and the high wall of the yard's eastern boundary. Griessel and Cupido walked closer to inspect them.

'I think they came over the wall there,' Riddles said. 'With handguns. Silenced, most likely, because the neighbours in front said they didn't hear a thing. And the neighbours on that side . . .' She pointed at the house on the other side of the wall from where the suspected attackers had come. 'They weren't home until just now. Husband and wife work in Cape Town, they only come home after six. So, I reckon the attackers jumped over from there. When the dogs attacked, they shot them. You can see, one shot to stop them, then the head shots were to make sure they were dead. Maybe Small heard the muffled shots and came out. Then they tasered him. Look . . .' She showed them a place with deep, ploughed footprints in the lawn.

'Why didn't they just shoot him too?' Griessel asked.

'That's the million-dollar question,' said Riddles.

'They wanted something,' said Cupido. 'Safe combination? Card PIN?'

'There's a gun safe in the bedroom, inside the wardrobe. Locks with a key, I haven't started looking for the key yet. But there's no sign of activity in that room.'

'Why the filler foam?' Griessel asked.

'That is a statement,' said Riddles. 'I'm sure of it.'

'A statement for who?' Cupido asked. Then: 'They grabbed him outside, and then took him inside. Why?'

'Maybe he got loose. Ran inside,' Griessel said. 'To get a gun from the safe?'

'Maybe they wrestled him inside. More private space, less chance of being seen or heard,' said Riddles.

'Benna, we can at least get bite profiles of the dogs,' said Cupido. 'Close that case.'

'Now, that's the other million-dollar question,' said Erin Riddles. 'Is *this* connected to your case?' She knew the details of the Le-Lanie Leibrandt investigation, because the detectives had to report their progress to Colonel Witkop Jansen at morning parade every day, so that the whole team would know about it.

Griessel looked at Cupido. They both shook their heads.

'Not impossible . . .' said Griessel. 'But . . .'

'Not very likely,' said Cupido.

'The brother, Arno. We never told him Small was a suspect . . .'

Cupido gestured at the murder scene, inside and outside. 'And I just don't see that guy doing this.'

'That investigation is at a dead end?' Riddles asked.

'The bite profiles on the girl were inconclusive as to species,' said Cupido.

'No DNA, the palm print on the phone was Le-Lanie's,' said Griessel.

'We never had enough for a warrant.'

'This is something else,' said Griessel.

'This is trouble with a capital T,' said Cupido.

'The colonel said it's your trouble now. Your docket,' said Erin Riddles. 'But I'm here to help if you need me.'

35

They asked Erin Riddles to check with the municipal CCTV control room for video material of all the vehicles entering and leaving the Dalsig neighbourhood in the twenty-four hours before two o'clock this afternoon. And they said Forensics and the videographer should continue with their work in the living room while Griessel and Cupido made a thorough and meticulous search of the house.

In the master bedroom they found the gun safe. It was locked. And, as Erin Riddles had said, no sign of any activity or struggle. The double bed was neatly made up, the wardrobes equally orderly. A large collection of sports clothes and shoes. And no sign of the safe key in the bedside cupboard drawer or between or under the clothes. On the wall was a console to activate the house alarm.

The second bedroom was set up as an office. It faced north. Through the lace curtains at the window they could see the front garden, and the wall that separated the yard from the sidewalk beside the street. Inside the room was a laptop and printer on a simple wooden table-top on trestles. The chair at the laptop was pushed far back. The computer was still on, a screen saver making swirling patterns. Small's cell phone was connected to it with a charger cable. The phone required a PIN code before it would open.

When they activated the computer's keyboard, a website appeared with a registration form for the Ironman 70.3 to be held in Mossel Bay in November – at an entry fee of R4,300. The page was partially filled in with Small's details.

The Outlook app displayed an inbox with only three emails: his services account from the municipality, a statement from Allan Gray for an investment, and one with the subject *This Might Interest You* from admin@vega-resources.com. The last two email attachments needed passwords.

In the wardrobe they found the house alarm box and backup battery. Everything was in working order.

The third bedroom contained only an unmade single bed. A built-in cupboard contained an ironing board and iron, a vacuum cleaner, two empty travelling cases and an empty military duffel bag.

The kitchen cupboards produced nothing of any note. Neither did the drawers under the cabinet of the widescreen TV.

Next to the door leading from the kitchen to the double garage was another alarm console, and a small panel for hanging keys. The safe key was not there. There were keys for the outside doors, and one for the vehicle in the double garage – a black Ford Ranger Raptor, polished and gleaming.

Against the rear wall of the garage was a work bench, a tool chest and a few boxes with equipment for reloading ammunition and cleaning firearms. Everything was well maintained and carefully organised.

In a tall cupboard beside the work bench they found backpacking equipment: a large Deuter hiking backpack, a sleeping bag, an ultralight mattress, a camping stove and extra gas cylinders, a folding pan, a headlamp. Also neatly stowed.

An aluminium ladder leaned against the wall. Beside it, mounted on bicycle hooks, hung a Canyon Speedmax CF SLX – a slim, feather-light carbon bicycle with peculiarly shaped handlebars. Griessel, who knew something about bicycles, googled it and confirmed that it was a model used by athletes in Ironman competitions. And it was a heck of a lot of dosh hanging up there.

At 21:35 the paramedics carried Basie Small's body to the ambulance, and the forensics and photography teams departed.

Griessel made certain that all the doors were locked. Cupido spanned crime tape across the gate and locked it behind them while two TV stations and various newspaper photographers snapped and recorded them. The street was crowded with people and cars.

They dodged the media questions, walked to Cupido's Golf, and drove to the KFC down in Adam Tas Road.

They knew that when they returned in twenty minutes to tackle the door-to-door footwork, the street would be mostly empty.

★ ★ ★

Tuesday, 25 May, eighteen days to the wedding.

Just before three in the morning they bought coffee at the Vida e Caffè at the petrol station in Adam Tas, and drove to the office.

At twenty to four in the a.m. they made and filed their final notes in the criminal docket. Cupido was just ten minutes from Desiree's house, he said goodbye and left. Griessel decided to lie down on the camp bed in the office for an hour or two. They had to report to the colonel at six, and at seven they had to continue the investigation; the first seventy-two hours were crucial. If he went home, it was ninety minutes there and back, with barely an hour to sleep.

He took off his shoes and socks, switched off the light and lay down. His mind was whirring. He thought about Basie Small's final moments, the fear and rage, the terrible inevitability of his end, the desperate desire to breathe, to live, and the primal scream on the way to death. Did he think about Le-Lanie Leibrandt then? Did he feel any remorse?'

He knew he was heading for trouble if he couldn't find a way to focus on something else. His psychologist had taught him some techniques, but she didn't know what it was like to be standing there, seeing and feeling it all. It was part of him, this visualisation. It was the source of his sole talent as a detective: the ability to live himself into the crime scene, reconstruct what had happened, to get inside the minds of the perpetrators.

And it was the root of his drinking too, because once you'd seen it, you couldn't unsee it.

He forced his thoughts towards questions of motive, but he found no clues.

He thought about his daughter. How much joy Carla was getting from his approaching wedding. He needed to try harder, to get over his anxiety about it all, start to enjoy this new connection with her. An opportunity that would never come round again.

It was around five before he finally fell asleep.

* * *

Quarter past seven. Colonel Witkop Jansen sat alert and ramrod-straight behind his desk, listening intently.

'Six suspects,' said Cupido. His eyes were red, his voice hoarse and he was ravenous: there had been no time for breakfast. 'Lean and mean motherfuckers. They parked around the corner in a Hyundai H-1 panel van. Ten past nine yesterday morning, according to the security cam on the garage of the house that side.'

'Just late enough for everyone who had to go to work or school to have left,' said Griessel. On his lap he held the light brown three-flap folder, the case docket. Or simply 'the docket' in the general lingo of detectives, state prosecutors and judges. Benny's eyes were just as bloodshot, his hair dishevelled, the dark shadow of his beard beginning to show. He wasn't hungry. Only the faintly nagging thirst of a man who remembered how alcohol had once helped him through days like these.

'Fake number plate on the Hyundai, it didn't trigger the municipal system's number plate recognition, so they were clever. We think it might be a van that was stolen the evening before yesterday in Salt River, and only reported this morning. They had fake logos on the sides of the Hyundai. Of a company called AfriFibre Internet. There is no such company.'

'The logos are professional, Colonel,' Griessel said. 'It must have taken time, money and planning. These guys are well organised.'

'I'm receiving you,' said Jansen.

'The van was parked in the street for only four minutes, then they suddenly jumped out,' said Cupido. 'Balaclavas, gloves, overalls. They went over the wall of the house opposite, the one next to Small's. In a very organised fashion. One *ou* stood with cupped hands, the next stepped on his hands and he was over. Not your common-or-garden-variety attacker. Professional. And they knew, if they went over Small's front wall that he could see them. They recced the joint, they had a plan.'

'We think Small was busy on his laptop in one bedroom,' said Griessel. 'It faces the front, so he wouldn't have seen them when they came over the wall into the back garden. They shot the dogs, possibly with silencers. He maybe heard something, and ran out. There are signs of a struggle outside and the sliding door between the sitting room and the swimming pool has a contact crack.'

'They tasered him, but from the defensive wounds you can see that he fought for his life. And we scheme he screamed, and they dragged him inside, just in case. And then they pushed him down and sprayed filler foam down his throat.'

Griessel passed over a photo of Small's face, the filler foam in his gaping mouth, eyes stretched wide and wild.

'*Bliksem,*' said Jansen.

'The cause of death must be suffocation, Colonel. There are no other serious injuries visible.'

'Horrible way to die,' said Cupido. 'And we scheme that was part of the plan. They could have shot him outside already. With the same firearms they used on the dogs, so why send six guys to taser and tackle a big man, just to spray this stuff down his throat?'

'As Sergeant Riddles said, they want to send a message,' said Griessel.

'And,' said Cupido, 'maybe they didn't shoot him because they wanted info. Six guys holding him down, tasering him a bit more, gun to the head, filler foam in his face. That should get a man talking. "So tell us, where's the key to your safe, Basie? What's your Internet banking code?"'

'We drew up a timeline,' said Griessel and passed an A4 page across the desk. 'They came over the wall of the neighbours' house at 09:14 according to the camera. The same camera shows them at 09:31 going back over it, and getting into the Hyundai. We reckon it took two minutes to get into Small's property, two minutes back out. That means the whole attack lasted only thirteen minutes.'

'Thirteen minutes, Colonel. That is pro-level action,' said Cupido. 'These *maaifoedies* are next level.'

'Sergeant Riddles helped us to follow the Hyundai on the municipal and provincial cameras. At 09:33 they left via Barry Street, then took the R44 until Root44, and then down Annandale to Baden Powell. The last camera that caught them was at the Baden Powell junction with the N2. Then they disappeared.'

'Into Khayelitsha?' the colonel asked.

'It's possible,' said Griessel.

'We put out a general broadcast on the van,' said Cupido. 'But we're not holding our breath.'

'Related to the Leibrandt case?' Witkop Jansen asked, but his tone suggested he wasn't convinced.

'We strongly doubt it, but we want to make sure, Colonel,' said Griessel. 'Today we will talk to the brother.'

'Be careful,' said Jansen.

They nodded.

'This is something else, Colonel,' said Cupido. 'This is Small's shenanigans. He was involved in something. Telling everybody he was a lawyer, but he's not on the roll. That's the first clue. We went to every neighbour in the street last night. They all sing the same song: he was a loner. No parties, hardly any visitors, they only saw him jogging with the dogs and riding that sci-fi bike. He moved in three years ago, said he was a lawyer, and that is about it.'

'What do you want in the press?' asked Jansen.

'Just a robbery, Colonel. Victim's name only to be released when next of kin have been informed. Nothing about the filler foam.'

'It's going to come out,' said Jansen.

'We know,' said Cupido. 'But it might buy us some time.'

Jansen was silent while he considered the matter. Then he nodded. 'Good. What's next?'

'We sent his laptop, cell phone and his sports watch to the Hawks. If Colonel would perhaps phone Captain Philip van Wyk of IMC there?' Cupido was referring to the Directorate of Priority Crime Investigation's Information Management Centre.

'There's a dude there by the name of Warrant Officer Lithpel Davids, he's the digital forensics expert, bit of a genius. We want Small's call register, his contacts, WhatsApps and text messages. Maybe the sports watch has info about exactly where he was the day of Le-Lanie Leibrandt's death, his heart rate, etcetera. The usual stuff.'

Jansen nodded, and made a note.

'Key of the safe must be in that house, we want to find it,' said Cupido.

'We hope his ID document is in the safe. We want to find out who he is,' said Griessel. 'Who are his next of kin. What he was really doing for a living.'

'So we can pinpoint the shenanigans.'

36

They drove to Vida e Caffè again, this time for breakfast. Griessel ordered a toasted sandwich with bacon, egg and cheese. Cupido chose the yoghurt with granola and blueberries.

In the car Benny said 'Sorry, Vaughn,' because he knew the aroma of his sandwich was making his colleague's dietary efforts difficult.

Cupido nodded. 'No need to be sorry, Benna. I ate myself this fat, not you. It's just . . . this job. The hours. The fucked-up routine. The pay. Desiree keeps telling me, "Lovey, you have to exercise, you should join a gym. Diet without exercise is twice as hard." Now I ask you, where must I get the money or the time to go pump iron with Volvoville's yuppies? The SAPS, it's a conspiracy to keep you fat. Or keep you drunk. I'm telling you.'

'Volvoville' was how Cupido referred to Stellenbosch, because so many residents drove that make of car. 'Rich whiteys,' he often said, 'I will never understand. You can afford any wheels, but you buy the most boring luxury vehicle known to man. Why?'

Now they both sighed deeply. Cupido noted the kilojoules of his meal in his diet app. Then they drove off.

* * *

Basie Small's house was silent as the grave. Only the crime scene tape, the blood spatter on the floor, the star in the glass of the sliding door and the remains of fingerprint dust on various surfaces remained to tell the tale of the previous day.

It always made Griessel feel uneasy, an interloper, intruding into a private space that had belonged to a victim. He spoke in a low voice: 'Let's do the car first.'

The Raptor was, like everything in the house, in excellent condition, clean, tidy and orderly.

At first glance the navigation system's history yielded nothing: they suspected that Small had probably used his Samsung phone and Android Auto for directions.

The glove compartment contained a vehicle manual and registration papers, a cloth, two writing pens and a container of chewing gum, half full.

There was an empty water bottle in the driver's door.

Then they found Basie Small's wallet in the console between the front seats. It was leather, slightly worn from years of use, the first small step to progress, because his driver's licence, ID and bank cards were all inside.

They learned that his real name was Arthur Thomas Small.

'No wonder we couldn't find him on the Law Society roll. Arthur Thomas. Like an English Lord. I would also tell people, just call me "Basie",' said Cupido, who had a thing about names.

The ID document showed that Small was forty-nine years old. And according to the debit and credit cards in the wallet, a Private Wealth client of First National Bank.

Griessel made a note in his book. 'For a man who didn't exactly work, he has a lot of money. This house is worth seven or eight million in this area. Private banking services . . .'

'Maybe one of those early-retired lawyers, Benna, from Gauteng. They make big bucks there and then they move to the Cape. To the pothole-free land of milk and honey.'

Griessel placed the wallet in an evidence bag. They locked the vehicle, put the key away, and went into the house. Their instincts were that the key of the safe was hidden somewhere in the master bedroom – close to the safe. If you were keeping firearms in the safe and you expected trouble, you wouldn't want the safe and key to be too far apart.

They began with the built-in cupboards that covered the whole rear wall. It was slow work, removing each item of clothing, every pair of shoes, a meticulous fingertip search. They had to guard against their lack of sleep, the weariness and the boredom that could break their concentration.

They talked softly while they worked. The subject of their conversation was, as it had been nearly every day for the past two weeks, speculation over where Colonel Mbali Kaleni was going. According to their former colleagues at the DPCI's (otherwise known as the

Hawks) unit for Serious and Violent Crimes, 'The Flower' had cleared her office the day after her announcement. Nobody knew where she'd gone. But the rumours ran riot: she was pregnant out of wedlock. She'd found a 'blesser' – a wealthy older man who was going to take good care of her. She was simply fed up with the corruption in the SAPS. She couldn't bear the poor management and political appointments in the Hawks' top structure. She had gone for secret training in the USA. And the rumour that amused them most – that she had bowed to some corrupt temptation. Nobody knew better than they that she was the most honest police officer in the country. She was frequently honest to a fault – she even refused point blank to exceed the speed limit when she drove or to park illegally.

Griessel's theory was that Eskom, the country's electricity supplier, had secretly appointed her to put an end to the large-scale corruption and theft at the power stations in the north. Cupido maintained that she had gone to KwaZulu-Natal to investigate the Minister of Police's alleged links to a notorious drug syndicate.

It took them a fruitless hour of searching the cupboards for the key.

Then they lifted up the double-bed mattress, searched the bottom of the bed, inspected the en-suite bathroom's cupboards and found nothing. Cupido suggested it might be in Small's study, but there was no obvious hiding place there. It was only when in desperation they removed both bedside lamps and turned the bedside stands upside down that they spotted the flat metal tin that was fixed to the underside of the right-hand stand.

'Arthur Thomas, you crafty bastard,' said Cupido, hopeful. He pulled on the tin and it slid outwards on two little tracks.

The key was there.

Griessel gave a sigh of relief and opened the door of the built-in cupboard wide. Cupido inserted the key in the Magnum MG8 gun safe and turned. The lock clicked. He turned the handle, pulled the door open.

At first glance the contents were not as impressive as they had hoped. On top was a rack with two wooden boxes. At the bottom was a pistol on another wooden box. It was the five firearms in the middle that held their attention.

Cupido pulled on his forensic gloves while Griessel took a picture with his cell phone.

'We have five contestants this morning, ladies and gentlemen . . .' said Cupido. He removed the longest of the five assault rifles. 'Number one is the good old FN FAL,' he said while Griessel wrote it down. 'Unexciting, unattractive, but well cleaned, well oiled, ready to go . . .'

Vaughn put the weapon on the bed, and took the next one out: 'Number two, the cute but deadly little Heckler & Koch 416,' he said and laid it beside the FN.

'Number three: another Heckler & Koch.' He had to study the firearm before he could identify it. 'This time the elegant but deadly G36, in mint condition. And, number four . . . Benna, I don't know this one . . . Steyr, bolt action, sniper scope . . .' Cupido set the rifle down on the bed, came back for the last one.

'And our winner is . . . the very sexy bad girl of assault rifles, the AR-15!'

'*Bliksem*,' said Griessel.

'Nice little collection, Benna,' said Cupido. 'This dude was not a biltong hunter.'

He put the AR-15 down on the bed too, and went back to the safe. He removed the pistol that was right at the bottom, on the wooden box. 'Glock 17. Impeccable taste.'

He picked up the bottom wooden box. On the sliding panel on top was the name and logo of the Rust and Vrede wine estate. Cupido slid it open. In the space, which was large enough for three wine bottles, were three neat piles of cash – rands, dollars and euros – and a passport.

Griessel was still taking photos of everything. 'The attackers didn't get into the safe, Vaughn.'

Cupido removed each bundle of notes and riffled through them. 'Looks like about twenty thousand each.'

Griessel totted the sums up in his head. '*Jissis*. Nearly three quarters of a million, in rand value.'

'Crafty, wealthy Arthur Thomas,' said Cupido. 'What were you up to?'

He opened the passport. It was seven years old, and in the name of Small. The visas and stamps showed that between 2014 and 2019 he had travelled twice to the USA, four times to the UK, twice to the Democratic Republic of the Congo, three times to Mozambique and once to Iraq. Since then he hadn't been overseas.

Cupido left the box on the bed too, went back to the safe and removed the two wooden boxes from the top shelf. They were smaller, two-bottle wine boxes, from Beyerskloof and Kanonkop.

He put both down on the bed and slid them open while Griessel took photos.

They contained only ammunition – for the rifles and the pistol.

* * *

The contents of the safe were not part of the execution of the crime they were investigating. Hence they did not want to hand them in as evidence at the SAP 13 store – so named because every item of evidence had to be booked in on form SAP 13.

They noted and photographed everything, and packed them back in the safe. Only the safe key would go to the store.

'He wasn't expecting trouble,' said Griessel. 'Or else he would have kept the pistol close at hand.'

'I smell mercenary, partner,' said Cupido. 'Congo, Iraq, Mozambique, that's mercenary territory. Add the assault rifles, foreign currency . . .'

'And to the neighbours, you're a lawyer, because that makes them careful of you, and it gives you a kind of identity.'

'Yes, something that makes a picture so they don't go dig further.'

Griessel nodded. 'And the six attackers. The way they planned the thing, the way they got over the wall. Professional, guys with training.'

'Military background would explain Arthur Thomas's prime condition at forty-nine too.'

Griessel shook his head. 'The thing is . . . He was last out of the country two years ago. He's been living here, according to the neighbours, a quiet loner.'

'So why put filler foam down his throat now?'

'If it is a message, it's a very strong one.'

'Hold your tongue?'

'But about what?'

'War crimes, Benna. They do unspeakable things, these mercenaries.'

'But why now, suddenly?'

'The money. Maybe he blackmailed them, and they schemed enough is enough.'

* * *

The second step in their progress came when they locked up the house again and walked to the car. Warrant Officer Reginald 'Lithpel' Davids, the specialist in digital forensic services at the Hawks, phoned Griessel.

'Congratulations on your promotion, Lithpel,' said Benny.

'Thanks, Cappy,' said Davids. He had, out of habit, never stopped calling them by their previous rank. 'I told you I would catch up with you. Especially if you keep getting demoted. Listen, I've only done the victim's phone. There's not much, but I have a call register for the past month, if that will help.'

'Nothing on his WhatsApp?'

'He didn't have WhatsApp on the phone, Cappy. Just Telegram and Signal.'

'Signal?'

'It's an open-source app with end-to-end encryption and self-destructing messages. That already seems suspicious to me, but it doesn't help us, because there is no way to see what he received or sent.'

'Nothing else?'

'Cappy, the Garmin sports watch data is macabre and fascinating. I can tell you, his heart rate increased dramatically at exactly 09:16:48 on the morning of the attack, and reached a peak of hundred-seventy-six beats per minute at 09:25:17. And his heart stopped at 09:27:13 exactly. The watch shows nothing of the day the Leibrandt girl died, because Small synced his watch every day with the Garmin Connect on his phone. And on the app there is zero activity for that whole week. Which might mean that he deleted it, or that he didn't use the watch.'

'Okay.'

'Then we have his call register, which is kind of interesting. There's one number that he called every Sunday evening at six o'clock. And then he chatted for at least twenty minutes. Mostly longer. In his contacts the number is listed just under "Emilia".'

'Thanks, Lithpel, just send it to my phone. How long before you can look at the laptop?'

'Cappy, things are a bit crazy at the moment. The power backup is in its *moer*, and we are on stage five load-shedding. I can't give you an ETA.'

37

In a farmhouse between Humansdorp and Oyster Bay, on the most fertile coastal plains of the Eastern Cape, Dewey Reed heard the vehicle approaching.

He checked his watch. Eleven. It must be the hunters. The six from Kouga Engineering in Gqeberha who were coming to hunt wild geese as a team-building exercise. They had made the booking at the last minute, but they were on time. It was a good sign. The kind of guys who usually came were big boozers who often started partying on the way. He wasn't in the mood for boozers.

Dewey got up from the long table in the farmhouse kitchen, picked up his broad-brimmed hat and walked to the front door. He was of medium height, lean and sinewy, fifty-two years old. He had a long thick dark brown beard and hair down to his collar, showing only hints of grey.

He walked out onto the long veranda, put on his hat and took his dark glasses out of the breast pocket of his hunting vest to fend off the bright African light. He saw a white Hyundai Staria bus enter the gate. It parked under the big milkwood tree. On the right side that faced him, he saw the logo and name of the company under a thin layer of red dust from the dirt road that they had to drive from the R102.

With his welcoming smile beaming through his beard, Dewey came down the steps. He heard the sliding door on the left side of the little bus open. Then they came walking around the rear of the vehicle. He was going to say 'Welcome to Iinyathi Hunting Lodge', but he saw that the four coming around the vehicle all had their right hands behind their backs, purposeful body language, an intense look in their eyes. The driver quickly opened his door with his left hand, keeping his right hand low, and the sunlight glinted off a pistol.

Thirty years of training and experience. Dewey didn't think, he reacted, instinct making him dodge left and run behind the dense growth of camphor bush. He had to reach the long, whitewashed building, the old milking shed. Where the shotguns were laid out on the table ready for the hunt.

He heard the muffled shots, the bullets hitting the shrubbery. They weren't shooting wildly, he registered. Controlled, single shots. Professional. He ran, zigzagging, at full tilt. Handguns, they had handguns, less accurate. They also had to run, difficult to aim, he had to move, move.

They shot him through the shoulder blade, he stumbled, a curse exploded from his lips, he straightened up. Seven strides to the milking shed door, six, five, four, zig, zag, to the door. A bullet slammed into the wood, he grabbed the handle.

Then he collapsed. Pain exploded just above his coccyx. His spine, they had hit his spine, his legs wouldn't work.

There could be only one reason why they were here. That was his final thought.

★   ★   ★

Nine hundred and seventy kilometres north-north-east of the Iinyathi Hunting Lodge, as the crow flies, was the Pretoria suburb of Faerie Glen. In a residential house more or less halfway between the upper and lower end of the endless Cliffendale drive, Emilia Streicher sat in her office. She was in her mid-fifties, but looked considerably younger. At just under 1.9 m tall, she cut an imposing figure, with the muscular leanness of someone who worked out often. Well groomed, her hair neatly cut, her light make-up expertly applied.

Emilia managed a company that specialised in supply, installation and servicing of Samsung air conditioners for household use. The name of the company was ComfortAir. And it wasn't doing well. The second half of May was usually the quiet time for her – the summer heat was over, winter wasn't biting hard enough yet for there to be a notable increase in orders and service work. But it was the accelerating pace of load-shedding that was doing the most damage. People were less and less willing to spend money on something that strained a basic backup generator too much. So now she was analysing her figures, trying to find ways to limit her costs. She knew the only realistic outcome was to retrench some of her workers.

And she would get the blame, not this useless rotten government that was responsible for the load-shedding in the first place.

On the desk beside her were two cell phones. The one that she reserved for private calls began to ring. Emilia used the Truecaller app to flag nuisance telemarketing calls, but she knew it was only partially effective. Which was why she answered irritably. 'Hello?'

'Good morning.' A man's voice. He sounded as though he was in a car. 'My name is Warrant Officer Benny Griessel of the SAPS detective office in Stellenbosch. Who am I speaking to now?'

It felt like an eternity for her to grasp the implications of who and where he was, and then fear clenched the pit of her stomach. She couldn't keep the anxiety from her voice: 'Emilia Streicher,' she replied.

'Mrs Streicher, we suspect you are acquainted with Mr Arthur Thomas Small?'

The fear flooded over her, paralysing. 'What's happened?'

'What is your relationship to Mr Small?'

'He's my brother. What happened?'

'Ma'am, I am genuinely sorry to inform you that your brother passed away yesterday.'

Breath escaped from her lips, loud and audibly, as the shock shook her. She was faintly aware that the noise of the policeman's car had stopped. She tried processing what he'd said, but her brain had turned to ice. Eventually she got it out: 'What happened?'

'There was a break-in, ma'am. A robbery. Yesterday, between nine and ten. Mr Small was at home.'

She just breathed, in and out, she had to regain control, Basie would have expected that of her. In and out, in and out.

'Yesterday morning?'

'We could find no information about his next of kin in the house, ma'am. Only this morning when we accessed his phone. I am so sorry.'

A robbery? It made no sense to her. 'What about Sulla? And Scipio?'

'Ma'am?'

'His dogs. Where were his dogs?'

'They . . . The robbers killed them.'

Her heart pounded wildly. She didn't respond.

'Ma'am, our investigation . . .' said the Griessel policeman. 'It would help us a great deal if you could come and see us.'

She tried to gather her thoughts. 'I'm in Pretoria.'

'I see. Ma'am, from the nature of the investigation . . . We urgently need information. About Mr Small. About his work, his background . . .'

She processed that slowly, as if from outside herself. A robbery, but they wanted to know about Basie's background? His work? Why?

'Just give me . . . Please. I will come to you, I can be there tomorrow. It's just . . . It's a shock . . .'

'I understand, ma'am, and we would appreciate it if you could come to the Cape. But in an investigation like this time is a big factor. Can I call you later? In an hour or two? I just have a few things I want to make sure of.'

'Yes.' That would give her time. Enough time.

'Thank you very much.'

'Goodbye,' she said.

She rang off. It felt as if her body was on fire. It felt as though a storm was raging in her head.

* * *

They sat in the car in front of the detective offices while Griessel stared absently through the windscreen, phone still in his hand.

'What?' asked Cupido.

'It's his sister. And . . . It's . . . I don't know . . . It sounds sort of . . .'

'What, Benna?'

'Like it isn't entirely unexpected?'

* * *

Emilia Streicher stood up. She felt her knees wobble. She must be strong now. For Basie's sake. She opened the cabinet behind her desk, took out the thick burgundy file, sat down again and opened it.

There was a thick stack of documents in it. Among others, Basie's will, concise and to the point. The list was at the bottom. She found it and examined it. Four names, as she remembered. Four telephone numbers. In Basie's handwriting. But now it looked like Basie had drawn a pencil line through two of them. What could that mean?

She decided to keep to his original, very clear instructions.

She began at the one at the top: Dewey Reed.

She called.

It rang. For a long time. Then it went to voicemail. 'Hi. This is Dewey Reed from the Iinyathi Hunting Lodge. I can't take your call right now, but please leave your name and number, and I'll get back to you as soon as possible.'

Emilia waited for the tone. Then she said: 'Dewey, my name is Emilia. I am Basie Small's sister. Please call me back urgently.'

She rang off. The next name on the list was Tau (Evert) Berger. She rang the number beside it.

Two rings, and a man answered. 'Hello, this is Tau.'

'Tau, my name is Emilia. I am Basie Small's sister.'

'Hi, Emilia, I remember, Basie talked a lot about you.'

'He died yesterday morning, Tau.'

'Christ,' said Berger. 'I'm so sorry.'

'He told me if something unusual happened to him, I have to let you know. Immediately. I only just heard now.'

'Unusual?'

'It was a robbery. Yesterday morning. They killed his dogs first.'

'Yesterday morning? Like after midnight?'

'They say it was between nine and ten.'

'In broad daylight?'

'Yes.'

A silence hung in the air.

'Tau,' she said, 'they want to know about Basie's work. Urgently. And his background. I have to call them back now.'

He hesitated before he answered. 'You're strong.'

'I have to be strong for him now. I called Dewey Reed, but he didn't answer.'

'Do you know why Basie asked you to let us know?'

'Yes. I know everything.'

'Who else is on his list?'

'Corrie Albertyn and Fani Dlamini. But it looks like Basie . . . The names have been crossed out with pencil.'

'They are both already gone, Emilia. Corrie six years ago, IED in Afghanistan. Fani died last year, in Cabo Delgado, he and five other soldiers, helicopter accident. Basie let me know, with each. Because I'm outside of the loop.'

'*Ai*,' was all she could say.

'Thank you,' said Tau Berger. 'Thank you very much. I'll take it from here.'

She said goodbye and rang off. Put the phone down.

The strength drained out of her, and she gave in to a grief so fierce that her whole body began to shake. Then she wept.

★   ★   ★

The SAP 13 store at Stellenbosch detectives' office was on the ground floor, in the western corner. It was a large room, the windows reinforced with steel mesh, the door was of heavy metal. Griessel and Cupido were busy filling in the register so they could keep the safe key there. They told the sergeant on duty that absolutely no one was allowed to withdraw it without their permission, and had they made themselves completely clear?

Before the sergeant could reply, Colonel Witkop Jansen's secretary called. They were being summoned. Urgently.

It was only when they saw Captain John Cloete, the SAPS provincial media liaison officer, that they suspected what kind of trouble awaited.

38

Griessel had known John Cloete since they were both rookie ser-
geants in their Murder and Robbery days in Bellville South. Cloete,
carrying the burden of dealing with the media all those years, had
nicotine stains on his fingers and permanent dark shadows under his
eyes. That was the price he paid for his seemingly unflappable calm,
his patient endurance of the long hours and enormous pressures of
his job.

When they sat down in the commander's office, Witkop Jansen
just motioned to Cloete that he had the floor.

'Julian Jenkins phoned. Just after nine,' said Cloete now, slow,
measured and a little weary, as always.

Julian Jenkins was a seasoned journalist from Media24 who reported
chiefly on crime in the Cape Peninsula. A few months ago he had
interviewed Griessel and Cupido about their case at the time, an investigation – still unsolved – into the sensational and mysterious
disappearance of Jasper Boonstra, billionaire and alleged corporate
fraudster.[5] For Jenkins's new book about murders in Stellenbosch.
The media and the whole nation seemed to have an insatiable appetite
for scandalous and sensational stories from this university town.
Probably due to the town's unique political and cultural history, its
world-famous vineyards and plethora of super-rich residents.

'Shit,' said Cupido. 'I saw him, yesterday morning, there in the
whole hubbub outside Small's house.'

Cloete nodded. 'Julian had only two questions for you. He wanted
to know if Basie Small was a suspect in the Le-Lanie Leibrandt investigation, and if it was true that the cause of Small's death was that
his throat was full of filler foam.'

'Shit,' said Cupido again.

'How,' said Witkop Jansen. 'How does he know?'

---

[5] More about that in the novel *The Dark Flood* (2021)

'Contacts, Colonel,' said Cloete. 'Julian always had contacts at the station. He's good.'

'How does he know about the Leibrandt thing? It has only been discussed here in the parade room. My people don't talk.'

'The woman next door,' said Griessel. 'We went door-to-door with the photo of Small and the dogs, the day the girl died. The neighbour must have made the connection.'

'Jenkins also went door-to-door, I reckon,' said Cupido.

'That's how he works,' said Cloete. 'Thoroughly.'

'What do we do now?' asked Witkop Jansen.

'Look, no matter what, Jenkins will write that sources close to the investigation have confirmed both statements – even if we deny it,' said Cloete.

'When is the story going to break?' asked Griessel.

'An hour after I phone him back. On Network24 and on News24 websites. And then tomorrow in the newspapers,' said Cloete.

'Could we just wait until I've talked to Small's sister again? So she doesn't hear it in the media.'

'When are you talking to her?'

Griessel checked his watch. It was just before one o'clock. 'If she hasn't phoned me by two o'clock, I will phone her again.'

'I can't wait any longer than that,' said Cloete.

★　★　★

She phoned at 13:47, when he and Cupido were busy in their shared office, updating the docket.

He answered, repeating his condolences for her loss.

She thanked him. She sounded calm now, as though she had taken herself firmly in hand. She called him 'Warrant Officer' and said she was ready for his questions.

'You can just call me "Benny", ma'am. First I have to discuss something else with you: The media . . . When something like this happens in Stellenbosch, there's a lot of attention . . .'

'I understand.'

'The thing is, there was an incident a little while ago, a student fell off her bike in the mountains. Mr Small's dogs . . . When we investigated the case, we thought they might have been involved.'

Dead silence on the line.

'The media wants to bring that up now,' said Griessel.

'Were they? Where the dogs involved?'

'We don't know. And that is what we will tell the media. But we can't control what they write.'

'I understand.'

'The other thing is about the cause of Mr Small's death. It will be upsetting, but I don't want you to hear it in the media first. Unless you choose not to know.'

He heard her intake of breath, as though steeling herself for what was to come.

'What was the cause?'

Griessel knew that there was no way to soften the truth, but he tried to soften his voice: 'They sprayed filler foam in his mouth, ma'am. We are waiting for the pathologist's finding, but we think that is what . . . He must have suffocated.'

She didn't reply.

'Ma'am, if you want me to call back later . . .'

He waited.

Her voice came back strongly now: 'What do you want to know?'

★ ★ ★

They were back in Witkop Jansen's office. Without Cloete.

'He was a Recce,' said Griessel. 'A major in Five Special Forces Regiment. In Phalaborwa . . .'

'Now? At the time of his death? I thought he was a lawyer?'

'No, Colonel. He left the army about ten years ago. In 2012. He went and stayed with his sister, in Pretoria. She'd just got divorced. And he never married. He helped her get her business going. Air-conditioning. In the evenings he attended classes at the University of Pretoria, for a law degree. She said he realised that wasn't what he really wanted to do, but he finished the course. And then he began doing consulting work – military training, safety, security. In Africa, America, the Middle East. She said he was very good at his job, everyone wanted to use him, he made a lot of money. Later he got his own place, a townhouse up there in a secure complex, and then, three years ago, he said he was sick of the chaos in Gauteng, and he had enough money. He wanted to scale down, take part in more triathlons and Iron Man competitions. He chose Stellenbosch, because here he could run and cycle without being on his guard all the time against thugs who wanted to steal his bike or his cell phone.'

'Ironic,' said Cupido. 'And she has no idea why anyone would want to pump him full of filler foam?'

'She said she has no idea,' said Griessel. 'She said he had no enemies.'

Cupido recognised that tone of voice. 'But you don't believe her, do you, Benna?'

'Not one hundred per cent.'

'Why?' asked Witkop Jansen.

'Colonel, it's just a feeling. When I phoned her the first time, she asked me three or four times what happened, when Small died. People ask that, I know. But it sounded to me like . . . it mattered a lot. And as if she expected it in a way. That something would happen to him, I mean. And now, when she called back . . . she had her story all lined up . . .'

Witkop Jansen shook his head. 'A feeling? People handle the news of a loved one's death in all kinds of ways.'

'Colonel, I trust Benny's instinct,' said Cupido. 'And we know six real pros came for our Mister Arthur Thomas Small, all very prepared, with a can of filler foam ready in the backpack. Nothing stolen, a small fortune in the safe, but no, they didn't even try to crack it. They just wanted to send a message to someone. If Benna schemes the sister knew something, then I believe him.'

Jansen was not impressed. 'No. Facts, *kêrels*. Feelings aren't good enough, we work with facts. What about friends? Acquaintances? Colleagues?'

'She said he was a loner, Colonel. Did his own thing.'

'Lone Wolf McQuade,' said Cupido. 'And six dudes came for him? I'm not buying it.'

'What's next?' asked Jansen.

'The sister is coming down tomorrow, Colonel. To go through the house with us,' said Griessel. 'Then we'll question her again. And we're going to get a subpoena for his bank records this afternoon, and for any other cell phone numbers in his name.'

'Lithpel Davids must finish the forensics on his laptop and his phone,' said Cupido. 'The Hawks must do their work. That's all we have.'

'Good. What do we tell Captain Cloete and the media?'

'Everything,' said Griessel. 'Except the bit about the safe.'

'Are you sure?'

'The cat is out of the bag, Colonel. Maybe someone out there knows something. About Small's shenanigans. Can't do any harm.'

'A Recce would know how to cover his tracks,' said Griessel.

'Damn straight,' said Cupido.

'It's going to be a shitstorm,' said Jansen. 'A Recce. The Leibrandt case, the dogs, the filler foam. God help us.'

★ ★ ★

Emilia Streicher wanted to lie down on the double bed in her bedroom and surrender to raw sobs of loss. The pain of knowing that Basie, big, strong, invincible Basie, was just gone. Dead, in that terrible way. The pain of knowing someone did that to him, knowing what his last moments were like. Did he think of her, before death overwhelmed him? About the message she would have to deliver now, his faith in her, that she would do it? Pain for the girl on her bicycle and Basie's dogs. She didn't believe it, she didn't believe it, he wasn't like that. The pain of being alone, the lone survivor of a modest middle-class, single-parent family from Groblersdal. Their father and mother both long gone. Now Basie. She was the only one left. Alone.

Pain, too, over the will in her office. Basie had left everything to her.

Including his secrets.

First, she had to be strong. She had to get up. She had to call Tau Berger again, and tell him about the filler foam. It was important, it confirmed all her fears, it confirmed that Basie had been right.

She wanted to be sure that Berger would contact Dewey Reed. Basie had been very clear in his request: she must contact everyone on the list and warn them. 'Promise me, Sis,' he'd said.

She'd promised, without hesitation, because what could happen to him? Big, strong, capable, invincible Basie. Besides: she owed him so much. After her divorce it was Basie who'd got her back on her feet. Bought the house, financed the business. Comforted and encouraged her. She'd promised, solemnly, without a second thought.

She got up slowly. Went downstairs like a sleepwalker, to her office.

She had to book her flight, to Cape Town. She had to pack. She had to harness all her strength for tomorrow. Get her story straight for the detective.

39

Benny Griessel parked under an oak tree right behind the old Magazine in Stellenbosch's Market Street. He looked at the upright structure with its rounded roof and thought it was an omen: apparently the VOC, the Dutch East India Company, had stored cannons, guns and gunpowder in the small building two hundred years ago, without ever needing it. For decades now it had been a museum, but this afternoon, when Julian Jenkins's reporting hit the Internet, Twitter was going to light the fuse. And then the explosions would follow.

As usual.

Social media was the very oxygen that Stellenbosch breathed. You saw the cell phone approaching first and then the student behind it, each one self-obsessed and self-absorbed. TikTok, Instagram, Twitter and YouTube, the unholy quartet, and the message of every post screamed: 'Look at me, look at me.' It fucked up everything.

When Le-Lanie Leibrandt died a whole crowd of so-called 'influencers' went up Stellenbosch mountain to perform their own 'investigations', to speculate, broadcast wild conspiracy theories, and to blacken the name of the SAPS. The station was overwhelmed with useless 'leads', inquisitive questions and hate calls.

He didn't understand it at all. In the first place, the terrible thirst for attention. The hunger to show how pretty and clever and successful and full of opinions they were. How many 'friends' and 'followers' they had. All the time and energy they poured into this.

He knew his perspective was strongly coloured by his humble beginnings in Parow, by a mother who had taught him never to blow his own trumpet. She'd felt shame over her own poor choice of a marriage to an unambitious railway worker, their inability to escape from a blue-collar middle-class life. Whatever you do, don't attract attention; that was the constant refrain.

And then there was his own poor self-image, honed and shaped through alcoholism, a failed marriage and a mediocre career – he was on his way to his fifties and here he was, a warrant officer with a sum total of seven hundred rand in the bank. Not the sort of thing you trumpeted on Facebook.

But even taking all that into account, the psychology behind social media still unsettled him: that all-consuming urge to be special, to stand out, to be seen. He had been a policeman for over a quarter-century and hc could testify as an expert, that the drive behind crimes of greed was often just that. Take a look at the profiles of swindlers and fraudsters on the Internet. The signs were always there, the same attempts to present themselves as more than they were. Secondly: nobody is special. Everyone is just another fucker muddling along. Some have a bit more luck than others. But special? Not really. And third: it was a drug, this attachment to social media attention. And he knew all about addiction. It stripped you of everything, of your grip on reality, your self-esteem, of your relationships with your nearest and dearest.

He locked the car, walked up Market Street to the pretty, white-washed magistrate's court building, and he knew that what he thought was really irrelevant. Alexa maintained it was a useful medium. Every evening she was on Facebook, she said that was how she kept up with what was happening in the music world, how she could measure the industry's 'zeitgeist'. He had to ask her what the word meant.

His children's lives revolved, like everyone of their age, around social media. Carla and Fritz both said people of Griessel's age had no business being on social media because they didn't understand it. And Cupido's mantra: 'Partner, opinions are like arseholes, everyone has one. And they usually stink. The only difference now, with social media, is that we all have to smell it together. Welcome to Selfie City, we're dinosaurs, let's just suck it up.'

He told the clerk of the court that he needed a magistrate to sign a request for a Section 205 subpoena, so that could get Basie Small's cell phone records and bank statements.

The clerk asked him to wait.

He sat down on a bench in the busy corridor, his elbows on his knees, head bowed. Thinking everything through. To be painfully honest, the root of his problem was the bile being spewed out over the SAPS. In the mainstream media as well as social media. Over the decay, the corruption, the incompetence of poorly trained, inexperienced people. It offended him, all this poisonous negativity affected practically every interaction with the public, and it made their lives very difficult.

Worst of all was knowing that so much of the vitriol was justified.

He waited for a quarter of an hour before the clerk came to call him. Just before he went into the magistrate's office Cupido called to say Arno Leibrandt, the agricultural student brother of Le-Lanie would meet them in the Neelsie at four.

★   ★   ★

The Neelsie was a student shopping centre, the busy heart of the university campus – loud rock music in the background, students coming and going, sitting around chatting.

Cupido waited for him at a table in the foyer. 'We have twenty minutes before Leibrandt comes out of class. Benna, my blood sugar is rock bottom, let's get a bite to eat.'

Griessel said he wanted coffee too. They decided on the Buzz Juice & Smoothie Bar's offer, bought their food and drink and walked out to sit on a bench in the relative quiet and open area of the Red Square.

Cupido read Julian Jenkins's news report out loud from his cell phone. It was full and accurate, including the details of the filler foam, Basie Small's background, and the connection with Le-Lanie Leibrandt's death.

'*Jissis*,' said Cupido, as he drank his strawberry smoothie, 'this will set the cat among the pigeons, *pappie*.'

'And we have nothing,' said Griessel.

'Lithpel will have to deliver,' said Cupido. 'There must be something, partner. I mean, that safe of his . . . It's what isn't in it that worries me. Where are the personal documents? All the usual suspects: firearm licences, title deed of the house, short-term insurance, life insurance?

'And if he's so rich, where're the investment papers? Some of it might be digital, but where're the originals? And wherever he parked the digital copies, there should be other stuff. About all his shenanigans.'

Griessel nodded. 'Maybe his sister knows.'

'But you say she's a little bit slippery?'

'Maybe Witkop is right. Maybe she's just in shock.' Griessel bit into his chicken wrap. 'I've been thinking, Vaughn . . . it might not be about his military background. The Ironman thing, the bike race . . .'

'What do you mean?'

'Stimulants, Vaughn. Steroids are old now. They are using much more sophisticated stuff, especially from Russia. And we're talking big money. Small was in Britain, the USA, he could have made contacts. He was in Mozambique, that's a good route to bring in the drugs. Sell them for cash, keep only enough for small change in your safe. And then there were guys who didn't like the competition . . .'

Cupido considered it. 'I don't know, Benny. Those six dudes were next-level pro. It doesn't feel like 'roids and gangstas to me. Too much sophistication, I scheme.'

'Maybe you're right.'

Cupido looked at Griessel, long and hard. 'Benna, are you okay?'

'Just a bit tired. Long day, not enough sleep . . .'

'Hashtag me too. But that's it? Nothing else?'

'Why are you asking?'

'Partner, you have to understand, I don't want to pry, I'm asking, 'cause you're my bro. A month or so ago you were *lekka*. High spirits, full of beans, despite our collective professional setbacks, you looked happy. But now, recently . . . You . . . And I'm not talking about the four o'clock fatigue that's kicking in now, I mean in general, past few weeks. You lost your mojo, partner. So I want to ask you respectfully: how do things stand with you and the bottle?'

Griessel put his empty coffee cup down. He sighed. 'I'm battling, Vaughn. But I'm holding on.'

'It's the wedding,' said Cupido, with certainty.

Benny sighed deeply. 'The wedding . . . it's not specifically the wedding. It's . . . I don't know, Vaughn . . . Now that it's happening, it makes you think. About yourself. About your life, about who you are and where you are and all the fuck-ups that you left behind. They are like road signs that say there's no way you can make a success of anything in your future. And you try to be positive and tell yourself that you are nearly four hundred and thirty days on the wagon, you are at least older and wiser, you've buried a lot of your ghosts, you're going to be okay. And then you remember: you're part of a police service that's on the skids. Musad Manie, pushed out of the Hawks. He was a rock, that man, he was the best example to me of what a commanding officer should be. Hard but fair. Now Mbali has gone too. The most unshakeably honest police officer that I know. What the fuck are we going to do without people like them? Crime stats are through the roof, every day there is new stuff about corruption and poor management, money being squandered, look where we are with load-shedding . . . When last did we have a Minister of Police or a National Commissioner that knew what he was doing, Vaughn? I won't even talk about a Provincial Commissioner, it's all just politics and infighting and pushing and shoving to get at the feeding trough. All the stories about the generals who're in cahoots with the gangs. There's too much smoke not to be a fire somewhere. Then I think, I have to get out, I have to do something else. But what? Being a detective, that's all I have, all I can do. So, basically, I'm fucked. And then I remember that when I last felt like this, Jack Daniels did a bloody good job of easing the pain . . .'

Cupido nodded with understanding. 'I feel you, Benna. Things don't look great. I also worry. But we both know this is a transition phase. Never as good as we hope, never as bad as we fear. And in this country we fix everything in the end. Crooked and skew, I grant you, but we fix it. Thing is, partner, I scheme, it's not the wedding that's eating you, and it's not politics. There's something else, and I know what it is . . .'

Griessel raised his eyebrows, questioning.

'It's a classic case of midlife crisis, *pappie*. That is your problem. Forty-nine, the big five-oh is just around the corner, and you scheme you're a failure, 'cause why, twenty years ago you thought you would be a general by now. But then life happens, and then the late forties arrive, and the midlife crisis. Classic. Very common, happens to us all. But here's the good news: there's a cure, Benna, a two-part cure, don't you worry. Part one is, you need a reality check, 'cause you're looking at the wrong things. Look at the great stuff: Alexa reckons you're the best thing since sliced bread, that woman is crazy about you. And why? Because of your heart, partner. It's beautiful. Yesterday when I phoned you and Carla answered, I heard how crazy that kid is about you. Very proud of her daddy, loves him a lot. And I know I keep saying you're the second-best detective in the service, but that's just jokes. You are the best, Benna. You make a difference. In this town, in this country. And then there's your music too, Benna. Bass player in a rock 'n' roll band, living the dream, following your passion. Not many can say that.'

'And part two?'

'Well, my first thought was, bachelor party, the wildest, biggest bachelor party in the history of the SAPS. But that's not gonna fly, given your history with the booze. So, I scheme, Benna, we are going to figure out something to make the wedding special for you. Something to look forward to.'

'Like what?'

'I'm still working on it. You can't rush genius . . .'

And then they saw Arno Leibrandt approaching.

40

It was Cupido who told Leibrandt everything, in a gentle, sympathetic tone.

He explained that they suspected that Basie Small's dogs were implicated in Le-Lanie's death. Their suspicion was that it wasn't deliberate, but that he did attempt to camouflage the scene, make it look like something else, and he could have been prosecuted for that. They'd done their best to obtain a warrant for the bite prints, but no magistrate was willing to sign. There was no other material evidence. Under those circumstances they could not talk to Arno or his family about their suspicions. But now they could. The imprints had been requested, hopefully there would be feedback in the next few days. And closure.

Griessel watched the student closely. Arno sat silently and listened: his distress seemed genuine.

Cupido said they were very sorry, they knew the uproar surrounding the Small murder was going to upset the Leibrandts all over again. 'The crazies out there are going to throw all sorts of wild theories around, and you are going to be the target of some, Arno. Our advice is, stay off social media for the next few weeks. Let us work the case, when we catch the culprits everything will go back to normal.'

'Thanks, *Oom*,' Arno said. 'I understand.'

'Now, there is something we want to ask you,' said Griessel.

'Because we have to do our jobs properly,' said Cupido.

'It's just for the record,' said Griessel. 'We are really sorry.'

Arno shut his eyes and nodded. He looked vulnerable, like someone expecting a physical attack.

'Where were you yesterday morning between nine and ten?'

'In class, *Oom*. Soil Science.'

★　★　★

Captain Philip van Wyk of the Hawks' Information Management Centre phoned while Griessel was on his way back to the office. He said he had good and bad news, but then the signal broke up.

Griessel sent him a voice note on WhatsApp: 'We have finished for the day, Phil, can I drop by? In about three quarters of an hour? Then we don't have to talk on the phone. The signals are bad with all this load-shedding.'

Van Wyk sent a thumbs-up emoji and the message: *Then you can just take the laptop and phone back with you.*

★ ★ ★

The Hawks' Western Cape head office was in A. J. West Street in Bellville. IMC was on the first floor. Only Warrant Officer Reginald 'Lithpel' Davids was still there.

He earned his nickname as a result of the speech impediment he'd had in the early years, before surgery had rectified it. He was tall and skinny, with a massive Afro hairstyle, and a brilliant white smile. He was unfailingly cheerful. This afternoon he was dressed in ripped designer jeans, sandals and a green T-shirt with big white letters spelling out: *If I said I'll do it . . .* Below, in smaller letters: *. . . there's no need to remind me every six months.*

Griessel said hello.

'Cappy, good to see you, even if you look like shit. They're working you hard there in Volvoville, *nè*.'

Griessel asked if anyone at the Hawks knew why Mbali Kaleni had resigned as head of the Serious and Violent Crimes Unit.

'Just a few new rumours. She had dirt on the brass, they forced her out. That sort of thing.'

'Who took over?'

'Uncle Frankie is temporary CO of Serious and Violent.' He was referring to Captain Frank Fillander, the oldest and most beloved member of Mbali's former team.

'That's good,' said Griessel. 'I hope he gets the job.'

'Okay, let's rock 'n' roll, Cappy. Did the boss tell you there's good news and bad news? He sends his regards, he had to go to Alfred Street for a meeting. He's going to try and protest the budget cuts, but I'm not holding my breath.' The headquarters of the South African Police Services were in Alfred Street in Green Point.

'Give me the good news,' said Griessel. 'I need it.'

'Dope, Cappy. So, the good news is, I cracked the passwords of both the email attachments. Wasn't rocket science, it was the Small dude's ID. First one is . . .' He passed Griessel a printout. 'A portfolio report from Allan Gray Investments. The man had a nest egg of four point two million, Cappy, not bad for a Recce, *nè*? That's what I heard, he was Special Forces?'

'He was.'

'Dope.' Davids passed the next printout to Benny. 'And this is the other attachment, in which the plot thickens. It's from a company in the US of A. Vega Resources. They call themselves a "non-financial risk management company", but I did a bit of research. They are basically a rent-a-soldier outfit for companies doing business in all the awkward little hotspots around the globe. Now, the attachment is a job offer from their chief of recruitment, a Mr Gordon Cameron. Made to Small, dated this Monday past. In a nutshell, it says: Long China was very impressed with your services back in 2019, they want you to come back, and do more of the same – training security teams at their new mining venture in the Democratic Republic of the Congo. I went and googled Long China, Cappy. "Long" means "dragon" in Chinese, and Long China is partially owned by the Chinese government, they're the second biggest cobalt producer in the world. And, just so you know, in the DRC there is a lot of cobalt, which is a mineral very much in demand in this day and age. They need it for all the EV's batteries.'

'EV's?'

'Electric vehicles, Cappy. The transport of the future. In countries that don't have load-shedding, of course. And check this out: they offered Small a salary of twenty-five thousand dollars a month. That is three hundred thousand in rands, Cappy. Per month. Not exactly chump change. No wonder this motherfucker had the fat nest egg with Allan Gray. But in the sent folder there was an email addressed to Vega. And in the email he said no, thank you, I don't want the job.'

★   ★   ★

It was already well past six when Griessel drove home. The peak-hour traffic on the N1 was heavy; he never thought he would miss the Covid lockdowns. In those days it took a mere twenty minutes to drive the deserted roads from Stellenbosch to Bellville. And thirty-five minutes to Alexa's house in Oranjezicht on the N2.

His whole body felt tired, and his thoughts wandered. From the Small case and what they now knew and just how little it helped, to the state of the Hawks' head office. Every time he went there it looked worse, the facade was dirty and neglected. Inside the corridors were silent, his footsteps echoed off the bare floors. There were fewer and fewer of them there, his former colleagues told him and Cupido, and the shortages were not being addressed.

Cupido said it was a transitional phase. Griessel was not so sure.

Midlife crisis.

He didn't agree.

If that were the truth, his had begun ten years ago. It was no midlife crisis. Look at the facts. Everything was rotting away in this swamp.

What was he going to do? Let himself be sucked in and swallowed up?

Griessel drove up Buitengracht and he thought, the Fireman's Arms is just over there in Mechau Street. What he needed, for strength, to feel better, for another perspective, was their chips with curry sauce. And a tall beer. He wouldn't touch hard spirits, just one tall cold beer. He felt suddenly hungry. And thirsty.

He made a U-turn at Somerset, then left into Mechau. Just one tall beer, he looked for parking at Chiappini Square, the Arms would be busy at this time of day, the atmosphere welcoming, the old familiar aromas. He felt a tingling anticipation.

His cell phone rang.

Alexa.

He didn't want to talk to her now. Because he couldn't lie to her. If he answered, the chips and sauce and the beer would not materialise. And he wanted them now with all his soul.

The phone kept ringing.

There were no vacant parking spots.

He answered.

'Benny, you must be dead tired. I bought lasagne at Woollies, it only takes half an hour in the oven, when will you be home?'

★ ★ ★

She opened the door and he threw his arms around her and clung to her for dear life.

She knew, as only a fellow alcoholic could know. So she said nothing, just hugged him tight. Until he let go.

'I've got delicious juice,' she said. 'Some of Woollies' ginger that you love so much.'

'Please.'

'Let's sit on the balcony.'

He walked up the stairs. Took off his jacket in the bedroom, hung it up. Went out the double doors, sat at the little table outside. He looked out at the view. On the right was Table Mountain, on the left the city stretched out. The Fireman's Arms down there.

Deep breath.

Lord, that was close. The lure of the bottle. A sly black dog slinking around in the dark corners of the mind, trying to convince him that all was lost. Drink was the only way out, the road to oblivion and relief. Fuck. He would have to be strong. And on his guard. He'd better see the shrink. And Doc Barkhuizen, his Alcoholics Anonymous sponsor.

Alexa came out with a tray of cold drinks and a bowl of cashew nuts. He started to rise to take the tray, but she said 'just stay there and relax'.

He watched her as she sat down and passed him his glass.

The first time he saw her was on television. Thirty years ago. As the singer Xandra. She sang 'Sweet Water', in a tight-fitting black dress, blond, sensational, with that voice like Marlene Dietrich: just a beautiful woman and the microphone in the spotlight of a smoke-shrouded stage.

> *A small glass of sunlight*
> *A goblet of rain*
> *A small sip of worship,*
> *A mouthful of pain*
> *Drink sweet water*

Each phrase was filled with romance and sensuality and longing. He remembered it as if it were yesterday, he was half in love and half filled with lust, as was every man who saw her that night on the box. And he knew she would become a star.

And she had. The darling of the nation.

He'd met her for the first time twenty-five years later, in this house, downstairs in the sitting room. He hadn't recognised her. She looked awful. Unkempt, traumatised, an inebriated alcoholic. A far cry from the alluring limelight thanks to a destructive marriage with a toxic man. Griessel had to interview her, because she had woken up that morning beside her murdered spouse. And then he recognised – beneath the ravages of time and the shock and humiliation and turmoil of that morning – her gentleness, beauty and the quiet strength of her personality. And the sensuality and romance still there somewhere, under all the bruising blows that life had dealt her.

And now here she was sitting across from him: her long hair now more grey than blond, life's traces in the creases around her eyes and mouth, but her eyes were young and full of love and compassion. He felt the powerful surge of his feelings for her.

'I nearly had a drink,' he said.

She reached across the table and took hold of his hand.

'It's . . . the wedding,' he said. 'No, not the wedding. To *be* married. The responsibility. I have to be able to take care of you. I know you're going to say we take care of each other. And it's true. But I want to be able to take care of you. And now everything is slowly imploding, Alexa. The country, the police, the entire system . . .'

'I understand,' she said.

'Six or seven years ago we might have had fifty dockets on the table. Nowadays there are many in Stellenbosch with a hundred and twenty or more. At the other stations it's more like two hundred. And people are leaving and they aren't appointing enough new ones and . . . I don't know how much longer I can . . .'

He gulped some juice.

She said: 'I saw. On Network24. About the man with filler foam in his throat.'

He didn't react.

'It's your case,' said Alexa.

Griessel nodded.

'Seeing him. That's what really upset you.'

'You know I don't want to bring that part of my job home.'

'When last did you see the psychologist?' she asked.

He shrugged. 'Maybe I just need a good night's sleep.'

'Make an appointment, so she can tell you again that you can't save everyone.'

'Okay.'

'I'm scared too,' she said. 'Of being married. Of what lies ahead for us in this country. But then I think, what scares me most of all, is being without you for the rest of my life.'

Griessel stood up and he bent over to kiss her.

Afterwards she asked: 'Can I put some music on for us?'

41

Twenty-five to six in the morning.

Wednesday, 26 May.

Seventeen days to the wedding.

Evert 'Tau' Berger was lying in the veld, on a rugged slope. His dark trousers and windbreaker rendered him near invisible against the hillside. It was still night, though not pitch dark. The glow from the town's streetlights, less than a kilometre away, and the starry expanse above was enough. He would be able to see, should there be any movement below.

Dawn in Clarens should be at 06:47:50 exactly. Tau knew the landscape would start showing colour and definition from half past six. Thanks to the long shadows of Mount Horeb, part of the Rooiberg range to the east of the town, the sun would only shine directly on the houses at seven o'clock, revealing the full glory of the 'jewel of the Eastern Free State'.

He was watching from its western flank, with a view over the Clarens Golf and Leisure Estate. And beyond that, the town itself.

Sunshine, Tau knew, would prove how this was the most spectacular time of the year in this scenic corner of the country, as autumn colours in all their beautiful shades blended in with the gold of the cliffs. The fairway and green of the golf course were still a verdant emerald, the winter frosts only due to strike in three or four weeks' time.

Tau was the greenkeeper. Every morning at break of day, together with his team, he made sure the sand bunkers were swept, the greens mown, the tees moved and the leaves raked up. So he was well acquainted with daybreak and sunshine.

But now he wasn't thinking of his daily tasks.

He was waiting for the attackers.

Tau was short, a deeply tanned one hundred and seventy-one centimetres tall. He weighed a mere sixty kilograms. However, he created the impression of being a much bigger man, thanks to the luxuriant beard and dense bush of long yellow-blond hair, which he mostly tied back in a ponytail, ever since he had left the army. That, along with his striking light brown eyes and general sense of fearlessness, was the source of his enduring childhood nickname. In Sesotho, Setswana and Sepedi, 'tau' was the word for 'lion'. Though some of his old mates alleged it was his terrifying snoring at night that was the real reason for the moniker.

He was waiting for an attack, because he had put two and two together: Basie Small's sister Emilia had described how Basie died. He was sixty per cent certain then. Only sixty, because in this country you never knew.

Then he phoned Dewey Reed. Three times. Only late yesterday did a man pick up. A captain from the Humansdorp police, who said that Dewey had been shot dead that morning. Nothing taken, a very strange affair.

Then Tau Berger knew, Basie had been right all along. This thing would come back to bite them.

It had. And now they would be after him too.

He'd thought it all through: Basie and Dewey. You don't just knock off Basie and Dewey. Basie and Dewey were hard men, pure steel, the best of the best. So, the assailants had to be good.

They knew where Basie lived, that he had dogs, and that he would be at home. They knew where Dewey was. They had managed to catch Dewey unawares at the Iinyathi Hunting Lodge and take him out.

That meant planning. Reconnaissance. Preparation. Skill.

So they would know what Tau's cell phone number was. And they would be watching it. His calls, his location, all his activity.

He crushed his phone under his boot and snapped the SIM card between his fingers and then he drove over to one of the spaza shops on the other side of the R711 and bought three unlisted, un-RICAed, black-market phones. And he sent Emilia a message. *My new number. Tau.*

They would know where he, Tau, lived. In a house on the Clarens golf estate, right at the back, right at the top, on Kgwadi Street. They would have researched what it looked like. Google Earth, the estate's website. They would certainly have sent someone to check out how everything worked, suss out the security, get the lie of the land.

Then he asked himself, if he were the one doing it, how would *he* take Tau Berger out?

You would send an army, that's how. Because Tau was a fucking handful.

You would consider coming in via the estate's front gate, with a few sets of golf clubs in the car and a reservation at one of the houses. Yes, just a bunch of five or six regular guys coming to play eighteen holes and have a bit of a *jol*, don't worry about us. Firearms in the golf bags. But there were risks. The CCTV cameras at the gate, the scanning of driver's and car licences. The credit card needed to secure the rental. All that left a trail. And you don't want a trail.

The alternative?

Come over or through the estate's electric fence. Practically speaking it was simple, only two metres high, the wire was easy to cut and the power was mostly off during load-shedding.

Strategically it was a little more complex because the fence ran alongside the R712 – the tar road between the estate and the town of Clarens – for almost two kilometres, and the chances were good that somebody would see you just when you wanted to get in.

The way he would take out Tau Berger was to park your vehicle or vehicles over at the Maluti Mountain Lodge beside the R712. In the dark, at four in the morning. Weapons in fishing rod bags, pretend you're going fly fishing. Then wait until the coast is clear, and you and your army run across the tar road in the dark, into the veld. All along the northern, electric boundary fence, to the foot of Mount Horeb, where you can see Tau's house from above. And you see that all is quiet, and you cut the fence and go through and surprise him, before he rises at six to start the day.

That is why Tau was lying in wait on the mountainside instead.

Not to stop or to kill the assailants.

The thing was, Tau had questions. Such as: why now, a decade later, did they take out Basie and Dewey?

Why now?

Something had happened. Or was about to happen. But what?

What did he have to do, to stop them wanting to rub him out? To make them leave him alone, forever?

There were other, less important questions, too, but he would begin with these key ones. And he wanted answers.

So the goal was not to stop them or kill them. He just wanted to catch one of the fuckers. And he suspected one of the fuckers would be at or near the fence breach, covering the rear. That's what a well-prepared crack team would do.

That was the fucker he was going to catch. And then ask his questions. And then he would decide what to do with him.

At exactly twenty minutes to the hour he spotted them approaching. Six men, in step. Out in the open, down below in the veld, heading along the fence. At a decent clip, but not too rushed. Ready and willing. In the glow of the stars and the town's light, no weapons in sight. Which meant handguns. With silencers.

Come if you want, you fuckers, come, thought Tau. Tau Berger is a handful.

★   ★   ★

He could see that they knew exactly where his house was, because they cut the fence directly behind it. Barely thirty metres from where he lay.

Tau began to move. He stood up slowly and carefully, shaking his joints loose, getting his circulation going. He picked up the golf club, the classic 1-Wood driver, a good, heavy head, still made of wood. He adjusted the fighting dagger, the Gerber Mark II, settling it in the scabbard on his belt. Shook the black backpack into the correct position on his back. Everything tightly packed, it wouldn't make a sound.

His eyes fixed on the six of them.

The men ran lightly through the gap in the fence, in the direction of the reservoir.

He was wrong, Tau thought. No one was staying behind.

Okay. Plan B.

He ran after them.

They didn't look back, not guarding their six o'clock: they weren't expecting anyone there.

First mistake.

He kept his distance, following them. Up to the reservoir. He heard their muted voices, saw the hand signs.

Five went down. One stayed at the reservoir.

Tau saw Rearguard looking for a ladder at the base of the round cement reservoir. He wanted to climb up.

Don't climb up there, you fucker. It will be harder to *bliksem* you.

Rearguard found the ladder. He stood still first, took off his rucksack, took something out. Tau crept closer. Lifted the old wood driver.

Rearguard had a night-vision scope in his hand. He was going to put it on.

Stand like that, thought Tau. Stand just like that.

He swung the driver. It made a swooshing sound. Rearguard ducked, but Tau had known that he would.

The driver made contact with Rearguard's skull, just above the right ear. The man collapsed like a house of cards.

Outstanding ball contact, thought Tau.

Gotcha, you fucker.

42

At seven minutes to six Vaughn Cupido stood at the stove in the kitchen of Desiree Coetzee's Welgevonden townhouse. His carefully measured hundred grams of oatmeal was cooking in a small pot, the milk and honey were ready, his cell phone lay alongside, the Lose It! app active.

He was annoyed at the Jungle Oats people, as he was every morning. One day he was going to phone up their consumer line and tell them, you people have no respect for us dumb donners on a diet. There on the red pack with your smug half-smiling tiger, you print nutritional info of no bloody use to anyone. A forty-gram serving? Give me a break, you can't be serious. Forty grams will barely keep you going till after morning parade with Colonel J, then starvation will stalk you like that smugly smiling tiger, and *then* you will *really* want to eat, *pappie*. Bye-bye, diet, it's pig-out day. Forty-fucking-gram serving, that's for infants, man, not the second-best, just-a-bit-overweight detective in the SAPS. Get real.

Then his cell phone rang, and he saw it was Griessel, and he thought, aha, now he could tell Benna his grand idea.

* * *

Griessel was in his car on the N2 on the way to Stellenbosch, rested, invigorated and refreshed after nine hours of sleep and the surprisingly tasty cheese and biltong omelette that Alexa had lovingly prepared and served him. She was an outstanding businesswoman, a formidable singer still and a good pianist. With, in her own words, 'a passion for cooking'. But she had no innate feel for it. At the stove she was easily distracted, and then forgot which ingredients she had already added to the pot. And her sense of taste was a bit suspect. But this morning, to Griessel's relief, she was on top form.

Despite the good start to the day, he was castigating himself. For the very narrow escape from the bottle yesterday. Allowing the murder scene and fatigue and the dead end they had reached with the investigation, and the trouble with the police and the whole country, to bring him just one step from the precipice. After all the hard work of the past year. But he wouldn't let it happen again. He would do all the right things now.

Like focus on the Small murder. And that reminded him that he must tell Vaughn about Lithpel Davids' findings, and his appointment with Emilia Streicher.

He phoned.

It had barely begun to ring when Cupido answered: 'Benna, I've got it.'

'Got what?'

'Part two. Of the midlife crisis cure. The thing to put a smile on your dial, a *huppel* in your *knuppel*, a spark in your arc.'

'There's nothing wrong with my *knuppel*.'

'Aha, I sense a hint of the old Benny we all know and love.'

'What is part two?'

'Right. I scheme, when a man is struggling, lead him back to his passion. And your passion, Benna, is music.'

'You'll have to be more specific.'

'You have to sing, partner. At the wedding.'

'No, no, no,' said Griessel patiently, 'Lize Beekman is singing at the wedding.'

'I don't mean during the ceremony. I mean at the reception. Afterwards. You've *mos* got a band for the reception.'

'*Ja*, but . . .'

'And you're *mos* going to invite all your band members to the wedding, right?' Griessel played bass guitar in a four-piece band called RUST. They sometimes performed at weddings and parties on Friday or Saturday nights for a bit of extra income. They were all middle-aged and rusty when they got together, hence the name of the band.

'*Ja* . . .'

'So there'll be instruments there with the band that's playing, and all the members of RUST sitting in the crowd. All you have to do is organise with the performing band that you will do one song yourself. Then you sing to Alexa. Very romantic gesture, you're following your passion, you'll bring down the house. 'Cause why, that is what you need. Confirmation of your worth, a little bit of being the centre of attention, and following your passion. Bye-bye, midlife crisis.'

'Just like that?'

'That's not what I'm saying. But it's a big step in the right direction.'

'I see . . .'

'So? What do you think?'

'I think it's not a bad idea . . .'

'Attaboy. Now you must just figure out what you're going to sing. Something close to your heart.'

'Let me think about it . . .' Then he added: 'Vaughn, thank you.'

'No problem. I may be fat, but I'm not thick.'

Griessel laughed. Then he told Cupido about his talk with Lithpel Davids – Basie Small's investment of four point two million rand, and the job offer from Vega Resources to return to training security personnel at a cobalt mine in the Democratic Republic of the Congo. For a Chinese company at three hundred thousand rand a month. An offer that Small had declined.

'That explains the house. The lifestyle. But not the murder.'

'That's the thing. Lithpel said something is bugging him. Something about "Small's digital footprint". He said it's not typical of normal people. Small's email, his browser history, his cell phone records, and the Signal app that automatically deletes messages . . . It's like Small was extra careful. Like someone who thought there were guys spying on him digitally.'

'Doesn't help us when we still don't know who he was afraid of.'

'Oh, and none of his personal documents were on the computer. Small had Microsoft OneDrive, but there was basically nothing in it.'

'So, we have nothing, except for the slippery sister.'

'Yes. She sent a WhatsApp at five this morning. She took the early flight. She will Uber from the airport. She should be at the office by ten.'

★ ★ ★

Just before six. The sun was shining now, high on the slope of Mount Horeb above Clarens.

Tau Berger squatted on his haunches and watched the fucker. The man lay on his back, the blood on the back of his head was dark and dry now, his eyes shut, but he was breathing.

Tau had whacked him good and proper with the 1-Wood, down at the reservoir. Then Tau had taken cable ties and the masking tape out of his backpack and tied the man's wrists and ankles, taped his mouth, picked the fucker up and thrown him over his shoulder. Carried him out through the gap in the fence and up the side of the mountain.

The attacker was heavy. Ninety, ninety-five kilograms along with the guy's own rucksack's weight. Tau was fit but sweated and strained as he struggled upwards. The higher up the slope the steeper it became. Knees trembling, time wasn't on his side. He had to get as far away as possible, as fast as possible. Ten minutes, that's what he reckoned, a minimum of ten minutes for the other five to get into Tau's house, to see that he wasn't there, and to run back to the hole in the fence. Fifteen, if he was very lucky.

He tried to keep time in his head, his watch arm was gripping the burden on his shoulder. When he felt twelve minutes had passed, he put the fucker down behind a rock, looked back down and saw they weren't heading back yet. But he was three hundred metres up the slope, it was still dark and this was a good spot to shelter. He waited. His watch confirmed it: seventeen minutes, then they came out.

Tau imagined them looking for their mate at the reservoir first, calling quietly. Then, the surprise and consternation. Where was he? Swearing. Waiting. Speculating. Then realising there were only two possibilities. Their mate had deserted, or Tau had got him. Neither would have been good news to them.

And now they had one choice left. Get the hell out of there. What if Tau called the police? Or came after them? They would know very well: he was a handful.

He watched them pass through the gap in the fence. Pause and wait. Two of them put on night-vision sets, scanned the mountain. Tau lay flat. They called quietly, watching, waiting, talking in worried tones. And then they ran off in the direction from which they'd come.

That left Tau to carry the fucker up the mountain, taking his time, stopping to rest, until he reached the place he had picked out yesterday afternoon. The ravine where no one would see him.

He searched through the attacker's rucksack. There was an electroshock device, a Taser, inside. And the container for the night vision, and a Glock 19 with a full magazine and a spare in a side pocket.

That was all.

He heard the man groan. Eyes flickering open.

Tau dragged his own rucksack closer, unscrewed the water bottle lid and held the spout to the man's mouth.

'You must be thirsty.'

Tau tipped the bottle until the water ran out. The man was very thirsty. He drank. Tau took the bottle away again.

'You're the motherfucker who killed my friends Basie and Dewey,' said Tau. 'So, I'm going to hurt you. A lot. If you answer my questions, I will stop hurting you. If you don't answer all my questions within the next thirty minutes, I will kill you.'

Tau pressed a button on his watch. 'Your thirty minutes starts now.'

'Fuck you.'

Tau lifted the heavy old driver and aimed for the man's genitals. He swung, a high and rhythmic stroke.

★　★　★

Griessel got the call as he left morning parade with the other detectives. It was one of the state pathologist's new people reporting: the bite marks on Le-Lanie Leibrandt's legs were in all likelihood caused by one of Basie Small's dogs. The jaw imprint was a perfect match.

He told Cupido before they went to share the news with Witkop Jansen.

'Bingo. We were right, Benna. We were right the whole time. Karma is a bitch.'

43

Just after nine Griessel and Cupido drove to Brandwacht Street to make sure the cleaners had scrubbed the murder scene. They planned to ask Emilia to walk through the house with them later, in the faint hope that she might notice something that the attackers had taken.

The media were camped out in front of Basie Small's house. Curious onlookers had parked their cars on either side of the street, forcing the detectives to weave through the vehicles to reach the gate. In front of the house various onlookers were taking pictures of themselves with the murder house in the background.

'*Jissis*. The crazies are out in full force this morning,' Cupido said when they parked in the driveway and walked to the gate. Cameras flashed and clicked.

Griessel merely sighed, unlocked the gate and went in.

Inside the house everything was clean. Apart from the starred scar on the sliding glass door, there was no sign left of the violence that had taken place in the living room.

They decided on a strategy for bringing the sister here. Cupido would take the garage remote with them, and they would get her to lie down flat on the back seat while he drove directly into the garage. To spare her the exposure.

* * *

Just after ten she arrived by Uber at the Crime Investigation Unit.

The detectives were waiting for her outside. She had a compact travelling case on wheels that she pulled behind her, and a black leather handbag over her shoulder.

They greeted her, introduced themselves and conveyed their sympathy again. Her handshake was firm, her eyes weighing them up. Benny saw features that reminded him strongly of her late brother. She was taller even than Cupido, and not at all self-conscious of her height. She carried it with a measure of pride, despite her red-rimmed eyes and the downcast mouth. The aura of a strong woman, he thought. They would have to bear that in mind.

In the parade room they offered her coffee. She said yes, please. Cupido took the suitcase and parked it beside the door. Griessel went to pour the coffee, Cupido offered her a seat, pulling out a chair so that the door was at her back. They took their seats facing her.

'Ma'am, we know this is a very difficult time for you . . .' Griessel said, taking out his notebook and pen.

'I'm okay. I'm here to help,' she said. She sat up straight, her body language hinting that she was steeling herself, that she had prepared herself for this assault on her emotions. She looked Griessel in the eyes.

'The big question we're facing is motive for the attack. We would be grateful if you would accompany us later to Mr Small's house to see if there might be anything missing. But it doesn't look like burglary to us. Could you think of any reason why someone would do a thing like this?'

'I think it could have been burglary. The guns . . . It's an exceptional collection. And I hear that it's the thing most often stolen in break-ins in this country. Basie would take them to the shooting range once a month, he believed weapons should be kept in use. Someone could have seen him there with the guns . . .'

A slight frown on Cupido's face; Griessel nodded patiently. 'It's possible. But the trouble is it doesn't look like they were near the safe. To be honest, there is no indication they were even looking for the safe. There were six of them. If they couldn't open the safe, they could have taken it with them.' He wanted to add that he and Vaughn had thought through the modus operandi. If the attackers wanted to force Basie Small to tell them where the safe keys were, they wouldn't have silenced him with filler foam. But he didn't say it out loud.

'Then I think it must have been a mistake,' she said. 'The wrong address, the wrong person . . . Basie was . . . He lived a quiet life. On his own. His dogs, his backpacking, triathlon, that was his life. He was really pretty asocial. Even more than I am. He used to say he didn't really like people. And he was always like that. When he was at school too.'

'I'm really sorry,' said Cupido. 'But there's nothing that looks like a case of mistaken identity. Everything points to very specific targeting.'

She looked at Cupido, and said quietly: 'I understand. I . . .'

Her coffee steamed beside her, forgotten.

'Ma'am,' said Griessel, 'may I ask . . .'

Emilia Streicher raised her hand, a mute plea for silence. 'Just give me a moment . . .' She took a deep breath. 'I don't know why they . . . I don't know everything about Basie's business. I loved him so much, he's been through so much. My little brother. Our father was in the military. We lived in Pretoria. Basie was a *laatlammetjie*. He was born in November 1973, six years younger than me. My father had been dead for over a month already. Killed by a landmine in Caprivi. Basie never knew our father.' She was silent for a moment, took another breath. When she went on, that hint of emotion was under control again.

'And then my mother moved to Groblersdal, and she raised us on her own, and it was . . . hard. There was no money. My mother was a strong woman, but she struggled, she had to work long hours. She was . . . quite absent. Basie had a hard time and I couldn't always . . . I had to run the household, I had to help raise him. He'd get into fights. He . . . I think he was angry and ashamed about our home, so he always kept to himself. And then he joined the Defence Force, and that was very hard on my mother. Because of Pa . . . And then . . . We didn't see much of Basie, especially when he made the cut for the Recces. My mother died in 1994. Cancer. Then there was even less reason for Basie to come home. It was only when he left the military, in 2012, that December. I'd just got divorced and he came to stay with me. I got to know Basie better then, as a grown-up. But only up to a certain point . . . He was a closed book in so many ways. Maybe because of the things he experienced in the Recces? I don't know. He didn't want to talk about it. But one thing I can tell you: he had a good heart. A very good heart.'

Griessel saw that her resistance was crumbling: tears ran down her cheeks.

'Excuse me,' she said, taking a tissue out of her handbag. She dabbed her eyes and blew her nose. She took a sip of the coffee. 'What I want to say is, maybe there were people . . . Basie went to train people in bad areas, maybe things happened there. Things that he saw. That he wasn't supposed to see. He . . . He never said anything, and I had no reason to ask him. So, I don't know. If there was someone who . . . I don't know.'

Griessel nodded sympathetically and consulted his notebook. Cupido sat like sphinx-like, his eyes on her.

'Mr Small left the military in 2012, is that correct?'

'Yes.'

'Did he say why?'

'He said he'd had enough.'

'Of what?' asked Cupido.

She looked at him. 'Basie felt the standards under the new government weren't . . .' She touched her head just behind her ear, instinctively, as if it made her uncomfortable putting into words the extent of her brother's criticism of the new regime. '. . . what he believed in.'

'He found another job?' asked Griessel.

'I asked him to come and work with me. After my divorce . . .'

In her handbag, her phone began to ring. 'Excuse me,' she said, took it out and checked the screen. A momentary hesitation, then she switched it off. 'Excuse me. It's . . . a friend. A friend of mine.'

★   ★   ★

Tau Berger stood, stripped to the waist, coated in dust and sweat, beside the shallow grave on Mount Horeb. He held the cell phone to his ear. It had been ringing, and then Emilia cut it off.

Okay. She couldn't take the call now. That made sense, she'd gone to Stellenbosch, probably busy with the police now. A difficult day.

He wanted to tell her that one of the fuckers who murdered her brother was now dead. But not before he sang. To tell the truth, Emilia, at the end you could hardly stop him singing. Funny how high the notes a guy could hit if you pressed the right buttons.

He wanted to tell Emilia that he'd spare her the details, but here are the key points, if you put the bullshit aside and read between the lines:

This fucker, who was now under four inches of rock and mountain soil, was called Robbie Matlala. Two years ago he was a sergeant, an instructor at SAASIC – also known as the SA Army Specialist Infantry Capability – at its Infantry School in Oudtshoorn. One Friday, totally hammered, he'd beaten up two *troepies* at the canteen. And one *troep* died in hospital, and the army prosecuted Robbie in the Military Court. Manslaughter, and things looked bad for Robbie Matlala, fifteen years in the brig, at least. But before the case was heard, a man came to his cell and said Robbie, you're just the sort of guy we're looking for. For an off-the-record team helping to protect our hard-earned democracy, continuing the work of redistribution of wealth and radical economic transformation that our deposed president was busy with before they so unfairly fired him. If you join us, Robbie, my friend, we'll make sure that nasty manslaughter business goes away. What do you say?

Robbie said yes.

Tau Berger wanted to tell Emilia that it was *this* covert team that took out Basie and Dewey.

And he, Tau, was going to get them all.

Trouble was, Robbie Matlala had no fucking clue why they had been ordered to take out Basie and Dewey and Tau as well. Nobody told them why.

But Robbie gave him two names. Right at the end. Two names and one address.

The first name was that of the guy who managed this covert team. Ishan Babbar.

Tau knew Ishan. From the old days.

Robbie Matlala couldn't tell him where Ishan was now.

The second name was the guy who actually held the reins. The second name was the guy who knew why they had been sent.

That name was Dineo Phiri. Yes, Emilia, *that* Dineo Phiri, who was in court in the Free State province over all the corruption. And that Dineo Phiri was living happily in the Cape. By the sea. Hawston, close to Hermanus. And he, Tau Berger, was going to pay Dineo a visit.

Because Tau wanted to know. Why now, after all these years.

And then he, Tau Berger, was going to take Dineo Phiri out.

★ ★ ★

'My ex-husband had an air-conditioning business,' Emilia told Griessel and Cupido. 'I worked with him for nearly fourteen years, we mostly did offices in the city. And new developments. I saw there was a gap for residential air-conditioning in Pretoria, but my ex said it was a waste of time. After the divorce I had a little capital, and

Basie also made a contribution. I started my own company, and I asked Basie if he wanted to come and help me. So, he worked for me, in 2013 and 2014. I wouldn't have been able to do it without him, if you have someone you can trust . . .'

'And then?' Griessel asked.

'By 2014 the business was up and running. Then Basie said he'd had an offer. From an American company that does military training. Vega. And it was good money and he could see a bit of the world. So he went.'

'Do you know how Vega knew about Mr Small's background?'

'No, I . . . I really don't know. I think Basie had been looking around for some time already. I think he sent them his CV.'

'And he never socialised?' asked Cupido. 'No girlfriends? He was studying law. No student booze-ups? No former Recce pals to shoot the breeze with about the old days?'

'Not that I know. He studied extra-murally, and there weren't . . . As I said, he was a closed book.'

44

She lay flat on the back seat when they drove into Small's garage. The number of people in the street had dwindled, but Griessel knew that if the media suspected that the victim's sister had visited the crime scene, they would make her life a misery.

She walked slowly through the garage into the living room. Emilia Streicher stopped, and closed her eyes.

They gave her time.

She broke the silence with: 'The dogs. They were such a . . . presence, so much life in the house. Along with Basie they made the place seem full. But now . . .'

They waited. Griessel thought about the dogs. And their 'presence' when they attacked Le-Lanie Leibrandt up on the mountain. He shook off those thoughts. He had to focus. On her. That was all they had left.

She turned to them. 'Sorry,' she said.

'Ma'am,' said Griessel. 'We understand it's hard to be here. We can come back later, if you don't feel up to it . . .'

'No,' she said. 'I want to get this over with.'

'We assume you've been in this house a couple of times?' Cupido asked.

'Every Christmas since Basie came down here. And now, a month ago, at Easter weekend.'

'So, you would know if something was missing? Something obvious.'

'I don't know. Maybe . . .'

'Can we walk through with you?' Griessel asked.

She nodded. 'Where do you want to start?'

★ ★ ★

They began at the safe in the bedroom. Cupido unlocked it and showed her the weapons.

Griessel saw no signs of tension in her over the contents of the safe.

'They're all here,' she said.

'So you knew about all his firearms?' Cupido asked.

'Yes. He showed them to me. Back when we shared the house in Pretoria,' she said.

'So he had all these rifles when he left the Recces?'

'No, no. He only had two then. He collected the others over the years. With his work overseas.'

'We can't find the licences for them,' said Cupido.

'They are in the file I brought with me.'

'From Pretoria?' asked Cupido. 'He kept them there?'

'Yes.'

'But why?'

She hesitated. 'Well, actually it happened like this. Ten years ago. When Basie came to live with me, because of the divorce. All my things were a mess. It was hard, I wanted to start the business, but my documents were with the lawyers, or still at my ex's house, or they'd completely disappeared. Basie said we should both make a new, clean start and get everything in order. So I started a filing system, and I scanned the documents so that we had digital copies too. Both my documents and Basie's . . . I wanted to do something for him, because he had stood by me. That's how it began. I just carried on taking care of his paperwork.'

'So he would send you the hard copy every time, and you'd file it up there. The house paperwork. Policies, the works?' Cupido, with a frown that gradually deepened.

'That's right. I have it all in my case.'

'You never thought he was storing it up there with you because he was scared someone would come for him?' Cupido asked.

'No. Never. I told you: that's the way it started back then, and we just kept on with our system.'

Cupido did not look convinced.

Griessel took the wooden boxes out of the safe and showed her the contents. She said it was the first time she'd seen them, but the cash made sense, because he did travel sometimes.

'But he hasn't travelled since 2019,' said Cupido.

'That was because of Covid. He had plans. He wanted to walk the Camino. Next year. He wanted to cycle the Canal du

Midi route in France. There were so many things he still planned
to do . . .'

'Ma'am, can we assume that you wouldn't know if there is anything specific missing from the safe?' Griessel asked.

'No, I wouldn't. Apart from the firearms . . .'

They locked the safe carefully and walked back through the house
with her. She stayed strong, looking at everything.

In the study she brightened for a moment. 'Basie's laptop. It was
always here.'

Griessel explained that they had taken it for forensic investigation.
Small's cell phone as well.

She stared at the desk for a moment and then looked at Griessel.
'You will return it?'

'Yes, ma'am.'

She nodded. She said it didn't look like anything was missing.
Except Basie. And the dogs. And then she went out, down the passage, to sit on the couch in the sitting room. Her hands covered her
face. Her body motionless, she didn't make a sound.

Eventually she looked up. She said: 'I should tell you, I brought
Basie's will with me. I am his sole heir.'

★　★　★

They inspected the documents in her file. All the firearms were
licensed. The house was registered in Small's name.

'There's no mortgage?' asked Cupido.

'No,' she said.

'Can you remember what he paid?'

'Six point three.'

'Cash?'

'Yes.'

'And he had an investment of four point two million?'

'That's right. Here is the documentation for that . . .'

'Ten million. He had ten million before he bought the house.'

'No, it wasn't ten million . . .'

'Must have been, ma'am. Add it up . . .'

'About fourteen million. There is just under four million at ABSA
in three cash investments. I have his statements here as well.'

Cupido whistled softly. 'Lot of money for a former soldier.'

'He worked hard for that money. In some of the worst places on earth. He earned every cent with sweat and blood.'

★　★　★

The detectives gave Emilia Streicher a lift to Neethling Street where she had reserved a room in a guesthouse. Griessel told her they would have to limit access to Small's house for at least another week, and that she would only get the keys after that.

She said she understood. She would have to fly home to Pretoria tomorrow and then come back to Stellenbosch when they were finished with the house.

They dropped her off and drove back to Brandwacht Street to pick up the firearms and the pistol, each occupied with his own thoughts about the morning.

Back in the bedroom, while they took out the firearms one by one, making sure each one was made safe and then wrapping them up in a blanket, Cupido said: 'Benna, something is off with this woman.'

'*Ja* . . .' said Griessel, still not certain how to voice his own suspicions.

'Let me present to you exhibit number one,' said Cupido. 'It's a little weird, but ultimately understandable that the sister up there in Pretoria, one thousand five hundred kilometres away, stashes all Arthur Thomas's vital paperwork. Story makes sense, back in the day they had that arrangement. But then, Benna, I make the connection with what Lithpel Davids said. About Arthur Thomas's laptop and cell phone. That it looks like he was paranoid, that someone would hack him. Add that to the equation, and all you have is the weird.'

'Okay,' said Griessel, thoughtfully.

They carried the rifles to the car, which they'd parked in the garage again.

'Exhibit number two,' said Cupido. 'She came prepared. With all the explanations. And they are all just a little too detailed, like they were rehearsed. That story about, no, they saw Basie's rifles at the shooting range, that's what they wanted to steal. Good story, granted. But when we wouldn't bite, she made one up on the fly. It was a mistake. Wrong address. And finally, when we wouldn't swallow that one . . .'

They got into the car and reversed out. Cupido drove. The street was empty now.

'Which brings me to exhibit number three,' said Vaughn. 'When her stories didn't hit the mark, suddenly it was "of course I don't know everything about Basie". And yet: they lived in the same house from 2012 to about 2018. Six years, partner, this pair of anti-social orphans, they only have each other in the world. And he never told her anything? 'Cause why, he's this closed book? I don't buy it.'

'*Ja* . . .' said Griessel.

'Just "*ja*", Benna? That's all you've got?'

'There was something . . .' said Griessel. 'I . . .'

Cupido's cell phone rang. He could see it was the SAPS forensic laboratory in Plattekloof. He pulled off the R44 opposite Die Boord Spar, parked on the gravel shoulder, and answered. Then he said: 'Hang on, I'll put you on speaker, Benna is here with me.' To Griessel: 'Jasmine January from the lab.'

He switched the cell phone to speaker. 'Okay, Jasmine, go ahead.'

'It's the ballistics for the Small-docket, *nè*?' she said. 'On the dogs.'

'Check,' said Cupido.

'Two different firearms, but both are your SP1. No history on either. Standard 9 mm Parabellum rounds, nothing funny.'

'Shit,' said Cupido. Because the Vektor Service Pistol 1 was locally manufactured by Denel Land Systems under licence from Beretta. Along with its predecessor, the Z88, and the latest version, the SP2, it was the most common handgun in the country. The SAPS, the SA National Defence Force and various private security companies issued it as standard. Consequently it was frequently stolen and widely used for criminal activities. It was also relatively easy to obtain highly effective silencers, like the modular Dead Air Wolfman, or the cheaper Banish 45.

They thanked her. Cupido rang off, and steered the car back into the traffic.

Only once he had turned left into Dorp Street, did he say: 'Benna, you were going to say, there was something about the slippery sister . . .'

'Yes. She . . . I need to first . . . The problem is we don't know her. We don't know what's she's normally like. And she looks so much like her brother that I keep thinking she's like him. The way he was that night at his house, about the dogs. A man in charge. Arrogant. A man who had just been responsible for the death of a young girl on the mountain. A man who felt zero remorse, only thought of covering his tracks. Interviewing her . . . I kept wondering, is she also . . . so controlled. If you think of their background, it's possible. You need to be strong, from childhood already. But now I just think she was stressed. And then I ask myself, why? Was she stressed because she's just lost her only brother, she's sitting with this huge loss, but she has to manage it all. There are lots of things to handle with the estate. Or was she stressed, because she doesn't know what we're going to uncover . . .? Am I making sense? I don't know . . .'

'You're making sense, Benna. But you know where my sentiments lie. She's hiding something.'

Griessel nodded.

And he thought, he still wasn't making complete sense to himself. There was something else. Something during the interaction with Emilia Streicher that had set off an alarm in his brain. But he didn't know what it was.

45

Tau Berger drove to Bloemfontein on his Honda Africa Twin. It was a 2017 model, a well-maintained motorcycle, ran like clockwork. With aluminium panniers from Touratech on either side, and the topbox at the back.

Under the inside of his right thigh he could feel the thin handle of the old 1-Wood driver – the club's head lay behind, tucked between the seat and the pannier.

Yesterday afternoon Tau had concealed the motorbike beside the R712, in a gully opposite the tower of the Titanic cliff. Already packed, tank full, ready to go, if his plans worked out. And his plans usually did work out.

Tau rode carefully. On the back roads. Keeping to the speed limit. He'd have to navigate the pockmarks of numerous potholes, because he didn't want to attract attention on the tar road. He kept his focus a kilometre or so ahead, scanning for road blocks, law enforcement, any philistines trying to waylay him. So that he could change direction in time. Head into the veld, if need be. They would be looking for him. With a vengeance, he knew. And they would be plugged in to police and traffic police and State Security, all the unholy alliances of this day and age. Dineo Phiri was behind this. And Dineo Phiri had been high up in the former president Joe Zaca's Daylight Robbery administration, he would still be connected.

Let them search all they liked, they wouldn't find him.

He was going to book into a guesthouse in Bloemfontein. Where he could pay cash. No credit card traces for the bastards to follow.

Then he would shower and eat and he would phone Emilia Streicher. And then he would take a pill, and sleep. For a long time.

And tomorrow he would hit the road to the Cape. Not the N1. He wasn't stupid. He would go via Petrusburg, Koffiefontein, Philipstown, Britstown, Carnarvon, Calvinia, Ceres. *Lekker*. Broad horizons. Quiet.

He would sleep over in Ceres. Do a little shopping. In preparation.

On Friday he would head for the sea. Hawston, near Hermanus. See how things were going with Dineo Phiri. Do a bit of reconnaissance, before he paid Dineo a visit. Pop in for a cup of tea. Talk about this and that. Because Tau would like to know: why now? And Dineo, buddy-boy, how do we make this all go away?

And then Dineo would have to pay. For Basie and for Dewey.

And so Tau Berger drove, weaving between the potholes, at a hundred kilometres per hour. With his golden-blond locks hanging from the back of his helmet, fluttering in the wind.

★   ★   ★

Griessel worked through the bank statements that they had obtained by subpoena. On the other side, at Cupido's desk, Vaughn was busy with the cell phone records.

They found nothing.

Benny knew his numerical skills were limited. So he worked slowly and thoroughly, using his cell phone's calculator, a pen and notebook beside him. Small had just less than four million in fixed deposits in three ABSA accounts, and a current account for running expenses. The monthly interest on the deposits was about R30,000 – the money Small lived on. And he had to be thrifty, every month he had to count costs to survive financially: municipal services, short-term insurance, groceries, fuel, a Virgin Active membership, garden services, and now and then food deliveries from Mr Delivery and Uber Eats. He was subscribed to the *Bike Run Tri* magazine. Here and there he spent money at a gun shop, clothing store or sports shop.

An unremarkable, ordinary, suburban life. Frustrating.

The cell phone records showed Vaughn that Arthur Thomas 'Basie' Small only had one cell phone and number. And Cupido could immediately see he wasn't very active on it. In the last three months he had called his sister, an electrician in Franschhoek, and Green Fingers Garden Services in Stellenbosch regularly.

Cupido called the garden services. They said Small contacted them every Thursday before they came to do his garden. 'Because of the dogs, Warrant, those dogs of his, he had to lock them up in the house first, or they would eat up our guys. So, he'd phone to find out what time we would be there.'

When Cupido contacted the electrician, the staff members took nine minutes before the penny dropped: Small had ordered a solar and battery system for his house because he was sick and tired of the load-shedding. But the company was waiting for the delivery of the panels and batteries that were in a shipping container, and the shipping container was in the harbour, and the harbour was 'like everything in this country, Mr Cupido, in bloody chaos. Nobody knows when we will get our stuff. We have a whole crowd of people waiting.'

He asked them how much the equipment would cost. Then he rang off.

'Arthur Thomas wanted to go solar,' he told Griessel and pushed the cell phone records to one side. 'Big system, three hundred K. Must be nice.'

Griessel looked up, frowning. 'Three hundred thousand?'

'*Yebo, pappie*, the full monty.'

Benny tapped the pen on the table. 'That's . . . interesting.'

'Not in these dark times, partner.'

'No, what I mean is . . . His bank statements show that he only just comes out every month on the R29,250 interest at nine per cent. If he reduced his fixed deposit by three hundred thousand . . .' Griessel tapped on the cell phone's calculator: '. . . his income would come down to R27,000. Okay, that's not a huge difference, he could probably make some savings here and there. But his sister said he wanted to walk the Camino, and go cycling in France. The same dude who told Vega in America that he wasn't looking for work.'

'Benna, maybe he schemed he was going to save so much on electricity with his full-monty solar system . . .'

Griessel mulled over it. 'It's possible. But what does he do if the interest rate drops? And somewhere he has to pay tax as well . . .'

'You think like a policeman on a warrant officer's salary, partner. Always worried about surviving. But Arthur Thomas had a loophole. A financial hack. If the moola ran out he took a little job with Vega again. Three hundred thousand a month, four months and he pays off his solar system and puts the rest in the bank. Easy peasy.'

Griessel nodded. 'You know what that means?'

'*Jis, pappie*. That means we have *fokkol*. No funny deposits or heaps of cash, no strange phone calls, so there goes the theory of smuggling sports doping drugs. All we have, is Mr Closed Book,

Mr Clean Living, Mr Small Life, pardon the pun, a former Recce with a law degree and a good heart taking early retirement in the land of milk and honey. Except for one small problem.'

'Le-Lanie Leibrandt,' said Griessel.

'Bingo, Benna. Except for the curious case of the girl on the mountain bike. That shows he was a *maaifoedie.*'

'And where there's *maaifoedie* smoke . . .'

'Exactly. Look at the facts, partner. We have six pro dudes who check him out first and then flawlessly execute him. Military precision. Note my clever use of the word "military". Nothing stolen, just one very big, clear message. Keep your mouth shut. Now add that to the proven fact that our Arthur Thomas was a mofo, a man who stays cool, calm and collected when his dogs are responsible for a young woman's death. No remorse, no sense of civil duty to report it, he just takes his dogs home for a juicy rump steak. Put all those things together and it brings us back to my original theory. Mercenary war crimes. He had the capacity. The inclination. Some sort of atrocity, in some backwater somewhere. Maybe civilians that were killed, something like that. All covered up.'

'But why now, Vaughn? He was last overseas before Covid. In 2019. Mozambique and Iraq. That's two years. Two years while he kept silent over whatever happened. Why now suddenly this message?'

'Fair question . . . Let's look at what we have. The sister says he doesn't want to be a mercenary any more, he just wants to chill. He turned down Vega's recent job offer. You say his finances are healthy, but there's no room for manoeuvring, for splashing out on a big solar project. He uses an app that destroys the messages. He keeps all his valuables at his sister's place, he's scared he'll be robbed or hacked . . .'

'Yes . . .?'

'What if he schemed he could blackmail his Vega colleagues. Or even Vega itself: pay me some money, or I spill the beans. About that atrocity in Wakanda. They offer him an alternative, a lucrative new contract, come and train some security people in the Congo, we will pay you well, just drop the shenanigans. And then he says no. Maybe he thought they would come after him, because of the blackmail. Try to hack him. So he kept his digital footprint small, and he sent all his crucial documents to the sister, just in case. And he tells her I might be living on the edge, something could happen to me. You said, that day when you informed her of his death that it was like she was expecting it. Then they came for him, full force, with a message for the other *maaifoedies* who were with him in the atrocity. Shut up. Or die.'

'Could be . . .'

'You don't sound convinced.'

'It's . . . a lot of speculation. Witkop Jansen will say it's thin. And how are we going to . . .? Vega is in America, and even if we ask them if they know anything . . .'

Griessel's phone began to ring. It was the provincial media liaison officer.

Cupido sighed. 'Why spoil a good theory with the facts, Benna?'

'John Cloete,' said Griessel and picked up his phone. 'Maybe someone has contacted the media. About Small.'

'That's what we need now. A miracle.'

★ ★ ★

John Cloete had no miracles for them. Only trouble.

'Benny, do you watch social media?' he asked.

'You know we don't have the time.'

'Better that way. Hell, Benny, the world is going crazy. Twitter . . . They are like hyenas. Thousands of hyenas, and they smell blood and they all want in on the kill. The theories are wild, far-fetched . . . And then the papers ask me if they're true.'

'What theories?'

'The brother of the Leibrandt girl . . .'

'Arno?'

'Yes. Do you regard him as a suspect?'

'No. Why?'

'On Twitter they say it was him and his soldiers.'

'His soldiers?'

'Apparently he's a member of the Boer Commandos.'

'The Boer Commandos?'

'I know, Benny. I've never heard of them either. Apparently a far-right Afrikaner group wanting revenge for all the farm murders. Now the media wants to know if we are looking into that.'

'*Jissis.*'

'Hyenas, Benny, I'm telling you. So, you're not looking at that at all?'

'Not at all.'

'That is what I will tell them. But it's not going to stop them baying for blood.'

★   ★   ★

Griessel and Cupido walked up the stairs. They wanted to tell Colonel Witkop Jansen that they had nothing, but they did have a plan. They wanted to go back to the beginning, start going through all the details again, calmly, no stone unturned.

They walked down the corridor. Cupido's cell phone rang. A number with a Pretoria code. He answered on the move.

'*Jis?*'

'Is this Warrant Officer Cupido?'

'Yes?'

'My name is Brigadier Vincent Cambi. I am with the JOD in Pretoria . . .'

'The JOD?'

'Joint Operations Division of the South African National Defence Force. I'm calling about your case. The Arthur Small matter.'

'Yes?'

'I have very good news. We have just solved it for you.'

46

Cupido stopped in his tracks, halfway down the corridor to Jansen's office. 'You've solved it?'

'Just about. Well, when I give you the information, you'll be able to solve it yourself.'

'What information, Brigadier?'

'Right, so, before I give you the good stuff, let me just paint a picture for you. So that you know where I'm coming from. As I said, I'm with the JOD. Now, in the SANDF, Special Forces falls under the JOD.'

'Check.'

'Late yesterday, my office started receiving a plethora of media requests concerning the victim of your murder case . . .'

'A plethora?'

'It means "a lot", Warrant.'

'I see.'

'The media was asking for background information on the late Arthur Small, who served in the Five Special Forces Regiment until 2012. Obviously, with Small having been discharged nine years ago, I had to consult our records. It took a bit of time, but we found it all this morning, and I wanted to call you first. To help you solve the case, and to consult about the way ahead.'

'Okay. Thank you, Brigadier.'

'Small's personnel file just says that he resigned. But there was a very interesting reference in the file to what turned out to be classified material, which I had to really dig deep for. And pull a few strings, if you know what I mean. It seems that our man was, shall we say, a little mischievous. In Mozambique. Back in 2010 and 2011, he was on loan to the FADM, the Mozambique Defence Armed Forces, to do training for them. Up near Pemba, in Northern Mozambique. And then, in late 2011, he was on his way back to his base at Phalaborwa, when he was caught with almost twenty-five kilos of cocaine. In a Defence Force vehicle, at the Giriyondo border post crossing, the one into Kruger National Park. Now, this was a real embarrassment for both countries, given the circumstances. You know, Small being a senior officer. And the politics of the time: the former Mozambican first lady married to Madiba, and him still alive in 2011. And the fact that our defence force was helping theirs with training, and arms supplies, and whatnot. The FADM and Mozambican law enforcement people decided not to prosecute, as a gesture of good will. So, Small was handed over to our side, and our side, in the same spirit of hush-hush diplomatic cross-border co-operation, and with a real reluctance to draw the media spotlight on an unsavoury matter, decided not to prosecute. But we did force Small to resign. Which he did, in early 2012.'

'Well, I never . . .'

'Now, I know what you're thinking, Warrant Cupido, being the seasoned detective that you are. You're thinking, one instance, all those years ago, does not prove anything. That is what I was thinking too, this morning, when I unearthed the material. So I did two things. I looked at how many times Small entered SA from Mozambique during his time on loan to them. And the answer is seven. Every time at Giriyondo. It is a small border post. Easy to grease the wheels, if you get my meaning. And I also put in a request for information about Small's travels since 2012, to the Department of Home Affairs. And ten minutes ago, they finally sent me the data. That, by the way, is why I am only calling you now. I wanted to comprehensively solve your case. It seems that Small has been back to Moz several times in the last few years. He also went to the UK, the USA, the Congo and Iraq. Now, I'm no detective, but it looks a lot like setting up smuggling networks to me. So, there you have it. A neat and tidy solution to your problem. Just look at the drug cartels in your area. Organised crime, Warrant. Small was obviously still involved, one way or another. I see on the Internet this morning, he was living in a very expensive house in a very expensive town. Ask yourself, Warrant, how does a former soldier afford that?'

'Right.'

'That's it. Case closed.'

'Well, I . . . Thank you, Brigadier.'

'It is my great pleasure. After all, we share the same passion for serving our country.'

'You said something about consulting on the road ahead . . .'

'Oh, yes, right. The press is waiting for information. I just wanted to consult with you about the appropriate timing. How long do you need? Before we release a media statement about Small's colourful history.'

* * *

'We think it's a plethora of bullshit, Colonel,' Cupido said.

'A plethora?' asked Colonel Witkop Jansen.

'It means "a lot".'

Jansen rubbed his snow-white Chaplinesque moustache. 'Why is it nonsense?'

''Cause why, we did look at smuggling. Benna schemed that Small might be selling sports doping drugs. But that wouldn't fly.'

'His bank statements,' Griessel said. 'No deposits except his interest for the past two years. Here's a guy who was living relatively well, but he just broke even every month. No signs of money laundering. The cash in his safe . . . It didn't seem enough to consider large-scale drug dealing.'

'And the timing,' Cupido said.

The white eyebrows lifted.

'Why now?' said Cupido. 'It's three years since he left the country. And then there are the cell phone records. No sign of calls to gangstas, no burner phones on the premises. It makes no sense. And let's say, okay, here was a guy running a cocaine-smuggling network, or importing drugs wholesale. Why would they spray filler foam down his throat? That's not gangsta style, Colonel. If the gangs wanted to take him out over competition, they would have hired two assassins from Kwa-Zulu and done a drive-by shooting, or ambushed Small at a traffic light. That is gangsta style. Not this military execution with a message.'

'I think you must take another look. I think you've missed something.'

'Colonel . . .' Griessel began, but Jansen held up a hand.

'*Kêrels*, you must receive me loud and clear. This morning I've had calls from the Provincial Commissioner, the Provincial Chief of Detectives, and the cluster commander. They all tell me, this thing is getting out of hand. CNN is even asking the Minister if the far-right Boeremag is involved. *CNN*. Asking the *Minister*,' he said with emphasis. 'International attention, and it's not positive. It makes everyone higher up look bad, it makes us look bad. There's crazy stuff on Tweeter and I don't know what else . . .'

'It's Twitter, Colonel,' Cupido said. 'And that Boeremag story is bullshit too.'

Jansen just shook his head. 'Ask yourselves, if the army man is right, and it appears that we haven't even looked at it, we will all three be back on foot patrol in Koekenaap. Are you receiving me?'

'Yes, Colonel.'

'What is his name?' Jansen asked. 'The man who contacted you?'

'Cambi.'

'Give me his number. I will call him and get him to send us the documentation. Let's see. In the meantime you go back to that house, and search all over again. Through the garden and in the ceilings and in the panels of his car. Any keys in the house that don't fit any doors? He might have storage somewhere.'

'We will make sure.'

'Colonel, could you call the Hawks and ask Lithpel Davids to an-alyse the GPS in Small's *bakkie* for historic data. His system only shows recents on the screen,' Cupido said.

'It should have been done already,' Jansen said and made a note.

'And we will talk to the slippery sister again,' Cupido said.

'What's this "slippery"?' Jansen asked.

'She knows something, Colonel. We don't know what, but there's something there.'

'How sure are you?'

'Just a suspicion.'

'Not good enough either. And what did you agree with the Cambi *kêrel*? About the media?'

'We said they can go ahead. Can't do any harm.'

'I will have to let Cloete know,' said Jansen. 'It's a mess, this matter. A big mess. So go, get your asses in gear. Go and do your job properly. I will call if I get anything from Cambi.'

★   ★   ★

'"Get your asses in gear. Do your job properly". That is not fair, Benna,' said Cupido, as they drove back to Small's house. 'The thing with Brigadier Bambi Cambi is that he's a smooth dude. One of those with the attitude "Oh, I just solved your case. Oh, I'm a lot smarter than you". *Plethora*. You're in the Defence Force, why are you chucking that word around, when you can just say "a shitload"? Anyway, that is one reason why the whole pile stinks. And then, the cocaine. Twenty-five kilos, Benna. Twenty-five. Even in 2011 that was a shitload of money. Don't tell me they wouldn't lock Small up and throw the key away. Cross-border diplomacy be damned. Makes no sense.'

'Who was our president in 2011?'

'Joe Zaca. Why?'

'I say in those days our former president and his co-kleptos would have given the twenty-five kilos of cocaine to the Chandas at half price and a share in the profit. And told Basie Small, you keep quiet, or we put you away.'

Cupido chewed on the thought. 'Okay. So you scheme it's genuine, this whole cocaine affair?'

'It's not impossible . . .'

'Despite all the evidence to the contrary?'

'All we can say with reasonable certainty is that he wasn't involved with drugs the last two years. That's what the evidence tells us so far. Maybe he stopped that three years ago when he moved to Stellenbosch. But maybe he did bring cocaine across the border in 2011 . . . Maybe he blackmailed them, Vaughn. Now, when he saw what the whole solar set-up was going to cost him, he had the idea. To make the guys who were in charge back then, who confiscated the cocaine from him, to make those guys cough up. Back then a kilogram of wholesale cocaine was worth about eight hundred, nine hundred thousand rand. Twenty-five kilos meant at least twenty million rand. Where did it all go . . .?'

'So they took him out? The military?'

'Maybe.'

'And now they scheme it's okay to tell the media about the cocaine, because Small and the evidence are long gone? Government under new management?'

'Something like that.'

'Could be, Benna. Could be. But that means we won't find a thing in his house. Never mind how hard we look.'

Griessel just sighed.

* * *

Emilia Streicher sat on the veranda of the guesthouse in Neethling Street, her laptop open in front of her, coffee and cell phone close by. She was writing an email to an attorney, the one who had handled her divorce. The one who would have to handle Basie's estate. She struggled to focus, swirling emotions, her mind returning to thoughts of her dead brother, and to the detectives who had questioned her this morning. It was the tall man of colour who worried her. He was clever, and he didn't believe her, she could tell from his attitude.

The other one didn't look like much of a threat at all.

Her cell phone rang.

Tau, the screen read.

She answered.

'Are you okay?' he asked.

'The police,' she said. 'They want to talk to me again. They know something.'

47

Griessel and Cupido paced the yard, centimetre by centimetre. They stamped their feet on the grass and paving, checking for possible hidden underground spaces.

Vaughn was still unhappy about the colonel's dressing-down. It was uncalled for, he said. They hadn't got this far by being lazy. They deserved more respect. As seniors, as part of the Stellenbosch Serious and Violent Crimes squad. As former Hawks. And, even though they came from an elite unit, they never traded on their reputation or rested on their laurels. They just put their heads down and worked. Shared their knowledge. Witkop Jansen was just full of shit.

They inspected the small structure that housed the pool pump. Found nothing.

Cupido said their former Hawks commander Mbali Kaleni was a by-the-book pain-in-the-butt, but at least she had respect for them. And appreciation. The words 'get your asses in gear' would never have passed her prim-and-proper lips.

Griessel suspected his colleague's blood sugar was low again, so he suggested they order some food. Cupido used the Mr Delivery app to order Kauai wraps, because the kilojoule counts of all their meals were available on the Internet. He could keep track easily and it was relatively quick.

Inside they took each key and fitted it in a door, cupboard and vehicle until they could account for every one. Then they tackled the rooms, searching the built-in cupboards for secret storage places. 'I'm getting claustrophobic, partner, in this fucking house,' said Cupido. 'All we do is theorise. Talk, talk, talk. We should be out there. Chasing the bad guys. But no, it's "get your asses in gear". I object, your honour. I object!'

They fetched the aluminium ladder from the garage to access the loft space via the trapdoor. They shone their cell-phone torches around the space under the tile roof. Nothing but spiderwebs.

The takeaways arrived. They sat down in Small's kitchen to eat. Cupido said he wondered where Kaleni had vanished to, along with their chances of being reinstated with the Hawks. First of all, he no longer had the stomach for Witkop Jansen and his shit. 'And secondly, I can still marry Desiree on a Warrant Officer's salary, 'cause my cherry earns good money. But what do we do if there's a baby, maybe, Benna? I mean, I want to be a family man. Have my own little ones. And Desiree says she's up for it, but she doesn't want to be a working mother this time. And her biological clock is ticking. What do I do? Survive on a single income warrant's salary? With little Donovan and my own *laaities*? No, partner, that won't fly. Something has to change.'

Griessel realised the food wasn't helping. He took out his phone. 'I want to play you something,' he said as he started the music app.

'The song you're gonna sing to Alexa?' Vaughn asked, brightening a little.

'No, I'm still thinking about that.'

'Please, not some prehistoric blues again. Today is blue enough.'

'No. Just listen,' said Benny. 'Then I'll tell you a story.'

'Okay, grandpa,' said Cupido, rolling his eyes.

Griessel found the song, turned the volume up as high as the phone allowed and let it play.

Vaughn's scowl slowly dissolved and his face lit up. 'Wow. Catchy,' he said. 'Nice.'

Griessel just smiled in satisfaction.

The song ended.

'Really beautiful, Benna. Not your usual "let's teach Vaughn some ancient culture" music.'

'This,' said Griessel, '*is* ancient culture. From 1977. Fleetwood Mac. "Never Going Back Again".'

'Okay, ancient or not, I like it a lot. So what's the story?'

'You remember Vince Fortuin. Who plays lead guitar for our band?'

Cupido nodded. '*Yebo*. That brother is a credit to my people.'

'About a month ago, while we were rehearsing, Vince started playing this song on the steel-string acoustic, he wanted us to add it to our repertoire. You've got to understand, if the band does a cover of a classic, it has to be good, because people know the original. And the guitar work for this song is difficult. Even for an expert like Vince. It's a form of *Travis picking*, where you play the bass strings with your thumb while your other fingers have to do the rest. Vince said he'd been practising for seven months to do it perfectly, and he still had trouble. You have to play every note purely and keep the exact tempo, all the time, through the whole song, or it won't work. But he said he could do what he liked, he would never attain the quality of the original recording. The dude who wrote the song and played the guitar is called Lindsey Buckingham. The day they made the recording, they replaced all the guitar strings every twenty minutes, to make sure it sounded perfect. The next day when they wanted to add the vocals to the guitar track, Buckingham realised that he had played the wrong key. And he had to do it all over from the beginning again.'

'*Bliksem*,' said Cupido.

'Vince says that's just the technical side of the story. The woman you hear singing with Buckingham is Stevie Nicks. She was lead singer for Fleetwood Mac – and the great love of Buckingham's life. And he wrote this song because she left him. Sort of to try and process it. And after all that, the two are singing it together here. *Been down one time, been down two time, I'm never going back again.*'

Cupido pondered Benny's words. 'Benna, great song, great story, but where are you going with this? Are you trying to tell me we're never going back to the Hawks? 'Cause why, I'm not buying.'

Griessel shook his head. 'After Vince told me the story, I played the song to Alexa. She knew it, but not the story behind it. Last night, when I was on the point of going back to the booze, she made me listen to it again. And she said, "hear the lyrics". That's the big difference between a vocalist and musician – they listen to the words because they have to interpret them. And Alexa understands things that I don't always get. She had to explain it to me. This song is saying sometimes there are things that happen, that show you where you were. You have to admit you made mistakes, but you have to see how far you've come. Everything you learned in the process. So you can make the choices. Not to make the same mistakes again, to never go back. Because you *do* have a choice.'

'Such as, bugger Witkop. He made us see where we've been, but we'll get through this?'

'Yes, but . . .'

'Such as, at the Hawks, we made our mistakes not playing by the book, even if it was fighting the forces of darkness? Now, we're paying for the consequences, but we're learning. We're not going back?'

'Yes, but it's more than that. I . . . Alexa told me last night that it's time I stopped thinking I have no value. I know it's one of my big problems, because fuck knows, I've made a lot of mistakes in my life. But the thing is, it's just as big a mistake to stop at the failures. I think it's time to move forward. I mean, we've served our time, Vaughn. Over and over. We've done our work well since we came here. Every case, from stolen bikes to abducted students. And if we can't go back to the Hawks, we can start fighting back at least. I think it's time to tackle Witkop. About our rank, and his attitude. About our future. Because I have to say, we have to do something about this mess, or I'm going back to work for Jack Daniels.'

Vaughn slammed his fist on the table. 'Damn fucking straight, Benna. I'm with you all the way.'

'Okay. When we've finished up here today, we're going to see Witkop.'

'Yes, baby, yes. But you'll have to do the talking. You know I can get carried away, fuck things up a bit.'

Griessel nodded in agreement. Cupido downed the last of his Citrus Glo smoothie. Then he added: 'That was deep, partner, that was deep.'

'It's not me who's deep. It's Alexa.'

'No surprise there. Okay. Good talk. I'm all fired up. Play that song again, one more time.'

★ ★ ★

Just after five p.m., Emilia Streicher sat on the guesthouse veranda. She was waiting for the detectives. She was ready for them.

Half an hour ago Tau Berger had told her over the phone just to stick to her story. There was no way that the police knew anything. No way.

Tau.

After the call she tried to remember all that Basie had said back then about Tau. An extremely odd character. Unpredictable, in everything he did, sometimes quite reckless. There was the story that Tau always had a couple of golf clubs with him and a bucket or two of golf balls. Even in the bush. He was always practising, fanatical, addicted. And always on the move, always talking, Tau the veritable Duracell bunny, the only difference being that Tau's battery never ran flat. Short man syndrome, Basie said. Bantam cock, he always picked fights with bigger men and then gave them a hiding. But with Basie he had quickly met his match. Afterwards they became bosom buddies. Mutual respect. The most important aspect of that was on the battlefield, Basie told her, when the pressure was greatest and the shit hit the fan, you could always depend on Tau. He was fearless. The man Basie would always choose to go into war with: 'If he says he has your six, then he has your six.'

Tau had been intense over the phone. Rapid-fire speech, fierce, urgent, unstoppable. He told her he was the one who'd phoned her, this morning when she was in the detectives' office. To let her know they had come for him early in the morning. He was ready for them, because she'd warned him in time, he was grateful for that. He caught one. He made the fucker talk before he buried him. He knew now who was be-hind the matter, and he would get them all. He would avenge Basie and Dewey's deaths. Yes, Dewey was dead too, they got him yesterday. And all the time he was wondering, how did they keep it so quiet? But Dewey was the last one, Tau swore on it. 'I need to warn you, Emilia, the guys behind this thing still have power. Influence. They are every-where still. And because they couldn't get me all hell will break loose now. Don't be surprised if you hear tomorrow that I'm wanted for some or other crime. That's how they work. Counter-propaganda, disinfor-mation, shit out of the Stalin manual. Just stick to your story, never mind what they say. I'll call you, every time I find out something, I will call you. They won't catch me. I'm a fucking handful.'

She saw the detectives' car stop in Neethling Street.

She took a deep breath.

Let them come.

* * *

Cupido did the talking. The classic method, Vaughn was the fierce one, Benny the sympathetic one. It created a dynamic they might be able to exploit, and gave Griessel more time to observe her.

They sat down at her table. She asked them if they would like coffee. They said no, thank you, because that meant interruptions, and gave her the chance to fiddle with cups and teaspoons, if she felt uncomfortable.

Griessel again recognised her resemblance to Basie Small. The quiet confidence of someone physically fit, of impressive stature. Successful. Well-to-do. And she was clearly more relaxed this afternoon.

Why?

'Ma'am, we would like to know why your brother left the army. In 2012,' said Cupido.

'You asked me that this morning,' but politely, without irritation.

'We think you weren't entirely honest with us.'

She frowned slightly. 'I was. Completely. Basie said he'd had enough. It was simply not good for him any more.'

'Why exactly would that be?'

Griessel noted the gesture, her fingers briefly to her head, just behind the right ear. Like a woman who once had long hair, reaching for it now. An old, instinctive response. This morning he thought it was discomfort because Vaughn was a man of colour, and she was going to criticise the government. He saw that sometimes with white people, that sensitivity, that assumption that people of colour stood with the government. But now it looked like something else.

Her hand dropped again. 'Do you really want me to spell it out for you?'

'Please do.'

'Basie said the army had become a cesspit of corruption and cadre deployment,' she said, her voice reasonably calm. 'He knew he would never be promoted on merit again. The standard of training and military preparedness had dropped so low that he was ashamed to be part of it. And everything that he'd tried to do to prevent this, all of that was just met with shrugs or resistance. By that time most of his best friends had already left the unit. The Recces were his life, Warrant. It wasn't an easy decision for him.'

Cupido gave no sign that he believed her. 'Was he involved in training in Mozambique in 2010 and 2011?'

She nodded. 'If I remember correctly, for about nine months.'

'And then they caught him with twenty-five kilos of cocaine?' asked Cupido.

Griessel noted the expression of complete astonishment – the eyebrows lifting, the widening of the eyes, the relaxation of the mouth and the delayed stiffening of her body. 'Cocaine?' she said. 'Cocaine?'

'And that wasn't the first time either, was it?' said Cupido.

Her mouth opened and closed, she was at a loss for words. Eventually: 'Warrant, that's . . . that's . . . complete nonsense.'

'And yet, his official army records say the opposite. Which leaves us with two options, ma'am. Mr Small never informed you of his shenanigans, or you're lying to us. And we happen to think it's the latter, 'cause why, there are a bunch of things that don't make sense.'

Griessel saw anger flash across her face and then recede, like a shadow. The look of consternation which followed was harder for her to control, but she did. She put her fingertips together, a steeple in front of her mouth, looked down at the table. Then, as though she now understood, as though she gained some insight, a sense of calm came over her. She looked up, straight into Cupido's eyes. 'I don't believe you. Show me the records.'

48

'Showdown at the Witkop corral, partner,' said Cupido in the car, on the way back to the office.

Griessel was driving, and said nothing.

'Benna? You *orraait*?'

'I'm working on my speech,' said Griessel.

'Check.'

'Respectful, but decisive.'

'Check.'

'And you stay calm.'

'Like a psalm, *pappie*. Just there for moral support. Your safety net. Your wingman.'

'Okay.'

*   *   *

The colonel's door was open. Griessel knocked on the door jamb and walked in, Cupido close on his heels.

'Colonel, the cocaine story . . .'

Jansen was standing behind his desk, phone to his ear. He held up his hand for silence. 'Yes, Commissioner,' he said.

The detectives went and stood behind the two guest chairs.

'Yes, Commissioner. We will have it ready.'

The call ended.

Griessel began: 'Small's sister knows absolutely nothing about the cocaine.'

'And we believe her, slippery fish or not,' said Cupido.

'We searched that house from top to bottom, Colonel,' said Griessel. 'Lithpel Davids came to analyse the Ford's GPS. There's nothing.'

Only then did he realise that Witkop Jansen was taut as a wire. Angry. Griessel had to take a deep breath and talk fast before the commander could get a word in. 'Colonel,' he said, 'we want to register our objection. We feel that our asses have been in gear from the day we started here. We have never done anything else but our best work. We understand the pressure is coming from the top, but we think we were unfairly criticised today. The Small docket is . . . It doesn't matter how good a detective one is, how hard and thoroughly you work, there are motives behind this that nobody can see yet. There's a reason they are spinning this cocaine story . . .'

'Listen,' said Jansen, forbidding.

Griessel knew he couldn't afford to waver, he had his speech straight in his head now. 'Colonel, with respect, we think our work can improve even more. If we have peace of mind. About our future. I'm on the point of getting married. Vaughn wants to start a family sooner or later. We feel we have the right to know where we stand in terms of promotion. We want a timeline.'

'Receive me very clearly now,' said Jansen, in a muted voice, thick with barely suppressed rage. 'You walk straight out of here and you fetch the Small docket. You bring it to me, chop-chop, so that I can copy it all. You are off the case.'

Stunned silence. Cupido was the first to regain his senses: 'Colonel, that is grossly unfair. That is . . . I mean . . .' Vaughn saw Benny's warning glance, but he wasn't going to be deterred, not now, this had gone too far. 'That's fucking mean,' he said.

Jansen walked around the desk, heading for the door. He slammed it shut, turned to the detectives, and vented his fury. He screamed at them. 'Do you think I don't know that, Warrant? Do you think I'm doing this to punish you? You have no idea.' He pointed at the phone in his hand. 'That was the PC on the line. They are taking over. They are going to give the case to the Anti-Gang Unit.'

The AGU? Colonel, that's crazy. That unit has a forty per cent vacancy rate, and anyway, they are compromised . . .'

Jansen walked back to his chair again, and sat down. Clenched his fists, wrestling with himself. 'That's why I want a copy of the docket, Vaughn. Because they are coming to fetch it. In half an hour. And then chances are very good that the case will be buried. So move your asses. I want a record of the case, because I'm not dropping it. I will investigate it personally. My pension *se moer*, I'm *gatvol* of all this monkey business.'

They just stood there, dumbstruck and amazed.

'Bring me the docket,' said Jansen. 'Now!'

Griessel looked at Cupido. 'Vaughn, the story of "never going back again" . . .'

'Yes, Benna?'

'Fuck that.'

'Attaboy.'

'What are you two talking about?' asked Jansen.

'Colonel, we will copy the docket ourselves,' said Griessel.

'We're with you on this one,' said Cupido and opened the office door wide.

'No, no, no, I can't put your careers in jeopardy.'

Griessel hurried out, Cupido behind him. Over his shoulder Vaughn told the commander: 'No need, Colonel, we're pretty good at that ourselves.'

★   ★   ★

At the photocopier, behind a closed door, they raced to finish the job.

Griessel's phone rang. He could see it was his daughter, Carla. He knew why she was calling. She had sent a few WhatsApp messages over the past two days. The people at Sew Elegant wanted to take the last measurements for his wedding suit, time was short – just over two weeks before the big day.

He didn't take the call, but he did think about his daughter. And the wedding. And the implications of what they were doing. He said, as he handed contents of the folder, page by page, to Cupido: 'Are you sure you're in, Vaughn? Are you absolutely sure?'

★   ★   ★

They waited until the Provincial Commissioner's courier came to collect the original docket, and then the three of them walked outside to the big oaks on the western boundary of the Crime Investigation Unit grounds. The short, almost delicate Witkop Jansen, Cupido, tall and sturdy, Griessel halfway between the two in height, with the rusty-brown and red autumn leaves dropping soundlessly around them.

Jansen rubbed his moustache. '*Kêrels*, I appreciate the solidarity, but it was my decision. And I didn't take it lightly. I'm not going to permit you to proceed with the case.'

'Colonel, we discussed it over the copier. And we scheme, Colonel has, what, forty-five years of service?'

'Forty-six.'

'And Colonel is seven months from retirement?'

Jansen nodded.

'Colonel, that is not worth it, to throw away a good pension so close to retirement. 'Cause why, that's what could happen. We are still spring chickens. If they fire us, we can still start over.'

'What about being on the point of getting married?' Jansen asked. 'And with starting a family?'

'I don't think my wife wants to marry an *ou* who is too scared to do the right thing, Colonel,' Griessel said.

'Same here,' said Cupido. 'How do I tell my girl child one day that her daddy was more worried about his rank than justice? And our democracy?'

'We are sick and tired. Of the rubbish in the Service. That these guys . . .'

'These forces of evil,' said Cupido.

'That took our docket. Our docket. To cover stuff up.'

'It's time to fight back,' said Cupido.

'And to be honest, we are addicts,' said Griessel.

'Addicted to the hunt. Can't let go.'

Jansen looked at them. For a long time. Weighing them up. Then he said: 'About your promotions: back in January already I recommended that you be reinstated as captains. All I've heard since is that "it is being favourably considered".'

'Thank you, Colonel,' said Griessel.

'And you understand, if the PC knew that you were still working on the case, the "favourably" would be out the window. To say the least.'

They nodded. They understood.

'Okay then. I phoned the Cambi *kêrel*. This morning. Three times he didn't answer. He only took my call after two o'clock. I asked him if we could see the records of Small's dismissal, the whole cocaine saga. He said he would get back to me, he had to work through proper channels. Of course I heard nothing. Until the PC phoned, just now. To say hand over the docket, it's now a matter for organised crime. Anti-gang business. Fact is, they are in panic mode, *kêrels*. Cats on a hot tin roof. Jumping all over the place. The big question is why?'

'Maybe they took out the wrong guy, Colonel,' Cupido said. 'Military operation gone wrong, now they're covering their tracks. Maybe this has nothing to do with Small.' Then he shook his head.

'Okay, bad theory, let's move on.'

'Colonel, we must look at blackmail. Let's say something happened in 2011 . . .' Griessel began.

Jansen silenced him with a wave of the hand. 'Enough theorising. You know I don't work like that. Go and get us evidence.'

'Before Cambi called, we wanted to tell Colonel that we would like to start from the beginning again,' said Griessel.

'What does "from the beginning" mean?'

'Colonel, you can't just take a Recce out like that. Military precision or not, you have to have your ducks in a row. You have to watch the dude, know his movements, his home perimeter. You have to know about the dogs, the alarm, the layout of the house inside . . .'

'They must have been watching him, Colonel. They must have driven past the house, more than once. They might have followed him. We want to go to the municipality control room. They keep video material for six weeks. There has to be something.'

'We also scheme that with this sort of pro-level assassination, they would have looked at the house plans. At the municipality. You have to sign for that sort of access, there will be some sort of paper trail.'

'The Hyundai H-1 panel van they were driving,' Griessel said. 'We could follow them on the provincial CCTV as far as the Baden-Powell intersection with the N2. It must be somewhere. We want to take another look . . .'

'No,' said Jansen. 'Nothing outside our jurisdiction. Nothing further than the municipal control room. You must listen to me, you are going to be very, very careful. Say nothing to your colleagues, say nothing at morning parade. Talk only to me. I want to know the moment you know, I want to know before you do anything. Are you receiving me?'

'Yes, Colonel.'

'But you go home now, like two detectives who have no case to investigate. And have a decent sleep and tomorrow you act and talk like a pair of grumpy cops whose case was taken away from them.'

49

Thursday, 27 May.

Sixteen days before the wedding.

At 06:35 Tau Berger pulled away from the guesthouse in Bloemfontein on his Honda Africa Twin.

It was still dark. The sun would only rise at seven, but he was in a hurry. Focused. It was over a thousand kilometres to Ceres, on the back roads, the dirt roads, and the clock was ticking. The philistines had begun their counter-offensive. Yesterday afternoon Emilia Streicher told him about the cocaine story. That was a clever one, it was what he had expected. They would make Basie a criminal, and Tau too. That's how they worked. Discredit the truth, create a new reality. Then hunt him down and shoot him.

But they had to catch him first. And he was a handful.

⋆ ⋆ ⋆

At half past seven Emilia called Tau, but he didn't answer.

Probably on the road already.

She sent him a WhatsApp message: *Detective called. The case has been handed over to the gangs unit. How stupid can they be? On the way to the airport now, home by two. Good luck.*

⋆ ⋆ ⋆

Just past eight Tau Berger was beyond Koffiefontein, on the road to Luckhoff. Ruminating over this desperate Basie-smuggled-cocaine story. The case being taken over by a gangs unit.

The more he thought about it, the more he realised that he must place it in the context of the bigger picture. Of what had unfolded ten years ago, and who had been involved. And still was. They could only blacken the name of the dead because the dead couldn't talk back. But he, Tau, could still tell the truth.

They couldn't tell the police and the media that this Tau Berger was a criminal on the run, go and hunt him down. What if Tau went to the newspapers and said the philistines are lying. Here's the truth, here's the scoop, this is what they're covering up. No, that risk was too high.

They would have to get to him themselves. And silence him. After that they would come up with some bullshit story, yes, this Tau Berger guy was also a drug smuggler, something like that.

Perhaps, because they were still hiding in the intelligence agencies and the police and the army and in government, they could use state technology to try to track him. But they would have to keep it quiet. On the down low. And that was his great advantage.

Beyond Luckhoff he had an idea. A wild idea. Crazy.

Basie Small once said to Tau, you're a madman. But you're the best madman that I know.

Basie rest in peace. Tomorrow you will see what Madman Tau is going to do to the philistines.

★   ★   ★

At just past nine a.m. Griessel was in the Sew Elegant shop in Plein Street, Stellenbosch, ready for his final wedding suit measurements.

Last night Alexa and Carla had each given him a serious talking-to about the wedding date: time was rapidly running out. He promised to come in directly after morning parade. So here he stood as they pressed and tweaked and measured, jotting down little notes and chatting about this and that.

He was barely listening. His mind was on Emilia Streicher. He knew there was something, something during the interview. The problem was you had to listen and observe at the same time and sometimes the two interfered with each other. It was not in what she said, he was sure of that. Probably not in any of her answers. His instinct said it was something else. The thing evaded him, slipped from his grasp like soap in the bath. He tried replaying all three interviews with her in his mind, hoping that somewhere there was a thread he could pull on. But all this fuss and bother around him was a distraction.

★   ★   ★

In the Stellenbosch municipal control room Cupido sat and worked through the data.

He focused on the fact that the Dalsig suburb had only two entrances – Piet Retief Street running from the centre of town, and Barry Street, connecting with Van Rheede near the R44.

The operators confirmed that both these routes were equipped with a camera capable of number plate recognition, and that they had just under six weeks' data of every vehicle entering and exiting. They had supplied this information for him on the screen as an Excel spreadsheet, and also emailed it to him as a digital file.

All good news.

But the bad news was the number of records – a considerable sum total of 21,389 over the period of forty days.

Only one was identified as a stolen vehicle – a grey Toyota Corolla at the camera in Barry Street, on Tuesday, 4 May, at 11:02. Nearly three weeks before the murder of Basie Small. The system showed that the SAPS and the municipal law enforcement were notified within minutes, and the vehicle was intercepted at 11:32 at Macassar. The two suspects, respectively seventeen and eighteen years old, were arrested. Both were unemployed first offenders who still lived with their parents in Kraaifontein.

Cupido made a note, but didn't think it was relevant.

His second task was to identify the vehicles of the residents of the suburb and take them out of the equation. They should represent more than eighty per cent of the traffic, which left him with only six thousand entries. Taking into consideration that they were all double entries – vehicles driving in and out again, he was looking at about three thousand number plates to identify.

It would take a while.

Fortunately Benna would soon come to help. One thousand five hundred per detective.

* * *

Griessel drove down Andringa Street, on the way to the control room, noting the newspaper posters broadcasting the news of Basie Small's involvement in drug smuggling and organised crime in four short words:

RECCE
INVOLVED
IN
COCAINE

He thought about the trauma that Arno Leibrandt and his parents had been through over the past few days. The wild allegations and conspiracy theories, the nastiness and wickedness of all the faceless people on social media who would move on now, without a moment's thought, not a care about the scorched earth they left behind.

Lord, it was a horrible world.

★　★　★

Friday, 28 May.

Fifteen days to the wedding.

Just after nine, Tau Berger pulled into the parking lot of Ceres Agrimark, opposite the hulking colossi of the grain silos.

He had some shopping to do. A few items that he must leave behind with Dineo Phiri tonight, items that the police certainly would try to trace. And that meant they would check the CCTV footage of the hardware shops in and around Hermanus. And he did not want to be on camera.

Just a few items. They would easily fit into the Honda's panniers.

★　★　★

At eleven Cupido and Griessel took a break. They were nearly half-way through the one thousand five hundred vehicle records that they each had to check. It was soul-destroying, digital drudgery, their eyes were tired from staring at the screens. So far it had produced nothing.

They walked to the tea room.

'I think I know what I'm going to sing,' said Griessel. 'To Alexa. At the reception. But first I want to hear what you think.'

'Shoot, partner. I'm your number-one romance consultant, your expert witness about matters of the heart.'

'Well, that's the thing. The song I want to sing is not exactly what you'd call "deeply romantic".'

'Mistake number one, Benna.'

'Vaughn, if I try to play "Unchained Melody" everyone will laugh at me. Alexa too. It's just not me.'

'Aha. You're going with "stay true to thineself".'

'Exactly.'

'Objection overruled. But I know you, Benna. That is risky.'

'I thought about what Alexa always says: "With music you have to stay where your passion lies . . ."'

'*O, Jirre,* here comes the classic blues again.'

'Yes, but . . .'

'Blues? Benna? Old school blues? That sort of "she broke my heart and now I'm gonna die alone" thing? On your wedding night?'

Griessel laughed. 'No, not that sort of blues. It's this old song of Sonny Terry and Brownie McGhee. 1973, E-key, and it's . . . I don't think it's unromantic. Listen . . .' Griessel took out his phone, searched through it.

'Heaven help us,' said Cupido.

They walked into the tea room.

Griessel let the song play.

It was the last part of the lyrics that made Cupido smile broadly: *You're a chocolate cookie, baby, and you bring out the boogie in me.*

'*Jis,* partner,' he said. 'I love it. Gonna bring the house down.'

'That's what I thought too.'

★ ★ ★

Two weeks before the wedding, on Saturday, 29 May, at 11:43. Griessel and Cupido in their office, at their computer screens. Despondent, fed up: the number plate data had produced nothing of any use and they were nearly at the end.

Griessel's phone rang. He looked at it, annoyed, he didn't want his concentration to be broken.

Mbali Kaleni was calling.

He answered: 'Colonel?' He couldn't hide his surprise.

'Benny, your CO is going to call you and Vaughn in the next ten minutes. He is going to ask if you will be willing to be seconded out of the Stellenbosch office. I just wanted you to know that the request came from me.'

Lion
(Panthera leo)
Benny & Vaughn

50

Witkop Jansen didn't call. He came to knock on their office door, six minutes after Kaleni had rung, while they were still feverishly guessing at the possibilities.

'*Kêrels*, think about this carefully,' he said a little out of breath. 'Annika Johnson, the director of the NPA's Investigative Directorate here in the Cape, contacted me. She's asking for you to be seconded to them. Completely voluntarily, your decision, I won't stand in your way. But they need an answer urgently.'

It took a while for this information – and the implications – to sink in. But Griessel knew why the colonel said they should 'think about this carefully'.

The country's current president had announced the establishment of the Investigative Directorate of the National Prosecution Authority seven months ago. It was his response to overwhelming testimony during the Agnew, Zamisa and RSA Savings Fund commissions of enquiry the previous year, which had exposed the astonishing scale of state looting during his predecessor's term. The purpose of that new entity, also known as the ID or the IDU, was to manage the investigation of the countless corruption cases that flowed from the commissions of enquiry, so that the NPA's public prosecutors could build watertight cases for the prosecution.

This development was not received with the same enthusiasm in all quarters. Many members of the SAPS – and especially the Hawks – took it as a vote of no confidence and a slap in the face to honest, hardworking policemen.

There were also reservations about the NPA's ability to handle complex cases. The Prosecuting Authority had been decimated, haemorrhaging countless skilled and experienced staff members during corrupt ex-president Joe Zaca's term of office. Virtually all the best state attorneys had been pushed out or fired and the powers of the new ID officers were curtailed by existing laws. Investigators couldn't carry out arrests or seizures, and ID staff appointments were short-term and temporary. Not the ideal solution to the deeply entrenched, and wide-reaching tentacles of state capture that still clung on.

And because the ID worked in secret, there was practically no media reporting or rumours doing the rounds on the police grapevine to change the sceptics' opinions.

'How urgent, Colonel?' asked Cupido.

'As in the next ten minutes.'

Griessel and Cupido exchanged a look. Nodded. If Mbali was the one asking, there was no question.

'We're in,' said Cupido.

'Good choice,' said Witkop Jansen. 'Here's the number you must call. Right now.'

★ ★ ★

Over the phone Advocate Annika Johnson said she and the IDU appreciated their acceptance of the secondment. But would they please check in at the main entrance of the Arabella Estate and Golf Club near Kleinmond as fast as humanly possible. Literally within the next hour, if they could. She wouldn't be there herself. Her duty was to welcome them and explain that everything from now on must be treated as highly confidential.

Griessel hurried to collect his murder case from the car boot.

'Arabella?' Cupido said. 'Arabella?'

They took Cupido's Volkswagen Golf, it was faster.

On the way, weaving through the traffic on the R44, then the frustratingly congested N2 through Somerset West, they wondered about their destination. Something must have happened at the Arabella Country Estate, playground for the rich. That could be the only explanation for the request to bring their 'equipment' along. At least they finally knew where Kaleni had gone. The NPA's Investigative Directorate. They should have guessed, precisely because her move had been shrouded by so much secrecy. It was a logical appointment for her, the scrupulously honest, incorruptible Flower. 'And we call ourselves detectives, Benna? How did we miss that one?'

They speculated about the fact that it was the two of them who were asked to join the ID. Was it just because the Directorate needed more help and Kaleni knew they were good, reliable detectives?

Or because the NPA suspected Brigadier Vincent Cambi of the army's JOD in Pretoria was one of the tentacles of the great state capture octopus, and he lied like his feet stank?

★　★　★

Cupido took the coastal road to Betty's Bay, because there were major roadworks in Sir Lowry's Pass again. Beyond Gordon's Bay Griessel said: 'Alexa says I need a best man.'

'She does?' asked Cupido.

'That's right.'

'Check,' said Cupido.

'So I was wondering if you're willing?'

'Little old me?'

'Yes. You will have to hold the rings, make a speech . . .'

'Benna, I thought you'd never ask.'

★　★　★

Past Kogel Bay they were silenced by the grandeur of the view: the towering cliffs on the left, False Bay's rugged coastline sweeping in a wide arc to the right. Above, the prefrontal clouds trailed spectacular wisps through the air.

'*Ai*, Benna, this is a beautiful country.' A sigh of relief in Cupido's words, echoing what Griessel was feeling – the release of a burden, a freeing, an opening up.

'Amen,' he said. It was because they needed to escape from the frustration of the Small case, he thought. At last a broad horizon after suffocating restrictions, narrowness and stagnation, the claustrophobia of Stellenbosch and the long hours they had spent cooped up in the confines of Small's house. Being seconded to the ID had something to do with it too: a kind of promotion, recognition, becoming part of an elite specialist unit. Even if it was only temporary. They both needed this, for their different reasons.

At Pringle Bay Vaughn broke the silence, thumping his palm against the steering wheel: 'I've got it, Benna, I've got it.'

'What?'

'Why we're wasting our time with the number plate data. We're not gonna find anything there. 'Cause why, we're trained to try to think like criminals. And that is our big mistake. These guys are pros, *pappie*. Military grade. Careful planning, perfect execution. That means, they would know about the CCTV cameras, the number plate recognition. So, what do you do if you want to spy out the lie of the land of a former Recce, in himself a dangerous dude? You can't fly a drone in there, your former Recce will know "here comes trouble". You can't park a car across the road, same problem. So, what you need, Benna, is a Trojan Horse.'

'A Trojan Horse?'

'Damn straight, your classic Trojan Horse. It just hit me now, I know how they did it. The garden services. The fucking garden services. You identify the team that checks in with Small every Thursday. Those guys are low-skilled, low-paid, hard-working blue collars from Khayamandi. You sit down next to one of them in the shebeen on a Friday night, buy him a beer. Tell him, brother, I'll pay you a thousand to take sick leave next Thursday, and tell your boss you're sending your cousin to stand in for you. Even better, you bribe two garden services team members, you join the Thursday-at-Small-call, you check what you need to check, take notes. Like how you get over the wall, where's the soft underbelly of the house where you can sneak in. What weapons you would need?'

'*Bliksem*,' said Griessel. 'Could be.'

'Not could be, *pappie*. Definitely. No other way, it all makes sense. Just one small problem . . .'

'It doesn't help us?'

'Bingo, Benna. The garden services staff will deny, deny, deny. The foreman might just give us a description, but pro-level, military-grade assassins will know how to disguise themselves.'

★ ★ ★

Colonel Mbali Kaleni was waiting for them in a golf cart parked next to the fancy stonework of the Arabella Country Estate's main gate. Three SAPS vans blocked the entrance, with seven uniforms on duty to control access.

She had lost weight since they'd seen her last. Griessel wondered if it was deliberate, or just the stress of her new post. Still wearing the familiar black trouser suit that he'd come to know over the years, always the same style, but a considerably reduced size now. Her big handbag over the shoulder, identity card on a lanyard, and service pistol on the hip. She didn't wear a scarf around her neck any more, even though the scar of her gunshot wound still showed. From their first case together, way back when, even before Griessel joined the Hawks. John Africa was Provincial Chief of Detectives. When the SAPS was still a proud organisation.

Kaleni gave them a warm but somewhat muted welcome. 'I'm so grateful that you agreed to the transfer,' she said. 'I just wish it was under different circumstances. Please, take a warm jacket, the wind is getting worse. You can leave the car here.'

Griessel put on his SAPS windbreaker. Cupido took out his winter coat, the long one that he called his 'Bat Suit' because of the way it flapped behind him like a cloak when he walked.

They picked up their murder cases.

'You won't need those for now,' said Mbali. 'I'll explain on the way.'

They left the bags and climbed into the golf cart with her. She operated the vehicle the same way she drove her car, slowly, with extreme caution and concentration. 'I'm taking you to a crime scene. It is a little disturbing. The reason why you won't need PPE suits, is that the Hermanus and Kleinmond police have been here since just after six this morning. Forensics and pathology since ten. The scene has been comprehensively processed, and we were just waiting for you before we cleared up. I need you to take a good look. With total objectivity. So, I'm not going to brief you now. However, I'm afraid we don't have much time. There's rain coming soon, and the golf club people are very anxious to reopen the facilities.'

They drove on the tar road, across broad fairways, perfectly manicured greens, past luxury houses, fynbos and trees. The wind ruffled Griessel's hair.

Then Kaleni turned down a narrow players' route that was just wide enough for the golf cart. Ahead there were more police vehicles, an ambulance, and the big white panel van of PCSI, the elite Provincial Crime Scene Investigation Unit.

Mbali stopped the golf cart. They got out and followed her.

The entire sixteenth green was cordoned off with yellow crime tape.

Behind it, like a picture postcard, the dark water of the Bot River lagoon where the wind whipped up a succession of increasingly large waves, with Olifantsberg looming in the distance.

Kaleni lifted the tape for them to duck under.

'*O, stop your groaning, o, stop your moaning*,' someone was singing off-key, beyond the sand bunker to the left of the green, between the videographers, paramedics and more uniforms.

Another voice, more in tune: '*The Stellenbosch boys are here . . .*'

They recognised the voices, then the two men, still in their white overalls – short, fat Arnold, and tall, skinny Jimmy, the forensic investigators. In police circles they were generally known as Thick and Thin, because of the tired old joke they loved to tell: the PCSI stands by you through Thick and Thin. Griessel and Cupido had often worked with the pair of them in their Hawks days, learning to put up with their constant, sometimes pretty pathetic attempts at humour, because they did brilliant work.

Griessel and Cupido said hello, but Kaleni silenced Thick and Thin with: '*Hayi!* Not now.'

She went to the edge of the bunker. Forensics had erected a wide gazebo over it.

They looked.

Under the tent, in the centre of the patch of pure white sand, a man lay on his back, his hands hidden under his backside. His bloody feet were bare, and there were dark stains of dried blood on his yellow sweatpants and white T-shirt.

Filler foam extruded from his gaping mouth.

51

'Before you look at the victim, I want you to see this,' Mbali Kaleni said and walked up to the body, pointing her index finger. On an untrodden patch of sand just to the right of the victim were large, clear letters drawn in the sand:

FOR BS AND DR
FUCK YOU

The sky darkened, as the wind tilted the gazebo.

Kaleni pointed to the body. 'You can turn him if you want,' she said.

They just nodded. From the marks in the sand it looked like the body had been turned over once already.

'I'll leave you to it,' said Mbali and went to stand on the grassy edge of the green.

The detectives bent over the victim.

'*Jissis*,' said Griessel, taking a deep breath: the man's eyes were staring, wide-eyed, a look of naked fear. There was a gaping wound on the upper left side of his skull.

'Steady now, Benna,' said Cupido.

'I'm okay.' But he felt his palms grow damp. He just had to focus.

Cupido gestured to the head wound. 'Blunt instrument,' he said.

'Nose broken too,' said Griessel.

His mouth had been crammed with filler foam, the characteristic sickly pale yellow bulging over his chin and up to his bloodied nose.

The wind plucked at their jackets, raindrops began to spatter on the gazebo roof and the sand beside it.

Griessel and Cupido examined the blood spatters on the clothes, then the feet. The man's toes and the arches of his feet were crushed.

It began to rain harder.

'Okay, partner, ready to turn him?' asked Cupido.

Griessel nodded. They rolled the body onto its right side.

His hands were fastened behind his back with cable ties. The fingers too were crushed. There were no defensive wounds on his arms, nor any marks that would indicate an electroshock weapon.

The heavens opened and the rain poured down, a dense curtain.

★   ★   ★

In a conference room of the five-star Arabella Hotel Griessel saw how Lieutenant Colonel Mbali Kaleni had changed. She had a calm self-confident air, as if she felt safe, at home in her new role. A sort of quiet determination.

He and Cupido sat across from her. She ordered hot chocolate, then paused till the waiter had shut the door behind him. Finally she said: 'His name is Dineo Phiri. You may have heard of him?' as she slid the sugar across the table to them.

'Sounds vaguely familiar, Colonel,' said Cupido, passing the sugar on to Griessel. He wasn't in the market for any unnecessary kilojoules.

'Back in 2014 he was the Provincial Minister of Agriculture in the Free State Province, overseeing the Ilima Projects, which were supposed to uplift black farmers . . .'

'Wait a minute . . . the Tweespruit scandal,' said Cupido. 'Something about a tannery?'

'Yes, the Kgololesego Cattle Farm and Tannery project. That was the big one. But there were five initiatives in total, and they were all failures. Not a single black farmer was ever uplifted. Not one. Thanks to Phiri and his cronies misappropriating more than seven hundred and sixty million rand. The Free State Premier was implicated, Phiri's chief financial officer at the Provincial Department of Agriculture was implicated, and they were all forced to resign. By our former president, Joseph Zaca, no less. And then, absolutely nothing happened. Until the Zamisa Commission testimony . . .'

'Yep, I remember,' said Cupido. 'The Chandas again, right? That terrific trio of crooks.'

'Just the ears of the hippo, I'm afraid. Phiri and his accomplices were never prosecuted: our ex-president protected them. Because some of the money found its way into his pockets. Via the Chandas. But then, of course, seven months ago everything changed, with the creation of our Investigative Directorate, and a president who actually wants us to prosecute these criminals. I became the leading investigator on the Phiri dockets, and we've slowly but surely been building a case against him and his cronies. And now he's dead . . .'

'You think it's linked to the Small murder, Colonel?' asked Griessel.

'I honestly don't know. There has been absolutely nothing to connect Dineo Phiri with Small . . .'

'Except for a mouthful of filler foam,' said Cupido.

'And the writing in the sand. The "BS" could be Small's initials,' said Griessel.

'Yes, those links were made this morning. But there has been nothing prior to today, nothing in our investigations that point to Small's involvement in the Ilima Projects fraud.'

'And that's why you brought us in now?' Cupido asked.

'Yes. Now that you work for the Investigative Directorate, you can continue your investigation into the Small docket unimpeded. The Provincial Police Commissioner's decision to hand the case over to the Anti-Gang Unit has no bearing on us. And as you well know, they are not going to do much. You will also support me in the Phiri investigation.'

'Damn straight,' said Cupido.

'I also brought you in because you are the two best detectives I know. And I trust you completely.'

★ ★ ★

Mbali Kaleni said the ID obviously knew Dineo Phiri was in Hawston. He had built a house for himself there four years ago, in Marine Drive. Built with his stolen fortune. A double-storey with a view over the ocean and a footpath straight to the beach. 'We think he chose Hawston because it's . . . pretty anonymous. Not quite the Golden Mile of Hermanus, but close enough to everything that mattered to him. His house is big, but from the outside, it's not flashy. It's as if he wanted to tell his friends he had a beach house, he wanted the luxury on the inside, but he didn't want to attract attention from the outside. The reason why the Hermanus SAPS called me when they identified him this morning, is that we've asked them to keep tabs on Phiri, through our NPA colleagues at the magistrate's court in Hermanus. They knew his face very well. We had no reason to expect that somebody was out to kill him. According to all reports, he was living a quiet life, under the radar. He shared the house with two men who used to be members of the former Free State Premier's bodyguard, and we can only assume that they acted as such for Phiri too. Both men were found dead in the house this morning, when the Hermanus SAPS went calling after finding the body here.'

'Same MO on the bodyguards?' asked Griessel.

'Not quite. Multiple stab wounds. No filler foam. They are waiting for you to take a look before they clear it up.'

'Colonel, what do you expect of us?' asked Cupido.

'I want you to find me the murderer. I want you to find me the motive. Because, if someone is willing to kill several people in such a brutal fashion, there must be something very, very big at stake.'

★   ★   ★

Kaleni said Sergeant Rivaldo Carolus from Hermanus' SAPS Crime Investigation Unit was the first investigator on the scene. 'He's a good detective, I'll send him in, and then I'm going to the Phiri house to wait for you. PCSI and the pathologist will be there too, if you need to consult them. Call me if you need me, and call me when you get to his house, so I can let you in,' she said and excused herself and left.

They drank their hot chocolate in silence while they tried to process everything.

'Revenge attack,' said Griessel.

'Check,' said Cupido. 'A lot of anger.'

'That "fuck you", that's a response. To the message that Small's murderers sent.'

'But Phiri's fraud was in 2014, Benna. Basie Small was out of the Recces for two years, he was working overseas. Makes no sense.'

They heard the soft knock on the door, then it opened. It was one of the men they had seen standing behind the crime tape: mid-thirties, athletic, holding a notebook, shaven head shining in the neon light of the conference room. 'I am Rivaldo Carolus,' he said, and held out his hand to shake.

'Come sit down, brother. Where are you from?' asked Cupido.

'I come from Tesselaarsdal, Warrant. My people are still there.'

'How long have you been in Hermanus?'

'About two years now. I was in Paarl almost eight years, became a detective there.' He opened his notebook, then looked at Griessel and Cupido.

'I just want to say, it's *nogal* an honour to meet two legends of the Service.'

* * *

Carolus told them the Arabella course supervisor made his inspection round of the course in a golf cart this morning at 07:40, just after sunrise. The course opened at 08:00, when players on the first and tenth holes teed off.

The caretaker only spotted the body in the sand bunker at the sixteenth hole just before eight and walked over to investigate. What he saw made him throw up beside the corpse, then he left the bunker and immediately called the resort manager. The manager called the SAPS at 08:09 and closed the course. The players who had already teed off were asked to leave. The first patrol vehicle from Hermanus arrived at 08:42, and Carolus himself only just before nine. He was the one who recognised Phiri, and alerted Lieutenant Colonel Mbali Kaleni.

'I will forward photos of the scene as soon as I get them,' he said. 'But I'm reasonably sure the suspects put Phiri here, and then raked the bunker. Because the only footprints or marks in the sand belonged to the greenkeeper and the first uniforms on the scene.'

'You think they brought a rake?' Griessel asked sceptically.

'No, Warrant, every bunker has a rake. They tell me, if you're a golfer and you hit out of the sand, you have to smooth it over again yourself, so the next guy doesn't get stuck in your hole. I gave the rake at the sixteenth to the guys from Forensics.'

Griessel nodded. As Kaleni said, Carolus was a good detective.

'The pathologist said she can only give us the cause of death after the postmortem. It might be the blunt force trauma to the head or the filler foam in the throat. She said time of death is not yet certain either. It could be anything between ten last night and four o'clock this morning. The injuries to the hands and feet were made before he died.'

'Looks like torture,' said Cupid.

'That's what I think too, Warrant,' said Carolus. 'My best guess is, they tortured and killed him at his house, and then brought him here. The problem is, you can't enter the estate if you don't use the gate. The fence right around is electrified. I asked them to check.

There's no damage to the fence. There's security at the gate, they scan the car and the driver's licences, and there are cameras. Sixteen cars left after ten last night, mostly people who came to play golf yesterday, or who came to eat at the restaurants. But they all arrived too early to be persons of interest. Just seven cars came in after ten, the last one eleven minutes after twelve. All seven were people who live here on the estate. The cameras show nothing suspicious, but I'm going to check all of them anyway. If you ask me, Warrant, I think they brought Phiri on a boat across the lagoon. There's no fence between the water and the estate. That is the easiest. And the sixteenth green is close to the water. As a matter of fact, it's the lagoon-side green that is furthest from the clubhouse too.'

52

Because of his suspicions, Sergeant Rivaldo Carolus said, at twelve o'clock this afternoon he had dispatched a patrol vehicle to the Lake Marina Yacht and Boat Club in Fisherhaven. It was the only place where boats for use on the lagoon were kept. By road, Phiri's house was less than two kilometres away. The uniforms notified him that someone had cut a hole in the boat club's fence, just beside the eastern gate. An IRB, an inflatable boat commonly known as a rubber duck, had been found this morning in the water at the boat club. All four inflatable tubes of the boat were punctured with a sharp object. It was upside down in the lagoon.

The owner of the boat lived in Kleinmond, and he confirmed that he'd last used it more than three weeks ago. It had been on a trailer under the club's shed, the owner had been intending to repair it, as there was a leak in one tube.

It would have taken a rubber duck only a few minutes to cover the four kilometres from the boat club to the shore next to the sixteenth hole.

'I think it's the boat they used,' said Carolus. 'The trouble is that the boat club has a very fancy name, but it's really just a caravan park with two large sheds where they store the boats. And the caravans are some distance away from the sheds. 'Cause of the cold front that was forecast for today, there were very few people who stayed in their caravans at the boat club this weekend. Looks like nobody saw or heard anything last night. I asked Forensics to analyse the rubber duck.'

'But why?' asked Cupido. 'Why take the risk of transporting the body all the way from his house to the boat club? Then steal a rubber duck, motor across the water, and then come put him down here in a bunker. And then you rake the bunker, like a good, solid citizen. Ride the boat back again and poke it full of holes. Why don't you just leave the body at home? Or in the boat, underwater?'

'I couldn't say why yet myself, Warrant.'

'I know, brother, I'm just speculating,' said Cupido. 'This thing is just as crazy as the Small docket. You can't make this shit up. Benna, what do you scheme?'

Griessel shook his head. 'I don't know. They wanted to make a statement. An answer? To the Small murder?'

'*Jirre*, Benna, if they keep communicating like this, one of these days there'll be no one left in this country.'

★ ★ ★

They thanked Carolus, got the address of Phiri's house, and drove there.

On the way they discussed the words in the sand. 'If the BS stands for Basie Small, what does the DR stand for?' asked Griessel.

'Maybe the BS stands for "bullshit",' said Cupido. 'And DR for "dirty rat". Who knows, with these crazy motherfuckers? Mind you, that filler foam speaks clearly and said, "this is in reference to Small".'

'Or the guys who killed Phiri want us to believe there is a connection.'

Cupido sighed deeply. 'Yes. In moments like these, I am reminded of the Witkop Jansen school of crime investigation, partner: forget the theories, get the evidence.'

★ ★ ★

Hawston looked pretty dismal in the wind and rain.

The eastern part, beside the R43 to Hermanus, was a densely populated blue-collar neighbourhood. To the west, closer to the sea, it was harder to define. Between the many undeveloped residential plots, densely overgrown with fynbos, the houses were mainly simple one-storey structures. Only dotted here and there were large new homes, creating the impression of a coastal town aspiring to prosperity, but still uncertain of the outcome.

It wasn't hard for Griessel and Cupido to find Dineo Phiri's house. SAPS and emergency services vehicles lined the street outside.

They parked on the pavement opposite and examined the building through the drenching rain. It stood apart, solitary between two empty plots. There was a plastered brick wall painted light green facing the street, with sharp-pointed railings on top. Down the sides, and behind, the wall had no railings but was two metres high.

Behind the wall the house was painted the same colour. A simple box design, with wooden window frames, a peaked roof and double garage.

'Not exactly a mansion or a fortress,' said Cupido.

Griessel looked at the surroundings. 'The distance to the neighbours . . . Even if Phiri screamed, I don't think anyone would have heard him,' he said and took out his phone to let Kaleni know they were here.

'Or seen anything,' said Cupido.

⋆   ⋆   ⋆

Kaleni asked them to put on their PPE suits, as Forensics still had to come and finish the house after they were done with the boat club.

When Griessel and Cupido were ready, she said: 'I need you to tell me what you see. In terms of what happened here last night. Take as much time as you need.'

It took them three quarters of an hour to study the scene and confer before they could offer her a theory.

Beside the smart, expensive leather sofa and two easy chairs, on a large, square coffee table in the open-plan living area, there were leftover takeaway boxes, tomato sauce and mustard sachets and two Johnnie Walker Blue whisky bottles, an ice tray, and three glasses, none completely empty.

On the carpet right beside the sofa was a cell phone. It was still on.

To the left was a dining-room table and matching chairs. Six of the chairs were still intact and neatly pushed under the table. A seventh was to one side, at an angle, an eighth lay overturned, splintered and blood-spattered.

There were fine spatters of blood across the table and the tiled floor, and two larger blood stains next to the table.

In the short passage on the ground floor, a bodyguard lay just outside a bedroom door, his rump pressed against the wall, an arm outstretched in the direction of the living room. He was wearing jeans and a T-shirt, barefoot. Blood on the wall, blood on the floor: they stepped carefully to get past. Stab wounds to the chest and abdomen.

The bedroom contained a three-quarter bed, unmade. A bedside
table was overturned, a lamp next to it on the floor. The other bodyguard was sprawled on the carpet, in a wide pool of blood, between
the glass shards of the shattered main window. Stab wounds in his
throat and chest. He was wearing tracksuit pants and a Bloemfontein
Celtics soccer shirt, a flip-flop on one foot. The other flip-flop was
half under the bed. There were blood spatters on the door frame, the
lampshade and the side of the bed.

Forensics had erected a gazebo outside the house to try to stop the
rain coming through the broken window. It was not entirely successful.

In the upstairs bedrooms and bathrooms there was nothing worth
noting.

A white BMW X5 and a silver Mercedes Benz E-class sedan were
parked in the double garage. Both vehicles were at least three years
old. On the wall was a large dual-battery backup system for electricity.

There were no signs of the murder weapons.

Just before they went to present their theory, Griessel checked the
load-shedding app on his phone.

★   ★   ★

They stood in the living room, just Griessel, Cupido and Mbali.

'Load-shedding was from ten o'clock until twelve in Hawston last
night,' said Griessel. 'I think they came sometime during those two
hours, over the wall on this side, where the bedroom is. Because
there are burglar bars in front of the small windows, they broke the
big one.'

'Phiri and the bodyguards had dinner here,' said Cupido, 'and
afterwards they were watching TV and drinking. One bottle empty,
the other one three quarters down, it must have been pretty heavy.
They heard the window break in the bedroom. Maybe the TV was
loud, maybe they were a little drunk, maybe both, because their
reaction was slow enough to let the attackers enter the bedroom from
outside first before they got there. Did you find any firearms in the
house?'

'No. There's a small handgun-sized safe in the main bedroom
upstairs,' said Kaleni. 'We haven't opened it yet.'

'Okay,' said Cupido. 'So, there are two possibilities: the bodyguards were armed, but too slow and drunk, and the assailants took

both of them out before they could shoot. And stole the guns on the way out. Or, the guards ran to the bedroom unarmed, and were killed. Either way, it means the assailants were good. Quick. We saw no defensive or bullet wounds on the bodyguards. No bullet marks on the walls. The attackers wanted to be as quiet as possible. Especially during load-shedding, because everything is quieter then.'

'If you want to torture a guy in his own house,' said Griessel, 'you must buy yourself time. By not attracting the neighbours' attention. So you don't use guns. We couldn't see any defensive wounds on Phiri either, which indicates that they took him without any resistance.'

'Probably plastered too,' said Cupido. 'Or just sh—' He remembered Kaleni didn't tolerate bad language. '—very scared.'

'They tied him to the dining-room chair,' said Griessel, 'probably with cable ties. Then they smashed his feet, hands and face with a blunt instrument. And then killed him.'

'We didn't see blood at the front door or in the garage,' said Cupido. 'They must have picked him up and carried him out. Which means they might have had an accomplice waiting in a vehicle nearby, who came to pick them up. If Sergeant Carolus is correct, they took him to the boat club, stole a rubber duck, crossed the lagoon and left him in the bunker.'

'There's a laptop in the main bedroom, and a wallet on the bed-side table,' said Griessel.

'So it wasn't a burglary,' said Cupido.

'And that's about it,' said Griessel.

Kaleni had listened intently. Now she nodded. 'That is a good assessment, thank you. My first question would be, how does this compare to the Small crime scene? Do you think it's the same people?'

'Probably not,' said Cupido.

'I agree,' said Griessel.

'Why?'

'No taser, Colonel,' said Cupido. 'They stunned Small with a taser several times. If you have a taser available, why not use it on these bodyguards before stabbing them? Or Phiri, to get him under control?'

'They shot Small's dogs with SP1's,' said Griessel. 'And they must have used silencers, because nobody in the neighbourhood heard the four shots. It would have been much easier to take out

Phiri's bodyguards with that, and still not attract attention. The house is more than a hundred metres from the next one. But they used blades.'

'No blunt instrument on Small either,' said Cupido. 'This looks like a lot of anger. The smashed hands and feet and face. The filler foam: on Phiri it looks like they used the whole damn bottle. The Small crime scene just looked very calm and controlled and . . . well, efficient. Professional.'

'And there's the message in the sand,' said Griessel.

53

In a room on the first floor of the Protea Hotel at the Cape Town Waterfront Tau Berger stood in the shower, the taps wide open. He waited for the hot water to refresh his body and his mind. It wasn't working.

He should call Emilia Streicher. But his thoughts were muddled. From a mere three hours of sporadic, restless and uncomfortable sleep in the veld, from all night operating on adrenaline, high-octane, flat-out, balls to the wall. All of it worked out of his system now, only the hangover remained.

Images flickered and leaped in his mind like electric charges – the violence he had unleashed, the things he had done. And the stuff that Dineo Phiri told him, which stoked his anger like dry wood on a fire.

What should he say to Emilia now? About Basie. And why he died.

And what was he going to do next? Now that he knew how matters stood.

Two names. And a ship. And a date.

And a situation.

That's what he got from Phiri.

Two names.

The first name wasn't new.

And the second one, fuck knew, he hadn't seen the second one coming.

The second one changed everything.

He knew, the day before yesterday, past Luckhoff, that leaving Phiri in that bunker would be a wild idea. He knew, if he went that route, it would be a tipping point. Crossing the line. Before last night the philistines would at best have only wondered. But now they would know: this was Tau, he was that one that did it. Tau, the

golfer, who made their man in Clarens disappear, and who found
Phiri. And his two fat-ass bodyguards, useless, drunken bastards.

This was his goal: tell the fuckers, come and get me if you can.
Before I get you.

What should he do now, with everything that Phiri had told him?

Two names. And a ship. And a date. And a situation.

He would have to think carefully. But not with this messed-up
brain.

Call Emilia first. Then sleep. If he could.

What would he say to her?

Basie was dead because of an assumption. A conclusion, a connection. Totally to *moer* and gone wrong, but certainly not illogical.

He needn't give Emilia any details about yesterday. The way he'd
first recced the whole place. Thinking how Hawston was a very
stupid choice for Dineo Phiri to go into hiding. One CCTV camera,
at the intersection from the R43 and George Viljoen Street. Probably
the province's. No cameras in Marine Drive, where Phiri lived.
Moreover, Phiri's house was isolated, the plots next to it lushly overgrown with head-high shrubs so you could sneak around there even
in broad daylight and the fuckers wouldn't see you.

A boat club with a tall wire fence, the kind that you could cut like
a knife through butter.

So he made his plans. Stealing the licence plate of a Mr Delivery
motorcycle in Hermanus, and putting it on his Honda. Then waiting
for nightfall.

He left the Africa Twin down by the dead-end circle next to the
sea. Like someone going for a moonlit walk on the beach. He waited
in the fynbos beside the house, until ten o'clock load-shedding began.
With his old driver and his knife. And his backpack containing the
gloves and cable ties, the filler foam and the pliers. He noted the
lights were still burning in there, some nice little backup battery from
all the stolen money. Up and over the wall, then he heard the soccer
match on the TV inside, the men cheering and shouting, saw the
curtains of the bedroom window left wide open.

Then he knew Phiri had not been warned. Phiri was not informed
of what had happened in Clarens the day before yesterday. And Tau
wondered, why not? Did the guy who now lay buried in the shallow
grave up on the mountain lie about Dineo pulling the strings?

Let's find out, he thought.

He smashed the window and leaped through, knife held ready, the Gerber Mark II. The two fatties came running, yelling and reeking of booze, unsteady, swaying, staggering. And he took them out and he ran in, and Phiri just sat there in front of the TV with a whisky glass in one hand, his cell phone in the other, and a dazed look in his wide eyes and he said to Tau, 'I've got money, I've got money.'

Dineo Phiri didn't want to talk at first. But he did. After a lot of encouragement. And then he really sang.

He was the one who pulled the strings, who completely screwed it up and came to the wrong conclusion, who gave the instructions regarding Basie and Dewey. And Tau made Phiri pay for it.

Only right before the end, Phiri gave him two names and the date and the ship. Thought it would save him.

But it didn't.

And then Tau went looking through the house and the garage. Found the X5 and the Merc's keys on a kitchen cabinet just outside the garage. He saw the two Z88 pistols lying there too, what were they thinking? You only carry your firearms if you're going to drive, because you're safe in this house?

Useless bastards.

He took the pistols and put them in his backpack. And he took eight black garbage bags from the kitchen and arranged them in the boot of the X5. So that Phiri's blood wouldn't stain the carpet. He knew he would have to use Phiri's car, he just had to bring it back and park it nicely. The advantage was, the police would think the guys who took Phiri out must have come with a car. They would be looking for someone with a car, not a dude on a motorbike.

He put Phiri in the back of the BMW, and he sprayed the filler foam down his throat, put the empty container away in the backpack. And he drove to the boat club, exactly as he had planned in his reconnaissance earlier in the day. He cut a hole in the fence.

He was familiar with rubber ducks and with Arabella. He'd played golf there a few times. Nice golf course. Not easy. Narrow fairway, the rough was fynbos, made you search for your ball. Lots of bunkers, plenty of water. He had to look up on Google Earth to remember which bunker was the safest.

He laid Phiri down in it. On the spur of the moment he traced the little message in the sand with his gloved finger.

A message for Ishan Babbar. The name he got from Robbie Matlala on the mountain. It was also the first name Phiri gave him.

Tau knew Ishan, and Ishan knew him.

So he wrote the little message, to let Babbar know that Tau Berger said: Fuck you. Come and get me.

Dineo Phiri confirmed that Ishan Babbar was still doing the dirty work, the one directly in charge of Basie and Dewey's assassination team.

The one that Tau, personally, was going to hunt down.

Finally Tau raked the sand pit, smoothing it over, no boot tracks, it was just good manners, if you played out of the bunker. And when he took the rubber duck back, he discovered that one side was now very soft. It struggled along, slowly, he had to hang on the other side, all the time thinking if this thing sinks here in the middle of this lagoon, he was in deep trouble.

But he made it, and he thought that trying to get the duck back onto the trailer now was going to take too long, he didn't have time. Instead he punctured the tubes and overturned it in the water and he got into the X5 and drove it back to Phiri's garage. He removed the garbage bags, put them in his backpack. And he wiped the BMW driver's seat down because his ass was wet behind the wheel. He took some of Phiri's clothes, because riding wet at night on a motorcycle, the cold could kill you. Stowed the wet clothes in the backpack too, and he was out of there.

He took a long detour, riding east first, around the foot of the mountain, towards Caledon. Along the N2 a while, then gravel road from Botrivier, towards Theewaterskloof. He lay low in the Van der Stel Pass, under a little bridge, at four o'clock in the morning. He took off Phiri's clothes there. His bloodstained wet clothes, the gloves and cable ties, the empty filler foam bottle and the pliers, he buried the lot there. His old driver too, stained with Phiri's blood. He dressed in his own, dry clothes from the Honda's pannier. He tried to sleep with his back against the motorbike's tank. The night's action played over and over in his mind, the things he had done to Phiri, he knew it would drive him crazy. His brain built walls that defended and rationalised his acts: Basie and Dewey were dead, all because of Phiri's fucking stupidity.

At dawn, he was on the road again, even before the farm workers were up. Franschhoek, Paarl, Malmesbury. Filled up with petrol, drank coffee standing. Checked his cell phone, still nothing in the media about Phiri. Wondering, how will the philistines spin this story?

He saw heavy rain incoming, he would have to push on. Via the N7 to Cape Town. To the Waterfront. Crowds of people, anonymity, the Honda safely down in the basement parking. He arrived hungry and thirsty. He downed two Big Champion burgers and chips with two strawberry milkshakes in the Wimpy and went to Woolworths to buy clothes to replace the ones he had buried. And then he went to the Protea hotel to ask if he could pay in cash.

He didn't want to leave any tracks for Ishan Babbar.

Tau washed his hair and scrubbed his body and rinsed it again. Even that brought no relief.

He got out, rubbing himself dry with the towel. Paced up and down in front of the bed. Up and down. His mind racing.

The second name. That's where he had to start.

When Dineo Phiri said the second name, Tau didn't know what he was talking about. Phiri's mouth was so swollen from the beating, it was barely intelligible.

'Who?' he asked.

'Wilhelm Brenner.'

'Who the fuck is Wilhelm Brenner?'

'Please. Please. You know him. He was your friend. In the Recces. At Phalaborwa. We got photos of you and Small and Brenner, together. From two thousand and nine.'

'Brenner? Billy Brenner? Five SFR?'

'Yes.'

He never knew Brenner's name was 'Wilhelm'. He thought Phiri was lying to him. Until Phiri told the whole story. Then it all made sense. Yes, Tau had been with Brenner in 5SFR. With Brenner and Basie and Dewey and Corrie Albertyn and Fani Dlamini.

All dead now.

But one guy was still alive, as far as Tau knew. One guy who definitely went with Brenner to steal the dollars, because they were big buddies, those days in Phalaborwa. Ops team members, comrades. Later too, at some of the Recce reunions that Tau attended. Brenner and his brother from another mother, heads together, deep in conversation, always.

Vernon Abrahams. Vern.

The only *ou* who called Brenner 'Billy'. To the rest of them he was just 'Brenner'.

And Vern, Tau had heard a few times through the ex-Recces' bush telegraph, was here in the Cape. Owner of a company that specialised in industrial security, making big bucks. Bravo Zulu, that was the company name. Because Vern had been in the navy, before he was selected for Special Forces. And in the navy, a Bravo Zulu flag meant 'well done'.

54

At the boat club Cupido and Griessel parked in the pouring rain alongside PCSI's big white panel van.

They got out and ran to where Thick and Thin were standing beside the black, deflated rubber dinghy under the shed.

'The old comedy duo,' said Cupido. 'Long time no see.'

'Hey, hey, hey,' said short, fat Arnold, busily packing his equipment away in a Pelican case. 'Not that we missed you. Benny, the final countdown! We hear you're getting married?'

Alexa had announced it to the whole world on Facebook a week ago. Everybody knew. It was no use denying it now. 'Yes, yes,' he said, and braced himself for what was coming.

'I hear,' said Jimmy, 'with marriage you become one. The question is, which one?'

'Dad jokes, Jimmy,' said Cupido. 'That's the best you can do?'

'Marriage is like a walk in the park,' said Arnold. 'Jurassic Park.'

Arnold and Jimmy laughed heartily. Griessel just grinned.

'Being married is give and take, Benny. You give and she takes,' said Jimmy.

'Marriage is not a word. It's a sentence. A life sentence,' said Arnold.

'I'm laughing on the inside,' said Griessel.

'My insides are cringing,' said Vaughn.

'Tough crowd,' said Jimmy. 'Nothing has changed.'

The forensic investigators took off their gloves and came over to shake hands.

'Get anything?' asked Griessel.

'Here? Just a cold.'

'Boat was overturned and half under water,' said Jimmy. 'They were clever.'

'We still have to go and do the house,' said Arnold. 'Hope you wore your PPE suits there.'

'At the golf course,' said Jimmy, 'we luminolised the bunker. No blood. Chances are good that he was already dead by then. The rake is a bit of a problem. Helluva lot of useable fingerprints and palm prints, but now they tell us every *ou* who hits out of the bunker has to rake it when he's done. So, don't hold your breath.'

'The writing in the sand?' asked Griessel.

Arnold shrugged. 'Best guess is, it was done with a finger. We took samples, we'll have to test for DNA.'

'Can you send me a photo of the words?'

'Sure.'

'Only thing that might help,' said Jimmy, reaching under the PPE pants to fish out his cell phone. He took it out. 'Sole prints.' He searched for a photo, turned the screen so the detectives could see. 'Just below the sixteenth green, between the grass and the water. There's a border of sand and grass . . .'

They looked. Two prints, a left and right shoe.

'You can't see it too well in the photo, but that's a word, just in front of the heel. "REBEL". We forwarded the photos and the measurements to the lab. They say it's your Black Hawk S3 Combat Boot, pretty common among guys who do manual work. Construction, that kind of thing. Waterproof. About ten places on the internet where you can order. Not the kind of shoe you put on when you come to play eighteen holes. Oh, and according to the length, a number nine. So, we aren't necessarily talking about a *moerse* big *ou*.'

'Just the two footprints?' asked Griessel.

'The section between the green and the lagoon is patchy,' said Arnold. 'Grass and sand. This *ou* was the only one of them who stepped on the sand. On the way back to the water. Probably in a rush.'

'Trouble is, the rain came before we could test the sand's consistency,' said Jimmy. 'We will look at the depth, and the distance between the two tracks. Maybe give you an estimate of his height and weight, but it's going to be a bit of a thumb suck.'

* * *

Tau was sitting on the bed holding the phone. The screen said it was 18:07. He looked up, to the long tracks of rain streaming down his hotel window. He couldn't put it off any longer. He called Emilia Streicher.

'I was starting to worry,' was the first thing she said.

'Sorry,' he said. 'Had a bit of a wild time.'

'Are you okay?'

'Yes. Listen . . . I don't want to go into detail now. I just want to say, I got him. The dude who gave the orders. For Basie. And Dewey.'

He heard her let out her breath. As if she was released too. 'His name was Dineo Phiri. One of the state capture gang. It will surely be in the news tonight. Big. He was notorious.'

'I'm glad you got him.'

He knew she was going to ask now. He wished she wouldn't.

'Why, Tau? Did he tell you? Why now? Ten years after.'

'Yes. He did.'

She waited.

'Can you give me a day? I know it's not fair, and I'm helluva sorry. But there's a guy I want to see tomorrow. Because I just want to make absolutely sure of one thing. Then I'll tell you.'

She was silent for a long time, but he knew he had to give her time for her feelings.

'Okay,' she said.

He said goodbye, and hung up.

What he couldn't tell her was that he wanted to check whether Basie Small had betrayed them. Make sure Basie Small wasn't part of this too.

★ ★ ★

Mbali Kaleni brought them Woolworths finger snacks – meatballs, samosas and curry vetkoek. She sat with Griessel and Cupido in her car while they ate. Vaughn knew about her own long battle with her weight, and so he felt awkward noting the kilojoules in his app in front of her. He tried to make notes in his head so he could do it later.

Across the road, Forensics were busy in Dineo Phiri's house. The rain had eventually stopped, the glow of the DPCI's bright spotlights through the windows making the place look like a spaceship at night.

'I need to tell you about the case we've been building against Phiri,' she said. 'Everything we've learned about the Ilima Projects fraud so far, tells us that he was responsible for managing and moving the money. He was the one with the knowledge of where it all went, who shared in the spoils. The one with the international contacts. We managed to trace some of the cash, and were granted court orders to freeze more than a hundred million in fixed assets. But there is still almost half a billion unaccounted for. Stashed away somewhere offshore, probably in a few tax havens. When I saw the body, my first thought was that he was tortured by someone who wanted to get to the capital: shell companies, bank account details, PIN codes, that sort of thing. And then, as a diversion, make it look like it's tied to your Small case, with the filler foam. But there are a few problems with this theory . . .'

'The laptop,' said Cupido. 'And the cell phone.'

'And probably the wallet, the safe and the general condition of the house as well,' said Mbali. 'Completely undisturbed, they certainly did not conduct a search. But that's just part of it. I think it's extremely unlikely that Phiri kept any incriminating evidence of his crimes in the house. He knew we were coming for him and his cronies, he knew we would eventually get a search warrant.'

'Maybe they were stupid enough to think that Phiri had the account numbers and codes in his head,' said Cupido. 'I mean, if you look at the crime scene . . . Bulls in a china shop.'

'It's possible. More likely, I think, is that they believed Phiri kept the account details somewhere else. A bank deposit box, in the cloud, something like that. And they tortured him to find out where. That would explain why they left the computer and the phone behind. It's something we need to keep in mind. But what I don't understand in such a scenario, is why go to all the trouble and risk of transporting his body to the golf course, and writing a message in the sand. If they wanted to simply create a Basie Small diversion, the filler foam would have been enough.'

'Was there any pressure from the NPA on Phiri to turn state witness?' asked Griessel.

'No. We approached some of his former subordinates, who all turned us down. We believe they are all still hoping the case will go away, and their big payday will come. And Phiri was too big a fish to recruit. He, the former Free State Premier, the Chandas, and, of course, former president Zaca, that's who we're after. The so-called Cabal. The network behind state capture. And even if they suspected he might turn against them, why torture him? And they would have ransacked the house for anything that might be incriminating evidence.'

'What's your best guess, Colonel?' asked Cupido.

'Well, with this case, our problem is that the Ilima Projects fraud represents just a fraction of the state capture pillage. As the commissions of inquiry indicated, they stripped every state asset they could get their hands on. Phiri wasn't involved in everything, but we know he was part of the inner circle of the Cabal. We are pretty sure he was the one who knew where the billions were hidden, the one who moved and laundered it. So, he must have been in contact with the Chandas and the former president. My best guess is that this is related to something in that broad arena. But that's all I have.'

'What about cocaine?' asked Cupido. 'I don't remember any of the commissions of inquiry evidence ever mentioning cocaine, but . . .'

'It never came up,' said Mbali. 'We think it is classic disinformation.'

They ate in silence, until Griessel asked: 'Is there any indication that they had ties with the Congo? The DRC?'

'No . . .'

A car pulled up next to them. A man got out and hurried over to them. Only when he was right next to Griessel's window did they realise who it was.

Julian Jenkins, veteran Media24 journalist.

'Shit,' said Cupido.

Jenkins raised his hand in greeting.

Kaleni rolled down her window.

'Then the rumours are true,' said Jenkins. 'The Basie Small detectives are here.'

Mbali's cell phone started ringing. 'We have no comment,' she said to Jenkins and closed the window again.

Jenkins just smiled at her. A photographer with a camera followed him.

'Yes?' Mbali answered her phone. She listened, then she said: 'Thank you, Jimmy.'

To Cupido and Griessel: 'They've found three long, blond strands of hair in the dining room.'

The photographer's flash blinded them.

★ ★ ★

When Captain John Cloete, the media liaison officer, called eleven minutes later, as they knew he would, Griessel was ready with the answer.

'John, no detective from Stellenbosch Crime Investigation Unit is involved in the Phiri investigation,' he said. Because it was true. They no longer worked – temporarily – for Witkop Jansen.

'And you are no longer on the Small docket?'

'Of course not. The Anti-Gang Unit took it over.'

'Benny, you know, if you're lying to me now . . .'

'I know.'

'Lord, Benny, Phiri and filler foam. It's blood in the water, we're talking feeding frenzy like you've never seen before. It's going to get ugly.'

'John, I give you my word of honour.' Which was probably of limited value, Griessel thought.

'But you're in Hawston?'

'Yes. We were asked to give an opinion.'

'And? What is your opinion?'

'Come on, John.'

'You know they're going to ask me that.'

'And I know you know the answer.'

★ ★ ★

They didn't drive back to Stellenbosch until after midnight.

Griessel stared at the photo on his phone, the one that Arnold from Forensics had sent him of the words in the sand:

FOR BS AND DR
FUCK YOU

'Do you see anything, Benna?' asked Cupido.

Griessel shook his head. 'Not what I was hoping for.'

'And that is?'

'I wondered if the DR might stand for Democratic Republic.'

'Like in DRC? The Congo?'

'Yes. As in, *For Basie Small and the DRC*. He was there twice. Maybe they still wanted to write the C, but then something happened. But this photo doesn't show any marks after the R. And besides, they had enough time to rake the bunker. Then they probably had enough time to write everything they wanted.'

'That was smart thinking, partner.'

'Not smart enough.'

55

Sunday, 30 May. Thirteen days before the wedding.

The National Prosecuting Authority's Cape Town offices were at 115 Buitengracht just a few hundred metres from the High Court in Keerom Street. The four-storey building, recently extensively renovated, gleaming white and modern, occupied an entire block, between Leeuwen, Bree and Pepper Street.

It took just six minutes to drive from Alexa Barnard's house at this time on a Sunday morning. So Griessel was early. He reported to reception at 08:55 with the full copy of the Small dossier in his murder case.

Colonel Mbali Kaleni was waiting for him. He said good morning, and asked her if she'd seen the newspaper posters. They were on all the lampposts in Buitengracht:

PHIRI
ALSO
KILLED
WITH FOAM

She'd seen them, she said, handing him his electronic access card and leading the way to the lifts.

He couldn't help thinking how starkly this place contrasted with the shabby dilapidation of the Hawks headquarters in Bellville.

* * *

In the open-plan living room of Desiree Coetzee's Welgevonden townhouse Vaughn Cupido sat with his phone in hand. He was trying to get hold of anyone at Green Fingers Garden Services – clearly an impossible task on a Sunday morning – so that he could look at their records in Stellenbosch before going to the NPA's office in Cape Town.

'So, Uncle was fired from the detectives,' said twelve-year-old Donovan, stretched out on the sofa, with one eye on a rerun of the previous day's game between the Stormers and the Blue Bulls. Donovan was a fanatical Stormers fan, especially of fullback Damian Willemse.

Every time Willemse performed a side-step, Donovan would say: 'That's magic. That's a Stellenbosch *boytjie.*'

'No, Donnie, I've been seconded,' Cupido said as he called another number on the website.

'What does that mean?'

'"Seconded" means a temporary transfer. Like . . . say now the Stormers are out of the URC semi-finals, and the Blue Bulls flyhalf is injured, and they say, can we borrow Damian, just temporary, then they second him . . .'

'No, Uncle, the Stormers will never lose. We rock. We go all the way. And anyway, Damian would never pull a Blue Bulls jersey over his head. That is, like, treason. He's a Stellenbosch *boytjie.*'

'It's just an example, Donnie. But you must listen to me carefully: you can't go telling anyone I've been seconded. It's very hush-hush.'

'Like a secret agent?'

'Exactly.'

'Extra!' Donovan said, shifted his full focus to the game, though he already knew the outcome.

Before Cupido could ask exactly what this meant, a woman answered his call.

⋆   ⋆   ⋆

After twenty minutes of driving around, Tau Berger finally found a patrol vehicle from Bravo Zulu Security in the Elsies River industrial area, close to the train station.

He stopped next to the Nissan NP200, opened his helmet and waited for the driver to lower his window. The man took a good look at him first before he did so.

'Yes?' said the security man.

'My name is Tau Berger. I have a message for Vern Abrahams.'

'What message?'

'I urgently need to talk to him about Billy Brenner.'

'Who's Billy Brenner?'

'Vern will know.'

'It's Sunday. Mr Abrahams is not in the office.'

'I know it's fucking Sunday. But your control room will have his number.'

The man shook his head. 'No. It's not protocol.'

'Is it protocol that your wife and children have food to eat? Because if Vern finds out you didn't let him know about his old Recce pal Billy Brenner, you'll be looking for a job tomorrow.'

* * *

On the phone, the woman from Green Fingers Garden Services told Cupido they sometimes used substitute workers when their own labourers had compassionate or sick leave. And she did remember they used the same two substitutes twice in April and May. Late April, early May, if she remembered correctly.

He asked her how she found the temporary staff.

She said they just turned up, on both days. They were sent by the two employees who couldn't be there. It happened. People were desperate to earn a few rand. 'And there's nothing wrong with that,' she said. 'This is how we help the community.'

'Who were the two people who couldn't be there?'

'I'll have to go and see.'

'How soon will you be able to check?'

'Tomorrow morning.'

'Ma'am, I'm working on a murder investigation. I can't wait until tomorrow.'

'Sir, I'm in Witsand. My husband is out on the boat, they only come back late in the afternoon. I can't be at the office until tonight.'

'Do you have CCTV at your office?'

'Of course. We are in Plankenbrug.'

'How long do you keep the footage?'

'A week? I'll have to ask Hennie, but I think it's a week.'

'Who is Hennie?'

'My husband. The famous weekend deep-sea angler who never catches anything.'

Cupido asked her to call him as soon as possible with details of how long they kept the video footage, and who the two absent workers were. He thanked her and hung up.

On the TV screen, Manie Libbok scored a try. Donnie pumped his fist. 'Yes!' Even though he'd already watched the game.

Sundays, Cupido thought. It's only policemen and secret agents who work on Sundays.

★　★　★

Kaleni showed Griessel the Investigative Directorate's Information Management Centre on the third floor. As he looked at the big high-resolution screens on the wall and the obviously brand-new computer equipment, a woman emerged from her office to meet them.

'Benny, I'd like to introduce you to Doctor Malime Duba,' said Mbali, 'the director of our IMC in the Western Cape.'

Duba was very small in stature, making her seem much too young for this position. Her eyes were wide behind heavy, black-rimmed glasses. 'Your reputation precedes you, Warrant,' she said and held out a delicate hand.

'Pleased to meet you,' said Griessel, wondering what part of his reputation preceded him here.

'This is state of the art,' said Kaleni. 'We can do anything Philip van Wyk and his team do at the Hawks, and a bit more, thanks to a high-speed fibre connection with the IMC at head office in Pretoria.'

'Which gives us very quick access to all the major databases in the country,' said Duba.

'I assume you've gone through the 405 process for Small's cellular data?' said Kaleni.

'Yes. Lithpel Davids ran it for us.'

'Good. Let's get the records to Doctor Duba. As soon as we have Phiri's too, she can start mapping.'

'Do you want me to apply for a subpoena, Colonel?' asked Griessel.

'No, thank you. Sergeant Carolus started the process in Hermanus this morning, after our director, Advocate Johnson, called in a favour from a magistrate there.'

★　★　★

Tau Berger was sitting in Ashley's Family Restaurant in Goodwood with a steaming black filter coffee when Vern Abrahams called.

'Tau. Long time no see . . .' Tau heard the caution in his voice. It meant Vern was treading lightly. And if he was treading lightly, he knew something.

'Vern, thank you for calling. And sorry that I was angry with your man. It's just . . . there's a bit of a deadline on this thing.'

'What thing?'

'I don't want to talk on the phone, Vern.'

'You know I'm in the Cape?'

'Me too.'

Silence.

Then: 'It's Sunday, Tau. We're *braaing*.'

'Three o'clock, at the Waterfront?'

'Billy is dead, Tau. Do you know that?'

'Vern, I think you'll want to hear what I have.'

More silence. Tau heard children squealing in the background.

'Okay. The V&A Amphitheatre. Half past three.' And he hung up.

Vern Abrahams knows, thought Tau. Vern Abrahams knows.

He reached for the menu. He might as well have a pizza.

*   *   *

Griessel's new office was at the rear of the building, a large room overlooking the Thule store in Bree Street. Ten workstations, partitions, pot plants. Kaleni said he should make himself at home by the window. Cupido's station was right next to him. She'd ask the office manager to bring him the computer and wifi passwords – and anything else he might need. There was a coffee and tea station next door.

She said she would be in her office and left him there.

He had never worked in a space like this in his entire career. Modern and pristine, not a single mark or blemish from the chaotic working lives of a multitude of detectives over the decades. Wait until Cupido saw this.

He sat down, took the copied Small file from his briefcase and began to lay it out on the desk.

He would have to start all over again. While he waited to hear from Vaughn.

Before the office manager arrived, Alexa rang.

'My master detective,' she said, 'is on the cover of *Rapport.*'

He'd known Julian Jenkins would report that they were there.

'It's better than the back cover,' he said.

'At least they could have used a more flattering photo,' she said.

'A photo?'

'I'll send you a WhatsApp.'

When the photo came through, it was the one of him and Vaughn in Mbali's car. Kaleni on the phone, him and Vaughn looking at the camera in surprise and confusion.

The caption read: *Stellenbosch detectives W.O.s Benny Griessel and Vaughn Cupido outside Dineo Phiri's house last night. Both are suspended former members of the Hawks' Serious and Violent Crimes Unit, who this week were also relieved of their duties investigating the filler foam murder of former Recce Basie Small in the Eikestad.*

And still she called him her 'master detective'. It was times like these when he knew that Alexa loved him completely blindly.

And that's what made him so terrified of the wedding. What would happen if she truly saw him for what he was?

56

Tau saw Vern Abrahams approaching, almost a quarter of an hour late.

Vern looked good. Fit. He always had been, but now he was more so, as in every-day-in-the-gym fit, as in I-have-the-money-and-I-have-the-time. And the personal trainer. And the expensive watch. And the tattoos, but underneath the tight jersey and the jeans and the expensive Nikes you could only see the tips of inky flames peeking out from the neck.

Vern had an attitude too. Like he wasn't in the mood for this. Not in the mood for Tau. Truth be told, Vern had never been his bosom buddy, even in the old days. 'You're a loose cannon, Tau.' Back then. In the bush.

But fuck him, he's here, thought Tau. That said it all. He rose from the Waterfront Amphitheatre bench and shook Vern's hand.

No 'how are you', just: 'Tau.'

'Thank you for coming, Vern.' He didn't want a confrontation. They were on the same side, even if Vern didn't know it yet.

Abrahams shrugged his toned gym shoulders in a gesture that said he didn't actually have a choice.

'Can I buy you coffee?' asked Tau.

Abrahams shook his head. 'You said I'd like to hear what you have.'

It wasn't an attitude, Tau realised. It was tension. Vern had a lot to lose. His Bravo Zulu Security gold mine, his prestige. Tension was a good sign

Tau shot from the hip, letting his rage show: 'Basie Small and Dewey Reed died because the philistines thought they were in on Brenner's robbery. Of the dollars.'

Vern's attitude dissolved. He looked at Tau, looked towards the wharf to the side. Then he sat down.

Tau sat down next to him.

'Dewey is dead?' asked Vern.

'Tuesday. A day after Basie.'

'Fuck. But . . . There was nothing about Dewey in the media . . .'

'The philistines kept it quiet. You know how things are in the Eastern Cape.'

'The philistines?'

'They tried to get me too. They didn't. Now they're looking for me.'

'Who are they, Tau? Who are the philistines?'

'You know who.'

Abrahams didn't answer.

Tau said, 'Basie and Dewey, were either of them in, Vern? On Brenner's robbery.'

'No.'

'But you were.'

'No.'

'Vern . . .'

'I wasn't in, Tau. He did ask me. But I said no. I don't need it.'

'The money?'

'And the risk. I told him, don't do it. But he . . .' Abrahams's gaze was distant.

'He what?'

'Why did they think you and Basie and Dewey were in?'

Vern was many things, but he wasn't a fool. 'Long story. And I don't trust you.'

Abrahams looked at him. Questioning and gauging.

'The thing is, Vern, you're lying to me.'

Vern said nothing.

'You were in with Brenner. Or you wouldn't be here. You wouldn't be so jumpy.'

Vern stared at the boats at the wharf. For a long time. Then he asked: 'Are they looking for me too?'

'No.'

'The "they". The "philistines". Are you talking about Babbar?'

'Amongst others.'

'And the Chandas.'

'No.'

'Not the Chandas?' With genuine surprise.

'The Chandas are out of the picture. It's higher up. Bigger. More dangerous.'

Abrahams thought for a long time. Then he said: 'I wasn't in. I just did Brenner a favour.'

'What favour?'

'I had to watch the pilot's wife and children. For one night.'

'Which pilot?'

'The one who was going to fly the dollars to the Cape.'

'And? Did you?'

'Yes.'

'And then the plane caught fire and they all died, except the girl.'

'No.'

'Did the girl burn too?'

'No. She and three others got away.'

That's not what Dineo Phiri thought. 'Three more?'

'Roger.'

'Fuck.'

'Okay, Tau, now you tell me. Why did they think you and Basie and Dewey were in on it?'

Tau didn't listen. He was thinking.

'Tau . . .'

'Can you make contact?'

'With who?'

'With those who got away.'

'I can. Why did they think you and Basie and Dewey were in on it?'

'Because we brought in the dollars and the gold.'

'The gold?'

'Almost ten billion rands' worth, Vern. In total. Dollars and gold.'

'Brought in?'

'I tell you what: you tell me the whole story about Brenner, and then I'll tell you about me and Basie and Dewey and Corrie Albertyn and Fani Dlamini. And the ten billion.'

★ ★ ★

Cupido was delighted with their new work environment. 'Befitting investigators of our stature, Benna,' was his comment. Wearing his NPA access card around his neck like a talisman.

Now they sat, heads together, documents and notebooks and a computer screen before them, and went through all that had come in during the day.

The pathologist's postmortem said Dineo Phiri was still alive, until the filling foam suffocated him. She estimated the time of death was between 23:00 and 02:00 Friday night/Saturday morning.

The trauma to the left side of the skull's parietal bone was most likely caused by a wooden object. She collected splinter residue from the object and forwarded it to the forensic laboratory in Plattekloof. This trauma was inflicted with considerable violence, presumably by a right-handed assailant. The concussion that it caused would have resulted in Phiri losing consciousness.

His fingers and toes showed clear signs of traumatic compression, with lesions indicating the use of pliers. The bones in his hands and wrists, specifically the proximal phalanges, trapezium, trapezoid and hamate, were fractured by blunt object trauma. As were the metatarsal bones in his feet.

He also had lesions from a blunt object on his thorax, which had broken or cracked the fifth, sixth and seventh ribs on left side – another indication of a right-handed assailant.

There was no sign of any defensive wounds.

The pathologist also forwarded her report on the postmortem examination of the two bodyguards. *Cause of death on both cases were SFT*, she wrote. This referred to 'Sharp Force Trauma', the term for stab wounds. She described the blade as possibly a knife, dagger, stiletto or bayonet. The blade was about three centimetres wide and at least sixteen centimetres long, but she said it was only approximate, especially due to the power of the blows. *The skin stretches on impact, which could lead to underestimation. Furthermore, both victims were stabbed in the chest, where the surface can be compressed, which could lead to the length being overstated.*

There were also lesions on the skin that indicated a stabbing weapon with a quillon – the cross plate between handle and blade, *which indicates a dagger or bayonet, rather than a kitchen utility knife. However, preliminary analysis of bone markings indicates the possibility of heavy serration on both sides of the blade. As this is rare, further microscopic study is needed.*

Thick and Thin's forensic report offered much food for thought: no fingerprints in the house, except those of the victims. The assailants in all likelihood wore gloves.

According to the BMW X5's GPS data, someone drove the car to and from the boat club on Friday night. The departure time at Phiri's house was 00:32. At 00:37 it was switched off at the boat club. Forty-nine minutes later it was turned on, driven back to Phiri's house, where it was switched off again at 01:31.

They also found a long blond hair in the car, on the driver's side, on the carpet just to the right of the seat. It was similar to the three blond hairs in the dining room.

'Which tells us they didn't wear balaclavas,' said Cupido.

'Or they took them off in the house,' said Griessel.

'And at least one of the attackers was white. But a female, Benna, I just don't see that.'

'Me neither. But anything is possible.'

'So, now we're waiting for Phiri's phone records. And the laptop.' Sergeant Rivaldo Carolus had notified them that everything was on its way. Also that there was no useful video footage from the traffic cameras around Hawston.

* * *

Tau was in his hotel room, half past seven in the evening, when his phone rang.

'Yes,' he replied.

'Tau?'

'Yes.'

'I was with Brenner.' A man's voice.

'Who are you?' asked Tau.

'First tell me, how did they know Brenner was involved?'

'You were stupid when you deleted the videos. And unlucky.'

'How stupid?'

'You should have taken the hard disk with you. They could still recover some of the video. And there was good footage of the girl. A traffic cam down the road got Brenner.'

'That's all?'

'It was enough for all hell to break loose.'

'Brenner and the girl were the only ones they could identify?'

'Yip.'

'Could they put a name to the girl?'

'No.'

'How did they ID Brenner?'

'They thought we were involved. Me and Basie, Dewey, Corrie and Fani.'

'Because you brought the dollars in.'

'Yes. And the gold. Then they looked for pictures of us. And they found it was none of us. Then they looked at the *ous* who were with us in the unit. They found Brenner's face in the records. And they ID-ed him.'

'Okay.'

'Who are you?'

'Igen.'

'Okay, Igen. I'm going to steal that gold. I'm looking for partners. What do you say?'

57

In the small office of Green Fingers Garden Services, eight o'clock on a crystal-clear Monday morning, Vaughn Cupido questioned the two workers.

He recognised the suspicion, their surly hostility. Manual labourer versus policeman. He was familiar with it, understood it. He said: 'Guys, you're not in trouble. I just need information.'

It didn't alter the tense atmosphere.

'So, you stayed home two weeks in a row, on a Thursday. Twenty-ninth of April, and sixth of May.'

'Yes.'

'And you sent two strangers to work in your place.'

'Yes.'

'That's okay. No problem. You're not in trouble.'

No response.

'How did they contact you?' asked Cupido.

'We were walking home after work.'

'From here?'

'Yes.'

'To Khayamandi?'

'Yes.'

'And?'

'They just started walking with us.'

'You've never seen them before?'

'No.'

'And they offered you money?'

'Yes.'

'How much.'

'Two five.'

'Two thousand five hundred?'

'Yes.'

'Each.'

'Yes.'

'For both Thursdays?'

'No. Two five for each Thursday.'

'Five in total?'

'Yes.'

'In advance?'

'No. Ten pinkies up front.'

'Five hundred?'

'Yes.'

'Five *isitina*, guys, that's a lot of money.'

'Yes.'

'And all you had to do, was to call in sick, and say you are sending someone in your place.'

'Yes. Don't blame the *umlungu*. We said we are sending our cousins.'

'I'm not blaming anybody. I just want information.'

'And we told the guys, no problem. Don't do a *bafana*. Work hard.'

'And you never asked why they wanted this?'

They shrugged their shoulders.

'Can you describe them?'

'Black.'

'How old were they?'

'Maybe thirty.'

'Or forty.'

'Tall, short? Thin? Fat?'

'No.'

'Well, what?'

'Just normal.'

'Beards, moustaches, funny hair?'

'No.'

'Tattoos? Scars?'

They thought about it first, then they shrugged.

'Clothing?'

'They had beanies.'

'And blue jackets. Like the people who work in construction.'

'What language did they speak?'

'Xhosa.'

'The other one was maybe Tswana. He didn't speak a lot.'

Hennie, the famous weekend deep-sea angler who never caught anything, told Cupido the hard drive for the CCTV video footage filled up every three weeks or so. He would probably have to get a bigger one.

* * *

In the Pretoria suburb of Faerie Glen, Emilia Streicher listened to a member of the Cape Anti-Gang Unit tell her on the phone that he didn't know when her late brother Basie Small's remains would be available for cremation. Because the case was still in the process of being handed over, Basie was still in the state mortuary in Salt River. And he didn't know whether she'd heard, but there was another filler foam murder. It could result in further delays.

She hung up and wept. All the pent-up pain and frustration.

It was a week, today. A week since she'd got the call. About Basie's death. The worst week of her life. And she still didn't know why he died.

* * *

The software that Malime Duba and her colleagues at the Investigative Directorate's Information Management Centre used, could swallow raw data from any cell phone records and conjure up spiderwebs with it – flow charts of thin lines and bubbles that systematically appeared on the big screens, and grew. It created records of contacts, it told stories of interactions and relationships, and their intensity.

It could also determine the location of the mobile phones in question, often indoors within just a few metres.

Benny Griessel sat at the screens and watched while the system analysed Dineo Phiri and his two bodyguards' cell phone activities over the past three months – and compared them to that of Arthur Thomas Small.

There was still no indication that any of their contacts or calls matched Small's.

He kept hoping. Even if his focus was not one hundred per cent on the spiderwebs.

Last night Alexa Barnard had asked him if he'd written his wedding vows yet. She'd already done hers. 'I think it's so beautiful, Benny. I can't wait for the ceremony.'

The trouble was, he hadn't known they'd agreed to do this. Two weeks ago he came home Saturday night after a RUST performance, a thirty-year school reunion in Brackenfell. Exhausted, ready for shower and bed. Alexa was already in bed, reading *The Wedding Book: An Expert's Guide to Planning Your Perfect Day – Your Way.* One of the four or five wedding books she'd gone out and bought, she was so excited about the momentous day. Then she said, 'Benny, I think we need to write our own wedding vows. It's so romantic. And . . . It will make it all so unique.'

He hadn't said a definitive 'yes'. He had, if he remembered correctly, made an evasive – but positive – noise. Alexa had a thousand ideas, and not all made it to the finish line.

And then he'd forgotten about it. Completely. And he was no good with things like that.

He couldn't disappoint her. Not in front of all her friends, not in front of Lize Beekman.

I think it's so beautiful, Benny.

This while he was planning to sing to her *You're a chocolate cookie, baby, and you bring out the boogie in me.*

He would have to start thinking of something. Something beautiful and romantic. And 'unique'.

And he only had twelve days.

Vaughn would have to help.

★ ★ ★

In the hotel room, Tau was packed and ready to roll, a man on a mission. He felt revitalised. Filled with a sense of relief: Basie and Dewey weren't part of the whole business. Thanks to a good night's sleep too, thanks to the pill that kept the Phiri monster out of his mind. And Igen's words – saying, tentatively, let's talk. In Barrydale. Where he was headed now. Time to get things going.

Time to forge ahead, move the front, initiate the big counterattack. Fucking philistines wouldn't know what hit them.

Eleven days was enough, but they couldn't waste time.

Time to call Emilia. She saved his life. She and Basie. He owed her. Big time.

She answered: 'Hello.'

He could hear she was hurting. He asked: 'Are you okay?'

'Yes.' But she wasn't.

'I can call later.'

'Thank you, Tau, but no. I want to hear.'

'It's going to upset you.'

'I want to hear.'

He started slowly, he knew he could get intense. He wanted to do it gently, soften it. But it didn't last, his own anger at the fuckers overtook him. He told her about everything, about why Basie and Dewey died. The whole story, his own actions too, unashamed, because he knew she wanted to hear how Phiri paid.

Afterwards she didn't cry. She just said: 'Thank you.'

'I'm not done yet, Emilia. But if I tell you what I'm gonna do, I'll make you even more complicit.'

'I want to be an accomplice, Tau.'

'Think carefully first.'

'There's nothing to think about.'

He wavered. 'The way to make these fuckers pay, the way to hurt them the most is to hijack the things they have stolen.'

'Lord, Tau, you are just one person.'

'No. I can't do it alone. The guys who were with Brenner, I'm going to see them now.'

'Can you trust them?'

'They know about my shit, I know about theirs. Knife to each other's throat.'

She remained silent for a long time. Then she asked: 'How can I help?'

58

The spiderwebs of Doctor Malime Duba's system showed no over-laps between the contacts, calls and text messages of Dineo Phiri, his bodyguards and Basie Small's cell phone records.

'I'm sorry,' said Duba, as if it were her fault.

'Par for the course,' said Vaughn Cupido. 'If you'll pardon the pun.'

Duba just frowned behind her glasses.

'Phiri. The golf course . . .' said Cupido.

'Oh. Right. Dark humour,' she said. 'I will try to get used to it. There is something I would like to point out to you,' she said, and walked towards the big screen where the spiderweb was displayed. 'We are looking at Dineo Phiri's call register. Only his.'

They nodded.

'You see these bubbles are red?'

'Yes.'

'The red indicates that those numbers were not registered according to the RICA Act.'

'Burner phones,' said Cupido.

'Yes,' she said. 'You will see the same thing in the spreadsheets of raw data. Red cells are non-registered numbers, green cells are RICA'd.'

'There's a lot of red,' said Cupido.

'Eleven different numbers,' she said. 'And just about all the calls made by them were short. Less than thirty seconds. There are a few exceptions . . .'

Griessel flipped through his notebook. 'Can we isolate the dates of those burner calls, Doctor? And the time they were made?'

'Yes, give me a minute.' She tapped a keyboard at one of the desktop computers.

Griessel made notes, then he said to Cupido: 'I have to talk to you. About my wedding vows.'

'Benna, I thought we were past that. You've already promised, you can't chicken out now.'

'No, I'm talking about what I have to say to Alexa in front of the *dominee*.'

'Ah. Those wedding vows.'

'Yes.'

Cupido gave a sigh of relief. 'Okay. What's the problem?'

'I have no idea what to say.'

'Got your back, partner. You know me. A master in the language of love. A poet, and I know it.'

'I have the data,' she said and pointed at the computer monitor in front of her.

They got up and went over to look.

Duba traced a fingernail across a row on the spreadsheet. 'These columns represent the calls Phiri received. And these are the calls he made. And, as you can see, with all the burner phone calls, they were incoming calls. He never called them once.'

They stared at the screen. Numbers, dates, times, in long columns. They were trying to make sense, find meaning.

'This is only the last three months?' asked Cupido.

'Yes. Everything since March. You want to go back further?'

'Well . . . I . . . Hang on. . . There are no burner calls in March. Looks like the fun only starts in April.'

'Saturday, April third,' said Griessel.

'Easter weekend,' said Cupido. 'Second-longest call of all. Seven minutes. Just past nine at night. And another, just before midnight.'

Griessel came to sit next to Vaughn.

'And then they chucked that burner. Sunday, April fourth, nine short calls, new number. Monday, April fifth, five short calls, new number. These dudes are cagey, Benna. *Kwaai* cagey.'

'They knew the NPA was watching Phiri. Must have. But look here . . .' Griessel tapped his finger on a new date. 'Look at the times.'

It took a moment for Cupido to make the connection. 'Hit me with a snot *snoek*,' he said.

'I beg your pardon?' said Duba.

★ ★ ★

Two hundred kilometres east of Cape Town, as the crow flies. Barrydale. Four thousand souls, several hundred houses scattered along the foothills, against the dramatic backdrop of the Langeberg in the Little Karoo.

Igen Rousseau stood in the overgrown garden of a large plot on the bank of the Huis River in Tinley Street. He was stripped to the waist, just wearing jeans and *takkies*. And the bandana over his head partly covered the long scar. He was sweating, spade in hand, the hole already thirty centimetres deep.

He heard the growl of Themba Jola's Audi A3 before he saw it approaching around the thicket of trees at his entrance, slowly and carefully, avoiding the potholes.

Jola stopped next to Igen, muscular arm draped over the door, the T-shirt as usual a size too small. Big smile.

'You'll have to work on your driveway,' he said.

'The driveway will have to wait at the back of the queue.'

Themba got out. 'I don't hug guys without a shirt,' he said and held his fist out for a bump.

'But you're wearing a shirt.'

Almost two months since they had last seen each other, both of them grinning at the joke to disguise their joy at the reunion.

'Good to see you,' said Igen.

'You too.' Themba looked at Igen's cheek and temple. 'It's healing nicely.'

'My dream of looking like Brad Pitt is shattered. Your hip?' He'd noticed Jola still had a slight limp.

'Only hurts when it rains. What are you planting?'

'Pomegranates. And figs.'

'With your house still looking like that.' He pointed at the dilapidated house at the back, in the corner.

'The roof's not leaking any more.'

Jola shook his head. 'Now I understand why it was so cheap,' he said.

Igen stuck the spade into the ground, and headed on towards the house.

'Come. There's beer in the fridge.'

* * *

It was the five calls to Dineo Phiri from a single unregistered phone on the day of Basie Small's death that caught Griessel's attention. In particular the two of them that corresponded to the times of the Small attackers' arrival and departure. More or less one minute before they jumped out of the van, and one minute after they left again.

He quickly flipped through his notebook to make sure, drew tables to compare them all with each other. Then he turned the book so that Cupido could see.

Vaughn studied the notes. 'Hot damn,' he said. 'Doc, can you do us a printout of these calls? Arranged in order of the date and time they were made?'

'Yes.'

Griessel continued to scribble at his own tables.

* * *

Igen Rousseau's kitchen was spartan and simple, clean and tidy. They sat at the four-seater wooden table, with a beer each.

'So,' said Igen. 'Tau Berger . . .'

'Only three of my contacts know him,' said Themba. 'And the opinions . . . Let's call it a mixed bag. Way back, his first few years at the Recces, they say he was cool. Eccentric, but cool.'

'How eccentric?'

'Well . . . Let's start with short and cocky. You know the sort, always trying to prove they're up for it. In your face. Aggro. *Windgat*. But they say he was the real deal. Incredible stamina, fearless, great under pressure. And a talker. When the shit hits the fan, the motor mouth starts racing. There's the story of his parachute training, when he chirped all the way up and all the way down. Also, a golf fanatic, he always carried a seven iron and a bunch of golf balls in a bag on his belt. And, no matter where they were, he made himself a range and practised his swing and he told everyone just how far and how accurately he could hit. Played off scratch, never cheated, that's the legend. And then, in 2013, something happened in the Central African Republic. Battle of Bangui, where the thirteen Parabats died . . .'

'I remember.'

'They say Tau saw stuff. Heavy shit. Then it was PTSD. Bad. Six months at 1 Mil for treatment, then he went to civvy street, and he became the greenkeeper at a golf club in Bloem. He later moved to Clarens. Attended a few Recce reunions, and one guy said Tau will never be the same again. The other two say he's fine, he always has been a bit *bossies*. But when shit goes down, he'll have your six.'

'And what do you think?'

'He told you he took Phiri to the golf course, just to send a message? Just to tell Babbar, "It was me; come find me."'

'Yip.'

'After he killed him.'

'Yip.'

'That takes cojones. Big cojones. Which I like. But I looked at the media coverage. He killed three people that night. Violently. Cold blood.'

'Not quite "cold blood". Revenge. For Small.'

'Still . . .'

'So, what do you think?'

'I think let's listen to him. Then we'll talk again.'

59

Cupido had the prints, Griessel had his notebook, and they let the data tell the story.

Almost all the calls from unregistered phones to Phiri could be divided into specific, separate time periods of a day or two, three – what Griessel called 'volleys'.

The first volley was Easter weekend, from the Saturday night to Wednesday. Three different phones.

The second volley, smaller, was more than three weeks later, 28 to 30 April. One phone.

The third volley, again smaller, was a week later, 6 and 7 May. One phone.

The fourth volley was suddenly more intense again and corresponded to a certain degree to Basie Small's death. Two phones.

The fifth volley, the day after. The times of the calls were very similar to the Small attack. Two phones.

The sixth volley was two days after the Small murder. It stood out, because it began much earlier in the day than any of the others – a quarter past four in the morning. It was also the volley with the most calls. The last, on that Wednesday, 26 May, was also the longest. At 08:20 Dineo Phiri talked to someone for almost eleven minutes. Two different phones were used in the last volley.

Three days later, Phiri was dead.

Cupido turned to Duba: 'Doc, do we know where those burner phones called from?'

'Not yet. Let me see what we can do.'

Griessel saw another possible pattern in the data. He checked his notes carefully, until he was sure.

'Look here,' he said to Vaughn. 'At the end of each volley of calls received . . . Phiri called the same two numbers within minutes every time.'

'Green cells, *pappie*,' said Cupido. 'That means they are listed numbers.'

'Gentlemen,' said Duba from in front of the computer, 'it looks like every one of those burner calls were made from Johannesburg. The best I can do is a range of about two to three kilometres. Which is typical when the caller is mobile, as in a vehicle. But I can tell you it's somewhere in the Fourways area. Fourways and Dainfern. And Kempton Park.'

'Jozi,' said Cupido. 'Who is in Jozi? In terms of the Phiri investigation?'

'You'll have to talk to the director. And Mbali. I don't know.'

'Doctor, if you don't mind,' said Griessel, 'could you determine who these two phone numbers belong to,' and he gave her a printout on which he'd circled the two numbers that Phiri called after each volley.

'Of course.'

* * *

'And Chrissie?' asked Themba Jola.

'It's not a visit any more. I'm going to fetch her. If she's there, Wednesday. In the restaurant. And if she wants to come, of course,' said Rousseau and drank the last of his beer. 'Flight leaves tomorrow night.'

Jola raised his eyebrows. 'That's cutting it fine.'

'I changed the return flight. For Thursday. With or without her. I'll be back on Friday.'

'You can Telegram her.'

'No. Risk is too great. I will only turn the phone back on in Rome. If she doesn't show up. Besides, it's an expensive ticket to cancel. And there's too much to say in a text message. She's Chrissie. She will have a thousand questions.'

'Do we have enough time, Ig? To plan this thing?'

'Let me talk to Jericho first. If he's in, the rest is pretty easy.'

'We thought that last time too.'

* * *

Malime Duba stood up in front of the workstation and said: 'I have to speak to the director first.'

She could see the detectives weren't sure what she meant.

'About the two numbers Phiri called.'

'Okay,' said Cupido.

'Because this is . . . complicated.' And she left the room swiftly.

'And that, Benna, is what they call in the movies a "cliffhanger" . . .'

* * *

On the veranda of Barrydale's Country Pumpkin, half past four in the afternoon, they waited for Tau Berger to arrive.

'You know, she's not the kind of girl who's going to settle down,' said Themba.

Igen just nodded.

'And emotions on an Op . . .'

Igen said nothing.

'Is it lust? Or is it love?'

'She saved our lives.'

'The way I hear it, you saved Brenner's ass in Zim, that time, with the rhino horn smugglers. And he didn't want to fuck or marry you in gratitude.'

Igen grinned. Shook his head.

'The great Igen Rousseau. In love. Sad, really . . .'

They watched a motorcycle stop on the gravel shoulder of the R62, on the other side of the restaurant wall.

Just one more of the many R62 riders who dropped in here.

The man kicked out the stand, dismounted. He was short and wiry. Bantam cock. Gloves off, helmet off. Shook his head and the long, yellow-blond hair tumbled down. Bushy beard. He pulled the key out of the bike, his eyes were searching, he looked at them. He shoved the key in his riding trousers pocket, made a pistol with his right hand and aimed it at Igen.

He fired off an imaginary shot.

That's when they knew Tau had arrived.

* * *

Advocate Annika Johnson, director of the National Prosecuting Authority's Investigative Directorate in the Western Cape, was a good-looking woman. Somewhere near sixty, the natural grey hair, twisted in a bun. Well groomed and elegant, a head taller than the two women at her sides, Kaleni and Duba. Johnson's voice was soft and authoritative, she repeated how grateful they were that Cupido and Griessel had accepted the secondment, and were working with such dedication.

And she reminded them that the ID's work was absolutely confidential. 'We don't share information with anybody. Not even our spouses. I do hope we are clear on this.'

They said yes, they understood it all.

'Good. Because I am going to share sensitive information with you now. The two cellular numbers you had Malime trace. They belong respectively to Ketso Sebego and Fikile Nkosi. Both these gentlemen have been persons of interest in our state capture investigations. They are known associates of the late Mr Phiri. So, I am not surprised that he called them. However, what you should also know is that Sebego is in the employ of the disgraced former Premier of the Free State Province, and acts as a sort of private secretary. He lives in Bloemfontein, in close proximity to the ex-Premier. Fikile Nkosi, however, lives in the compound at Ukuphumula.'

'Wow,' said Cupido. Because Ukuphumula in the rolling hills of KwaZulu-Natal was the most notorious homestead in the country – the retirement farm of former president Joseph 'Joe' Zaca. 'Ukuphumula' meant 'to rest' in Zulu.

'Indeed,' said Johnson. 'Nkosi is a former member of the State Security Agency. We are not exactly sure what his responsibilities were, but we believe he had a senior position within the Domestic Branch, and was mostly responsible for keeping our former president informed about threats from within his own party. We also believe he is fulfilling a very similar role for the same man today. As you know, Joe Zaca is facing corruption charges, some of them dating back to his time as deputy president. So, both Nkosi and Sebego are part of what we see as the Cabal, the inner circle of the state capturers.'

'Are there any of the Cabal members living in Jozi?' asked Cupido. 'Fourways? Dainfern? Kempton Park?'

'At least five live somewhere in the greater Sandton area,' said Johnson. 'Two ex-ministers, and three former chief executive officers of state enterprises. Why?'

Duba answered the question: 'The burner calls to Phiri came from that area. The callers were mobile, so we can't pinpoint any of them.'

'Not specific enough to jump to conclusions,' said Johnson.

'What exactly have you found, Benny?' asked Mbali Kaleni. 'Concerning Nkosi and Sebego.'

'Colonel, to be honest, I don't know. Some of the calls from burner phones to Phiri coincide almost perfectly with the Small attack . . .'

'Benna doesn't believe in coincidence,' said Cupido.

'And the burner calls came in very time-specific volleys. After every volley, Phiri called them, specifically. Sebego and Nkosi. Only them. Every single time.'

'As if he was reporting to his bosses?' Kaleni asked.

'Something like that.'

Johnson asked him to point out the calls that so neatly matched up with the Small attack. Griessel showed her his tables in the notebook.

'Can we tie any of the other bursts to something significant?'

'No.'

'Just those two calls that coincide?'

'Yes.'

'It's way too little to build any kind of theory on, Warrant.'

'Perhaps, Advocate,' said Cupido. 'But if you also look at the filler foam and the message in the bunker . . .'

'We're going to need a lot more than that.'

It was the story of his life.

60

In the late-afternoon sun of the Little Karoo, on the Country Pumpkin restaurant's veranda, Igen asked: 'How sure are you Phiri didn't lie to you?'

Tau brushed the hair from his face, drank more coffee. 'He lied, in the beginning. Then . . . he stopped. Because he thought the truth would save him . . .'

They saw Tau's unease. As if he didn't want to linger with those memories. He moved on: 'Besides, what do we have to lose? Worst case, we wait, and the trucks don't come. That's all.'

'A few hundred thousand bucks to finance the Op. That's what we have to lose,' said Themba. 'For us that's a lot.'

'I'm telling you: he didn't lie. I fucking know. You don't sit there bleeding and weeping and still invent such detail.'

Igen and Themba looked at each other.

'And,' said Tau, 'I put in what you put in. I have money.'

Themba nodded silently at Igen.

'Okay,' said Igen. 'Exactly what did he say?'

'That Friday from one o'clock in the afternoon, they are loading the gold and the dollars at the warehouse into three trucks . . .'

'We're talking about Friday, June eleventh.'

'Roger. They will load the cargo into three twenty-foot containers. One container on each lorry . . .'

'Why only then? On that date?'

'The ship. It can't be here in the Cape before that Friday night. They don't want the trucks to stand and wait. Too risky, too many eyes at the harbour. The trucks must arrive Saturday afternoon, they want to load the ship, along with the Gripen. Saturday night it sails.'

'The Gripen?' asked Themba.

'Yes, bro, as in the fighter jet.'

'The Gripens we bought from Sweden? For the air force?' asked Igen.

'Yes. Fucking crazy, I know. That's where the Russians come in. Here's the story: Sweden wants to join NATO. And then the Russians sit with a problem, they have to fight the Gripens if there is shit with Sweden. Now the Russians are desperate to get their dirty little hands on a Gripen. So they can take it apart and work out how they can shoot down a Gripen. Or jam it, or whatever. So Vladimir Putin told his long-time buddies in our government, boys, you have twenty-six Gripens just sitting there, rotting away, how about it? Then our government said, sure, no problem, come and get yourself one. So the ship was actually sent to retrieve the Gripen. But the Gripen can't be in Simon's Town until one o'clock Saturday, they are driving it down from Waterkloof. Separate truck, separate route. That's why they have to get the timing of the other trucks right. The gold and the dollars are secondary cargo.'

'Jeez,' said Themba.

'I'm telling you,' said Tau, 'fucking crazy. Okay, they load the gold and the money in the three container trucks, then they go. Three shotgun vehicles with the muscle, one with each truck. Each about twenty, thirty minutes apart . . .'

'One truck, one vehicle with muscle, half an hour apart. Why?' asked Themba.

'Phiri's instruction. He called it "risk management". Three eggs, three baskets. It's twenty-four hours on the road, it's one thousand seven hundred kilos. Shit happens.'

'Which route?' asked Igen.

'The Gripen will probably go down the N1, the other stuff will go via the N12. Because the Gripen truck has papers from the government, the gold trucks don't. And if you don't have papers, it's easier to bribe traffic cops on the N12 in the North West and the Northern Cape, at the weighbridges, or if they are pulled off. So our guys drive Klerksdorp, Kimberley, Britstown, to Victoria West. Then they turn off the N12, they want to spend as little time as possible in the Western Cape, because in the Western Cape the traffic cops are not so corrupt. And it's a quieter road, through Carnarvon, Williston, Calvinia, as far as the N7, down to the Cape. Simon's Town. That's where the ship will be waiting. The *Lady R.* Russian.'

'Where does the ship go once it's loaded?'

'Ust-Luga. In Russia.'

'So, the Russians take the dollars and the gold?' asked Themba.

'Roger. The Russians transfer money to three bank accounts. Caymans, Bahamas and British Virgins, once the ship's captain has checked the containers. Agreement is for five billion. Dollars, not rand. The philistines are taking a hell of a knock on the true value, but beggars can't be choosers. Nervous beggars even less. And after Phiri's death they are going to be very nervous.'

'What time do the trucks leave from Spartan?'

'They load at one o'clock on Friday afternoon, they want to hit the road at two o'clock. Phiri said, according to Babbar, they will struggle to average seventy kilometres per hour, what with the road works and the stop-and-go's on the N12, the traffic up to Kimberley, and the mountain passes beyond Calvinia.'

'What time are the trucks expected in Simon's Town?'

'Two o'clock in the afternoon. The Gripen will be loaded first. One o'clock in the afternoon.'

'What kind of shotgun vehicles?' asked Igen.

'Phiri didn't know. He just transferred the money to Babbar to pay for trucks and the muscle's vehicles.'

'How much muscle?' asked Themba.

'Don't know. As much as Babbar wants. But we'll have an idea. Before the time.'

'How?'

'Basie's sister. In Pretoria. She knew the whole story. She's keen to help, to make the fucking philistines pay. We can ask her to take a look at the warehouse. Between one and two on Friday afternoon.'

'They're going to see her.'

'She has an air-conditioning business, and she has a panel van with the logo and everything. She'll be okay. Just a drive-by with a cell phone on video. You don't load all those dollars and gold in less than an hour.'

'You trust the woman?'

'They killed her brother. She hates them. She's the one who warned me.'

'Okay . . .'

'And she has to share. In the profit.'

'How much?'

'Full share. It's for Basie. And Dewey.'

Igen nodded. 'Do you have anyone who will buy the gold?' he asked.

'No. But you did,' said Tau.

'We had a guy for the dollars. One of Chrissie's contacts. But he'll never work with us again.'

'What the hell, bro? That's what brings you to the party.'

Themba laughs. 'That ship has sailed. Without a Gripen.'

'Why?'

'Chrissie told our guy we're bringing at least twenty million dollars. In cash. So he got a whole syndicate together, made all the arrangements. Then we didn't come through with it He lost a lot of face, he'll never trust us again.'

'Fuck.'

'Talking about what we bring to the party,' said Themba. 'If we do this, we do this with Ig's planning. If he's not in charge, none of us are in.'

A strange, fleeting moment: for a split second Tau's eyes were wild, as he looked at Themba, looked away. 'Ig is the one who planned the Brenner job,' said Tau.

'Not fair,' said Themba. 'The job went perfectly. They were blindsided from Brenner's side. His contact, his brother-in-law.'

Tau looked at Igen, calm, weighing it up. 'Okay. Whatever. Let me hear what you have.'

'We only steal the gold,' said Rousseau.

'Why?'

'Better return per kilogram than dollars. And we think it's easier to sell.'

'Okay. But it's not "stealing". It's taking. It was never the philistines'.'

'Whose was it?'

'Didn't Vern tell you?' asked Tau.

'Only that you were riding shotgun when it was brought in.'

'How's the food at this place? It's not a story you tell on an empty stomach.'

'Bobotie is great.'

'Okay.' Tau looked around, scanning for a waiter.

'So you have a contact for gold?' he asked.

'We think so.'

★ ★ ★

On the way home in the late-afternoon traffic from Buitengracht and New Church Street Griessel thought of wedding vows.

He would have to start thinking about what he was going to say.

And he was pretty hopeless with that sort of stuff.

Now just might not be the right time for all this. He was under pressure. Frustrated. He felt powerless. And shy.

Mbali Kaleni had brought them in. Put her reputation on the line. Had them seconded because of their knowledge and experience and instincts. And the fact they could keep their mouths shut. And until now the Benny-and-Vaughn mountain had only produced a molehill.

And this mountain couldn't afford to produce a molehill at the altar. What was he going to say to Alexa?

I promise I'll try not to drink?

Even when I drive past Kloof Nek Blue Bottle Liquors and I think the solution is there on a shelf, because I'm not even a 'master detective's' ass.

A week since the Small murder, and all they had was certainty that his dogs were responsible for Le-Lanie Leibrandt's death. They knew two phantoms had used garden services to spy on the house. They had video footage of six men going over a wall, times and causes of death. Two suspiciously timed calls to Phiri, which could be something or nothing. And four long blond hairs. Which could just as easily be from some woman there to relieve Phiri's loneliness. Or from her wig.

Forensics would let them know if they could DNA it, the hair. But it would take weeks to get the final results.

They had nothing, and, even worse, they had no prospects of anything more.

Unless Phiri's laptop yielded something, but he doubted it. A man who knew the NPA was watching him closely, that they could descend on him with a search warrant at any moment, would keep his digital life clean. As did his henchmen, who only used unregistered phones, while they were mobile – fully aware of all the risks.

What was the connection between Basie Small and Dineo Phiri?

State capturer and former Recce.

Fraudster, and a man who watched his dogs attack a young woman. And then tried to cover it up at all costs.

Why? Why did Basie Small take that decision in those moments? Survival instinct? Special Forces training kicking in?

Was there really a link between him and Phiri?

And: when was he going to tell Mbali he couldn't work on any docket on Saturday, 12 June? Because he was getting married.

And not the week after that either. Because he would be on honeymoon.

* * *

Desiree Coetzee, the love of Cupido's life, was smart *and* beautiful. By day she was project manager at a tech company that developed mobile apps at Stellenbosch's Techno Park. She was tall and slim, with long jet-black hair falling down her back, and dark eyes that still mesmerised Vaughn with their shades and flecks of gold and copper, like a lion's.

When he arrived, she was in the kitchen, at the stove, wooden spoon in hand.

'Desi, you're irresistible in an apron.' He kissed her hello, breathing in the spicy scent that enveloped her.

'That's sexist, Uncle,' Donovan commented from the couch.

'It's only sexist if he never wore an apron, Donnie,' said Desiree.

'What smells so good?' asked Cupido.

'Harira.'

'*Jirre*. Low cal and delicious. You're a keeper. Thanks,' and he hugged her.

'Tough day, lovey?'

'Secret agents aren't allowed to say,' Donovan said.

'Yes. Tough. And the traffic . . .' said Cupido. 'But at least one nice thing. Benna asked me to help with his wedding vows . . .'

'What is that?' Donovan asked.

'That's what the couple say to each other in front of the pastor. During the ceremony.'

'But Uncle V, you don't have any experience with that,' said Donovan.

'I've got the gift of the gab, *pappie*. I'm the maestro of *l'amour*, a silver-tongued devil in the language of love. You have to hear my best man speech, it's going to rock your world.'

Desiree laughed. 'Really?' she said. 'And? Any thoughts on the vows?'

'Yes, baby, I think I've nailed it. She calls Benna her "master detective", *nè*. Now, I thought, something that connects to that, but not too heavy and serious. He can read her her rights. You know, like when we arrest someone. As in, "you are under arrest for loving me; you have the right to remain silent", but just not the part where you have to say "yes" . . .'

'Lovey . . .'

'Cool, huh?'

'Lovey, do you have Carla's number?'

'Carla? Benna's Carla?'

'Yes.'

'Why?'

''Cause I think you must leave this in the hands of the women.'

'That's also sexist,' said Donnie from the couch.

61

Just after midnight, Tuesday, 1 June.

Themba slept in Igen Rousseau's small spare room, weary after the long drive from Johannesburg to Barrydale the previous night.

Rousseau stood outside, under the stars, coffee mug in one hand, cell phone against his ear. He was telling Jericho Yon the whole Tau Berger saga, from the beginning.

When he was finished, Yon cried out to heaven, protracted, and with feeling.

'Yes, Jer,' said Igen. 'Crazy story. Crazy country. And now it makes sense that Babbar only came to show you the videos of Brenner and Chrissie on Wednesday . . .'

'In what way does that make sense?' asked Jericho Yon.

'It was the morning that they tried to take out Tau. The day one of Babbar's crew was buried in the mountain.'

'You think?'

'Babbar got desperate, Jer. One of his guys just disappeared, he didn't know if he was taken out or if he had deserted. Things started to unravel. We think Phiri also started panicking, he put pressure on Babbar to find out who the hell was behind our robbery.'

'I swear Babbar knew I was lying.'

'Jer, if he thought you were lying, you wouldn't be talking to me right now. According to Phiri's story, they decided on that Wednesday night to approach the Russians about the gold and dollars. It had become too big a risk, that it would all be exposed. Too many people in the know, too much uncertainty, too much messing around. And the Russians agreed to the gold, said no thanks to the dollars.'

'Fuckit,' said Yon.

'Now you have to think this over carefully, Jer. You're the one with the family.'

'I'm in.'

'Jer, sleep on it . . .'

'I'm in.'

'Are you sure?'

'Ig, here's my reasoning. Babbar looked at all the dots, and then he connected them. And this is what he concluded: if it was Brenner, Small and Tau and the other guy had to be in. Sooner or later he will learn that those connections were way off the mark. Then he will start looking again. New dots. New connections. He will look where Brenner was, six years ago. And if he looks carefully, he will find me in that equation, and he's going to connect me. And you and Themba too. I don't want to spend the rest of my life looking over my shoulder, or worrying about my family. And the country is fucked anyway, Ig. I want out. To go to America. Citizenship by investment. Eight hundred thousand dollars, and you're sorted.'

'This one is going to get rough, Jer. Kill zone. Firefight. Blood.'

'I don't care. As long as my share is more than two million. In dollars.'

'It will be,' said Igen.

'Then I'm in.'

'Great. Because the only way is to fly out the gold.'

'Where to?'

'Jamba. In Angola.'

'Who chose the place?' Yon asked.

'Schmidt.'

'That Schmidt?'

'Yip. He can take the gold. Everything.'

'I need to know what weight we're talking about,' said Yon.

'Tau said, when they brought the stuff in, there were twelve pallets of gold. Each pallet is more or less one thousand kilograms.'

'It's too much, Ig. For twelve tons you need a hell of a plane. And a tarred runway. And that means a big airport and . . .'

'Yes, don't worry. They are moving the dollars and gold in three trucks, and we will only be able to take out one truck. We don't have numbers for more than one. So, if they divide the load evenly, we are talking about a maximum of four pallets. Schmidt said he can give us five hundred thousand rand per kilogram. That's two billion total. Divided by six . . .'

Igen was busy doing the calculations in his head, but Jericho Yon interrupted him: 'Six? How do we get to six?'

'I'm going to get Chrissie. I fly tomorrow . . . Tonight, I mean. And there's Basie Small's sister. She's going to help. And Tau said she has to have a share. Because she is going to check, at the warehouse, that Friday afternoon. When they load.'

'Risky.'

'I know. But it's important to him. Recce loyalty, payback for Small's murder. He's a little weird, Jer. But he's okay. So: to calculate what you should get, that's two billion divided by six, that's . . .'

'Three hundred and thirty-three million, three hundred and thirty-three thousand rand,' said Yon. 'About nineteen million dollars.'

'I don't know how you can do sums so quickly.'

'I'm a pilot, Ig. I have to do it. Who's flying with us?'

'Just five.'

Jericho Yon thought for a while. Then he said: 'Okay. But only four tons. Four thousand kilos. Absolute maximum. It could work.'

'Right. Let me explain the route . . .'

★ ★ ★

Two o'clock in the morning. Igen sat at his small kitchen table with his cell phone, using Google Maps and Google Earth to study the route.

He thought of three big trucks, each carrying a six-metre shipping container.

They were big trucks. Four men could ride in the cab. Two to take turns as drivers. That's what he would have done.

One vehicle with security accompanying each truck. Six guys in each security vehicle? A total of thirty?

Maybe that was too many? Would attract attention. And be expensive. It would be harder to assemble such a big team. Thirty guys with the right skills, thirty guys you could trust? Too many with a story they could tell afterwards. A story that could never come out.

He guessed, three minimum per truck. Four maximum. Three minimum per security vehicle, four more likely. Twenty-four guys. Armed to the teeth.

But he only had to worry about eight. Maybe ten. The four in the last truck, and the four or five or six riding shotgun in the last vehicle.

Ten guys.

Eleven days to plan.

Actually only eight. Because he was going to get Chrissie.

★   ★   ★

Seven o'clock.

Griessel was on the way to Stellenbosch to pick up Cupido, so they could drive out to Hawston again. Sergeant Rivaldo Carolus from Hermanus was bringing a man who could open Phiri's safe. And after that they wanted to search the house from top to bottom, without the stress of contaminating the crime scene.

He didn't know what they were looking for.

Anything.

His phone rang. Carla. He answered via the car's Bluetooth connection.

'Hi, Carla . . .'

'Are you still at home, Pa?'

'No, I'm on my way to Stellenbosch.'

'I thought Pa was working in the city now?'

'Where did you hear that?'

'From Aunty Desiree.'

'Aah . . .'

'She called last night. Apparently Pa asked Uncle Vaughn to help with the wedding vows . . .'

'I did . . .'

'Why didn't Pa ask me?'

He knew he could never tell Carla a lie. 'I just never thought that far. This past week has been . . . rough.'

'Well, Uncle Vaughn's ideas were a bit out there . . . Pa can always ask me these sorts of things.'

'Thank you, Carla. I will be glad if you can help.'

'Aunty Desiree and I have got you covered. Give us a few days . . .'

'Thank you, Carla.'

'Oh, and the suit. Pa must come for a fitting on Friday.'

★   ★   ★

Afterwards, he wondered, what did she actually mean by 'Uncle Vaughn's ideas were a bit out there'? So 'out there' that Desiree called Carla. He was going to ask Vaughn.

He thought about his colleague. Always a bit left field, outside the box. Back when they started working together for the first time as Hawks on the Sloet case.[6] He'd known of Cupido's reputation in the Service as a loose cannon. At first he struggled to like him. And then he got to know him. And understand him.

Now they were like brothers.

He once asked his shrink, why was it that he struggled so much with PTSD because of the murder scenes and violence, but it seemed as though Vaughn just let it roll off him?

She said there was interesting research done in America about policemen with more cheerful dispositions, higher levels of extroversion and lower levels of neuroses. They simply handle the stress better, as if they have some kind of bulwark against evil. 'Detectives who have higher levels of positive emotions before they go on duty,' she said, 'also have better resistance to the stresses.'

That was Vaughn. In a nutshell.

But it wasn't him. He would have to make another appointment with the shrink.

Before the wedding.

Even if he didn't like going. There was a teddy bear in her consulting room, large and brown, with glass eyes that always stared at him. As if it wanted to tell him something. Like: Get your ass in gear, Griessel.

He tried. Every day. And then along comes Le-Lanie Leibrandt and Basie Small and Dineo Phiri and then he was a mess all over again.

The shrink taught him that he had a fear of harm coming to others. She said it was common among policemen and soldiers, people who are exposed to violence and death. In him the PTSD caused the full spectrum of ills: survivor's guilt, separation anxiety, over-inflated sense of responsibility, and self-hatred. He often saw the dreadful things people did to each other, things he knew he couldn't protect his loved ones from. And so he drank.

One of the solutions, she often reminded him, was to discuss his job and work situations with his loved ones.

But now he worked for the ID. He couldn't breathe a word.

He would make an appointment with the shrink, as soon as these dockets were under control.

Before the wedding.

---

6   The murder of Hanneke Sloet is the subject of *7 Days* (2012).

62

Tau Berger stood on the balcony of his first-floor room in the Karoo Art Hotel. Barrydale stretched out in front of him, behind it a backdrop of mountains. He didn't see any of it, his attention was all on the phone conversation with Emilia Streicher. He said to her: 'I don't have a choice, I have to trust them. We can't do it without them.'

'You know, it's actually their fault. That Basie is dead.'

'Yes, I know. They and the philistines. But we'll worry about that later. We have to do this thing first . . .'

'Is there a plan?'

'I'm talking to them about it at ten o'clock. But what we spoke about; you spying out the warehouse. You'll have to do it. Next Friday afternoon. At the warehouse. We need to know what vehicles are driving shotgun. And more or less how many guys we're talking about. Are you up for it?'

★ ★ ★

'Benna, my wedding vows idea was genius, *pappie*. Pure genius. Romantic and topical, and the people would have loved it. Because it's sharp, but serious, if you get my drift.'

They were en route to Hawston, Griessel driving. 'What was your idea?'

'No, partner, I've been gagged and muzzled by the Court of Female Romantic Superiority. But that's okay, 'cause why, the one you are addressing your vows to is also a woman. Desi is right. It's the bride's day, really. The groom is just there to keep the numbers even.'

'So you're not allowed to tell me.'

'No, I can. But only after the fact. And it won't be wasted, partner. My wedding is on the horizon too.'

★ ★ ★

The Karoo Daisy was a restaurant that looked like it was once a church – though it never had been – next door to Barrydale Cemetery.

They sat outside, Igen, Themba and Tau, drinking coffee that steamed in the morning chill. They were each waiting for a Karoo-Sant – a croissant with bacon, scrambled egg, cheese and tomato.

'Good news,' said Igen. 'We have a buyer for the gold. If we are willing to take five hundred K per kilo. In rands. That's a little under half of what it's worth, but he can take everything we bring.'

'Great,' said Tau. 'Who's the bro?'

'Schmidt. German. We know him from the old days, when Brenner and I did anti-poaching work in Zim for John Ehrlichmann.'

'Where does Schmidt get the money?'

'He's the biggest trafficker in illicit arms, gold and diamonds in Africa,' said Themba. 'Very, very rich.'

'Schmidt is plugged into Zimbabwe's gold-smuggling network,' said Igen. 'With the sanctions against Zim, they can't sell gold internationally. So, senior guys in the Zim government supply the gold, Schmidt provides the couriers. They smuggle the gold to Dubai, the smelters pay with bank transfers. Schmidt can take all our gold, but he'll have to give the Zim guys a cut. That's why we get half price.'

'Overheads,' said Themba. 'The cost of doing business.'

'Why didn't you use him for your dollars with the Brenner job?'

'Schmidt was our Plan B,' said Igen. 'First prize was to do it locally. Faster. Easier flight plan, easier to control. And speaking of flight plan, Jericho Yon, the pilot, is in.'

'Fucking A, bro,' said Tau. 'It's the only way. To fly it out.'

'Yip. But he said, absolutely no more than four tons. The only plane he can get his hands on, that can land on a small airstrip and fly to Angola, has a capacity of four and a half thousand kilograms. Maximum. So, four thousand gold, and the weight of the five of us.'

'Five. So, is the girl still coming?' asked Tau.

'I'm going to get her tonight.'

'Roger . . . Okay, how does it work? We give the gold to Schmidt, and how does he pay?'

'Internet Bank Transfer.'

'There? In Angola? In the middle of fuck all?'

'Schmidt is geared up. Satellite Internet, the works.'

'And he pays into what account?'

'We all have our own offshore accounts,' said Themba.

'You give us your offshore account,' said Igen, 'Schmidt pays your share into it. Immediately. Once he's checked the gold.'

Tau Berger's eyes darted, from Igen to Themba to Igen. 'Okay,' he said.

'Next,' said Igen, 'the place where we are going to do it. Jericho and I think there's only one realistic possibility . . .'

A woman arrived with two of the breakfast dishes. They thanked her, Igen waited until she was back in the restaurant again. 'Let's say, we take out the guys riding shotgun. And we stop the truck. The clock starts running then. Time is everything. The longer we take for the goods . . .'

The woman came back with the last breakfast. Igen waited again. When she'd gone, he said: 'The longer we take to get the things to the Dak and on the Dak, the bigger the chance of a fuck-up . . .'

'A Dakota?' asked Tau. 'A DC-3? You're not serious.'

'Jer said it's a Dakota that's been retrofitted and upgraded. It has turbine engines, new avionics. Basler. They call it a Basler.'

'A Dak. Fuck me. Back to the future, bro.'

'There's only one place with a runway long enough for the Dak, and close enough to the road. The other advantage is, Babbar and his merry men will have been on the road for at least eighteen hours, they will be tired and *gatvol*. And they'll be thinking they've almost made it.'

'Where?' asked Tau Berger.

'Calvinia,' said Igen. 'Themba is going to drive there now to have a look.'

'Roger, I'm going along,' said Tau Berger, loading a fork with bacon, egg and croissant. 'And you're absolutely certain Schmidt isn't going to double-cross us?'

'As certain as I can be,' said Themba. 'Schmidt knows we can tell every mercenary in Africa he fucked us over. He wouldn't want that.'

'And if that's not enough,' said Igen. 'Schmidt knows us well enough to know, if he tries any monkey business . . .'

'We'll hunt him down and kill him,' said Themba.

★ ★ ★

The angle grinder made a deafening high-pitched squeal, and sent sparks flying across the bedroom carpet. Griessel and Cupido were standing with Sergeant Rivaldo Carolus from Hermanus, watching the locksmith cut open Dineo Phiri's Rottner Powersafe.

'That's the fastest way,' he said, after trying the factory master code without success.

He switched the grinder off, put it down, and reached for the safe's door, just thirty centimetres high.

'No, thank you, I'll do that,' said Carolus, who was wearing his forensic gloves.

He carefully removed the door so they could see the contents.

The interior was divided horizontally into two compartments.

Carolus took out his cell phone and began to take pictures.

On the top shelf were stacks of fifty-rand notes, tightly and neatly packed. On top of the money was a single piece of white cardboard, the size of a medium-sized cell phone.

On the bottom shelf, watches were lined up next to each other, in their original packaging – Breitling, Rolex, Richard Mille and Patek Philippe.

The locksmith whistled softly.

'Yes, brother,' said Cupido. 'The state capture guys like their watches. Probably easy to trade in Dubai, when the shit hits the fan.'

Carolus put his cell phone in his pocket and carefully took out the white card.

There was a number on it. *4033 667 872.*

'Could this be the safe combination?' Carolus asked the locksmith.

'No. This one works with eight digits maximum.'

Griessel's phone began to ring. He saw it was Mbali Kaleni. He answered: 'Colonel?'

'Benny, are you at the Phiri residence?'

'We are.'

'Found anything?'

'Too early to say.'

'Are you with Sergeant Carolus?'

'Yes.'

'I need you to discreetly ask him if it would be possible to make a copy of the Phiri docket. Someone from the SAPS Criminal Intelligence Division in Pretoria has just released a statement to the media. They are saying they have been suspecting for some time now that Phiri was involved in international drug smuggling. Especially cocaine. They're saying that was the main reason why he had moved to Hawston. The town has been closely linked to the illicit trade of abalone, and it is common knowledge that this is part of the larger trafficking networks of synthetic drugs, since the nineties. Phiri, they say, wanted to be close to a harbour, and the gangs of the Cape Flats. And they believe he was killed by the same organised crime people who killed Small.'

'Could that be true?' asked Griessel.

'No, Benny,' said Kaleni. 'It's a lie. More misdirection. A diversion. Same as with Small. And the question we need to answer is: a diversion from what? Because I am more and more convinced it is something very big.'

⋆   ⋆   ⋆

Igen Rousseau in his *bakkie*, the single-cab Toyota Hilux, on the Op de Tradouw Pass, en route to the airport. His backpack lay next to him. It was all he was taking.

A three-hour drive. Three hours to think. Of the operation ahead. And of Chrissie.

Chrissie had been on his mind for the past two months. From the moment he regained consciousness.

Would she be there, on a Wednesday? He'd memorised her words, that day of the robbery, on the road to Brits. *Caffè Greco. Every Wednesday. Torta della Nonna. And their perfect coffee.*

Because he wanted to see her again.

63

Outside in the street the press were back again for more photos and video footage of the Phiri house, now that it was connected to dealing in abalone and cocaine.

Griessel and Cupido were left alone inside. They searched the house systematically and thoroughly.

They saw the signs of blatant consumption of wealth. The expensive furniture and electronic accessories. The gold and diamond-encrusted rings and chains in bedside tables. Expensive brand names in the wardrobes, rows upon rows of jackets and trousers and shirts. Bottles of Bollinger and Krug champagne, Glenfiddich and Johnnie Walker whisky, Sïku Glacier Ice vodka.

Booze and bling. But that's all they found.

They talked about Mbali Kaleni's call.

They knew, despite her grave doubts, there was a direct connection between the trade in abalone and drugs. The same gangs from the Cape Flats were involved in both.

And Phiri had opted to come and stay in Hawston. Of all the places he could choose.

True, there were no signs of involvement in any trade with Basie Small. Not here either.

But what if Kaleni was wrong?

What if there was something they were all overlooking? There was always something.

★ ★ ★

On the other side of Ashton, Igen Rousseau called Themba.

'Where are you?'

'Clanwilliam,' said Jola. 'Another two hundred kilos.'

'Okay. I have a preliminary shopping list. Tau, can you hear me?'

'You're on speaker, Ig,' said Themba.

'Right. Tau, is your motorbike in your name?'

'Roger.'

'Then we'll have to find another one.'

'Why?'

'Because we're going to need you on a bike to take out the shotgun guys. And we'll have to leave the bike at the contact point. If they check the engine number . . .'

'Okay.'

'Talk to Themba, it must be a bike with storage space. What do you call those cases?'

'Panniers.'

'Right. A bike with panniers. Themba, we have to make stickies. See what you can get. Semtex. PVV. And also some RGD-5, or M26s, something like that . . .'

'Got you,' said Themba.

'See what the road looks like past the airport. We'll need a truck long enough to block the road completely. Sheep lorry or something.'

'Got you.'

'And a forklift. And a ramp to get the forklift onto the lorry and off again.'

'Yes.'

'And firepower. AKs. Two or three with RGD-5 launchers, if you can get hand grenades.'

'*Jissis*,' said Tau Berger. 'Guy Fawkes.'

'Handguns too,' said Igen. 'See if you can get five MP-443s.'

'Got you.'

'Body armour for everyone. And satellite phones, Themba. At least three.'

'Yes.'

'And burner phones. At least three for each.'

'Leave that with me,' said Tau.

★   ★   ★

Cupido wanted to drive back to Stellenbosch on the N2, so that they could eat 'some of those next-level meat pies' at the Peregrine farm stall.

By half past five they were sitting inside, each with a pie and salad. Benny drank Coke, Vaughn had a can of Coke Light.

'How's the diet going?' asked Griessel.

'Very close to six kilos off. Then nine more to go. I'll get there. Damn it, Benna, it's not easy. Let's face it, I like to eat, *pappie*. And the thing that I have the biggest craving for this past week is *dhaltjies*. Fresh *dhaltjies*, like my mammie used to make. Still hot out of oil, you have to blow on them. Crunchy on the outside, soft on the inside, with a *lekker* chili bite, raises a bit of a sweat . . .'

His juicy reverie was interrupted by the chirp of his phone.

He checked it.

WhatsApp messages from Sergeant Rivaldo Carolus. The first one said: *AGU taking over docket. Just heard now.*

And then the pictures started coming through. The contents of the docket.

★ ★ ★

On the way to Calvinia, Tau Berger questioned Themba Jola. He wanted to know what he was dealing with. And going to be dealing with.

'So, you have a military background?'

Jola nodded. 'Pathfinder Platoon, 16 Air Assault Brigade.'

'Together? You and Igen?'

'Same six-man stick.'

'Seen action?' asked Tau.

'Afghan deployment in 2010. Helmand.'

That was all he said.

Tau knew big mouths and bullshitters couldn't stop talking about all the wild action they'd seen. Jola's silence said it all. To Tau, it meant he would have to tread carefully. Around Jola and Rousseau. Because Helmand was rough.

He watched Jola when they stopped five kilometres before Calvinia and got out at the airfield gate, just twenty metres from the tarred R27. Jola took in the ordinary farm fence, the ordinary farm gate, secured with a chain and padlock. And the windsock, west of the gate, beside the runway.

He saw Jola looking at the dirt path beyond the gate. 'It's a week since anyone went in here; there are no tracks.'

Jola took pictures of the gate with his mobile phone. Then he turned to the road. A minibus drove past, followed by two large trucks. Jola took a video of the vehicles. 'Road is quite busy.'

They climbed over the gate and walked on, towards the single, lonely, small white building.

'Listen, bro,' said Tau, 'the motorcycle and the sheep lorry, where the fuck do we get them without doing papers?'

'I know a guy,' said Jola. 'In Mamelodi. He needs a week's notice. And he's not cheap.'

'He steals and delivers?'

'Yes. With fake plates and papers. Good enough for short-term use.'

'And he can get them to us in time?'

'*Yebo.*'

'Forklift too?'

'*Yebo.*'

'The weapons?'

'Schmidt.'

'The guy who's going to take the gold.'

'*Yebo.*'

'How is he going to get the weapons here?'

'From Luanda. They smuggle it in on fruit trucks.'

'What fruit trucks?'

'Apparently, fruit is in short supply in Angola. Very expensive. So there are people who export fruit from Cape Town, at a huge profit. The trucks come back empty, except for the diesel. Fuel is cheap in Angola, so all the trucks are fitted with extra tanks, to fill up at the border. They hide the arms inside the tank . . .'

They stood beside the tarred runway. Tau watched Jola scan the dry plain, and the mountains, south, north and east. He took pictures and video. Made notes on his note app. Then he said: 'We'll have to make sure what the weather is going to do next Saturday. I don't think Jer wants to fly in here with zero visibility.'

Good brain. Good observation, good strategy. Tau would have to tread warily. Pathfinders were a handful.

★ ★ ★

Dense fog on Sir Lowry's Pass. Griessel drove slowly.

'It's like these dockets, Benna,' said Cupido. 'Small and Phiri. Everything is foggy. We can't see. Not forwards, not backwards.'

'That's true,' said Griessel.

'If we only . . .' said Cupido, thoughtfully.

'What?'

'Benna, you trust my instincts, don't you?'

'Just not when it comes to wedding vows.'

Cupido smiled. 'Fair enough. We have to get through the fog. We need to look further. Further back. Because the connection lies beyond that. 'Cause why, I've got this feeling about Arthur Thomas Small and his fourteen million. If you can believe the sister. Fourteen million, *pappie*. That is a lot of money. In a short time. Small's last international action was three years ago, in Mozambique. His first American trip was 2014. Seven years ago. We have no clue what they paid mercenaries back then. To make fourteen million between 2014 and 2019 . . . Almost three million a year. After tax? My instinct tells me those guys don't get that much money.'

'Could be,' said Griessel.

'I think, let's clear the fog. Let's take a look.'

'How?'

'Tomorrow morning I'll go to his bank. And I'm going to ask if our subpoena is good enough for ten years of bank statements. And if it isn't, I'm going to call The Flower and ask her to get us a new subpoena. So I'm going to be a little late to the office.'

64

He dropped Cupido off at the Welgevonden gate and drove home. He worked out the shortest route with the least traffic. Just before he turned left on the Kromme Rhee road, he realised Carla lived and worked very close by, on a wine farm beside the R44. She did marketing and PR, good at her job.

She takes after her mother, he had often thought.

Her working day was over, he could go and speak to her. This morning's conversation with Carla had made him think throughout the day, he would have to call her. About the song he wanted to sing to Alexa. If his daughter and Desiree had reservations about Cupido's wedding vow proposal, maybe he ought to run the song by Carla first too.

Women are different in the way they think about things.

★ ★ ★

Through the large glass doors of the wine-tasting centre, he could see Carla sitting around a table with four colleagues, glass in hand, laughing and chatting. His beautiful daughter, so carefree, so full of life. And he saw himself in the reflection, his wrinkled jacket and his dishevelled hair and the traces of his history all over his face, and he thought, Turn around, Benny. Don't embarrass her in front of her friends.

He halted.

She turned her head and saw him.

Her face transformed with sheer joy. He saw her mouth form the words form: *My pa*. As though she was proud of it.

She jumped up, hurried to the door, came out. 'Pappa!' she said. And she hugged him.

He hid his feelings well.

★ ★ ★

Carla listened to the song and the lyrics with her eyes shut.

Then she said: 'I think it's *so* cute.'

Relief washed over him.

When she walked him to the car, she said: 'Pa, have you thought of asking Fritz to play bass? When you sing it?'

His son had once played bass for Jack Parow's band. He was a much better musician than his father.

'No,' said Griessel. Because his relationship with Fritz was better than it once was, but still shaky. 'Do you think he would?'

'I think he'd love to. And then Pa will also be including him in the wedding.'

He looked at her. Barely twenty-five, and she had more emotional intelligence than he would ever have.

'I'll call him now,' said Griessel. 'Thank you.'

'Love you, Pa,' she said as he drove off.

★ ★ ★

Twenty kilometres east of Calvinia, just beyond the T-junction of the R27 and the R63, there is a layby next to the road. Three eucalyptus trees, five pepper trees, two small, thatched shelters with concrete tables and seating. All these cast long late afternoon shadows across the tarmac.

The Karoo wind was cold. Themba Jola and Tau Berger sat in the Audi, Jola with his phone in his hand, staring at Google Maps telling him Williston was one hundred kilometres away.

'It's going to be tricky,' he said, and typed something into his phone's note app.

Tau waited for the Xhosa man to explain.

'Too many moving parts,' said Jola. 'The plane, the trucks . . . Our biggest problem is, the Dak can't stand and wait at Calvinia. An aircraft that size is going to attract attention. Which we don't want.'

'He can circle. Until he sees the trucks.'

'Not that simple. Jericho said fuel is a problem. The Dak's range, fully fuelled, fully loaded, is enough to get us to Jamba in Angola, and from there to Luanda, after we've unloaded the gold. But he has to do low level, which burns more fuel. And if there's a head wind . . .'

'Shit.'

'One or two snafus, and we're fucked.'

'Shit, bro . . .'

'No, don't worry. Ig will sort it out.'

Tau wanted to know about Ig. Because Ig, he reckoned, was the smartest of this lot. And Tau, he had to be smarter.

'You think he's the bee's knees?'

Jola looked up from his phone. 'Warfare is like chess, Tau. You need the pieces, you need the hand that moves them, and you need the brain that can look at the game: the board, the spaces, the pieces, and the opponent. The brain that can think twenty moves ahead, and plot an outcome. Igen is that brain. Best I've ever worked with.'

'Then what was Brenner?'

'Brenner was the hand. He gave the orders, moved the pieces. Good leader. Brenner was able to take the plan and execute it.'

'And you?'

'I can be any piece you need me to be. I'm the Swiss Army knife of soldiering.'

'Who's going to be the hand, with this Op?'

'If you want the job, it's all yours. As long as you stick to Ig's plan.'

★ ★ ★

On the N1, Griessel called Fritz.

'Pa?' That touch of anxiety, as always, when Griessel called. Less anxiety than a year ago, less each time they spoke, but it was still there. The concern: is my father sober? What's happened *this* time?

'Hey, Fritz. How are you?'

'Mad, Pa. I'm on deadline.' Fritz had graduated from AFDA, the film school in the Cape last year. To Griessel's huge relief; the tuition fees were crippling. Now he worked as a junior editor at The Refinery, a company in the Cape that did post-production in film and television.

'Should I call later?'

'No, I could do with a break.'

'The deadline. Something interesting?'

'No. Just grading an ad. They still don't trust me with the big projects.'

'And how is Kayla?'

Kayla was Fritz's girlfriend. She was a vegetarian, with tattoos on her arms, Chinese characters spelling out 'strength', 'love' and 'courage'.

She'd studied with Fritz, a vivacious young woman and Griessel and Alexa liked her a great deal. Even if she had inspired Fritz to get himself tattooed as well – a compass on his left breast, because it 'celebrated the journey of life', and a feather on his right arm, because it meant 'free-spiritedness, courage, and strength'. According to Kayla.

'Kayla is cool.'

'Has she found a job yet?'

'She had an offer, but it's ridiculous. This industry is such a patriarchy, Pa.'

'Fritz, I want to sing something for Alexa at the wedding reception.'

'Okay.' Cautiously.

'It's one of my favourite blues songs. Sonny and Brownie . . .'

'Yes.' Enthusiastic. 'Which one?'

'You know them?'

'I love them.'

'Where did you hear them?'

'Some of Pa's LPs were left behind with Ma. Pa must have been . . . I listened to them all, when I was at school. Which one do you want to sing?'

'"You Bring Out the Boogie In Me".'

'*Jis*, Pa, that's sick.'

'Sick? You mean it's no good?'

Fritz laughed. 'No, Pa, "sick" is great. "Sick" is dope.'

'Oh. OK. Now I'm wondering, would you be willing to play bass if I sing?'

'*Jinne*, Pa, I think it will be goat.'

'Goat?'

With great patience: 'Greatest of all time, Pa.'

★ ★ ★

On Nelson Mandela Boulevard, Griessel watched the sunset over the sea, spectacular clouds in deep orange, the sun making a halo behind Signal Hill. On his left, the glass in Cape Town's tower blocks reflected the colours in a thousand diamond facets.

It filled him with a kind of longing, a strange mixture of sadness and regret and joy. This city. It made him and it broke him. This city which he loved so intensely. The last bastion against the country's decline. The last hope.

He thought about his conversation with Fritz.

Some of Pa's LPs were left behind with Ma. Pa must have been . . .

What Fritz was going to say was that Griessel was probably too drunk to remember he'd left some of his records with Anna, when she kicked him out, years ago. But then: Jinne, *Pa, I think it will be goat.*

He suspected Carla and Fritz desperately wanted his marriage to Alexa to go ahead. And work. So that the burden of their worry over him could be relieved.

Sick. And *dope.* And *goat.*

And the tattoos. In his rookie constable days tattoos were just for sailors and *dagga* smokers.

The world had changed.

It made him feel old.

Next year he would be fifty.

Fuck.

Leo
Leon Nemeios)
Chrissie

65

Wednesday, 2 June. Ten days before the Great Gold Rush. Eight minutes past twelve in Rome.

Christina Jaeger and Igen Rousseau were sitting in the corner of Caffè Greco's largest room.

'The first point is, it wasn't the Chandas' dollars,' said Igen.

Chrissie just stared at him.

'The story,' he said, 'is much more interesting.'

'What about Babbar? Themba sent me a message. He's hunting us . . .'

'It's true. Babbar is after us, but not for the Chandas. They are sitting in Dubai. And our new president is tightening the screws, they might well be extradited to South Africa. Ishan Babbar has been back with his old bosses for over a year already.'

'Who?'

'I'll get to that, Chrissie. The second thing you need to understand is that I can only tell you the rest if you're in.'

'In what?'

'In the next job.'

'What next job?'

'We're going to steal four thousand kilograms of gold.'

'Whose gold?'

'The same guys that the dollars belonged to. Are you in?'

'Fuck you,' she said.

'Why?'

'After everything, you even ask if I'm in? After everything? Well, fuck you.'

'You're right. Sorry, I just meant . . .'

'You're such a total bastard.'

'I am, I am. Sorry. Brain fart, I wanted to . . . Sorry.'

She punched him on the shoulder with her fist. Hard.

'I deserve that. You may hit me again.'

He was so genuinely sorry that she couldn't stay angry. 'Go buy me more coffee and torta. And then you're going to tell me everything. Bastard.'

⋆   ⋆   ⋆

'In 2011,' said Igen Rousseau. 'That's when the whole thing started. In North Africa. I had to google some of the stuff again, because at that time Themba and I were in Afghanistan, in a bubble where you only think and live Afghan, the rest of the world didn't really exist for you. In any case, North Africa. Uprisings in Tunisia and in Egypt, February 2011, and the shit spills over into Libya. Muammar Gaddafi, remember Muammar Gaddafi, the Libyan dictator? The Colonel. "Brother Leader"?'

Chrissie nodded.

'Now, his people started to rebel against him as well. Gaddafi tried to quell the uprisings, called in the army and the air force, the whole shebang. Shot the hell out of his own people, and the whole world turned against him. Sanctions and resolutions and pleas, and all this to no avail. And then, in May, he had a visit. From that great messenger of peace, his great bosom friend, President Joseph Zaca of South Africa. It's a friendship that goes way back, Gaddafi gave a lot of money to the ANC during the apartheid era. And Joe Zaca was going to talk to Brother Leader in Tripoli. And afterwards Prez Joe says to the world, don't worry, the African Union has this helluva road map that will sort out all the Libyan troubles, peace is just around the corner. But the blood bath only gets worse. A month or so passes, and Joe is back to Tripoli again. Same story, the great mediator, major promises that everything's going to come right. But while Joe and Muammar sit down together, Brother Leader says, "Joe, the paw-paw is nearly in the fan, how about a little retirement spot there in Camps Bay, a bit of asylum, when it's game over for me?" And Prez Joe says, "My brother, our door is always open to you, come when you're ready." And Brother Leader says, "Cool bananas, just one more thing. I made a bunch of money with all our oil, I built a little nest egg, just a few billion in dollars and gold that I need to get out of here pretty fucking fast. Because I do want to enjoy a little luxury in my old age, and . . ."'

'You're not serious,' said Christina.

'Oh, I am. Prez Joe says: "Brother Leader, let us sort it out for you."
And Zaca flies home to sunny South Africa, and his cabinet says no,
we can't grant asylum to Brother Leader, we would become pariah of
the world. Why don't we ask Angola to help with that. And Prez Joe
says, "Good idea." He doesn't breathe a word to the cabinet about the
dollars and the gold. He played those cards close to his chest, he only
shared them with one or two of his most reliable henchmen. Because
Prez Joe had sussed out the whole Libyan affair long before, and he had
a strong suspicion the paw-paw had already hit the fan, the game was
over for Brother Leader. And there was money to be made out this
mess. So he got the ball rolling. He told his Minister of Defence he was
looking for the biggest cargo plane they had, and he was looking for the
best guys in the army to ride shotgun, all the way to Tripoli, on a special
mission. In support of their great friend, Brother Leader. And who were
the best guys in the army to ride shotgun on a special mission?'

'Tell me.'

'Special guys, Chrissie. And who's the most special of all? The
Special Forces. The fucking Recces, that's who. And the Minister calls
the guy in charge at Five Special Forces Regiment in Phalaborwa, and
he says: "I'm looking for at least five of your most special men." And
the guy in charge sends him five: Tau Berger, Basie Small, Dewey
Reed, Corrie Albertyn and Fani Dlamini. But our Prez Joe knows if
you are sending a flight crew and a bunch of Special Forces to collect
a fortune like that, you need someone to keep an eye, who can manage
it for you. To make sure all hands remain in pockets, and mouths
shut. And he knew just the man for the job. Ishan Babbar.'

'*Bliksem*,' said Christina Jaeger.

'Yip. Our very own Ishan. I researched him again. The rumour is,
Babbar was a new face at the National Intelligence Service in the late
nineties. Very smart, very ambitious, flexible moral values, with a good
ear to the ground in KwaZulu-Natal. And Babbar picked up the stories.
That Joe Zaca, still deputy president at that time, was a corrupt bastard.
And well on his way to becoming the next president. And Babbar
decides he was a potential soul mate, exactly the kind of horse he should
hitch his wagon to. He waited until he had a juicy bit of intelligence
which would be useful to Joe, and then he went to see him. And he said:
"There's more where this came from. We can help each other." They
say Babbar is the one who introduced the Chandas to Prez Joe, and who
is the invisible middle man in much of the state capture stuff. And Prez

Joe kept Babbar invisible – no senior appointments when National
Intelligence became State Security. Just mid-level, blending in, an ear to
every door. Always willing to do the dirty work; a little blackmail here,
removing an annoying telltale there. In any case, when Prez Joe had to
pick a man he could trust with the Libya trip, Ishan was his boy. And
then Babbar and the five Recces and the flight crew got into the Flossie
– you know, a Hercules C-130 aerie – and Babbar tells them: "Okay,
gentlemen, here's what we're going to do . . ."'

'Wait, wait, how do you know all this stuff?'

'I'll get to that.'

'It's all genuine?'

'About the Libya trip, it's right from the horse's mouth. Just give
me time.'

'Okay.'

'Right, now they're on the Flossie, and Babbar says: "Gentlemen,
we're going to collect all these billions of dollars of gold and dollars.
We're going to fly to Tripoli, in Libya, twice. And you're never going to
talk about it again. But I know nothing is free. That kind of silence
comes at a price, and we are perfectly willing to pay that price. Five
million each for you. Five million, tax free, because we have the right
people in place at the taxman. And if any of you ever says a word about
this, then we'll send that same taxman after you. And you know, that's
the one man you don't want to mess with." And they flew to Tripoli.
Refuelling stops in Angola and Nigeria. They loaded the dollars and the
gold, all on pallets. A C-130 can take about sixteen tons, and they loaded
that Flossie up to the max, it nearly ran out of runway on take-off.

'But it all happened so fast that Babbar hadn't had time to find a
place where they could store it in the long term. They parked the pallets temporarily in an old hangar at Waterkloof air force base, and they
left two Recces to stand guard. The other three flew back a day later,
and collected another sixteen tons. And they unloaded that cargo, and
then all five Recces had to stand guard there, at the old hangar. Day
and night, to make sure no one came snooping, and no one took anything away. Two months, until the warehouse in Spartan was ready,
with the special rooms and safes. Then they moved the cargo. The
same five Recces, they were the guys who transported it there.'

'We stole Gaddafi's dollars,' said Chrissie in amazement.

'No,' said Igen. 'Gaddafi died four months *after* the Recce-op. We
took Prez Joe's dollars. And now we're going to steal his gold.'

66

Vaughn Cupido drove in from Stellenbosch. He said to Griessel: 'A week, partner. The bank says we have to wait a week for Small's statements. Last three years' they will send tomorrow, but everything before that, not until Monday, at the earliest.'

'How far back can they go?'

'I asked for ten years.'

Griessel's phone rang. It was Forensics. He answered.

'Heard of the two cell phones that got married, Benny?' asked Jimmy, the tall thin one.

'No . . .'

'They say the reception was great.'

'Good one, Jimmy.'

'I know. Okay: your blunt object, Benny. The one that caused Phiri's head injuries . . .'

'Yes?'

'We've identified the wood fragments.'

'And?'

'*Dadelpruim.*'

'*Dadelpruim?*'

'Persimmon. It's the type of wood. In Afrikaans it's Virginia *dadelpruim*. Or *tamatiepruim*. Helluva hard wood, heavy and strong. Very good shock resistance. Exotic. They still use the stuff to make drumsticks. But, and that's where things get interesting, in the old days they made golf clubs from persimmon. The head of the stick, the part that hits the ball. We talked to the pathologist again this morning, and we think they used a golf club. Possibly on his hands and feet too.'

'*Jissis.*'

'If you look at the shape of the trauma to the head, it fits beautifully. But it has to be an old golf club. They haven't made clubs out of wood since the eighties.'

'Okay,' said Griessel. He sighed inwardly. This introduced a whole bunch of new possibilities.

'Trouble is, we can't tell you exactly which golf club it was. Could be a one-wood, or a two, or three . . .'

'What do you mean?'

'That's what they call the things. Your driver that you use to hit the ball the longest distance is a one-wood. You hit off the tee. All the others are called "fairway woods", because you hit off the fairway. You get a two-wood, but it's rare, and a three and a five. All in those days made of persimmon. That's what the Internet says. I don't play golf, I just drink at home. That's all I've got, Benny. Don't know if it helps.'

'Okay. Thank you, Jimmy.'

'Also, where are you going on honeymoon?'

'Goodbye, Jimmy.'

'We've got lots of honeymoon stories. Do you know the one about . . .'

'Goodbye, Jimmy,' and Griessel hung up.

★ ★ ★

'Now you have to fast-forward,' said Igen Rousseau. 'To January this year. Nicky Berry goes to see his brother-in-law, Billy Brenner. And tells him about the dollars he saw in the warehouse. Nobody has a clue where the dollars came from, but he recognised Babbar on TV, from the Zamisa Commission's hearings. And he came to the logical conclusion that it has to be the Chandas' dollars. And Brenner and I also thought, it must be the Chandas', I mean, it's common knowledge that they stole billions.'

'Brenner was a Recce too,' said Chrissie. 'And he didn't know anything about the Gaddafi thing?'

'Good question. If he ever heard anything, he didn't mention it to me. Remember, Brenner had already left the army in 2010 to go to work for Ehrlichmann. In the bush. Far from everything and everyone. The Tripoli flight was only mid-2011.'

She nodded.

'Right. So we steal the dollars. And Babbar finds out, and he has to let Prez Joe know. You have to remember, we're talking about the year after the Zamisa Commission. Prez Joe was indicted on criminal charges, and he was using the Stalingrad tactic to postpone his court cases, but he was worried about his future. The Chandas had fled, the Free State Premier was fired, most of Prez Joe's corrupt cronies were out of government jobs. Everyone was under investigation. The pincers began to bite. Zaca was feeling the pressure, Babbar was feeling the pressure. Cats on hot bricks. And it was under these circumstances that Prez Joe hears his Gaddafi fortune was now a bit smaller. And there are people who know where it is. Suddenly the stress is a bit bigger. You get the picture?'

'Yes.'

'Okay. Now there's one more guy I have to tell you about. Mr Dineo Phiri. A numbers guy. Clever bastard. Always a kind of a behind-the-scenes *ou*. He's the one who conceived and executed all the state capture frauds for the Chandas in the Free State. And then all the corruption was exposed and they fired his ass, and he went to lie low. In Hawston, there near Hermanus. Very low profile, while the media focused on the big guns. So low profile that the media and the Zamisa Commission never really twigged that Phiri was the Prez-Joe inner circle's mastermind. The strategist. The one who knew where all the money was parked, the one who moved it around, the one who had the contacts in Dubai and in Moscow. And Phiri was Ishan Babbar's new boss because Prez Joe couldn't afford to speak directly to Babbar . . .'

Chrissie saw the fire in Igen, how much he enjoyed telling her the story. That smile of his.

'What?' he asked.

'You're a bastard. But it's nice to see you too.'

★ ★ ★

On the N2, on the way to the Arabella Country Estate, Cupido called Sergeant Rivaldo Carolus of Hermanus.

'Have the Anti-Gang men come to get the docket yet?' asked Cupido.

'No, Warrant. I'm still waiting,' said Carolus.

'Goes to show,' said Cupido. 'Lip service. No urgency. That is messed up, my brother.'

'Yes, well, as they say in the classics, Warrant, things work in fits and farts.'

'Sarge, now there's a new development. Forensics say the blunt object used on the victim was an antique golf club, which they made out of wood in the old days.'

'Well, I never . . .'

'You looked at the residents of Arabella, *nè*?'

'Just at the people who were there around the right time, Warrant. Found nothing obvious.'

'You didn't ask if Phiri was a member of the club?'

'No, Warrant.'

'There wasn't any golf equipment at his house, but maybe he left it there at the course. Anyway, we're on our way to Arabella now, we'll let you know if we find something.'

67

'So,' said Igen Rousseau to Chrissie, 'we carry out the heist. Brenner got the info about the CCTV system from Nicky Berry, he thought he knew how to delete the video. But it didn't really work because afterwards Babbar recovered just enough on the hard drive to hi-res parts of the video and get screenshots of you. And a traffic cam down the road got a nice shot of the Hino, and Brenner's face. Then Babbar set to work to identify you and Brenner. And where does he start? He starts with the guys who know. As in, who flew with him at the time to Tripoli. As in, who helped to move the gold and the dollars to Spartan back then?'

'How do you know what Babbar did?' asked Chrissie.

'Just let me finish, please.'

'Okay.'

'I don't know if this was the first thing that Babbar did, but what we do know is that he went to Phalaborwa to work through Five Special Forces Regiment's records. And he found pictures. Photos of Brenner, thirteen, fourteen years ago, but you know, Brenner looks like Brenner still. And in some of the photos, Brenner was with some of the five Recces who flew with him. And Babbar came to the logical conclusion: some of these five were involved in the raid. Maybe all five. He called his boss Dineo Phiri, and asked him, what do we do now? And Phiri told him, we don't take any chances. We do two things. We start making plans right now to sell the Gaddafi gold and dollars; we don't want to sit with fixed assets, because the risk of it all coming out now is too high. And we take out the five Recces. And we send a message to anyone else that was involved. Shut up, or you're next.'

'Take out? As in?'

'As in permanently silence. As in, Babbar sends his team around to kill them. But first he finds out that two of the five Recces are already dead. A few years back, nothing to do with the Gaddafi operation. Only three Recces left. Basie Small, Dewey Reed and Tau Berger. His team takes out Small first. Spray filler foam down his throat to get the message out to "shut up". Then they take Dewey Reed out. We're not sure how, but Small apparently told his sister, if anything ever happened to him in peculiar circumstances, she must let the others know. She called Tau Berger, and he ambushed Babbar's team. Caught one of them, and made him talk. And this guy mentioned the name of Dineo Phiri. And he gave his address. Tau Berger – I have a lot to tell you about Tau Berger – drove down to Hawston, took out Phiri's two bodyguards, and he got Phiri talking. And Phiri sang, he told him everything, the whole thing. That's how we know everything, Chrissie. And then Tau told us.'

'When?'

'Last Sunday.'

'But Themba's message. About Babbar looking for us. He'd sent that the Wednesday before.'

'That's right. Wednesday was when Ishan Babbar started to panic. That morning, Babbar's team tried to kill Tau Berger, and they didn't find him. And Tau eliminated one of Babbar's guys. As far as Babbar knew, the guy was just gone. Either deserted, or dead. And all that Babbar could do was . . . Okay, let me rewind a bit: the night when Nicky and Co ambushed us, with the fire. Themba was just focused on getting me and Jericho Yon out of there before the fire brigade and the police arrived. He didn't have time to see what wasn't burning. I think what happened is that the heat of the fire caused air currents. Or something like that. Because the police found dollars. Outside the hangar. Not a lot, the media said a few hundred notes, most of them damaged. And of course what remained of the weapons. Babbar must have heard about the fire, and the dollars and the weapons. And he put two and two together. Why he didn't show Jer the screenshots then, I don't know. Maybe he thought if the police didn't believe Jer was involved, then he wasn't. Maybe he was too busy locating and eliminating his five Recces. But then, last Wednesday, he had a problem. Tau had vanished, one of his guys had vanished, and Phiri told him he'd better sort out the mess. What I think is that Babbar revisited the only other lead he had. The plane, the burned dollars and the weapons. Then he went to see Jer. With the screenshots and the video. In the hope that Jer might have seen something. And Jer said no, he'd never seen these people. And Jer called Themba, and Themba sent you the message. And he dumped the phone, because we didn't know how much Babbar knew.'

'Okay. But that doesn't explain why you never sent me a message.'

'Because I wanted to surprise you. I'd already bought my ticket to Rome three weeks ago. And when Themba told me about Babbar and Jer, and we didn't know what Babbar knows, I decided, I will only turn on the phone one more time. In Italy. If you're not at Caffè Greco on a Wednesday.'

She thought that over. Then she asked: 'And this Tau? How did he find you?'

'You remember Vern Abrahams? The guy who had to watch Jericho's wife and kids while Jer was sitting with all the money?'

★   ★   ★

Cupido and Griessel spent nearly three hours at the Arabella Estate and Golf Club.

They produced Dineo Phiri's identity number and the registration of his two vehicles, they also showed a photo of Phiri from his days as a Free State politician. They questioned the hotel, the estate and the golf club's helpful, patient staff. And the sum total of it all was that not one could remember seeing him there. Phiri had no official connection with the place. He wasn't a signed-up member, he'd never booked a round of golf there in his name, and he'd never turned in an official scorecard.

Neither Phiri's BMW nor his Mercedes had been through the gates in the past three months. He could have come in with someone else because the estate only scanned the vehicle and drivers' licences. But no one recalled his face.

Arabella's resident professional golfer was a weatherbeaten, tanned man in his fifties. He said he didn't see Phiri on the national database of registered golfers, the Handicaps Network Africa. 'He might have been here before, he might have played here, with someone else, without handing in a score card, or registering his handicap.'

'Are there golfers here who play with antique clubs?' asked Cupido. 'Like those they made out of the persimmon wood?'

The man smiled. 'No.'

'Why are you smiling?'

'Amateurs all make the same mistake. They focus on strokes off the tee. That's all they practise, they think the further they can hit the ball off the tee, the lower their score will be. They buy the latest drivers and hybrids they can afford. And all the pros are sponsored with the latest stuff.'

'Who else would own such an old club?'

'There must be people who collect them. Here and there you see a few old clubs hanging above the fireplace in a clubhouse.'

'But not here?' asked Griessel.

'No.'

'Any collectors here on the estate?' asked Cupido.

'Not that I know of.'

'If I wanted to buy such an old wooden club, where would I be able to find it?' asked Griessel.

The man shrugged his shoulders. 'Gumtree? Facebook Marketplace? I don't know. Maybe in an antique shop or a pawn shop. Can I ask why you'd want to know about the old-style clubs?'

'We're not at liberty to say.'

68

Seven o'clock in the evening, on the big bed in a second-floor room of Rome's Hotel Genio in Via Giuseppe Zanardelli, Chrissie lay on her stomach. She felt the leanness of Igen's body against her, his finger tracing the brown hyena's lines on her bare back.

'I fantasised about this a lot,' he said.

A long silence before she answered. 'Perhaps, if I didn't think you were dead, I would have too.'

'Perhaps?'

'Perhaps.'

'And what would your fantasy have looked like?'

She shook her head.

'Too wild to say?' he asked, teasing.

She shook her head again.

'Christina Jaeger. Enigma,' he said.

'I'm not sleeping with you again until this thing is over,' she said.

He kissed her behind her ear. 'It's okay. I'll wait.' Then, seriously: 'Before you decide you're in, I have to tell you a few things.'

'Tell me.'

'This time it's going to be rough. There's no other way.'

She doesn't respond.

'I'm talking war. I'm talking fixing a homemade bomb to a car carrying four or five or six people. I'm talking, they're going to shoot to kill. We're going to shoot back.'

She nodded.

'The risks are high, this time. Very high.'

She nodded.

'War means things always go wrong. Always. You understand that, Chris?'

She turned around. 'I understand.' She drew his head towards her and kissed him on the mouth. 'And you understand, I'm not sleeping with you again until this thing is over?' she said.

★   ★   ★

Griessel ate Woolworths' chicken fajitas in the kitchen. Alexa hadn't touched her food yet, all her attention was on the large notebook and pen beside her on the table, next to the open *The Wedding Book. An Expert's Guide to Planning Your Perfect Day – Your Way.*

'You're going to fit the suit on Friday?' she asked.

'Yes.'

Alexa made a tick in her book.

'Will you also collect the rings from Daneel's? It's just around the corner from Sew Elegant.'

Not quite around the corner, but close enough. 'Okay,' he said.

Another tick.

'And make sure you give Vaughn the rings.'

'Yes.'

Tick.

'Vaughn's speech?'

'He hasn't said anything yet.'

'I'll call Desiree. She can remind him,' said Alexa, and made a note. 'And you put in for leave? For the honeymoon?'

He'd applied for leave from Witkop Jansen, but he no longer worked for the Stellenbosch station. 'I'll have to apply again, to Mbali.'

'Benny, will you do it tomorrow, please?'

'I will.'

'Remember to pack the bag. We fly early.' They were leaving on honeymoon the Sunday morning after the wedding. He didn't know where. Alexa was keeping it a surprise. All she'd told him was they'd be gone for a week, and he didn't have to 'pack very warm clothes'.

'Okay.'

'Carla will pick up your luggage when it's ready, she'll take it straight to Zorgvliet, the morning of the wedding.'

'Thank you.' He loved her focus, the evident pleasure which she drew from all the arrangements.

'Will you have your hair cut next week? Maybe Wednesday or Thursday?'

'Okay.'

'Remember you're alone here next Friday night? I'll make sure there's something nice to eat.'

'Thank you.'

'All right. The day of the wedding: The ceremony is at four o'clock. I will be fashionably late, but only about ten minutes. You and Vaughn must be there at two o'clock. To get dressed, pinning on your corsages . . .'

'Okay.'

'And your wedding vows?'

'I'll be ready.'

★　★　★

In the hotel room, Chrissie and Igen were looking at her phone, checking flights to Cape Town. There was no space on Rousseau's flight the next day. She could only fly on Friday.

'Just to be sure: from when does this ban on sex apply?' he asked when she'd made the booking.

She smiled. 'From the moment I set foot in the Cape.'

He pulled her closer.

69

Thursday, 3 June.

Griessel felt a bit awkward approaching Mbali Kaleni to tell her about the wedding. Because he'd been working for barely a week at the Investigative Directorate, but also because she wasn't invited to the ceremony. There was simply no room on the guest list. And she wasn't married herself, though he knew it was ridiculous for him to feel guilty about that.

He knocked and entered.

It was the first time he'd been in her ID office on the second floor. It was smaller than the office she'd had at the Hawks, but the gallery on the wall behind her chair looked exactly the same – a perfectly spaced, framed photo chronicle of her life and career. One item was new: just to the left of the door was a framed movie poster of *Captain Marvel*, with a large photo of actor Djimon Hounsou. The poster was signed by him, with the message: *To Mbali. With best wishes.*

She was working on her computer, her desk fastidiously tidy, as ever. She said: 'Please, Benny, take a seat.'

He sat down. 'Colonel, Alexa and I are getting married next Saturday. The twelfth . . .'

Her face lit up, her joy genuine: '*Iyamangalisa*, Benny! I'm so happy for you two. Congratulations.'

'Thank you, Colonel. But it does mean I won't be at work that day.'

'Of course.'

'The problem is, I applied for leave with Colonel Jansen, for the week after the wedding. He approved, but I'm not sure it's valid now . . .'

'Ah. The honeymoon!'

'Yes.'

'How romantic. Where are you going?'

'I don't know,' he said. 'Alexa is keeping it a surprise. Also, I have to go for the final fitting of my suit tomorrow morning. I'm sorry . . .'

Mbali leaned forward, her elbows on the desk, her fingers forming a steeple. 'Benny, with both these cases, we are in the fortunate position that the pressure and the attention is not on us. It is now on the Provincial Commissioner and the Anti-Gang Unit. At the NPA, we play the long game. We build cases for the prosecution, meticulously and methodically. We have time on our side. So, you go do what you have to do. I'm sure Vaughn will hold the fort.'

Relief flooded over him. 'Thank you, Colonel.'

He was surprised to find Cupido just outside the door as he left. His partner looked a touch guilty. 'See you now-now, Benna, I just have something a bit private to discuss with the colonel.'

Benny pondered on this all the way to the stairs. It must be that Vaughn wanted to discuss their future with the Hawks.

★ ★ ★

Eight city blocks north-east of Kaleni's office, at a cell phone store in Adderley Street, Tau Berger asked the owner if he could buy fifteen cell phones and sim cards. Cash. 'But I don't have time for any paperwork.'

'I understand, sir,' said the man. 'I have a special on the Xiaomi Poco F3. Very good Android phone.'

'You've got fifteen?'

'Yes, sir. Six and a half each.'

'Too much, bro.'

'I can maybe do six, sim cards included.'

'Deal,' said Tau. The phone rang in his motorcycle jacket pocket: he took it out, saw that it was Themba Jola calling.

'Yes?'

'My guy can get us a Suzuki V-Strom, a Triumph Speed Triple or a BMW. The F750 GS.'

'The BMW,' said Tau. Because he knew it was the only one of the three motorcycles with a seat low enough for him. Not that he was going to say that.

★ ★ ★

'Everything okay?' Griessel asked as Cupido returned to his workstation.

'Yes, Benna, all hunky dory. Have you seen the Djimon Hounsou poster?'

Before Griessel could answer, Malime Duba approached. 'We've just completed the analysis on the Phiri laptop,' she said. 'Can I give you the nutshell?'

'Please, Doc,' said Griessel.

'Right,' she said. 'So, let me start with his browser history. It shows online gambling, mostly sports betting, and pornography. And a lot of searches for escorts in Cape Town and Hermanus. That, sadly, represents just about everything he used the computer for.'

'Ah,' said Cupido. 'The sweet fruit of state capture.'

'Indeed,' said Duba. 'He was on Gmail, but he kept that very clean, it seems. A few emails in his sent folder to former colleagues, wishing them well for elections, and complaining that he misses what he calls the "action". Most of them did not respond, or he deleted their responses. He also seems to have deleted all statements sent by the bank. But the latest one, for May, arrived in his inbox yesterday. It shows a balance of just over one hundred and fifty thousand rand in his Standard Bank cheque account. His expenses are, generally speaking, for groceries, alcohol, eating out, municipal services, gambling, and escorts. However, there are two items of interest. The first is his income during the past thirty days. On Monday the third of May, he received a payment from the United Arab Bank in Dubai. For twelve thousand five hundred US dollars. About two hundred thousand rand.'

'Wow,' said Vaughn Cupido. 'Must be nice.'

'The second item of interest is the fact that he did not use his laptop or his mobile phone for online banking. Which begs the question: how did he manage his financial affairs? We hope to find out soon. Colonel Kaleni filed a subpoena with Standard Bank yesterday, and we should have three years of statements by tomorrow, and more on Monday.'

'Thank you, Doc,' said Cupido.

'We are also analysing the GPS data from Phiri's two vehicles, and comparing that to the data on Small's Ford Ranger. I should have something for you soon.'

*　*　*

Chrissie parked the Panda outside Poggio Nativo's centuries-old town gate, took out the bags of cat food and walked up the hill to her apartment.

She stood still for a moment and looked out, over the *Tre valli*.

Down there, somewhere, was her patch of soil. The one she was going to buy. The one with olive and cherry and fig trees on it. The vegetables and herbs she would plant herself.

She would build a shed. Buy a tractor and a trailer. Like every self-respecting smallholder farmer in the Sabine hills.

And invest in a few more houses and flats here in town. That she could fix herself. And rent out. Luca told her, there were lots of people who came to the Santacittarama, the Buddhist temple in the southern valley. They were always looking for places to stay.

She would finance Luca's restaurant. So that the people who rented her cottages would have a good place to eat.

She heard Katse and Sebini meowing.

She carried on walking.

70

On Friday morning at Sew Elegant in Stellenbosch, Griessel stood in his wedding suit, the seams of the jacket still just tacked. But everything fitted.

Eight days to the wedding.

Carla looked him up and down. 'It looks nice,' she said, 'but, Pappa, you're going to get a haircut?'

'Thursday,' he said.

'Okay. Can we quickly look for a tie to match Aunty Alexa's dress?'

He shook his head. 'I have to go to work. And then pick up the rings.'

'Okay, will Pa trust me with the tie?'

'Of course.' He took off the jacket.

Carla picked up her handbag, took out a sheet of folded white paper. 'I tried something, with the wedding vows . . .'

She handed him the sheet. 'Aunt Alexa's song,' she said. '"Sweet Water". I tried something . . . Pa must tell me if it doesn't work.'

'Thank you, Carla.'

He unfolded the paper, and read.

Carla waited, on edge.

He had to take a deep breath to hide his feelings.

'Do you like it, Pa?'

He walked over to his daughter, and hugged her tight.

'It's beautiful. You are . . . you're such a precious child.'

She could hear the catch in his voice. 'Pa, now you'll make me cry.'

* * *

Cupido sat at his workstation. Kaleni had drawn Griessel's empty chair closer. Malime Duba was standing beside the desk holding a yellow file, from which she pulled a stack of printed spreadsheets: Dineo Phiri's finances.

'You will see, it's been the same pattern of income and expenditure for the past three years. The same payment, once a month, every month. Always from the United Arab Bank in Dubai. For twelve thousand five hundred US dollars. Paid from the account of an LLC, or limited liability company, called Shawka Trading. We are trying to ascertain who the owners are, but it will take time.'

'Check,' said Cupido.

'It's reasonable to surmise,' said Kaleni, 'that the Shawka Trading account is part of the state capture web of money laundering. And connected to the Chandas. This might be our first small breakthrough in unravelling that web. Bear in mind that we have always suspected that Phiri was the man who knew where the money was. And the man who was moving it around.'

'Check,' said Cupido.

'So,' said Kaleni, 'bear in mind that we have now ascertained that Phiri did not use his personal laptop or his cellular phone for any banking activities. We've searched his house and his vehicles, and came up with nothing. Which begs the question: how did he do it? What did he use? When did he use it? And where did he use it?'

'Got you.'

'Please proceed, Malime,' said Kaleni.

'Right,' said Duba. 'My team has now concluded the mapping of the GPS history for both Phiri's vehicles, the BMW and the Mercedes. The first thing we did with this data, was to compare it to Basie Small's movements. I can tell you that there are no similarities or overlaps. Small seems to have had no set routine, day to day, week to week. However, Phiri very definitely had. And this is where it gets interesting . . .'

She placed a printout of Google Maps on the desk. It showed the area from Hawston to Cape Town. 'Every Thursday, like clockwork, for the last six months at least, his BMW travelled from Hawston to Cape Town. The car left Hawston around two-thirty in the afternoon, and arrived in Cape Town at around four, give or take fifteen, twenty minutes. The BMW always parked in the parking garage of the Lifestyle on Kloof shopping centre. It stayed there until about seven, moved to Long Street, and went back to Hawston about two o'clock the next morning.'

'Right,' said Cupido.

'He also made this trip on the day before he died. That Friday of
his murder, the BMW arrived at his house at three twenty-seven in
the morning. And that night, as you know, the same car was used to
drive to the boat club, presumably with his dead body inside.'

'Yes.'

'Was that coincidence?' Kaleni asked. 'Did he get something in
Cape Town every Thursday that was worth killing for?'

'Now,' said Duba, 'the GPS data in itself has only limited value.
We know where the car went, and we know at what time. Nothing
more. However, this morning, we took Phiri's cash and credit card
transactions, and made an overlay of time, places and amounts on
top of the GPS information . . .'

'Very clever work, Malime,' said Kaleni.

'Thank you, Colonel. We're not sure exactly what it means, but it
definitely opened up a few new avenues of investigation.'

71

On Flight EK770 from Dubai to Cape Town, Igen Rousseau sat at the window, thinking about Christina Jaeger. Of her scent and her taste, the feel of her skin, the contours of her body. Her eyes, in those moments of intensity, and her voice, the raw depth of it when she came.

And he thought: I'm addicted.

From that moment at the stop sign after the robbery. When she pulled the wig off, threw it on the back seat and turned to him and took his face in both her hands, and kissed him. The electric current of her being flowed through him. And he wanted *more*.

You know, she's not the kind of girl who's going to settle down. Themba's insight.

He knew that. She was a brown hyena, an alpha female, a loner. She was a heartbreaker. And he was addicted to it all.

Is it love or is it lust?

Why not both of them, Themba? Isn't it that very combination that made it perfect? To intensely desire the one you love?

There had to be a space, somewhere, between *settling down* and nothing. A dynamic which could work. For him and for Chrissie.

Because she felt something.

I'm not sleeping with you again until this thing is over.

It meant she wanted to. When the Op was over. And he could see it, he could *feel* it, she liked him. Maybe more than that. Despite her casual facade, her protests, her hardass attitude. It was all a front, a shield, a mechanism. He just had to show her, she could trust him, she was safe with him. All she had to do, was to give him a chance. He would talk to her, when this Op was over.

Safe with him.

Good one, Igen, he thought. You bring her into an Op with helluva high risk, and you want her to feel safe.

Focus on the Op. Because if it goes fucking wrong, you lose everything.

Focus on the Op.

★ ★ ★

Cupido, wearing his long black coat, waited at the main entrance of the Lifestyle on Kloof shopping centre. He saw Griessel walking towards him, and stood up to greet him.

'How does the wedding suit fit, Benna?'

'Like a glove.'

'Attaboy. Rings?'

Griessel put his hand into his jacket's left inner pocket, and took out two black leather pouches. He solemnly handed them over to Cupido.

'Let the record show, your honour, that this sacred moment happened on the corner of Park and Kloof,' said Vaughn, stowing each pouch safely in his coat's inside pocket.

'Come on, Benna, I'll stick you for a burger over there.' He pointed at the Tiger's Milk restaurant.

'That's why we're here? For a burger?'

'Patience, Benna. All will be revealed . . .'

★ ★ ★

On the plane, Igen focused on the operation. First of all he carefully went over the notes, photos and videos that Themba Jola had sent him on Telegram.

A lot of moving parts, Ig. You have to think carefully, Themba wrote at the end. *High reward, but extreme risk.*

Their greatest advantage was also their biggest enemy: the R27, the tar road running through Calvinia, to the Cape. Because the airfield's runway was barely a hundred metres from the road, which meant moving the gold between the truck and the plane would be quick and relatively easy.

But the road was busy. Big trucks carting ore. Cars, one every few minutes, according to Themba's observation. He said tomorrow morning he was going to watch the Saturday traffic passing the airfield, from six to twelve. To get an indication of what they could expect.

A busy road meant a lot of prying eyes. People who needed to be kept away from the 'scene of the accident'. They had only four people to transport and load the gold, because Jericho Yon would be sitting in the Dak. They didn't have the manpower to contain the curious. And he didn't want bystanders to get hurt.

Problem number two: the three trucks and three security vehicles had to pass through Calvinia first, then just five kilometres on, pass the airfield. They would of necessity drive slowly through the Karoo town. It was possible they could concertina, get closer to each other. Five kilometres might be too short a space for them to still keep their distance by the time they reached the airfield. Too close, and the second truck or security vehicle would be able to see what was happening behind them, with truck number three.

Unless they could manage to keep faithfully to half an hour or more apart.

That was his hope.

How were they going to determine how far apart they were? With just four people on the ground?

He would have to figure that one out.

Get another truck. Or a *bakkie* that looked like a police vehicle, to block off the scene of the attack on the other side.

They were going to need some luck.

And good flying weather.

Five kilometres. To take out a vehicle with three or four or five heavily armed guys. To stop a truck in just the right place. To neutralise the armed occupants. To block the road on both sides, keep the busybodies away, load the gold. And fly away.

No matter how you looked at it, there was only one way.

Rapid dominance. That's what the Americans called it in Afghanistan. *Shock and awe.* Hit fast, hit hard.

Rapid dominance with four team members and a pilot.

Fuck. He had to be smart. They would have to execute the plan to perfection.

But there was always a snafu. He knew that from bitter experience. Always.

72

Cupido let them sit at a table outside, under the roof, so that they could see the street. After the waiter had taken their orders, he said: 'Partner, we have ourselves a little conundrum. It's a complicated one, so I'll take it from the top: you remember, The Flower swears high and low that Dineo Phiri was the money mover and launderer for former president Joe Zaca and his merry men of the state capture club?'

'Yes.'

'And we searched that Hawston house, we took Phiri's laptop and analysed his phone, and there's not one single bit of evidence that he did online banking anywhere, or talked to someone who could do it for him.'

'Okay.'

'And the billion-dollar question is, how did he do it? When? Where?'

'Yes.'

'Right. Then Doc Duba looked at the GPS data of Phiri's cars. And, lo and behold, that data shows that Dineo went to Cape Town every Thursday in the BMW. Like clockwork. And he parked over here at the Lifestyle on Kloof shopping centre, about four o'clock in the afternoon. Then, just before seven o'clock in the evening, the Beemer drives out of here, down Kloof, makes a turn in Loop Street to negotiate the one-ways, and parks in Long Street, or very close to Long Street. You get the picture?'

'Yes.'

'Cool bananas. Then Doc Duba took Phiri's credit card statements. And that shows, every Thursday, like clockwork, Phiri buys his first drink at Bob's Bar in Long Street, at around seven o'clock in the evening. Same credit card statements show, eight o'clock every Thursday night, that Phiri moves on to The Waiting Room, very popular night club where all the Cape celebs hang out, also in Long Street. Then it is party time, lots of drinks, big tab. Until two o'clock in the morning, which is Waiting Room closing time. Then it's back in the Beemer, back to Hawston.'

'And the question is, where was he between four and seven?'

'Damn straight, Benna, where was he between four and seven? The Flower's theory is that he clocked in somewhere in that time. To do his money laundering. By phone, by computer, in dialogue with someone. Somewhere. Every Thursday. And I guess it has to be somewhere near here. 'Cause why, he always parks across there.'

'When was the last time he was here?'

'Last Thursday. A day before he died.'

'Parked at four in the afternoon?'

'Yes.'

'Never before four?'

'No.'

'Banks close at four o'clock.'

'And that, partner, that's the conundrum. And that's why we're here at Tiger's Milk.' Cupido pointed at the CCTV camera on the restaurant's outer wall, just above the veranda roof. The camera faced south, up Kloof Street. 'If they keep the footage for more than a week, we'll be able to see if Phiri passed by here. And in which direction. And then we'll have to take it from there. And hope.'

* * *

On flight QR132 from Rome to Doha in Qatar, Christina Jaeger sat in an aisle seat. Listening to *La Traviata* on her headphones, with Pavarotti, Studer and Pons.

On her lap was a book about Greek and Roman myths that Luca Marchesi had lent her.

She read about Heracles and the Nemean lion.

She saw the mighty beast in her mind's eye, with its supernatural strength and rage, in the huge dark cave. And Heracles, blocking off first one entrance and then entering the other.

The lion charges. Heracles stands, massive club at the ready.

Chrissie smiled. She remembers the night Igen arrived at Letsatsi Lodge. While she was telling the Americans what you do if a lion charges you.

Ask Heracles, she should have said. He knew. By not showing fear. By facing it. Direct confrontation.

She read that the Greeks had named a constellation after the Nemean lion. The Romans took over the name, and renamed it in Latin.

Leo.

You could only see the constellation in the Northern Hemisphere. It was easily recognisable, with many bright stars in the shape of a crouching lion.

She would look for it in the night sky when she returned. So that she could remember Heracles. And her old life. A life she was leaving behind.

⋆ ⋆ ⋆

The video footage from Tiger's Milk's street camera showed Dineo Phiri and his two bodyguards cross Kloof Street and walk past the camera the previous Thursday afternoon at eleven minutes after four.

North. Towards the city.

'Swanky,' said Cupido: all three men were flamboyantly dressed, collared shirts and jackets.

They walked purposefully. Phiri was a metre ahead of the guards when they disappeared from view.

Thirty hours later, all three would be dead, Griessel thought.

⋆ ⋆ ⋆

When flight EK770 landed in Cape Town at 16:59, Igen Rousseau switched his phone from airplane mode.

His Telegram app indicated he had a message.

From Themba. *Apartment 23, The Belmont, Holmfirth Road, Sea Point. Key lockbox code 76947.*

The address of the Airbnb where he would stay until D-Day.

⋆ ⋆ ⋆

At six o'clock the detectives gave up. Load-shedding had started in Cape Town and all the possible cameras in Kloof Street were now behind closed and deserted shop and office doors. The one in front of Tops was focused on the liquor store entrance. The footage from the previous Thursday was available, but all it showed was that Phiri and the bodyguards hadn't gone there to buy alcohol.

The detectives walked back to their cars in the mall parkade.

Benny remembered the folded sheet of paper in his jacket pocket. 'Do you want to hear my wedding vows?' he asked.

'Benna, this is so sudden.'

Griessel laughed. 'Do you want to hear them?'

'Of course I do!'

Griessel took out the paper, smoothed the page. With cars, mini-bus taxis and a Golden Arrow bus passing by, pedestrians milling about them, he read the words to his partner, as they walked.

When he had finished, Cupido stood and looked at him. '*Fokkit,*' he said.

'It's Carla,' said Griessel, shaking his head in wonder. 'That child . . .'

'Partner, I now see the error of my ways. That's next-level beautiful.'

73

'I might have been a bit heavy on the salt,' said Alexa.

She cooked a big breakfast every Saturday morning – scrambled eggs and bacon, butter-fried mushrooms and roasted tomatoes, with toast, jam and mature cheddar – because she didn't have to go to the office.

'On the egg?' asked Griessel.

'Yes. I don't know how it happened.'

'It tastes good to me,' he said. These were the only times he ever lied to her, because she put such enthusiasm into the preparation, she was so eager for him to enjoy it. 'And the mushrooms are fantastic.'

'Really, Benny?'

Before he could answer, his phone rang. It was Mbali calling. Quarter past seven in the morning.

'Colonel?'

'Benny, I want you and Vaughn to take the weekend off.'

'Colonel, we have to go back to Kloof . . .'

'Well, Benny. On Thursday, Vaughn told me you've been work-ing seven days a week for the past six weeks. I didn't know that. Remember what I said: the pressure of the murder dockets is on the AGU. You both need family time, you both need to recharge. Espe-cially you, just a week before the wedding.'

What was he going to do, for a whole weekend?

'Thank you, Colonel.'

When he hung up he told Alexa.

'That's great, Benny! Then tonight we will eat at Scala. I hear it's sublime.'

★ ★ ★

Tau Berger, in a hotel room in Sea Point, swearing, frenzied and frustrated. Busy on the new, unregistered phone. All he wanted was to open a bank account. Overseas. A bank that would welcome a billion-dollar transfer with open arms, a bank that didn't ask questions, a country or an island where they didn't have bothersome tax regulations and the extradition of criminals.

He'd googled 'offshore' and 'tax haven', he'd looked at the options. And it was all fubar. The fuckers wanted documents. References, IDs and passports, bank letters, proof of income. And big deposits, just to get the account up and running. What was he going to do?

He only had a week.

His Telegram app was tinkling. He checked it.

Emilia Streicher was sending him videos. Images of the warehouse in Spartan at Kempton Park.

Six o'clock this morning, she wrote.

He watched the videos. She must have held the phone against the driver's window, she wasn't driving too slowly. That was good. And the image was clear: in front of the warehouse in Spartan were three double-cab Toyotas. All three black, all three facing the street. Two men in the front seats of each one. A guy was leaning against the middle *bakkie*. Combat boots, bulletproof vest, Heckler & Koch UMP on a band over the shoulder.

These are the guys who are going to ride shotgun, thought Tau. The Toyotas are the shotgun vehicles.

And they were already there, six days before the trucks were due, because Phiri was dead and they weren't taking any chances.

He called Emilia.

'Hello, Tau,' she said.

'Great work.'

'I stuck a piece of black cardboard over the lower part of the window, with a hole for the camera. They wouldn't have seen anything.'

'You're a star, you know. Listen, we have a bit of a problem. There's no way I can open an offshore account. Not in time anyway. And then we're screwed.'

Silence on the line.

'Are you there?' he asked.

'I have one,' she said.

'An offshore?'

'Yes. It was Basie's. But I have access.'

'Still? The bank doesn't know about Basie's . . .'

'No. I haven't let them know yet.'

He clocked the implications. All the money transferred to an account to which only she had access.

'I don't know if it's going to work,' he said.

A moment's silence. As if she understood: 'Tau, you were like a brother to Basie. How can you not trust me?'

'You're right, sorry. It's great, it's great. Then I can take Igen and the rest of them out.'

'The pilot too?'

'Only in Luanda. No loose ends, Emilia. Trust no one.'

★ ★ ★

It was cloudy and cold in the city, the north-wester tugging and shoving. Griessel rode his Giant mountain bike, up Kloof Nek, then left, into Tafelberg Road, past the cars parked at the cable car station.

He was struggling, his legs aching. It had been two months since he'd been on the bike, there'd been no time for cycling. He'd had to get up too early to be on time for morning parade in Stellenbosch.

Where the tar turned into gravel, at the sign that said *Devil's Peak*, he stopped to catch his breath. He looked out over the city. Beyond the harbour, in a single pool of sunlight, Robben Island looked like a green jewel in the grey sea.

His thoughts wandered.

The wedding. Carla's beautiful wedding vows. Fritz saying it would be 'goat' to play bass while Griessel sang. Alexa, who took such delight in the arrangements. Cupido, who'd gone to tell Kaleni they deserved a weekend off.

He wondered if Vaughn thought the wedding was causing him to lose focus. That and the long hours, the hard work. Because it wasn't.

It was the NPA and Mbali Kaleni's mission, their passion, to unravel state capture, to slowly build watertight cases against the suspects.

His own mission was to solve the Small and Phiri murders. That's what he was passionate about. He didn't want to lose focus now, he didn't want time off now. Murder investigations were about momentum, about *living* the dockets, until your whole mind was filled with them, and you could see everything, feel everything. Make the connections.

Even if it fucked you up.

He didn't want to look through lists of digital data and numbers. He wanted to do footwork. Old-school footwork. Door-to-door, ask questions, think, measure, adjust.

Footwork.

That gave you perspective. Thinking time. It let you see and experience everything, build an image with all your senses.

He wanted to do footwork.

He rode on again. By the time he reached the King's Blockhouse on Devil's Peak Mowbray Ridge, he'd made up his mind to go back to Kloof Street later this afternoon and take a walk. Just to see if there were cameras they could follow up with on Monday.

74

Flight QR1369 from Doha landed in Cape Town at 10:50.

At 11:14 Chrissie was standing at passport control. Her heart raced. The passport was forged. She'd bought it in Gaborone, four years ago, for a thousand dollars.

The customs official scanned it, looked at the photo, looked at her.

'Welcome to South Africa,' she said.

'Thank you,' said Chrissie, took the passport and walked through.

She didn't have to wait for luggage. She only had the backpack. And the hope that Igen would be waiting for her in the arrivals hall.

* * *

In the Santa Ana Spur at the Cape Waterfront, Vaughn Cupido was engrossed in his Lose It! app. He wanted to know what a two-hundred-gram sirloin would cost him in kilojoules. This morning the scale told him he was very close to another kilogram off. He didn't want to screw it up. Only just over eight to go.

The sirloin was approximately two thousand kilojoules. His limit for the day was just over nine thousand, and breakfast cost him two thousand eight hundred this morning.

He would have a salad with the sirloin. No chips, no onion rings. Then at least he could still eat something tonight.

Desiree sat beside him, a Stormers scarf around her neck. Opposite was Donovan wearing his Stormers jersey with the number fifteen on the back, his nose buried in the menu. Cupido had bought tickets for this afternoon's game, a URC quarter-final against Edinburgh at the Cape Town Stadium.

'What's a prego roll?' Donovan asked.

'Donnie,' said Desiree, 'stick to a burger, a prego roll has hot sauce, you won't like it.'

'Uncle V, do you think Damian would eat a prego roll?'

'No, Donnie,' said Cupido, 'I think he's a steak man. For the protein. All those muscles need protein.'

'*Djas*,' said Donovan. 'T-bone for me.'

'You eat everything you order, Donnie,' said his mother. 'You know the rules.'

'*Djas*?' said Cupido. 'What is "*djas*"?'

★ ★ ★

In Themba Jola's Airbnb apartment in Hill Street, Green Point, half past four in the afternoon, Tau Berger met Jericho Yon, and thought: This Chinaman won't be a problem.

It didn't matter that Igen Rousseau said he's the 'best bushpilot in Africa'. No, Yon was a walkover. Small skinny ass, long black hair and the dragon tattoo, he knew the type. Super concerned with a certain 'see what a cool and alternative pilot dude I am' image, but with a fucking Tokarev against his head he would do what he was told.

A knock on the door.

'That's Chrissie,' said Igen and opened the door.

Tau was curious, but hid it well, taking a look, casual-as-you-please.

A wildcat walked in. Pretty face. Common streak in there somewhere. Black hair cut very short, tight black jeans, tight black polo-neck sweater, nice ass, nice tits. Fuck you attitude.

Jis, jis, jis, thought Tau. What have we here?

★ ★ ★

Everyone sat around the table. There was Coke, bowls of potato chips and peanuts. Igen Rousseau, carving biltong with his big pocket knife, swivelled a laptop around so they could see the screen: Google Maps displaying practically the whole of South Africa.

'At one o'clock on Friday afternoon they start loading the cargo at Spartan,' said Rousseau. 'Basie Small's sister will drive past the warehouse at a quarter past one and record the trucks on video for us, and see if the shotgun vehicles are the same Toyota *bakkies*. According to Phiri, the trucks leave at two o'clock. Then they drive to Potchefstroom, Klerksdorp, Kimberley. . .'

He ran a finger along the route.

'In Potch there is a security company called North By Northwest. I spoke to the head honcho, told him we wanted someone to cast an eye over three of our trucks that are passing through Potch on Friday. We will send video of the vehicles at around half past two, we expect them in Potch around half past three. All we want from them is a photo of each vehicle, and the time they passed through, because we suspect our drivers are not being completely honest with us. We will pay North By Northwest two thousand for the job, but it's worth it. Because we don't have the manpower or the time to be everywhere, and we want to know more or less what time they got away, how far apart they are, and their average speed.'

Igen scrolled the map south, and tapped on Kimberley: 'In Kimberley, Diamond City Security will do the same for us.'

'What about the shotgun *bakkies*?' asked Tau. 'How do we know if they'll be driving in front or behind the trucks?'

'Right,' Igen said and moved the map east, pointing to the town of Williston. 'Tau and Chrissie, you ride the motorcycle to Williston on Friday. Sleep in the Lord Willis Guesthouse. It's right next to the R63. The convoy has to pass it. With the information from Potch and Kimberley, we'll have a good idea of roughly what time they'll be coming through Williston. If you take their ETA of two o'clock in Simon's Town, and an average speed of between sixty and ninety, it will be somewhere between four and eleven o'clock in the morning. From two a.m. one of you must be permanently on watch, take shifts, try to get enough sleep. When you see the convoy, call me. Tell me what the convoy's composition looks like. Williston is a hundred and twenty kilometres from Calvinia. More than an hour's warning before the trucks reach us, but I estimate at least an hour and a half. Wait fifteen minutes and then follow them, and pass the convoy, go as far as Calvinia. Wait at the Caltex Calvinia. When you see the first truck coming, you call me again. Wait for the last shotgun guys to pass, then you go after them. Keep close to the last shotgun pick-up, past the golf course. Wait until the *bakkie* comes to the Ceres turn-off, the R355 which turns left. Chrissie, that's when you plant the sticky . . .'

'The sticky?'

'Magnetic explosive device,' said Themba. 'Originally developed by the Brits in World War Two, the modern version is what the

Afghans used in Kabul. I'm making a few. Plastic explosive, packed in a box. You will have to stick it to the car magnetically, right on the driver's door.'

'That's how we take out the shotgun vehicle,' said Igen. 'Then I'll pull the sheep lorry in front of the truck. And Themba closes the pincer with a police van.'

'Which you'll get where?' asked Tau Berger.

'Final Cut Movie Cars,' said Themba. 'It will be fake, but good enough for our purposes.'

'Themba is going to wear a blue uniform, a fake police uniform,' said Igen. 'Maybe it will help keep the mob away, maybe not. Can't do any harm. Anyway, then Tau and I have to take out the truck guys. And you . . .' he pointed at Chrissie, 'are going to ignore it all. You go and fetch the forklift.'

They heard the roar of the crowd in the Cape Town stadium, just a kilometre north.

'Sounds like the Stormers are kicking Edinburgh's ass,' said Igen.

★ ★ ★

Benny Griessel was standing in front of Workshop17 at 32 Kloof Street. Two old, classic storeys of red brick and white plaster from the 1920s at the bottom, two new floors of glass and steel recently added above. Front and centre, the large main entrance with a sign that said *Members Entrance*, but he had no idea what business it was. It was the only puzzle in this street, all the other buildings were clearly shops or restaurants.

He took out his phone and did an internet search.

He found that Workshop17 was renting out office space. 'Your choice of flexible workspaces.'

Could Phiri have had an office here? Where he came to do his 'dirty business', to use Vaughn's words?

He found a phone number on their website, and called. It rang for a long time, no answer. Probably closed for the weekend.

He sighed. He would try again on Monday morning. He had to head home now. To get dressed for tonight's dinner at Scala.

75

Chrissie made the bank transfer on Sunday morning. Four hundred thousand rand, to Igen Rousseau's 'Op account'. Her part, her contribution to the fund they needed to finance the entire operation – the vehicles, the plane, the fuel, the weapons and the accommodation.

She had less than five hundred thousand rand left in her account. Maybe eighteen months of survival money, if she lived very conservatively.

This Op better work. She had listened closely, yesterday, to Igen's plan. There was so much that could go wrong.

At the very least, if this thing didn't work out, it was going to be a wild ride.

A very wild ride.

★ ★ ★

The Cessna 210 came down on the abandoned dirt landing strip of Skoorsteenberg in the desert landscape of the Tankwa Karoo.

Jericho Yon let the plane roll up to the single hangar on the northern end of the strip, and cut the engine.

'As you can see, there's nothing here,' Yon said to Igen Rousseau, who was sitting beside him. 'Just the plain. The cottages are two kilos away, that way. On AvCom they say there are no people here in the winter.'

'Yes.'

'Fuck all cell reception. Satellite phone is the only thing will work.'

'Covered.'

'If the trucks are slow . . . I can land here with the Basler, and wait. But only when there is light, from ten past seven. Because there are no landing lights here . . .'

'Right.'

'One thing I worry about. The weather forecast said there's rain coming Tuesday. Big rain.'

'Here too?'

'Yes. And this strip. If it's very wet, it's all mud. Smooth and sticky.'

'Shit.'

'Wednesday to Saturday is partly cloudy, it should dry out.'

Yon reached for a tablet computer on the back seat. 'Saturday looks okay. Cold front arriving in the evening, strong north-westerly only in the afternoon, but visibility is fine until around noon.'

Yon activated the SkyDemon app on the tablet, and showed Rousseau. 'We are here. Sixty-eight nautical miles to Calvinia. When you let me know the trucks are past Williston, I wait forty minutes, then I start up. Pre-flight, take-off, straight to Calvinia. It's the leg we're going to fly now, I want to take a good look at their landing strip and the approach. Saturday I do a holding pattern above the airfield until you tell me they're through the town. Then I bring her in.'

'Yes,' said Rousseau.

'Yes, just one thing. If it's a fuckup . . .'

'It's going to be okay, Jer.'

'If it's a fuckup. I will wait as long as I can . . .'

'That's cool, Jer, I understand. You're the one with the wife and children.'

'My wife and children are flying to America on Thursday, Ig. It better not be a fuckup.'

'It's going to work. Rapid dominance. Shock and awe.'

76

Monday, 7 June.

Five days to the wedding.

At eight o'clock Griessel was at the entrance to the beautiful old Workshop17 building in Kloof Street. He waited for a young man to arrive at the door and enter the access code. He showed him his identification card and asked where the building's administration office was. The man led him to the first storey.

The interior was beautiful. Tasteful furniture, modern artwork on the white walls, an office area behind glass, set against the original brickwork.

He identified himself to the woman at reception and asked if she had any records of a Dineo Phiri renting space from them.

She checked her computer, but found nothing.

He took out his cell phone, found a picture of Phiri dating back to his political career, and showed it to her.

She said she had never seen him in her life.

$\star$ $\star$ $\star$

Chrissie took an Uber to Trac-Mac in Paarden Eiland.

Tau Berger was waiting for her there, with his motorbike.

She had watched him, Saturday, during the planning meeting. He was quiet. Focused.

She had tried to compare this reticence to the story that Igen told her in Rome. About Tau's killing spree, his golf club fury. It didn't fit. Maybe it was like her own madness, the red fog of battle, in the hangar at Brits. When she shot Nicky Berry.

But when he led the way into the Trac-Mac store, when he helped her choose the crash helmet, motorcycle jacket and trousers, warm undershirt, neck warmer and gloves, the bantam-cock hyperactivity and intensity began to surface.

He talked swiftly, non-stop. 'On the bike, everything is ten degrees colder,' he said. 'Wind chill. Williston to Calvinia, early in the
morning, in the winter. Forty minutes at one-sixty, or faster, we're
talking about minus two, minus three degrees. Constantly, it creeps
up on you. You have to keep the wind out, you have to keep the
body heat in. Layers, that's all that works. Three layers, on the legs
and the torso. Four is even better. Cold is your enemy, cold is
trouble. Because cold means you lose concentration. Cold makes
your muscles stiff, and stiff means you miss the sticky on the door.
Light layers. Light and dense. Because we have to move, on the
bike, and afterwards . . .'

'What about boots?' she asked as they paid for their purchases.

'We won't buy boots here. Biker boots are useless if you have to
run. And when we hit the truck, we're going to have to run.'

She liked the way he thought.

Transaction complete, he told her to go to the fitting room and
put on the motorcycle gear.

'Why?'

'Time to practise.'

★ ★ ★

In the city, Griessel at the junction of Kloof and Rheede Street.
Thinking. Footwork. Door-to-door. But which doors? Why couldn't
he work out where Phiri went?

He knew this city. Especially this part of the city. Kloof Street was
basically Alexa's backyard. She often dragged him along for Saturday lunches at Cafè Paradiso or The Black Sheep. Sunday morning
shakshuka breakfast at Our Local. Occasionally a midweek burger at
Hudsons. Across from where he was standing they'd attended
Alcoholics Anonymous meetings in the Reformed Church before the
pandemic. Before it moved a few streets up, to Upper Union's NG
Church. Lifestyle on Kloof was where Alexa went grocery shopping
at Woollies, the Engen was where he filled up with petrol before he
drove to Stellenbosch.

But where would you go in Kloof Street if you were moving
money around and didn't want to be seen? Making transactions?
Apart from the office space at Workshop17?

Griessel closed his eyes, tried to picture it: Phiri and the body-guards parking here at Lifestyle on Kloof. And then walking down, towards the city centre.

Why had they parked here? Because they were lazy bastards. And didn't like walking far. He knew this because three hours later they drove barely seven hundred metres to Long Street, to be close to the drinking spots.

They parked here to be close to a specific location. Deliberately.

The camera showed them pass Tiger's Milk. Further down Kloof?

No. There was no reasonable money-moving destination further down. He just couldn't see it.

It was one of the side streets. It had to be. Rheede, Dorman or Beckham.

Footwork. He would fine-comb all these streets. One by one. Looking for cameras. Places that made sense.

He waited for the traffic, crossed Kloof, to walk down Rheede.

His cell phone rang. It was Vaughn.

'Benna, Basie Small's bank statements. The slippery sister lied.'

*   *   *

Chrissie was in her motorcycle gear, next to Tau's Africa Twin out-side Trac-Mac.

Tau took a plastic shopping bag out of the pannier. The contents weighed heavily in it.

He reached into the bag and took out a cardboard box, the kind you can buy at gift shops, in bright yellow. There was masking tape wrapped around it.

'Right,' said Tau. 'I jerry-rigged eight stickies. So we can practise.'

She saw that he had stuck a magnet on the flat bottom of the box, and on the top side a key ring on a piece of string.

'We're going to ride down the highway. Hold the bag in front of you, on your lap You're not going to be wearing your gloves, because you need to grip. I'll show you a car. You take a sticky out of the bag. When you're ready, tap me on the shoulder. I drive up to the car. You stick the sticky against the driver's door, with the magnet side. Then pull the ring, until the string comes loose. Then you slap my back. Hard. Because then I have to get the hell out of there before the sticky explodes. You with me?'

'Yes.'

He handed her the box to hold. It was heavier than she antici-
pated.

Tau said: 'Okay. The real sticky is going to be bigger. Heavier.
Stronger magnet. Easier. You're right-handed?'

'Yes.'

'You have to do all this with your left hand. In the cold. It's hard.
That's why we have to practise. Because we only get one chance. We
can't fuck up.'

'Okay. What's in the box?'

'A glass paperweight. And a note.'

'What does the note say?'

'Boom.'

She laughed. She liked Tau.

77

In Mbali Kaleni's office, Cupido arranged the bank statements in piles on the desk. Griessel and the colonel watched.

'Keep in mind,' said Cupido, 'his sister said he made fourteen million in five years, between 2014 and 2019. By training people, and fighting overseas. These statements . . .' and he pressed his index finger on one pile, '. . . are from that period. And sure enough, he made good money. A total of nine million bucks, coming in from overseas. And he paid tax on it too. Like a good boy.'

'And the other five million?' Kaleni asked.

'That's the conundrum, Colonel. That's the conundrum. These statements go back nine years. All the way to May in 2012. And in May of 2012, Arthur Thomas Small had a balance of just over four million in his account.'

'When he was still in the Defence Force?' Kaleni asked.

'Damn straight. That was seven months before he left the Recces. So, maybe there was a bit of cocaine smuggling after all. 'Cause why, how did he get that rich? I've asked the bank for more statements, we need to go further back in time. At least 2010. We have to know when exactly he won the lotto. The bank told me it's going to take another week. Maybe, if you could make a call, exert some pressure?'

'Which bank?'

'FNB.'

'I'll ask the director to call their CEO. You'll have your statements by tomorrow.'

'Thank you, Colonel.'

'But it's not cocaine, Vaughn.'

'Colonel, we don't know that.'

'It's not.'

'Why?'

'Brigadier Vincent Cambi at Joint Operations Division of the South African National Defence Force called you about Small's cocaine smuggling, right?'

'Yes.'

'He's a member of the Cabal, Vaughn. He's one of Joe Zaca's men. The cocaine is pure disinformation.'

Cupido wanted to use a swear word, but he knew The Flower would scold him. He just made a gesture of frustration.

Kaleni saw it, spoke calmly. 'The fact that Cambi lied to you, the fact that he's creating disinformation, is significant, Vaughn. It means he's hiding something, and it means Small is probably tied to state capture, one way or another. But not cocaine smuggling. We need to find the truth. And when we find the truth, we will find the connection between Small and Phiri, and we will find the motive for the killings. That's why we need the bank statements going back even further. To 2009. When Zaca became president. And I'll get them for you. By tomorrow.'

'Colonel, why didn't you tell us? About Cambi and the Cabal.'

'I told you what you needed to know, didn't I? That it was disinformation.'

Cupido shook his head.

'Vaughn, I am simply not at liberty to share everything the NPA knows or suspects. You know, the Cabal still has people everywhere. And your secondment is temporary. You have to understand that.'

'You don't trust us, Colonel?' Deeply hurt.

'*Hayi*,' said Kaleni. 'Of course I trust you. It's not that simple. I have to honour the pledge I made to the director. To be extremely careful and discreet. I told you all you needed to know, in terms of the investigation. That the cocaine smuggling was a smokescreen.'

Cupido sat down next to Griessel. His body language said he was giving up on the argument.

'You've done good work,' said Kaleni.

Cupido just nodded.

'Follow the money,' she said.

★ ★ ★

First time, Chrissie struggled.

On the motorbike they wove through the traffic on the N1, past Century City. Tau pointed to a Volkswagen Polo in front of them. She took out the box. Slapped Tau's shoulder. He drove up beside the car. She stretched out, planted the box, couldn't get a firm grip on the key ring. She saw the driver stare at her, then he swerved away.

Tau accelerated through the traffic.

With the second one, an old Nissan *bakkie*, she dropped the box before she could plant it.

On the third attempt, a Land Rover Discovery, everything went well, but her hands were cold, her fingers stiff. She took too long to get a grip on the key ring and pull it, forgetting to slap Tau on the back when she was done.

He took the exit to the shopping centre at N1 City, stopped at Caltex Vasco.

She got off and slid up her helmet visor. 'Sorry,' she said.

'Don't stress,' said Tau. 'That's why we practise. Take your time. Do the next five slowly.'

'Okay.' Grateful for his patience.

'Tomorrow I will make more. Bigger. Heavier.'

★ ★ ★

Cupido smacked the stack of bank statements down on his desk. 'It hurts, Benna. I mean, I get it, pledge of discretion, the walls have ears and all that jazz, but it still hurts.'

'I know,' said Griessel. 'But she's right.'

'Yes, yes.' Vaughn sat down. He spread the documents out, one by one. 'So. Let's follow the money . . .'

Griessel dragged his chair closer and sat next to Cupido.

They stared at the columns. Dates and amounts, codes and abbreviations.

'Two types of deposits into Small's account,' said Cupido. 'Local, from his investment, and overseas. Overseas payments are always in dollars. Same origin, every time, but we don't have a clue who did it. It's all just codes. How do you follow that?'

'Doc Duba,' said Griessel. 'Give her the codes.'

'No way. She's surely also made a pledge of discretion. We are fucking Hawks, *pappie*, temporary secondment or not. Rogue detectives.

On our own. We are going to google the hell out of these codes, until we can figure it out ourselves.'

★ ★ ★

With the seventh and eighth imitation sticky bombs, Chrissie placed them perfectly on the doors of a Kia Sportage and a Peugeot 3008, on the N1 between Brackenfell and Parow.

Tau gave her a thumbs-up. Then he drove to South African Military Surplus store in Stellenberg Road, Parow, so she could buy a pair of Black Delta boots.

When they dismounted from the motorcycle, she asked him if he wasn't worried that one of the drivers they'd targeted would take a photo of his licence plate.

'That number plate was still on a Checkers Sixty60 delivery bike last night,' said Tau with a manic grin. 'Tonight I'll steal another one.'

78

After three in the afternoon, Griessel and Cupido knew that all the forex payments to Basie Small's bank account between 2014 and 2019 came from a single source – an account at the APS bank on the island of Malta which belonged to a Maltese company called MilSec Solutions.

Cupido typed the name of the company into the Google search box. It didn't produce a single reference.

It took them another half-hour to find out there was a website, the Malta Business Registry, where they could enter the name of the company. All it provided was:

Company Registration Number: C 18667
Company Name: MilSec Solutions LTD
Registration Date: September 16, 2014
Registered Office: 24 Mancini Street
City/Locality: Birkirkara
Country: Malta

'Benna, what was that company that offered Small the military gig?'

Griessel had to consult his notebook. 'Vega Resources.'

'Remind me, that email said they were looking for him again? Because he did work for them previously?'

Again Griessel looked at the notes he had made at Lithpel Davids'.

'Yes. In 2019. In the Congo.'

'And yet, he was paid by MilSec Solutions in 2019. As he was every other time.'

'That's probably how Vega pays their people. Out of Malta.'

'Let's call Bones,' said Cupido. Lieutenant Colonel Benedict 'Bones' Boshigo was connected to the Statutory Crime Group of the Hawks Commercial Crime Branch in the Cape. A bigger expert about financial monkey business than anyone they knew.

Griessel nodded.

'Benna?'

'Yes?'

'Where's your mind, partner? You're just not in the game. Not even a little scrap of indignation when The Flower shafted us.'

'Sorry, Vaughn. It's just . . . The sister. When you called, and you say the slippery sister lied . . .'

'Yes?'

'*Jissis*, Vaughn, there's something she said. In our first interview, something that bothers me all the time. I know it's important, I know it's . . . there. Somewhere. That's where my mind is. I'm trying to remember, but I just can't get a handle on it.'

'It will come, partner, give it a chance. Take all the time you need. I'm calling Bones. So long.'

⋆ ⋆ ⋆

Eight kilometres east of the NPA offices, in a warehouse on Inyoni Street, Ndabeni, the large refrigerated fruit truck stood behind the closed doors. Beside Igen's *bakkie*.

At the back of the truck were the driver and his passenger, each with a 9mm Sig Sauer P226 pistol in hand, aimed at Themba Jola and Rousseau.

Nine armoury chests were neatly displayed on the cement floor, all open. Jola and Rousseau were inspecting the contents.

They counted: five AK-47s, each with two thirty-round magazines. Three soup-can-sized grenade launchers able to screw onto the front of an AK. A hundred boxes of ammo for the AKs – two thousand rounds in total. Twenty-four rust-brown RGD-5 hand grenades. Five MP-443 Grach pistols with a thousand 9mm Parabellum rounds. One box with twenty sticks of Russian PVV-5A plastic explosive. When they started to inspect the two RPG-30 'Kryuk' missiles and launchers, the big lights on the roof suddenly went out.

Everything was suddenly plunged into a deep twilight.

'Easy now,' said Themba. 'Just your usual four o'clock load-shedding.'

⋆ ⋆ ⋆

Lieutenant Colonel Benedict 'Bones' Boshigo earned his nickname because he looked like a living skeleton – a reed-thin long-distance athlete who'd completed the Comrades marathon nineteen times. His favourite Afrikaans word was '*nè*'.

'They do that, *nè*,' he told Cupido over the phone. 'A lot of the internationals, they have a shell or a subsidiary in Malta, or some other tax haven. For that very purpose. To pay less tax. Malta is popular, because it's cheap to set up the company, and annual fees are low. So, it's possible, *nè*.'

'Okay, I get that. But here's the conundrum, Bones . . .'

'They teach you big words at the ID, *nè*.'

'Who said we're at the ID?'

'Grapevine, Vaughn, you know how it works.'

'I can't confirm or deny.'

'What's the conundrum?'

'Vega Resources was founded in two thousand and one. When the Yanks were in Afghanistan. But this MilSec Solutions was only registered in 2014. Which is very convenient for a particular South African mercenary soldier, who just happened to start working overseas in 2014 . . .'

'That's a murky world, *nè*,' said Boshigo. 'Big, international military contractors. They change tax havens all the time. To stay ahead of the game. I won't bet big money that it means anything.'

'But wait. There's more,' said Cupido. 'MilSec Solutions was registered on the sixteenth of September 2014. My mercenary guy got his first payment on the thirtieth of September 2014. Coincidence? I think not.'

'Sounds a bit fishy,' said Bones.

'Damn straight. And, there's proof that my mercenary guy has a propensity for criminal behaviour. Crafty. *Skelm*. Bit of a psycho.'

79

'How was Tau?' asked Igen.

They were sitting in the Hussar Grill at Mouille Point, half past eight in the evening.

Chrissie shrugged. 'He was fine. Very focused, very patient. He wants this to work. It's hard to imagine it's the same guy that . . .'

'With Phiri?'

'Yes.'

'It's the same guy.'

'Maybe his anger is over now.'

'PTSD doesn't work like that,' said Igen.

She nodded. 'I know. But he was genuinely okay with me. There was just a moment, this afternoon . . .'

'What?'

'When he dropped me off at the apartment. I walked to the door and . . . You know how your subconscious kind of expects you to hear him ride off. You don't think about it, it's just, suddenly you realise, you haven't heard it. And when I looked around, he was just sitting there watching me. His eyes . . .'

'What?' asked Igen.

She didn't put it into words, just shivered.

'But that's all?'

'I can handle him.'

'I know you can.'

The waitress came to take their order. As she walked away again, Chrissie said: 'Do you remember, in Pretoria, after the *braai* at Brenner's, you gave me a lift?'

'I remember.'

'You asked me why I said yes to the robbery?'

'You said you wanted to leave before Africa broke your heart.'

'Why did *you* say yes to this one, Igen?'

He looked down, smiled.

The waitress brought his beer and her water. He took a slow swig. Chrissie knew he was buying time.

'Why are you asking about this one, and not the Brenner job?' said Igen.

'With the Brenner job, we were ninety per cent sure that no one would need to shoot. No one would die.'

'And yet . . .'

'You know what I mean,' said Chrissie. 'This one . . . It's unavoidable. The sticky on the *bakkie* . . . Those guys are dead.'

'Yes. I know.'

'So?'

'It's complicated.'

'Try me.'

He kept on turning the beer glass in his hands. 'There's the fact that the Brenner job is unfinished business. There's the issue that . . . I know you thought Brenner wasn't the most loveable guy in the world. But we walked a long road together, he and I. I kind of owe him. I don't want Brenner to have died for nothing . . .'

'The bond between soldiers.'

'Something like that. And then there's the issue of not making enough out the Brenner job to buy my farm in the Klein Karoo. A smallholding in Barrydale was never my dream.'

'But that's not all.'

'No, that's not all.'

She waited.

He looked outside, said: 'There's the numbing effect of two tours in Afghanistan, where you see and experience things and do things that make you . . . It's a funny thing, Flea. That process. Your enemy. You don't think about them as human beings any more. The Americans speak of "moral disengagement", of "the demonising of the enemy". That's how you can carry on doing what you have to do. To survive. The state capture guys, it's easy to do that with them. They are scum. They are looting this country, the damage they do is permanent, and the poor suffer the most. To demonise them, to take them out, is not hard.'

He took another swig of his beer.

'Thank you,' she said.

'For what?'

'For being honest. And a little bit vulnerable.'

He smiled. 'I'm still waiting to see you vulnerable.'

'It's not going to happen. Is that all? All the reasons why you're doing it?'

'No.'

'I think I know what the other is.'

'Oh?'

'You're an adrenaline junkie.'

'Yes.'

'And this is your thing. Your superpower. The planning and execution of the impossible.'

He smiled. And nodded. He said: 'And you, Flea of my heart, why are you doing this one?'

'Don't call me that.'

'Flea? Or of my heart?'

'Both.'

'Okay. Why did you say yes to this one, Christina Jaeger?'

'Heracles,' she said.

'Heracles?'

'There is nothing so fucking intense as standing still while the lion charges, Igen. Nothing.'

80

At a quarter to five on Tuesday morning, Griessel woke to the sound of rain drumming on the roof.

Alexa was fast asleep beside him, her breathing even, her hand resting softly on his shoulder.

Last night she'd played Willie Dixon to him on the hi-fi, brought two big mugs of hot chocolate and snuggled under his arm on the sofa. 'I'm so looking forward to being Alexa Griessel,' she said, with relish.

Alexa Griessel.

It hadn't even crossed his mind that she would want to change her surname. The idea affected him in a strange way. She was a household name, a brand. Alexa *Griessel*. He felt the pressure of it, a vague discomfort, at the weight and enormity of it. An added sense of responsibility that he couldn't explain.

He shouldn't dwell on such things now; it just messed with his mind.

He'd better get his ass into working gear.

Emilia Streicher.

What was it that she'd said?

And Kloof Street.

Where had Phiri gone?

⋆　⋆　⋆

On the N2 on the way to work, in the pouring rain, Cupido called Bones Boshigo again.

'Hey, I was wondering, last night, Bones, if you wanted to register a company in Malta, do you have to go to Malta? Do you have to do it there?'

'Like in physically being in Malta?'

'Yes.'

'Not necessarily.'

'Bingo. 'Cause why, my guy never clocked in to Malta. So, how do you it? How do you register a company in Malta, when you've never been there?'

'You work through Maltese consultants, usually a law firm, *né*? Through the Internet. There are a lot of them. They would need a copy of your passport, a bank reference, proof of address, that sort of thing. Digital copies, certified, would do the job.'

'The proof of address. That address could be anywhere? South African too?'

'Yeah. For the initial registration. But your Maltese company must eventually have a Maltese address. The law firm will arrange that for you, it's really just a postal address, a letter drop.'

'And you never have to go there?'

'Only if you really want to.'

'*Djas*. Thanks, Bones.'

'*Djas*?'

'That's how we youngsters roll, Bones. That means "cool".'

'*Né*.'

* * *

Just before eight, Griessel found a parking space in front of the main entrance of the Kloof Street Hotel, which is not in Kloof, but in Rheede.

It was raining. He got out, locked the car, jogged to reach cover. He stopped suddenly, took three steps back, looked again. There was a sign on the pillar in front of the hotel, with a camera icon on it, and the words *These Premises Are Protected by CCTV Cameras*.

He walked into the hotel, clocked the camera on the wall behind the front desk. It faced the street.

* * *

Chrissie was towelling her hair dry, still in her underwear, when Igen called.

'New plan,' he said. 'It's going to rain all day, you and Tau aren't practising stickies. But put on your biker gear anyway, I'll pick you up in half an hour.'

'What for?'

'I'll tell you on the way,' and he hung up.

She was relieved. She hadn't been looking forward to a day on the motorcycle in this weather.

★   ★   ★

The purpose of the camera at the Kloof Street Hotel front desk was to cover the reception area – and people entering and exiting the front door.

But Rheede Street outside was visible. Slightly overexposed in the daylight, completely underlit at night. The image quality was too poor, the distance between camera and the opposite side of the street too great, to be able to identify individuals beyond reasonable doubt.

Unless you knew what you were looking for.

And Benny Griessel knew. He was looking for Dineo Phiri and his bodyguards. Who might have walked past the previous Thursday afternoon between eleven minutes past four and half past five, in broad daylight.

And he found them.

Fourteen minutes past four, on the other side of the street, moving in an easterly direction. The faces were unrecognisable, but it was definitely that trio, in formation, in the right shades of fancy clothes.

And then they turned right, just before they would have disappeared from the image. Right into Faure Street.

Faure Street? He had never been in Faure Street in his life.

As far as he knew, there was nothing to see in Faure Street.

He thanked the hotel manager and jogged out, crossing the street. Right into Faure, the rain sifting down as he quickened his pace. Barely twenty metres from the corner of Rheede, on his left, he spotted the discreet sign on the wall of a renovated white-painted Victorian building which might once have been a grand mansion.

Safestore. Your personal vault.

There was a steel gate with a camera eye, a code panel and a call button.

He pressed the button. The rain sluiced down, drenching his hair, his shoulders.

'Yes?'

'Police. Please open.'

'Show me your ID.'

He took out his identification card, wiped the raindrops off the camera eye with his thumb, and held out the card.

⋆ ⋆ ⋆

The lobby of Safestore was practically empty – just the two security men in black uniforms behind a counter. Griessel, dripping over the grey tiled floor, said: 'I want to know if a Dineo Phiri rents a safe from you.'

The older one of the two shook his head. 'We will have to call management.'

'Thank you,' said Griessel.

The man was reluctant. 'It's confidential information.'

'This is a murder investigation,' said Griessel.

The man picked up the phone and dialled.

Griessel took out his own phone, looked for the picture of Phiri. He showed it to the younger man. 'Have you seen this guy here before?'

The way the security man looked at his colleague was all the answer Griessel needed.

81

Down Helen Suzman Drive the rain was a curtain and the windscreen wipers in Igen's *bakkie* juddered back and forth.

'Can you turn the heater down?' asked Chrissie. She was perspiring in her motorcycle outfit and its four layers of clothing.

'Sure,' said Igen, adjusting the climate control. 'Better?'

'Thanks.'

'Right,' he said. 'About today. What I'm going to tell you, you need to visualise. See it in your mind's eye. Every night, in your bed, see it your mind: you and Tau are on the bike. Behind the shotgun truck. Just past the Ceres turn-off, you plant the sticky . . .'

'Why the sticky, Igen? There are other ways.'

'The chances are very good they will be armoured. Bulletproof windows, armour in the bodywork.'

'Will the sticky be enough?'

'What Themba makes will be more than enough.'

'Okay.'

'So, you plant the sticky. Tau opens the throttle. Ahead of you I pull the sheep lorry across the road to stop the truck, Themba parks the police van across the road behind the truck. You pass Themba and the police van, Tau stops just behind the truck. Themba gives him an AK because he couldn't carry it on the bike with him. But don't you worry about that. The airfield gate is directly on your left. Get off the bike, take off your helmet, you can take off your jacket, just leave it there. Speed is everything. No matter what happens behind you and around you, just run through the gate, down the road, to the small building at the airfield. There's only one building, small, white, three metres by three metres. If you hear shots, you hear explosions, don't worry, run to that building. It's about a hundred metres from the road. Behind it you'll find the forklift. Start the forklift, and bring it. If you see it's all a fuckup, we're dead, ditch the forklift and run to the Dak. Do you understand?'

She nodded.

'No saving our asses. You hear?'

'I hear.'

'Right. You and Tau will have pistols with you, on the bike, but we'll leave you an AK in the forklift. If everything's fucked up and someone's coming after you, use the AK while running to the Dak. Okay?'

'Okay.'

'You see it all in your mind?'

'Yes.'

'If we're not fubar, then bring the forklift to the road, as fast as it can go. To the back of the container. Themba and I will be inside the container, we'll push the gold crates to the back. You load the crate on the forklift, and drive to the Dak. First time Tau will go with you, he has to help with loading into the Dak. You come to the Dak, you lift the crate, up to the door. Tau and Jer drag it in. When the crate is down, you race the forklift back to the truck. If you see there's trouble, you leave the forklift, you run to the Dak. Tell me you understand that part.'

'I understand.'

'You see it? In your mind.'

'Yes, Igen, I fucking see it.'

'Right. Then you drive back to the road, pick up another crate. Until Themba or I say it's done, our time is up. Or you see it's a fuckup, you leave the forklift, you run to the Dak.'

'Okay.'

'What we're going to do now: we're renting a warehouse in Ndabeni. The forklift came this morning. I assume you don't have a clue how to operate a forklift.'

She nodded.

'You're going to practise. All day.'

'To run when there's a fuckup?'

He laughed. He said: 'Reason why you're wearing your biker clothes is . . .'

'Yes, I know. That's how I'm going to be dressed during the Op. Don't mansplain.'

'Okay. Sorry. Old habit.'

★ ★ ★

Lieutenant-Colonel Mbali Kaleni did not arrive with the search warrant until after nine.

Griessel and Cupido were waiting for her, along with the depot manager of Safestore, a lawyer and the two security people.

The lawyer studied the warrant. He nodded to the depot manager.

'This Phiri guy didn't rent space under his name,' said the depot manager. 'It's under a company.'

'What company?' Kaleni asked.

'Morago Trading.'

'Show us the space.'

'We couldn't do that. There's a code on the door. Only the client has the code.'

'*Hayi*,' said Kaleni angrily. 'What do you do when the client loses the code?'

The depot manager looked at the lawyer. The lawyer sighed.

'We have the code,' said Griessel.

They all looked at him.

'It's ten digits, right?' asked Cupido.

'Yes.'

Griessel took out his notebook.

'Show us which door,' said Kaleni.

★ ★ ★

Griessel read out the numbers from the card they'd found in Dineo Phiri's safe. Cupido typed them in.

The door clicked open.

'Thank you, you can go now,' said Kaleni to the manager, the lawyer and the two security personnel.

They reluctantly turned and left.

Griessel pushed open the door.

82

'It's really easy,' said Themba to Chrissie in a loud voice, because it was raining hard on the tin roof. 'You have one forward gear, a neutral and a reverse, here,' and he tapped the lever to the left of the steering wheel.

She was sitting in the forklift, Themba standing beside her.

Igen, Yon and Tau were spectators, some distance away in the large warehouse.

'We have a problem,' said Igen.

'She looks fine,' said Yon.

'No, not her. The forklift. Themba said top speed is twenty kilometres per hour, but with a pallet of gold she'll be lucky to get fifteen. It's too slow. She has to go from the truck to the Dak . . .'

'It's not a Dak, it's a Basler,' said Yon. 'Big difference.'

'I know, Jer. She has to go from the truck to the Dak. The Dak will be at the end of the airstrip, the closest point to the gate . . .'

'Eastern end, and we pray for a westerly wind,' said Yon.

'It's half a kilometre from the truck. It takes her . . .' He tried to do the mental arithmetic.

'Two minutes, if she can get fifteen kilos an hour,' said Yon immediately.

'Jeez. You're good,' said Tau Berger.

'Two minutes is a problem,' said Igen. 'Because it all adds up: let's say, two minutes to load the pallet from the truck. Two minutes to the Dak . . .'

'The Basler.'

'Jer, please. Two more minutes to offload. Two minutes back. It's eight minutes per pallet, from truck to Dak and back again. Four pallets, thirty-two minutes. It's too long. Add the time from the moment that we take out the shotguns, and we're talking about almost three quarters of an hour. The police will be well on their way there. Or already there.'

'What's the solution?' asked Jericho Yon.

'Another forklift. With Tau driving. But that will mean you're alone in the Dak to load.'

'Not a problem,' said Yon. 'There's a winch up in the Basler's cargo hold. They load in, I connect the winch, I pull up the pallet and I wait for the next one.'

'You sure?'

'Yes. It's going to be fine. We should rather worry about the rain.'

'Why?' asked Tau.

'The landing strip at Skoorsteenberg,' said Yon. 'It's gravel. If that gets wet, it's mud. If I skid on the landing . . . The Basler is a tail-dragger, at least that should help . . .'

'Shit,' said Tau.

In the forklift, Themba tapped the lever just to the right of the steering wheel: 'Left lever is up and down. Next one is your tilt, and this one is side to side. OK. Start her up.'

★ ★ ★

In the centre of the Safestore walk-in safe there was a work surface, like an island, neatly constructed from stainless steel and polished maple wood.

The shelves, from floor to ceiling, covered all four walls, made of the same material.

The vault was empty. Except for a laptop on the middle shelf against the opposite wall. A cellular modem stick was inserted into a USB port. Beside it, the computer's power cable, neatly rolled up.

'Bingo,' said Cupido. 'Less is more.'

'I'll go fetch my gloves,' said Griessel.

'Benny,' said Mbali Kaleni, 'this is brilliant work.'

'Yes,' said Cupido. 'Not bad for temporary secondments.'

★ ★ ★

Christina Jaeger loaded an empty pallet with the forklift on one side of the warehouse, driving at maximum speed across the concrete floor to the other end, and offloaded it. Then she repeated the process. Back and forth, back and forth.

In the middle of the space Themba, Igen, Yon and Tau stood and watched her.

'She's a natural,' said Themba.

'You'll have to teach Tau as well,' said Igen. 'One forklift is going to take too long. We'll have to get another one. That he has to operate.'

'Now you tell me. Four days to go.'

'Sorry. My bad.'

'We'll have to buy one, Ig. Cash. Second-hand. That way, maybe we can avoid the paperwork.'

★ ★ ★

They had to wait for Malime Duba and her team to analyse the Phiri computer. Which could take all day, because Duba said the security that Phiri used on it was good.

Griessel and Cupido, each at their own desk, heads bent. Benny did the admin for the new ID docket, filed the search warrant and his latest notes.

Cupido had the photocopies of Basie Small's passport in front of him. He systematically worked through it.

Griessel heard him cry out in triumph: '*Aitsa!*'

'What?'

'Come look here.'

Griessel stood up and went over to him.

Cupido had a sheet of paper in front of him, lined with four columns. 'I just wanted to check first, if Small had ever been near Malta. And then, when he did work, when did MilSec pay him? Just to get a clear picture in my head The problem with a passport, Benna, is lazy customs people just stamp it wherever they choose. Nothing in sequence, many, many stamps, higgledy-piggledy, all *deurmekaar*. You have to check carefully. So that is what I did.'

'Okay.'

Cupido pointed to the columns. 'This one is the dates that Small left the country. Next one is date of arrival in the other country. America, UK, Congo, Mozambique, Iraq, right?'

'Right.'

'This column is the date of when he checked out of that country again, the last one is the stamp when he was back in South Africa.'

'Okay.'

'A bit of a conundrum, Benna. Because our Arthur Thomas Small was never over there for more than two weeks at a time. In the Congo, Moz and Iraq, less than a week. And yet, MilSec paid him a million bucks every time. For five days of work? That's fishy, Benna. That is very fishy. Hence the "*aitsa*".'

83

In a swish office in Lynnwood, Pretoria, the investment broker told Emilia Streicher it wasn't a good idea to sell ComfortAir now. The current economic climate, load-shedding and the poor performance of the company over the past twelve months meant there would be little interest. And a very poor price.

'It doesn't matter,' Emilia said. 'I want to sell. My brother has recently passed away. I'm the only heir. I don't need the money.'

The woman offered her condolences, gave her documents to sign, and promised to do her best with the sale.

Emilia headed over to Tashas at Lynnwood Bridge for cake and coffee. Her cell phone rang. When she took it out of her handbag she saw it was the detective. Griessel. Her stomach clenched.

She took a deep breath. 'Hello, Warrant,' she said.

'Afternoon, ma'am. How are you?'

'Not good, Warrant. My brother is still in your mortuary and no one at the Gangs Unit is returning my calls.'

'I'm really sorry, ma'am. I'll see what I can do.'

'Thank you.'

'Ma'am, I'm calling to find out if you are going to be back in the Cape soon.'

'Why?'

'We still have a few questions about the docket.'

'I thought the Gangs Unit were on the case now?'

'Yes, it's their case, ma'am. We're engaged in the handover process, and just wanted to clear up a few last things.'

'What things?'

'About Mr Small's work overseas.'

'I already told you what he did.'

'Madam, the dates of his foreign visits don't make sense to us.'

It took a moment for the shock of it to wash over her. And she thought, not now, not so close to Saturday. She had to buy time, one way or another she must gain time.

'I . . . I have to be in Cape Town on Thursday.'

She held her breath, she listened carefully, could he hear she was lying?

'When on Thursday?' asked Griessel.

He believed her, she thought he believed her.

'I should be in Stellenbosch by noon.'

'We will pick you up at the airport, ma'am. What time do you land?'

'I don't know anything about Basie's travel dates, Warrant. I don't know if I'll be able to help.'

'We would still like to talk, please.'

She hesitated for a fraction of a second, her brain whirring frantically. 'Ten o'clock? I think it'll be around ten o'clock, I'll have to check. I'm not at the office now.'

'Would you Whatsapp me the flight and the time?'

'Yes.'

'Thank you, ma'am. Goodbye.'

She stood stock still, petrified, the phone to her ear, in the middle of the little square. She had to think, she had to think.

She would have to book a flight. Now. Because if she forwarded the flight number and time, Griessel would be able to check with the airline.

She couldn't tell Tau about this. He would ask what was wrong with Basie's travel dates. And he must never find out about that.

On Thursday she would call Griessel. Thursday morning. And tell him sorry, the estate, Basie's estate, there were urgent things she had to sign. She wouldn't be able to be there until Saturday.

And on Saturday she would be on a flight to Kuala Lumpur.

Where not even Tau Berger could find her.

It was because of him that she was leaving the country. Because of what Basie had told her about Tau back in the day. His recklessness. His unpredictability. Now Phiri's murder. She had read about it, in *Rapport*, that Sunday after Phiri's death.

It frightened her, that horrific violence.

And now, just how casually Tau had said he was going to take out the entire gold heist team. The girl too. *No loose ends, Emilia. Trust no one.*

Tau's share had to be paid into Basie's foreign account. She still had access, until he got his money. And then? Then she was just another loose end too. Someone who knew the whole story. Someone who was no longer of any use.

She turned and ran to her car.

84

Griessel sat with the phone in his hand, staring out of the window, at the Rook Cycles shop on the corner across Bree Street.

'What did she say?' asked Cupido.

Benny didn't answer, his mind on the call. And the connection that he'd suddenly made.

'Benna?'

'She . . . She's coming to the Cape on Thursday. We'll meet her at the airport,' he said, his mind clearly elsewhere.

'Hey, why so pensive, partner?'

'I think I . . . Just wait . . .' Griessel scrabbled for his notebook among the paperwork on his table. He found it, started flipping through it. 'The day we interviewed her in Stellenbosch. With us. In the parade room . . .'

'Yes?'

'Just wait . . .' Griessel flicked the pages until he found his notes. He read quickly, knowing he had to be sure.

Then he found what he'd been looking for. 'Here it is!' he said, and stood up, excited. He walked up to Cupido, notebook in hand. 'Now, when I was talking to her, on the phone. She was the same . . . She was stressed, Vaughn. I could hear it, in her voice. And then I remembered. Since that day, in Stellenbosch, something bothered me. And every time I try to remember, then I think it's because of you . . .'

'Because of me? Partner, you've lost me.'

'Okay, okay. Do you remember asking her why Small left the army?'

'Yes. Kind of . . .'

'And she said . . .' Griessel read from the notebook, '. . . "standards under the new government weren't what he believed in." Remember?'

'Yes, I remember.'

'And then I noticed she was uncomfortable, the way she touched her head like that, and I thought that's what some white people do when they criticise the government in front of a man of colour.'

'True that.'

'But that's the mistake I made. Every time I try to remember what it was that bothered me, then I think it was that moment. Because with interrogation, we try to read people, we look for signs of lying.'

'Check.'

'But it's what happened right after that that made her stressed. That made her lie.'

'Remind me.'

'Her phone rang. And then she looked at her phone, and then she put it down. And then she said something about "it's a friend". That's what bothered me. How she said it. And why she said it . . .'

'Slight over-elaboration.'

'Exactly. And . . . Now, over the phone, it was the same tone. Same stress. She said . . . I told her, the dates of Basie's overseas visits don't make sense to us. The logical reply would be "I don't know anything about that", or "I'll have to think". But first she was silent, and then she said: "I have to be in Cape Town on Thursday." In that exact same tone. Stressed. Afraid.'

★ ★ ★

'No,' said Mbali Kaleni. 'It's too flimsy.'

'Colonel, you have to trust Benna's instinct,' said Cupido.

'As much as I admire Benny, I am not taking his instinct to a judge for a 205 subpoena. If you want to invade a grieving woman's privacy, you will have to bring me more.'

'We just want to look at her calls received on that specific day, Colonel,' said Cupido. 'Just that day. That's not invasion of privacy if she has nothing to hide.'

'No. I'm sorry. Bring me more.'

Griessel's cell phone made a sound.

It was a WhatsApp message from Emilia Streicher: *FlySafair FA604. Landing at 11:20.*

★ ★ ★

Igen took Chrissie back to her apartment, at a quarter to six in the afternoon. It was almost dark, the rain no longer falling, but the sky was dark and ominous, rush hour traffic heavy.

They drove in silence.

'Are you okay?' she asked him.

'Tell me again: if you see it's all a fuckup, we're fubar, what do you do?'

It made her angry. 'You can't do that, Ig.'

'What?'

'Worry more about me than about the Op. You focus on your job, I focus on mine. What happened in Rome doesn't count on Saturday. Do you understand?'

He just stared at the car in front of him.

★ ★ ★

Griessel was in the lift, on the way to his car in the basement of the NPA building, when Fritz called.

'Pa, we have to practise the song tomorrow night. I talked to Uncle Vince, we'll meet the band at the MOTH. Seven o'clock.'

The MOTH hall in Woodstock was where RUST usually practised.

'Fritz, I might have to work. Our investigation is now at a difficult . . .'

'No, Pa, I'm not going to make a fool of myself in front of everyone on Saturday. Please. Just half an hour.'

'I . . . Okay, I'll make a plan.'

85

Wednesday morning's sky was clear and deep blue, the day bright as crystal. The sea still bore the after-effects of the cold front – massive, leaden-grey waves broke over the thousands of dolosse on the sea front behind the big parking area at Victoria Quay.

That's where Tau Berger now stood, beside the stolen and delivered black-and-silver BMW F750 GS with its silver aluminium panniers on either side and a top box behind.

Three days to Operation Gold.

Tau gave Chrissie the new fake magnet bomb. Slightly larger than a brick, twice the size of the one they'd practised with on Monday. The metal ring, attached to a stronger cord, was also significantly wider. And this one had a plastic handle on the side – like what you'd find on kitchen cupboards.

'This is exactly how Themba has made the genuine one,' he said. 'Same size, same weight. With the handle, because this one is too wide to hold in one hand.'

She took it from him with her left hand, gripping the handle. It was considerably heavier. An ominous dead weight.

'Saturday,' said Tau. 'We're behind the shotgun truck, we've left Calvinia. You are already holding the handle in your left hand, like this, between us, on your lap. I wait for the shotgun *bakkie* to reach the turn-off. I open up, reach the side of the *bakkie*. You make sure the ring doesn't hook on anything. You press the magnetic side to the door, and pull the ring as hard as you can, you hit me on my back. Loud and clear, I have to be sure. Then we have five seconds to get the hell out . . .'

'Five seconds?'

'It's longer than you think. That's all we need. We don't want to give them time to pull the sticky off. Okay, then you prepare yourself, bend low, because the blast wave can be quite fierce and shrapnel is a possibility. Not big, but it's there. The top box should protect you.'

'Why did we practise with small stickies on Monday?'

'Because small is difficult. If you have confidence with the smaller one, then the big one is easy. Are you ready?'

She nodded.

'Same as last time. I point out the car. You hit my shoulder to say you understand. Then I drive up to him. Immediately. I want to put pressure on you, so you can get used to it. You stick the sticky, pull the ring hard, the cord *must* come loose. Then you slap my back.'

★   ★   ★

Phiri's laptop wasn't the big breakthrough, but it laid a solid foundation.

In the large room of the National Prosecuting Authority's Information Management Centre Malime Duba told Mbali Kaleni, Cupido and Griessel that they'd worked through the night to unravel the various levels of encryption. From the computer's interface, and the multiple folders and files in which Phiri kept the account numbers, PIN and access codes.

But when they finally succeeded, they could expose Phiri laundering money step by step – the bank accounts, the massive sums, the network of holding and shell companies, investments, payments and quite a number of those involved.

'Wonderful, wonderful,' said Mbali Kaleni.

Duba said the one that really excited her was the evidence of the monthly settlement of ex-president Joseph Zaca's accounts at his respective lawyers and advocates. Now they knew how he was able to afford his extended legal battle.

'Are there any payments directly to Zaca?' Kaleni asked.

'We haven't found anything yet.'

'Any payments to an Arthur Thomas Small?' asked Griessel.

'No.'

'What about a company called MilSec?' asked Cupido.

Duba looked at her list. 'No.' She noted their disappointment. 'Please give us more time. We are now researching ownership of all the companies, and trying to trace all the payments. The problem is, we can only see the financial history of the past eighteen to twenty-four months. Anything older than that, we will have to request archive statements. And we are worried that such an act

could alert whoever might have taken over the laundering from
Dineo Phiri.'

★   ★   ★

The breakthrough came at lunchtime. When Cupido finally received
Basie Small's bank statements for the period 2010 to 2012 by email.

Griessel was sitting at his desk, eating the Woollies sandwich that
Alexa had packed for him. He heard Cupido shout: 'Yes!'

Cupido pressed his index finger to the screen, turned to Griessel.
'Yes, *pappie*, yes, yes, yes. Thirtieth of November, 2011. Five
fucking million.'

'*Bliksem*,' said Griessel, putting down his sandwich and getting
up. He wanted to see for himself.

'Amen, Benna. It's a single deposit, into Small's account. Five
million one hundred rand, to be precise. From something called
Lago Holdings.'

Cupido jumped up, ran to the door. 'I knew it. I knew it. Slippery
sister, *pappie*, we're going to nail her.'

'Where are you going?' asked Griessel.

'Doc Duba. I want to know if Lago Holdings was one of Phiri's
money laundering companies.'

Griessel jogged after him.

★   ★   ★

'And lo and behold, Colonel,' said Cupido to Mbali Kaleni. 'Lago
Holdings is a Cabal company, right there, still active on Phiri's laptop. Still the same Dubai bank account. Phiri paid Small, thirteen
months before he left the Recces. In dollars. Which translated to five
million bucks. There's your connection between the murders, right
there.'

'*Hayi*,' said Kaleni, leaning back in her office chair.

'We don't know what it means, but we'll get there. Once the sister
spills the beans.'

'This is proof,' said Griessel. 'She lied to us.'

'We want those phone records, Colonel. Surely, this is enough for
the subpoena.'

'Maybe. The judge will have to decide. But you can go try.'

'Thank you, Colonel.'

'We'll confront her tomorrow, Colonel. She's coming to Cape Town.'

Griessel thought about the anxiety in Emilia Streicher's voice. He thought how smoothly she'd lied. He said: 'I'll have to check that she actually did make the booking.'

86

In the warehouse in Ndabeni, Igen Rousseau and Themba Jola unpacked the firearms, and cleaned them one by one, oiling and testing the mechanisms. Loading the magazines.

They were inspecting the two RPG-30 'Kryuk' missile launchers when Chrissie banged on the big steel door just after four.

Igen went to unlock the door for her.

As Tau rode in on the BMW, Igen asked: 'And?'

'Twelve astonished *bakkie* drivers in the Cape today,' said Chrissie.

He laughed. 'Twelve out of twelve?'

She nodded, pleased with her success.

Tau dismounted, removed his helmet. He looked at the RPGs. 'You know that thing will blow a truck to hell and gone.'

'It's just insurance,' said Themba. 'In case they are armoured. Ever used one?'

'Once or twice,' said Tau. 'In the Congo. Just for fun. Took them off the rebels.'

'Show me,' said Igen.

★ ★ ★

They didn't get the Section 205 subpoena signed until after five, because the details of the case were complicated, and the judge sceptical. Cupido did his best to charm her, but it didn't help. She adapted the application, limiting their access to Emilia Streicher's phone records to the past month.

'That's all we're looking for, Judge,' said Cupido. 'Thank you.'

He finally received a lukewarm smile.

They drove to work to send the subpoena to MTN. The mobile phone company supervisor on duty said he would do his best, but it was after hours, they wouldn't be able to provide the records until the following morning.

★　★　★

Griessel was late for band practice because Alexa wanted to talk about wedding arrangements first.

'Did you make an appointment for your hair?'

'Not yet. I'll just run into a salon tomorrow morning, there's one around the corner, in Church Street.'

'Benny, it's important . . .'

'Alexa, I have to go, I have an appointment with Fritz. Can we talk later?'

'Did Vaughn put the rings somewhere safe?'

'I'm sure he did.'

'His speech?'

'He will be ready,' hoping Cupido had remembered.

'Remember to pack the bag.'

'Okay.' He kissed her. 'See you just now.'

'Enjoy it,' she said.

★　★　★

He opened the front door of the MOTH hall. The silence in the foyer made him uneasy. Usually the band members were there before him, already busy tuning up and strumming away.

He opened the inner door.

Cupido pounced on him. 'Stag party, Benna!' he yelled.

On the stage, behind Vaughn, loud cheering erupted. Then the band started to play.

Cupido also ran to the stage.

Benny saw Fritz there, bass guitar around his neck, huge smile on his face.

Alongside the RUST band members Vince Fortuin, Japie Blom and Jakes Jacobs, stood his former colleagues from the Hawks. Frankie Fillander, the new acting chief of his old unit. Philip van Wyk. Vusi Ndabeni. Mooiwillem Liebenberg. Bones Boshigo, Lithpel Davids. And Thick and Thin from Forensics.

They all sang together. A Sonny Terry and Brownie McGhee song, one of his all-time favourites.

When they got to 'You just a white boy lost in the blues . . .', Benny Griessel did his damnedest to keep it together.

They had done all this for him.

And then he heard how out of tune Vaughn was singing, and he had to laugh.

87

Griessel walked to the hair salon in Church Street just before eight on Thursday morning in the hope that if he was early they would be able to help him out quickly. Because he'd forgotten to make an appointment.

His thoughts were on last night.

The whole thing had been Vaughn's idea. He'd arranged everything, invited everyone. An alcohol-free stag party with music – the world where his comrade Benny Griessel was most happy. So that he could play the blues with his son and his band mates, could laugh and chat with his former colleagues, his people. And when he thanked Vaughn after one in the morning, Vaughn hugged him and said: 'That's what you do for your brother.'

Griessel walked to the car with his heart overflowing.

Cupido called after him: 'And don't worry about my speech on Saturday. It's going to be brilliant.'

On the corner of Bree and Church, twenty metres from the salon, Griessel's phone rang.

It was the man from MTN. He was calling to confirm he had just sent Emilia Streicher's cell phone records for the past month to Benny's email address at the ID.

Griessel said thank you. Stopped in his tracks. Emilia was landing in three hours. There was no time to waste. He turned and jogged back to the office.

*　*　*

Hastily printing out the call register, he and Vaughn took it to Dr Duba.

The first call he was looking for was the one that Emilia Streicher received during their interview on Wednesday, 26 May, somewhere between ten and eleven in the morning in the parade room at the Stellenbosch detectives' offices.

Griessel found it. He called the number on his cell phone, Duba typed it into the system.

It rang. Nobody answered.

'Not registered,' said Duba. 'It's a burner.'

Griessel's shoulders slumped, deflated. That was the call that had rattled Emilia.

'One of the burners that called Phiri too?' Cupido asked hopefully.

'Let me check . . .'

They waited.

'No,' she finally said.

'Damn,' said Cupido.

'That same number called Streicher several times,' said Griessel. 'On Wednesday, Thursday, and Friday. Could we trace the locations?'

'Let me see what I can do.'

Griessel ran his finger through the call register, hopefully: there must be something there. He recognised his own number, the calls he made on Tuesday, 25 May, to let Emilia know her brother had passed away, at 11:51. And when she called him back later.

He saw Emilia had called two numbers within three minutes of their first conversation. The first was apparently unanswered, no indication of duration. She made the second call less than a minute afterwards.

He called the first number.

A man answered. 'Hello?'

'Good morning. I'm Warrant Officer Benny Griessel of the National Prosecuting Authority Investigative Directorate in Cape Town. Who am I talking to now?'

'It's Robbie.'

'And your last name?'

'Reed.'

'Mr Reed, on May twenty-fifth at 11:54 you received a call on this number from a Mrs Emilia Streicher . . .'

'No, it wasn't me . . . You . . . The Investigative Directorate? I thought the Hawks in PE took over the investigation.'

'The Hawks in PE?'

'Yes. Gqeberha. Port Elizabeth. And it seems to me they are useless . . .'

'Sir, what investigation are you talking about?'

'My brother. Dewey.'

'What about him?'

'They shot him dead. Farm murder. On the day you mentioned. Twenty-fifth of May. This is his phone.'

'It's . . . My sympathy for your loss, Mr Reed.'

'Thank you. Are you taking over the investigation now? Because we hear nothing from the Hawks.'

'We are investigating the murder of Mrs Streicher's brother. Basie Small.'

'Basie Small? He's dead?'

'That's right. He was killed on the twenty-fourth of May. In Stellenbosch. You didn't know? It was all over the media.'

'I work in England, sir . . . Tell me your name again?'

'Benny Griessel.'

'I work in Bristol, Benny. I didn't get back here until Monday. For the funeral yesterday. Do you think there's a connection? Between Dewey and Basie?'

'Mr Reed, how do you know Basie Small?'

'I only know him from Dewey's stories. They were in the Recces together. Left together too. Ten years ago.'

Griessel's pulse quickened. 'What did your brother do afterwards? When he left the Recces?'

'He bought a game farm. Iinyathi Hunting Lodge. Past Humansdorp. He specialised in birds, for shooting. There's quite a demand, from overseas. Wild birds. Wild ducks, Egyptian geese, guinea fowl, partridges . . . He had everything on the farm. And he led safaris now and then. To Namibia. Zambia, Botswana. The bush was his life.'

'Do you know if he'd ever been to the Congo?'

'No.'

'Iraq?'

'No.'

'England or America?'

'No. Tell me, do you think there's a connection?'

'Yes. We just don't know how it works yet. Do you know why your brother left the Recces, back then?'

'He said the army's standards were no longer what they used to be. And they gave him a golden handshake. Big money.'

88

'Mr Reed,' said Griessel, 'there's one thing I don't understand. It was in all the papers that Basie Small was an ex-Recce. And your brother was killed one day later, but no one in the media made the connection that another ex-Recce was killed . . .'

Griessel saw Cupido trying to get his attention, waving frantically.

He held up his palm to show, not now, just wait, he wanted to finish the conversation first.

'Benny, how do you know someone wasn't in the Recces?' Robbie Reed asked.

'I don't know.'

'When he tells you he was. Recces don't walk around telling people they were in the Special Forces. Neither did Dewey. In Humansdorp people only knew him as a hunter.'

* * *

Robbie Reed said he was flying back to England the next day, but would Griessel please keep him informed if there were developments. He gave him his UK phone number, and hung up.

Griessel looked at the Cupido, fizzing with excitement.

'We have a golf connection, Benna,' said Vaughn, pointing at Duba's computer screen.

Griessel got up and went to look. On the *About Us* web page of the Clarens Golf and Leisure Estate was a photograph of a man in his fifties, with long yellow-blond hair, a bushy blond beard, tanned face and a white Titleist golf cap on his head. Unsmiling, he stared with manic intensity at the camera. The headline read: *Meet our greenkeeper – Evert 'Tau' Berger.*

'That's the *ou* she called next?'

'*Yebo, pappie.* RICA's database says his address is number five Kgwadi Street, Clarens Golf and Leisure Estate.'

'Clarens?' asked Duba. 'In the Free State?'

'Yes.'

'That's interesting. That burner number. The first call came from Clarens too.'

'Fucking bingo,' said Cupido.

'Language,' said Duba, but she smiled.

'Sorry, Doc.'

Malime Duba consulted her data: 'That same number called Streicher at 15:56 that afternoon, from Bloemfontein. The duration was eleven minutes. The next morning at 07:31, Streicher called the burner number, which went unanswered. Three days later, the same burner called Streicher at 18:07 in the evening, from Cape Town. Looks like the Waterfront. The call lasted just three minutes. And then, one day later, a final call. Sunday, thirtieth of June, again from the same Waterfront location. Nine minutes.'

'It has to be this Berger guy,' said Griessel. 'Clarens couldn't be a coincidence. And the long blond hair they found at the murder scene . . .'

'*Yebo*,' said Cupido.

'Let's call the golf estate,' said Griessel. 'Let's find out if Berger owned an antique golf club.'

'Benna, I'm driving to pick up Miss Slippery.'

Griessel saw that it was already half past eleven.

★ ★ ★

The sheep lorry – a Nissan UD 440 with a long body and a trailer – was parked in the middle of the Ndabeni warehouse. Igen Rousseau paced out the length of it, from the horse's nose to the trailer's tail. Then he walked to where Evert 'Tau' Berger was standing next to Chrissie, Themba and Jericho Yon.

'Long enough,' he said, 'to block the road completely.'

'Great,' said Yon. He pointed at the pile of rucksacks and duffel bags lying next to it. 'Is that all the luggage you want to take with you?' He had to take it with him now, to pack it in the Basler tomorrow.

They all confirmed, that was everything.

'Do you all have cash for bribes in Luanda?' asked Igen. Just in case the Angolan customs and immigration officials noticed their passports hadn't been stamped in South Africa.

'Yes,' said Themba. The rest just nodded.

'Passports packed?'

They nodded, one by one.

'Everyone's flights booked from Luanda?' asked Rousseau.

'Yes,' they said, in unison.

Only two of them would need the bribes, a passport and a flight from Luanda, thought Tau Berger. Himself. And Jericho Yon. Because, as he'd told Emilia, he was going to take everyone out. Just not the pilot. Not even once Yon brought him to Luanda. Because if he shot Yon there at the airport, and the Angolans found the body before Tau could get the fuck out of Dodge, it would cause trouble.

He must remember to pack the cable ties. To tie Yon up in the back of the plane.

★ ★ ★

The resident professional golfer of the Clarens Golf and Leisure Resort was called Dylan Botha. 'Tau. We just call him Tau,' he said to Benny Griessel. 'Did you find him?'

'What do you mean?'

'He's been gone since Wednesday last week. He and his bike. The door of his house looks like it was broken open . . . We got the police in, but they say all they can do is file a missing person report.'

'Mr Botha, do you know if Mr Berger owned an old wooden golf club?'

'Yes, he has a few of them. More than one driver, a Wilson and a Spalding. And, I think, a two-wood and a three-wood. He played with them sometimes.'

'Do you know if any of the clubs are missing?'

'No. I'll have to go and see.'

'How long has Mr Berger been working there?'

'Probably about four years.'

'And before that?'

'He was greenkeeper at the Bloemfontein club.'

'Do you know if he was in the army?'

'Oh, yes. Tau was a Recce. That's what he said, I couldn't swear on it. He's a bit weird.'

Griessel felt his phone vibrate. He looked at the screen. There was a WhatsApp from Emilia Streicher.

So sorry, missed my flight. Car broke down. Can we move it to Saturday? Or call me.

89

Emilia Streicher sat in her home office, phone in hand.

Would he believe her?

She'd lain awake last night wondering what they knew. They surely suspected Basie's overseas trips were too short to be for training. But that was all. And they hoped she would have information about it. Which she wasn't going to give them. She would just say Basie was very private. Mysterious. Like all Recces are. He never shared the details with her.

What could they do?

Nothing. She just needed to stick to her story. Over the phone.

She couldn't face the two detectives today, not in person. They would spot her tension. Her stress about what she had to do tomorrow morning.

Her stress that Tau and the gang would fail in their heist because it sounded almost impossible to pull off.

Her stress that, if the detectives found out where Basie's money really came from, she would lose her inheritance. And then she would have nothing.

Her stress over all the secrets she had to keep.

Her phone beeped.

Griessel's answer: *It's okay. Can I call in 10 minutes?*

She exhaled slowly.

Thank you, Lord. He believed her.

★   ★   ★

For three hours, Griessel and Cupido worked speedily, but with laser focus. Then they took the plan to Colonel Mbali Kaleni.

Step One, they told Mbali, was to ensure Emilia Streicher believed that they knew very little. And that they believed her.

So Benny only called her back twenty minutes later. So they didn't seem desperate for the information. Griessel told her they were just scratching their heads a bit about Small's short visits and the large payments. Maybe she knew something about it?

No, she didn't know. Basie was so private. But she was sure there was a good explanation.

Didn't she perhaps know who he went to work for? Or more or less what he did?

No. All Basie said was 'military and security training', that's really all she knew. She was so sorry.

He said he understood completely. If she could think of anything, he would appreciate it. Otherwise they would see her on Saturday, when she came to Cape Town. Then they would show her the passport and the dates and the payments, between 2014 and 2019. Maybe something would jog her memory.

Definitely, she said. She really wanted to help.

And then he thanked her, and hung up.

Step Two was they would fly to Pretoria. Tomorrow morning. To confront her. With all the information: They had evidence that in 2011 her brother, Basie Small received a payment of five million rand from Dineo Phiri. They knew she'd called the late Dewey Reed and Evert 'Tau' Berger immediately after being notified of her brother's death. Both were ex-Recces, just like Basie. They were pretty certain Berger was involved in the murder of Dineo Phiri. There was the wooden golf club, the filler foam, the corpse on the golf course, the blond hairs found. And the message in the sand, which they had now deciphered.

FOR BS AND DR. *For Basie Small and Dewey Reed.*

So, they believed she knew about Basie and Phiri and whatever happened in 2011.

They were going to her because they believed she had no intention of coming to Cape Town on Saturday.

Step Three: tighten the screws, exert greater pressure. Tell her they were going to arrest her for obstruction of justice, false statements and aiding and abetting. Unless she told them everything. About Basie, about Tau Berger and Dewey Reed. And about Dineo Phiri.

Step Four was an application to the court for the extension of the Section 205 subpoena regarding Emilia Streicher's cell phone. So that they could constantly monitor its location. And intercept any further calls. Just in case she and Tau Berger contacted each other.

Step Five, Colonel, was tracking down this Berger bloke.

The trouble was, he seemed to have used at least four different unregistered phones to contact Emilia Streicher. From Clarens, Bloemfontein, the Cape Waterfront, Barrydale and somewhere in between the high-density residential apartment area of Green Point.

What further complicated the situation was that they couldn't send out a General Broadcast for Berger to the SAPS to help find him. The state capture Cabal and all their cronies in the police and the army and wherever, would immediately smell a rat, and sabotage the whole operation.

'We want to go rogue, Colonel,' said Cupido.

'What does that mean?'

'We want to give Julian Jenkins a call.'

'The journalist?'

'*Yebo.*'

'No.'

'Colonel,' said Griessel, 'just tell us: what is the alternative?'

Griessel saw her waver. He said: 'I understand that your priority is to build cases against the members of the Cabal. But you brought us in to solve two murders. Please, Colonel, help us to do our job.'

★ ★ ★

'This is Julian,' Jenkins said as he answered the phone.

'Brother, this call never happened, do you understand?'

'Who is this?'

'Warrant Officer Vaughn Cupido, formerly of the South African Police Service Crime Investigation Department in Stellenbosch.'

'How do you like it at the ID?' Jenkins asked.

'Damn, brother, you're good.'

'You were in the car with Kaleni at Hawston. Elementary, my dear Watson.'

'We're off the record, right?' asked Cupido.

'If that's how you want to roll, we're off the record.'

★ ★ ★

Carla called at six o'clock. 'Did you cut your hair, Pa?'

'I will tomorrow morning, there really wasn't time.'

'Pa!'

90

Friday.

Seven o'clock in the morning.

Griessel's phone alarm went off. He was awake instantly, scrabbled for the phone, missed, finally shut down the alarm.

Alexa stirred beside him. He didn't want to bother her, quietly lifted the duvet to slip out. Alexa grabbed his arm, pulled him back. 'Just hold me tight for a little bit.'

He turned, put his arms around her. Her body was warm and soft.

Last night she'd played the seductress. 'Our last extra-marital romp,' she said, 'some bedroom shenanigans.' That's what she sometimes called it, with that mischievous glint in her eye that gave him so much joy. Because that meant she was happy. She felt safe with him.

The shenanigans were, as always, magical and surreal to him. He still couldn't believe that such a beautiful, sexy woman found him desirable.

'Tomorrow I'm yours,' she whispered in his ear. 'Forever.'

He just held her tighter because he never could find the right words to respond to her sweet talk.

'I love you so much, Benny.'

'You too.'

'I know. And remember, I won't see you tonight. There will be food in the fridge.'

'Thank you.'

'Are you definitely flying back tonight?'

'Definitely.'

'Okay.'

He held her a moment longer. Kissed her on the forehead, then got up.

He took a shower, dressed, and came to kiss her again before leaving.

'Remember your hair,' she said.

'First thing this morning.'

★　★　★

07:52

Malime Duba walked into the NPA's Information Management Centre, her heels echoing in the silence.

The assistant who worked the night shift looked up and greeted her.

'She's still at home?' asked Duba.

The assistant pointed to the screen in front of him. It showed the location of Emilia Streicher's cell phone on the map software. A small, red triangle flashed more or less halfway between the top and bottom of the endlessly long Cliffendale Drive in the Pretoria suburb of Faerie Glen.

'She hasn't moved since five o'clock yesterday.'

'Good. Any calls?'

'Nothing so far.'

★　★　★

08:03

In the apartment in Green Point Tau Berger was at the stove, egg lifter in hand, scrambled eggs in the pan. His phone lay nearby.

His Telegram app beeped. He put down the egg lifter, picked up the phone.

It was from Igen. A screenshot, from the Network24 news page. A photo, of him, Tau Berger. The one on the golf course website. There was a caption above the photo. *Ex-Recce wanted for Phiri murder.*

Shock and adrenaline. His first thought was: How the fuck?

Then, a Telegram text message from Igen. *Shave your beard. Cut your hair. Now.*

How the hell?

★　★　★

08:05

'I don't have fucking scissors or a razor, bro,' said Tau Berger.

'I'll bring them to you,' said Igen Rousseau on the phone. 'Wait until the shops open. But you stay inside.'

'I'm not stupid, Ig.'

'How did they connect you, Tau?'

All the tension, the suggestion that they'd made the connection because he'd been stupid, made Tau lose it. '*Jissis*, bro, how the fuck would I know?'

Igen kept his cool. 'Could it have been Vern?'

It took a moment for Tau to regain control and consider the possibility. 'No. He can't afford to . . . He helped Brenner, he would have to admit that. It's not him.'

'How sure are you?'

'He has too much to lose.'

'Okay. Keep thinking, how they made the link. And keep your head down.'

★ ★ ★

08:30

On the corner of Bree and Church Street, in the Mop Hair salon, the pretty young woman told Benny Griessel they could only help him late that afternoon.

Because it was Friday. Everyone was having their hair done.

He said: 'I'm asking a big favour. Just a quick cut. I'm getting married tomorrow.'

She heard the distress in his voice.

'Genuine?' she said.

'Four o'clock tomorrow afternoon. Please.'

'Come sit down,' she said. She called a red-headed woman over. 'Bernise, this man is getting married tomorrow. No nonsense about "just a quick cut". Make him handsome.'

Jissis, thought Benny Griessel. *Handsome.*

'Thank you very, very much.'

91

08:46

Tau opened the door for Igen, who strode in with a Clicks shopping bag.

'Sit,' said Igen. 'We're shaving everything off.'

'Bro, I don't like your tone. There's no fucking way they could connect me with Phiri through something I did.'

Igen took an electric clipper out of the Clicks bag and put it on the table. Then a razor and shaving cream. 'Come sit down,' he said.

Tau took off his shirt and sat down. Then he said: 'Let me tell you why it couldn't be Vern. Because I didn't tell Vern about Phiri. Because I'm not fucking stupid. And us, me and Billy Brenner and Dewey, we didn't know anything about Phiri, back then. We didn't know he was one of the fucking philistines behind the scenes. So, it's not Vern, and it's not me. And now I'm wondering, is it one of you?'

Igen plugged in the clipper. He switched it on. Above the droning noise he said: 'Just give me one good reason why we would do it.'

*   *   *

09:14

Cupido looked up as Griessel walked in. His face brightened when he saw Benny's haircut.

'Not a word,' said Griessel.

'Benna, you look so cute, I want to marry you.'

'Fuck off,' said Griessel, and began to gather up the paperwork he needed for their confrontation with Emilia Streicher.

*   *   *

09:41

In the Information Management Centre, Cupido told Duba they were on their way to the airport.

'Streicher is still at home,' said Duba.

'No calls?' asked Cupido.

'Just one,' said Duba. 'To Edelstein Business Brokers in Lynnwood, Pretoria, about half an hour ago.'

'We're landing at OR Tambo at one forty,' said Cupido. 'If you can update us then?'

*   *   *

10:26

In the living room of Themba's rented apartment, Chrissie looked at Tau Berger.

His beard was gone, his head was shiny and shaven, his eyes intense under the deep scowl. All of it conspired to give him a look of ferocious coldness. For the first time she could see the Tau who had tortured and killed Dineo Phiri.

But at least he was unrecognisable, totally different from the photo in the media.

'The fact is,' Igen told the group, 'they don't know where Tau is. They don't have a clue.'

'Why?' asked Chrissie.

'If they knew, they wouldn't have said anything to the media. If they knew, he would be in custody.'

'Okay,' she said, because that made sense.

'You all know what the situation is,' said Igen. 'Go, no go?'

'Go,' said Yon.

'Go,' said Chrissie.

'Go,' said Themba.

Tau just nodded. His mind elsewhere.

'Okay,' said Igen. 'Now we're waiting for Emilia.'

*   *   *

11:41

On FlySafair flight FA112 Griessel and Cupido continued their speculation from yesterday afternoon: what had Basie Small, Tau Berger and Dewey Reed done for the Cabal in 2011?

'A month's salary, Benna, that it was assassinations. They paid the Recces big money to take out problematic, honest people in government. There are many who have disappeared in suspicious circumstances. That's what Recces do, *pappie*. They are trained for only one thing. Killing people. And making it look like accidents or natural causes.'

'And then Basie Small blackmailed them?'

'Exactly.'

Consensus.

* * *

12:22

'She's moving,' said Duba's assistant in the Information Management Centre. Duba came to stand at the screen. She saw that Emilia Streicher's cell phone was on the R21, south of Pretoria, heading towards Kempton Park.

Not until seven minutes later, when Streicher passed the Olifantsfontein off-ramp, did Malime Duba realise that this was the road to the OR Tambo International Airport.

She turned to another assistant. 'I want to know if Emilia Streicher has a reservation on any flight today. And I want to know quickly.'

'Yes, Doctor,' said the assistant and began tapping at her keyboard.

92

13:13

Four kilometres from OR Tambo International Airport Emilia Streicher drove her ComfortAir panel van past the Spartan warehouse.

She was rigid with tension, her palms sweating.

Against the window right beside her, she had taped her company cell phone, behind a narrow strip of black cardboard. There was a hole cut in the cardboard, just big enough for the cell phone camera lens. She had activated the video function on the phone three minutes ago in Kelvin Street.

She drove at a constant speed, so as not to attract attention. She didn't look at the warehouse. In her peripheral vision, she noticed activity. Three shipping containers on three trucks. Forklifts going back and forth. Three black Toyota *bakkies*. Many armed men.

Suspicious eyes looking her way.

She drove past, down to the corner with Newton Street.

Then she exhaled slowly.

She parked, to stop the recording with a trembling finger.

★　★　★

13:14

'This is strange,' said the assistant to Duba. 'An Emilia Streicher booked two flights for tomorrow morning.'

'Tomorrow? Not today? Are you sure?'

'Absolutely. The first is a flight from Johannesburg to Cape Town, tomorrow morning at eleven o'clock . . .'

'Yes. And?'

'The second flight is from Johannesburg to Kuala Lumpur in Malaysia, via Singapore, on Singapore Airlines. That flight leaves tomorrow afternoon at 13:45.'

'She couldn't be on both. Show me.'

The assistant showed her the bookings on the screen.

The other assistant at the terminal monitoring Streicher's location said: 'She's not going to the airport; she's on her way back north again.'

'How curious. Please send the information about those two flights tomorrow to Warrant Cupido.'

* * *

13:21

Tau Berger's cell phone was on the breakfast counter, the others were gathered around, everyone was watching the video that Emilia had sent.

'Play it again. In slo-mo,' said Igen.

Tau started the video. The parking area in front of the warehouse appeared. For a moment, Chrissie relived the robbery, more than two months ago – walking from the white Hyundai Atos, in stiletto heels, to the warehouse.

'Stop,' said Igen.

Tau froze the image.

'Count them,' said Igen.

Everyone counted the armed men they could see.

'Sixteen,' said Themba.

'Yes,' said Igen. 'Sixteen that we can see. There must be guys inside loading.'

'But only three shotgun trucks.'

'Great,' said Igen. 'Let's roll.'

'Wait,' said Tau.

Everyone looked at him.

'I think I know how they found me.'

* * *

13:32

The tension slowly drained out of Emilia, on the R21, on the way home.

She'd played her part. Now it was all in Tau's hands.

She still had to send Griessel a message, with the flight number and arrival time of the Cape Town flight tomorrow morning. Then he could check whether she'd made the booking. She still had to pack for the flight to Kuala Lumpur.

Tomorrow she would be safe. Tomorrow it would all be over.

She heard a Telegram message come in. She picked up her phone while driving and quickly peeked at it.

It was Tau:

Watch Network24. They are looking for me. Think it's because you called me, 1st call after Basie's death. Think they are checking your phone. Delete everything!!!!! Don't call, don't answer the phone. Don't say anything to the police! Lie low until Sunday. I will be ok. Telegram you Sunday.

She heard the sharp sound of a hooter next to her, realised she was veering into the right-hand-lane traffic, swerved back, the shock shuddering through her.

★ ★ ★

13:41

On the runway of the OR Tambo International Airport Griessel and Cupido switched on their mobile phones in the plane.

Cupido had a message from the Information Management Centre.

Emilia Streicher booked two flights for tomorrow. One to Cape Town (11:00) and one to Singapore and Kuala Lumpur in Malaysia (Flight SQ479 at 13:45).

'*Aitsa*,' said Cupido.

93

Griessel and Cupido stood at the Hertz car rental counter. Griessel signed the forms and waited for the keys.

Cupido's cell phone rang. It was Duba.

'Doc?'

'She just switched off her cell phone. We lost her on the N1 near Menlyn. I believe she is going home, but we don't know for sure.'

'Okay, Doc, thanks. We're almost on our way. Call if she gets back on your radar.'

'Now we have to move it, Benna,' he said to Griessel. 'She's gone offline.'

★   ★   ★

14:13

Emilia took the Atterbury off-ramp. She concentrated on her breathing, she had to stay calm. Basie would have expected it of her, to be able to handle this crisis.

She just had to gather her thoughts.

She was going to pack her suitcase now. Use the landline to call a hotel at the airport and book a room for tonight. In case the police sent someone to her home to come and talk to her.

And pray they didn't catch Tau before the heist.

It was impossible for them to know about the gold and the robbery. Impossible.

They were only looking for Tau because he killed Phiri. They had no evidence that she was involved.

Yes, she had called Tau. And Dewey. Because they were Basie's best friends.

Never mind. They wouldn't find her. All that mattered was that she was on that plane tomorrow. And that Tau got away with the gold.

Because if she was in Kuala Lumpur, she would be safe. Malaysia didn't have an extradition treaty with South Africa. Malaysia didn't require a visa for South Africans.

Just one problem: all the money she had access to now was the six thousand dollars in Basie's foreign account, and the ninety thousand rand in her own. If they knew about everything, and she fled, she would forfeit Basie's estate.

Tau and the rest *must* get away with the gold.

Tau. Unpredictable, reckless Tau, as Basie had described him.

It was very reckless of him to trust her.

*   *   *

14:29

Tau and Chrissie were on the motorbike. He rode within the speed limit, past Piketberg, on the way to Williston.

He could sense that, behind him, she was keeping as much distance from him as she could. She didn't want to touch him. A fucking ice bitch, all of a sudden this morning. They were all different with him this morning, as if he was toxic. It was nothing, he could handle it, he would sort that out very quickly on the Dak tomorrow. His real worry was Emilia.

All the money from the gold would go into her account. Every cent. Two billion of it.

What if the police squeezed her?

It had taken him hours this morning to work out they'd got to him through Emilia. He'd gone over everything, from the beginning. He knew he hadn't made mistakes. Not in the mountain at Clarens, not at Phiri's house. And then he thought about Emilia, and the police who were on her case. They were on her for a reason. They thought she was hiding something, lying or something. He remembered, that day when he called her from Bloemfontein. She'd said: 'The police want to come and talk again. They know something.' And if they knew something, they started checking cell phones. And he remembered she tried to call Dewey first. Dead Dewey. And if the police looked at Dewey's phone, they were going to start wondering. And if they checked Emilia's phone, they were going to find him: Tau.

Emilia was a loose end.

What if the police squeezed her?

He'd fucking go to Pretoria and squeeze her much harder, that's what. Tau was a handful.

★ ★ ★

Under the crash helmet, Chrissie was wearing her headphones, listening to Shostakovich's Fifth Symphony. It perfectly mirrored the rolling turmoil she felt.

★ ★ ★

14:51

Emilia deleted all comms with Tau on both her cell phones. She used the landline in her study to book a room at the airport hotel. She would stay at the City Lodge tonight.

Tomorrow she would wait there. If Tau let her know the robbery was a success, she would board the plane, to Kuala Lumpur.

And if she didn't hear anything?

She had yet to decide.

She packed frantically. First of all, in a small carry-on case, the file with Basie's documents. And her laptop, her lifeline, her security, her only way to a foreign account and the financial independence of two billion rand. If the raid succeeded.

The amount was unreal to her. Mythical. What do you do with that much money?

Everything.

She left the case at the front door, along with her handbag, containing her passport, wallet and mobile phones. On to the bedroom, a single large suitcase on the bed. She packed almost exclusively summer clothes, it was always hot in Malaysia, she'd read.

She was in two minds about taking a shower now, wanting to rinse away the morning's sweaty panic, but the sense of urgency was too great. She decided against it, she would shower at the hotel.

She zipped the bag shut, her hands trembling as she jiggled the combination lock into place.

She picked up the suitcase, extended the handle, dragged it out of the bedroom, down the hall, to the front door. Opened the front door, ran out to her car, a white Volkswagen Tiguan, parked in the driveway ready to go, behind the tall electronic gate. She opened the back hatch, hefted the heavy suitcase inside. Jogged back, fetched the carry-on and her handbag. Set the burglar alarm, out of sheer habit. Locked the front door, stowed her carry-on beside the big suitcase. Pushed the button to close the boot. Pressed the remote control to open the gate. Walked round to the driver's side, handbag slung over the shoulder.

Out of the corner of her eye, a movement at the gate. She turned to look.

The detectives were standing there, beside a small grey Suzuki Swift.

'*Jinne*, ma'am, looks like we nearly missed you,' said the Coloured one. Cupido.

94

Griessel saw the shock flash across Emilia Streicher's face.

She stood there in her black Nike sports shoes, a black Nike tracksuit, keys in hand. Frozen, dumbstruck. And he knew their suspicions were correct. She was on her way to Malaysia because she was involved in the Phiri affair, one way or another. They would have to play their cards very carefully. They didn't want a lawyer involved now. She had the right to insist on one, but then it could turn into a very long day. Which he definitely couldn't afford.

They remained standing on the other side of the gate. 'Mrs Streicher, we'd just like to have a chat,' said Benny, his voice as calm as possible.

She looked straight at him. At the file in his hand. Back to him.

A jingle of keys, her hand was shaking. She gripped them tightly. The sound stopped.

'We just want to clear up a few matters,' and he gestured at the file. Then he lied: 'Nothing serious. Ten minutes. That's all we ask.'

She looked at Cupido.

'Just look at my partner's cute new haircut,' said Vaughn. 'It's for his wedding tomorrow. So, we'll genuinely just be in and out. We have to go back to Cape Town. Flight leaves at eight thirty-five.' And he tapped his watch.

She looked at Griessel. As if she couldn't believe someone would wish to marry him, haircut and all.

Seconds ticked by. He knew she was considering her options.

Her shoulders sagged. 'Come in,' she said.

★   ★   ★

15:04

They sat in her dining room.

Griessel laid out the documents on the table in front of her, one by one. Spreadsheets of Basie Small's income from 2014 to 2019. A spreadsheet of his travel dates. Then the registration summary for MilSec Solutions.

He explained their dilemma, the short stays and the large sums. He kept his voice soft, no hint of confrontation. He asked if she could shed any light on it all.

She told him Basie was a closed book. She knew nothing about these things. And then she started explaining. Without them asking, and in detail, how Basie did his own thing in that period, between 2014 and 2019, completely. He just dropped in on her sporadically, here at her home and office. Or called and said he was somewhere overseas. And it didn't seem strange to her, because he'd been secretive about his comings and goings, ever since he became a Recce, years before. That's how they are, Special Forces people. They're not talkers.

They nodded, as if they understood.

Had she ever heard of MilSec Solutions in Malta?

No, never heard of it.

Again, a nod, a gesture, of course, it was all perfectly understandable. They believed her.

Griessel gathered up the documents. 'Thank you, ma'am,' he said, and put them away in the file.

'I'm sorry I couldn't help.' Her voice a little lighter now.

'How are the funeral arrangements going?' asked Cupido.

'I . . . Basie's . . . remains. They haven't let me know anything yet . . .'

'Should be any day now,' said Cupido.

'I will be so grateful.'

'So you're coming back, for the funeral?'

'Back from where?'

'Malaysia,' said Cupido. 'Bit of a weird time for a holiday, if I may say so.'

'It looks like you might want to make a run for it,' said Griessel. He watched her closely. Her body language betrayed nothing. She was a sphinx, staring at Cupido. You have to respect that, he thought. That inner strength.

'Ma'am, you know what Basie was involved in,' said Griessel. He slipped a bank statement from the file. 'The thing that happened in 2011, when he was still in the Recces. The thing that Dineo Phiri paid him five million rand for, on the thirtieth of November that year.'

He placed the bank statement in front of her. 'We know these are things he did. Not you. He and Evert Berger. Tau. And Dewey Reed.'

He took out her cell phone records, put them on the table. 'The two guys you called, on the twenty-fifth of May.'

'And then the Berger guy went and killed Phiri, just four days later,' said Cupido. 'And he called you repeatedly, non-stop, on burner phones. That implicates you. Directly. In two murders. Reed and Phiri. You're looking at multiple charges. Obstruction of justice, false statements, accessory to a crime. Five to seven in chooky. Minimum.'

'We're looking for Berger,' said Griessel. 'Help us, and we'll help you.'

She looked past them. The room was dead silent, only the cooing of a pigeon audible outside.

'I want a lawyer,' she said eventually.

'Of course,' said Griessel.

'And you probably have travel insurance, right? Because if the lawyer comes, it's bye-bye, Malaysia. Those dudes charge by the hour. They like to stretch things out. It's a game we know. And we're good at it.'

'Feel free to call, Mrs Streicher,' said Griessel. 'That's your right and privilege.'

95

Emilia thought. About her choices.

Basie's inheritance. His house, his investments. Ten million rand. That's what she would have. If she could get an indemnity from the police, if she stayed in the country, if the high-risk gold heist failed.

Versus two billion rand. If the high-risk gold heist was a success. But she still needed that indemnity to catch her flight to Kuala Lumpur.

Then she realised, she didn't have to choose. She could keep both options open. With an indemnity she could fly to Kuala Lumpur. And come back, if she wanted.

'I can give you information about President Joseph Zaca's corruption,' she said. 'Billions of rands.'

She had their attention.

'I will tell you everything I know. About Basie and Dewey and Tau. And Corrie Albertyn and Fani Dlamini. They were the five Recces involved.'

'Involved in what?' asked Cupido.

'I want indemnity,' she said.

'For what?' asked Cupido.

'For all the things you mentioned. Obstruction of justice . . .'

'False statements, and accessory to a crime?'

'Yes.'

'That's it?'

'Yes.'

'Only the National Director of the Prosecuting Authority can give you indemnity,' said Griessel.

'Well, I hope you can get hold of him before your wedding,' said Emilia Streicher.

'Her,' said Cupido. 'The National Director is a woman.'

★ ★ ★

15:41

Griessel called Mbali Kaleni and explained the situation.

Kaleni said she would have to talk to her boss, Advocate Annika Johnson, to get this ball rolling. They would have to wait. It would take a while. In the meantime, he could chat with Malime Duba. The good doctor might have information that could help them.

* * *

15:59

Emilia asked if she could make them coffee.

There was a new sense of calm about her now.

They said, yes, please.

'Rusks with your coffee?'

'Please,' said Cupido, who was ravenous.

And so they sat and waited. Over coffee and rusks, while the pigeons cooed outside and the shadows cast by the leafless jacarandas next to Streicher's dining-room window lengthened, minute by minute.

* * *

16:25

Driving up Piekeniers Pass, Igen Rousseau shivered in the cab of the sheep lorry, the Nissan UD 440. It was cold and the heater wasn't working.

His cell phone rang on the worn seat next to him. He answered.

'The last of your three trucks has just passed through,' said the security officer from North By Northwest in Potchefstroom. 'I'm sending you the pictures.'

Igen looked at his watch. 'Okay, thanks,' he said.

He did the sums in his head. The gold convoy was travelling at approximately seventy kilometres per hour.

Perfect.

He could only look at the photos beyond Citrusdal, that was the first straight stretch of road where he could safely stop.

Then he would see, in two of the photos, a black Toyota double-cab pick-up driving a hundred metres behind each truck. Two of the shipping containers were red. The last one was blue.

* * *

16:48

Mbali called. She said the National Director had approved the indemnity. They prepared a document for Streicher to sign. She sent it via WhatsApp.

It took another ten minutes to fetch Emilia Streicher's laptop from her Volkswagen Tiguan, transfer the document, print it out, study it, and sign it.

96

Emilia told them the story of the Tripoli mission, the five Recces who flew out to collect Muammar Gaddafi's dollars and gold. For which they were each paid five million rand. She didn't know it was Dineo Phiri who made the payments. Basie had just spoken of an Ishan Babbar.

Griessel and Cupido listened in stunned amazement. Then Benny started taking down notes in his notebook.

Cupido watched her, her whole demeanour had changed. The tension was gone, she spoke with a new confidence, laid-back, almost nonchalant.

That's good, he thought. Let her relax.

She said her brother was one of the two Recces who were left behind while the rest went on the second flight. To guard the gold and the dollars in the old aircraft hangar at Waterkloof air force base. The other was Corrie Albertyn.

At night while Albertyn slept, Basie stole some of the dollars. He stowed the contents of his army duffel bag – mainly clothes – underneath the gold, shoved into the cavity between the wooden pallet boards. And packed the bag full of notes. Just enough so that the weight wouldn't attract attention. Twenty kilograms in cash. One million dollars, give or take. With some dirty underpants on top.

And then the second consignment arrived, and they offloaded it. Worked shifts to guard the hangar. When Basie got a breather two days later, he brought the duffel bag to her.

Basie was on edge. He didn't know if there was an inventory of the money. He didn't know if anyone would realise he'd stolen some.

They stood guard, for weeks, and then they helped to move the gold and dollars. To a warehouse in Spartan, here at Kempton Park.

And then Babbar sent them back to Five Special Forces Regiment in Phalaborwa, and the payment of the five million came through.

It didn't take the five Recces long to work out who Ishan Babbar was, and who he was working for. And after Muammar Gaddafi's death they made the logical deduction: Joseph Zaca and his followers were the new owners of the fortune.

★ ★ ★

17:48

Griessel interrupted Emilia. He said he was sorry, but he quickly had to send a message. So that they could get a later flight to the Cape, because they weren't going to be in time for the one at 8:35 p.m.

He sent Kaleni a WhatsApp.

Then he said: 'Thank you. Please continue.'

She said there were two reasons Basie gave her all his documents. And a list of names and numbers, should something happen to him.

One was because he always worried that they would find out he had stolen a million dollars. And that they would come for him. The other was that Joseph Zaca and his henchmen would want to silence all those involved in the Gaddafi mission. The pressure on the then president was increasing, his days were numbered.

Basie used his five million to help her start ComfortAir. He went to study law, planning to make a career of it. But he hated it. And he realised his nest egg was not going to last. Not if he wanted a house and a vehicle and a certain lifestyle.

And he didn't know how to convert his one million dollars into rands in a way that wouldn't attract attention.

'Then, in 2014, Gordon Cameron contacted him. Gordon was with Basie in the Five Special Forces Regiment at the time, but in 2014, he was working for Vega Resources in America. It was the year President Obama announced that America's troop numbers in Afghanistan would be reduced. The private military contractors were already starting to take over more and more duties, and they needed people with experience. Cameron offered Basie a job, in Afghanistan. Basie came to talk to me, and I told him he shouldn't go. It was dangerous in Afghanistan. He should rather ask Cameron to help him with the dollars.'

Benny's phone vibrated. He ignored it, he let her talk.

Emilia said between her, Basie and Gordon Cameron they developed the system. The establishment of MilSec Solutions in Malta. With a bank account there.

Cameron emailed each time, from Vega Resources, to offer Basie a job. That was to signal where he would be, and when, to take delivery of the dollars.

Basie smuggled the dollars out of the country, in quantities he was able to stow in his luggage. To locations where Vega Resources had a presence. The USA. Britain. The Congo. Mozambique, and Iraq. Cameron or one of his colleagues would come to collect the dollars, and make a payment to MilSec Solutions. That was how Emilia and Basie laundered the dollars. With MilSec 'paying' him, income he could declare and on which he owed tax.

★ ★ ★

18:09

Griessel picked up his phone. A message from Kaleni. *No other flights tonight. Looking at tomorrow morning.*

That was when he began to worry.

97

'Okay, chilla vanilla,' said Cupido. 'All of that makes sense. But why did ex-Prez Joseph Zaca's people wait until now to take out Basie and Dewey Reed?'

'They thought Basie and his friends were involved in the robbery,' said Emilia Streicher.

'What robbery?'

She realised she would have to be very careful now. Calm. Because she was going to hold something back for the first time. Tell a little lie. She wasn't going to give them Igen, Themba, Chrissie and Yon's names. That could mean the end of the gold heist.

'I can only tell you what I know. I only have two names. Billy Brenner. And Nicky Berry. Brenner is also an ex-Recce. He and four other people broke into the warehouse in Spartan to steal dollars . . .'

'When was this?' asked Griessel.

'In April. Early April. And then the Babbar guy got video of Brenner, and they identified him. And then they thought, because he was a Recce, Basie must be involved.'

'But they weren't?' asked Cupido.

'No. Definitely not.'

'Weird coincidence,' said Cupido. 'Another Recce.'

'That's true,' said Emilia. 'But you can go and see. This Nicky Berry was a security guard at the warehouse. He was Brenner's brother-in-law. That's how Brenner knew about the dollars.'

'Can you prove that the heist happened?'

'All I know is that they wanted to steal a plane from the Brits airfield. And then there was some kind of shootout between them, and the plane caught fire, or exploded, or something. You can ask the police in Brits. It's true. It was in the papers and everything.'

'Okay,' said Cupido. 'Let me make a few calls first.'

★　★　★

18:35

Cupido was still on the phone talking to the Brits SAPS office when Mbali Kaleni called Griessel.

'Benny, are you almost done?'

'No, Colonel. We'll be at least another hour or two.'

'Oh, my goodness. What time is your wedding tomorrow?'

His heart sank as he said it: 'Four o'clock.'

'Oh, my goodness.'

'Why, Colonel?'

'I'm so sorry. We couldn't get you on any flights tomorrow morning. It's the rugby. Apparently, the Blue Bulls are playing the Western Stormers, and the Blue Bull people are all flying down for the game. The earliest available seat is at twenty past two.'

Fuck. If they rushed to the airport now, they might still catch the 20:35 flight.

But they couldn't.

'We'll keep trying, Benny. I'm so very sorry. Maybe there's a cancellation.'

He couldn't work with 'maybe'. Not today, not tomorrow.

'Colonel, we have a rental. If we don't get a flight, we'll have to drive down.'

'Oh, my goodness.'

Cupido came back from outside. 'Okay. Your story checks out. Now, let's talk about Tau Berger and Dineo Phiri.'

★ ★ ★

18:52

Emilia told them Dineo Phiri confessed to Tau Berger that Ishan Babbar killed Basie. The same Babbar who killed Dewey. And sent the team to get Tau.

That's why Tau went to Dineo Phiri. He wanted to find out why.

And he wanted revenge, because Tau was a wild man.

And then Griessel caught her out.

In the silence after she finished the story, he flipped through his notebook.

He said: 'Can you give us the address of the warehouse in Spartan?'

She gave them the address.

He looked at his notebook again, then added: 'We are going to send a team to check the warehouse. If the gold and the dollars are there, we know you are telling the truth.'

'How would I know? I've never been there.'

'Never?'

'No.'

'According to our Information Management Centre, you were at that address this afternoon,' Griessel said. 'In Spartan.'

'*Heito,*' said Cupido.

Surprise blazoned across her face. Shock. She couldn't hide it.

Griessel said: 'They were scratching their heads, our guys at the IMC. They said it was an odd route to take. You know, only the day before you wanted to leave the country. They couldn't understand it. Neither could I. Not until you gave me that address just now.'

'Maybe that explains all the burner calls from Tau Berger, this past week,' said Cupido. 'As well as the flight to Malaysia.'

And Griessel added: 'You signed an indemnity agreement that is only valid if you tell the whole truth.'

★ ★ ★

19:05

While Emilia talked, Carla called.

Griessel didn't answer.

A minute later the WhatsApp came through: *At Pa's house. Where is Pa?*

He hurriedly replied to her: *Jhb. Call soon.*

All he got back were big red exclamation mark emojis.

98

Griessel went outside, first of all to call Mbali Kaleni, and tell her the whole story. About Gaddafi, about the robbery in April, about the three trucks on the way to Cape Town with a fortune on board. And a Russian ship.

The Flower listened to all of this in silence. Then she congratulated them, and said the ID would get to work immediately.

Griessel called Carla. He felt guilty that she'd had to wait. The eve of his wedding, and her alcoholic father was not at home as he should be. He could understand her concern.

She replied with: 'Johannesburg? What on earth is Pa doing in Johannesburg?' She was clearly upset.

'We had to come and do an interrogation . . .'

'Is Uncle Vaughn there too?'

'Yes, Carla. Don't worry, everything is okay.'

'When are you coming back?'

'We're driving now.'

'Driving? From Johannesburg?'

★ ★ ★

19:39

Desiree Coetzee called Cupido.

'Vaughn, tell me it's not true.'

'What?'

'Johannesburg? And you're driving down?'

'Don't worry, lovey, everything will be fine.'

'Don't "lovey" me now. I'm telling you, if you're late for *this* wedding, you will sleep in the spare room until December. Do you understand me?'

'Lovey . . .'

'No, you don't "lovey" me now!'

★ ★ ★

21:41

In the Oudeklip guesthouse in Nieuwoudtville, Igen Rousseau was just about to have a hot shower to drive the chill from his body, when Diamond City Security finally called him: 'We can confirm that your last truck has just gone past.'

'Great, thank you very much. Can you do me a favour? When you forward the photos, can you tell me exactly what time each was taken?'

'Sure. I'm doing it now.'

When the photos came, it was hard to see the black *bakkies* behind them, because it was dark, and the trucks' lights so bright in the foreground. But the order of the trucks was still the same. Red, red, blue shipping containers.

The time stamp showed the convoy's average speed was now much slower. They were barely maintaining sixty kilometres per hour.

Roadworks? Fuelling up? That meant they wouldn't pass through Williston until seven o'clock tomorrow morning. Eight thirty at Calvinia. That was good news. That gave Jericho Yon some daylight.

But the fact that the trucks were only ten minutes apart was concerning. Too close.

He must call Themba, who was still in Cape Town. And then Tau. And Chrissie.

★ ★ ★

21:54

The Lord Willis bed and breakfast was the very last building beside the R63 before you left Williston on the road to Calvinia. Christina Jaeger and Tau Berger were standing in the dark behind the electric gate. They could see the road clearly through the railings from there.

'Feel how cold it is?' asked Tau. His shaven head gleamed dimly in the yellow light of the street lamp across the road.

She nodded.

'You stay inside. Keep warm. I'll take the watch, from four o'clock. Sleep in your gear. When I see them coming past, I'll call Igen, then I'll wake you up. You put the pistol here . . .' He put his hand behind his back, sliding his fingers inside his waistband. 'So it doesn't get in the way. The sticky is everything. We can't fuck this up.'

She let his slightly patronising tone roll off her. She recognised the strain in Tau, the same tension and apprehension that she felt.

Not much sleep to be had tonight.

★ ★ ★

21:59

The two detectives from the Investigative Directorate in Pretoria who came to relieve Benny and Vaughn were women.

In the driveway of Emilia's house, beside the rented Suzuki Swift, Griessel said they must just make sure Streicher didn't leave the house until everything was confirmed. The warrant for the Spartan warehouse would take another hour or two, it was Friday night. And in the Cape their colleagues were looking for information on a Russian ship.

'But if we don't hit the road now, we won't make it.'

'Benna is getting married tomorrow,' said Vaughn.

'Oh, wonderful!'

'*Ag* shame. Congratulations.'

Ag *shame.* Griessel just shook his head. Then he got in the car, so they could be ready to drive.

'ETA, according to Google Maps, is quarter to three tomorrow afternoon, *pappie*,' said Vaughn. 'It's a piece of cake.'

'Will you tell that to Carla?'

Griessel called his daughter.

'Ask her to please let Desiree know. I'm totally in the dog box with her.'

99

Chrissie listened to Mozart's clarinet concerto, in search of a bit of peace and calm.

A message came in: *Awake?* From Igen.

Her answer: *Yes.*

He called. 'You okay?'

'Do you have some kind of technique? For sleeping, on the night before an Op?'

He laughed. 'No. Don't worry. Tomorrow you run on adrenaline.'

'I'm glad you're calling. Because I wanted to tell you, I lied.'

'Oh?'

'About Heracles and the lion.'

'What makes you think I believed you?'

'You did.'

'So? What is the truth?'

'You're not going to like the truth.'

'Then don't tell me now.'

'Okay.'

Both were silent for a moment.

'Tell me at Caffè Greco. On the twenty-third. Twelve o'clock.'

★ ★ ★

22:12

Emilia could wash off the perspiration at last, but the tension remained in her body, despite the stream of hot water.

She wasn't telling the whole truth. A calculated risk. Offer just enough for them to believe her. Enough for them to verify. But no information that would directly harm Tau and the others.

She told them that Tau had asked her to go and see if Ishan Babbar was loading the gold and the dollars, this afternoon just after one. That's why she had been in Spartan.

Yes, she saw the trucks, and people busy at the site. But she didn't hang around, it was too dangerous. Two trucks. Big. White. Then she sent Tau a message on Telegram. No, she couldn't show them the message. She deleted it immediately. Here are both her phones, the personal one, the work phone. They could look.

The tall detective googled pictures of trucks. She tapped on one, one that she imagined would be able to carry ten tons of gold. One of a make you'd see in their hundreds on the roads. A Tata with a white horse, double rear axle and a long white trailer behind.

Cupido forwarded it on to someone.

She told them Tau was going to ambush one of the trucks. Tau and his crew. He didn't say where. He didn't say when.

That's all she knew. That's really all she knew.

★ ★ ★

23:19

Cupido was playing Diana Krall to Griessel on the Swift's sound system as they crossed the Vaal River, when Benny's phone rang. It was Mbali Kaleni. He turned the music off and answered.

'Are you making good time?' she asked.

'Yes, Colonel, we should have an hour to spare.'

'I'm so sorry, Benny.'

'It's really okay.'

'I'm just calling to tell you that they have searched the warehouse. And it looks like Streicher told the truth. The space was converted into a series of fourteen strongrooms, with state-of-the-art surveillance and security. And we know Ishan Babbar well. He is the enforcer of the Cabal, the doer of the dirty work. So, her story is holding up.'

'Okay,' he said.

'Also, Doctor Duba asks if you can remember the dates of the burner phone calls to Dineo Phiri.'

'Yes . . .?'

'She said that first big burst of calls on Easter weekend very much corresponds with the alleged robbery at the warehouse, and the fire at Brits airfield.'

He remembered. 'Yes,' he said. 'That's right.'

'But the trucks are going to be impossible to find. We don't know the route, and we couldn't risk a general law enforcement broadcast.

However, we have sent a national GB to all stations requesting any information about truck hijackings in the next forty-eight hours.'

'And the ship, Colonel?'

'So far, we haven't found a single Russian vessel coming to the Cape Town Harbour.'

100

Saturday, 12 June.

01:02

In Green Point, Themba Jola made sure the rental agreement was in the Ford single-cab pick-up glove compartment – the document that said the vehicle belonged to Final Cut Movie Cars. He'd said it was to be used as a police van for a film production in Calvinia. A movie with the name *Gold Heist*. Just in case he had to go through a road-block somewhere.

It would also explain why there was a cop costume lying on the seat beside him.

He shut the glove compartment, started the engine, and set off.

It was about four and a half hours' drive to Calvinia.

★ ★ ★

03:03

Griessel woke up when Cupido stopped at the Engen next to the N1 at Rayton, Bloemfontein, to fill up.

'Coffee and a meat pie?' asked Vaughn.

'Please. And I'll take the next shift.'

'Damn straight. I'm basically a zombie. Oh, and Carla called.'

'Again?'

'*Yebo*. Made me promise I'll get you to the church on time.'

★ ★ ★

04:51

Jericho Yon unlocked the rear port-side cargo door of the Basler BT-67. The plane was parked in front of the Douglas Street hangar at the now almost deserted General Aviation section of Cape Town

International Airport. The steel-grey hull glistened in the bright yellow lights of the area.

He climbed in to activate the parking brake, then fetch the big black PVC tote bag and the step ladder.

He came back out with the ladder and placed it under the port engine, removed the propeller brakes, and the plugs over the turbine intakes and exhaust pipes. He placed all the articles in the tote bag, and repeated the process at the starboard engine.

He checked that the wheel chocks had been removed and the single wheel at the back was unlocked. He looked at each of the two wheels in the front undercarriage for any possible previous damage. He tested the tyre pressure; he didn't want them to be too hard, because he had three different runways – the possibly muddy Skoorsteenberg, the tar surface of Calvinia, and the sand of Jamba – to negotiate.

Yon pulled off the two pitot tubes' covers, and put them in the bag as well. He inspected the flaps, trimmers, elevators and rudders, tested them by hand, and pulled out the red rudder stopper.

When he was satisfied that everything was in order, he climbed in through the rear loading door, hoisted up the ladder, and secured it. He pulled all three sections of the cargo door shut, and made sure it was securely locked. Then he walked to the cockpit with the tote bag, careful not to trip over the electric winch on the cargo area deck, and stored the bag in the box just behind the cockpit, under the axe and fire extinguisher, against the partition.

He would start his pre-flight checklist now. So that he could be ready, if Igen called and said the trucks were early.

If he didn't hear anything, he would take off at 06:20.

★　★　★

05:25

In the darkness, Themba Jola stopped the movie prop police van at Calvinia airfield's locked gate.

He reached for his cell phone, and called Igen.

Rousseau answered immediately. 'Yes.'

'I'm at the gate. Did you get any sleep?'

'About an hour.'

'Ready to roll?'

'I'll be there in fifteen.'

* * *

05:32

Forty kilometres before Colesberg, Cupido was fast asleep. Griessel looked at the Google Maps screen on Vaughn's phone.

Their arrival time in Cape Town was 14:26.

There wouldn't be enough time to go home, pack his honeymoon bag, shower and drive to Zorgvliet.

He would call Carla, at about at seven o'clock. And see if she could help.

He changed the destination to Zorgvliet. They would have to drive straight to the wedding venue. There would definitely be somewhere he could shower and change there.

* * *

05:39

Chrissie sat on the armchair next to her bed, clasping a mug of instant coffee.

She thought of Katse and Sebini. In the summer heat of Poggio Nativo.

Was Luca taking care of them? Would they have gone wild again when she got back?

She wished she could call Luca now. Just to hear his voice.

She wished she could call Igen, and tell him the truth.

She said yes to this whole thing because he'd asked her.

That was the one and only reason.

101

07:02

High in the sky above Ceres, Jericho Yon saw the eastern horizon change colour.

He drew back the two throttle levers. The roar of the Basler's turbine engines dropped an octave.

His altimeter began to move downward. He contacted Cape Town air control for the last time, then he switched off the Basler's radio.

He looked at the satellite phone.

Nothing yet.

★ ★ ★

07:07

From behind the gate, Tau Berger saw the first truck pass. He read the registration number, he looked at the black Toyota *bakkie* a hundred metres behind the truck. He noted the exact time.

Then he looked at the photos that Igen had sent, of the trucks in Potchefstroom and Kimberley.

Same truck, same registration.

He called Igen.

★ ★ ★

07:10

Jericho Yon was on the final approach to the airstrip at Skoorsteenberg. He saw the satellite phone's screen light up, though with his headphones he couldn't hear it ring.

He took off the headset, answered, pressed the phone to his ear, his eyes still on the instruments.

The noise of the engines was too loud, he couldn't hear what Igen was saying.

But he knew it was to say the trucks were in Williston.

He shouted: 'I'm on final approach, I'll call you in ten.'

★ ★ ★

07:12

Carla was calling. 'Where are you, Pa?'

'Just beyond Richmond.'

'Are you guys going to be on time?'

'Definitely, but . . .'

'No buts, Pa. Not one single but.'

'Carla, I won't even be able to go home. Could you go and pack my honeymoon bag? One huge big please?'

'Wasn't that on Pa's list?'

'Yes. I'm sorry. Oh, and my wedding shoes too, please. There's a key in a security box at the back door.'

★ ★ ★

07:43

'The last one is past now,' Tau said to Igen over the phone. 'They are about fifteen minutes apart.'

'Great. Still red, red, blue?'

'Roger. But the last one – the shotguns are right on their ass. It's going to be tight.'

Igen heard the strain in Tau's voice, so he tried to keep his own voice calm. 'I expected them to be close to the trucks, passing through a town. And tight is okay if we only have one truck and shotgun *bakkie* to deal with. Could you see how many are in the truck?'

'Just the two in front that I could see. The *bakkie* windows are tinted, I think it's four.'

'Okay. We stick to the plan.'

'Roger. We leave in fifteen.'

He hung up to call Chrissie.

★ ★ ★

07:45

On the satellite phone, Igen said: 'I take it the strip wasn't too wet?'

'Strip is fine,' said Jericho Yon.

'Everything quiet?'

'Like the grave.'

'Great. The last truck's ETA is ballpark nine fifteen.'

'Roger. I'm wheels on the tarmac by nine ten.'

'It should distract them. A Dak on the airfield.'

'Basler,' said Jer.

102

07:58

Themba also parked the second forklift behind the small white building at the airfield outside Calvinia.

Igen dragged the steel ramp, the one they used to get the forklifts off the sheep lorry, to the side of the building. He walked back to the lorry to collect Chrissie's AK, and put Tau and Themba's in the police van.

Themba jogged past him. 'Wardrobe call,' he said, and went to get the police uniform, so he could put it on behind the building.

Igen saw how relaxed Themba was. Loose-limbed, easy in himself. Like he always was before an Op.

★ ★ ★

08:20

Starting at the southern end of the airstrip at Skoorsteenberg, Jericho Yon began his checklist before he started the Basler's engines.

He looked to the heavens. The weather looked good.

★ ★ ★

08:23

On the back of the BMW motorcycle, Chrissie adjusted her bandana to keep the icy wind away from her neck and the inside of her helmet. They were halfway to Calvinia, Tau riding at a hundred and forty. The road was quiet.

Tau touched her knee with his left hand. He pointed to the road ahead. At the black Toyota double-cab. And two hundred metres ahead of it, the rearguard truck, with a blue shipping container on it.

Her heart beat faster.

They caught up with the *bakkie*. Passed it.

She tried to look without being too obvious about it.

She saw four men behind the tinted glass. One was resting his head against the window. He seemed to be asleep.

They drove right behind the truck. There was a thick chain and lock on the shipping container door.

Tau accelerated, they passed the truck. The cab was too high for her to see anything more than the driver. A hard face, with a full beard.

*   *   *

08:33

A hundred metres from the Calvinia airfield gate, on the sloping road shoulder, Themba Jola sat in the police van. The front of the van pointed west and he could see the sheep lorry, parked in front of the gate. But Themba kept an eye on the rear-view mirror.

He saw the truck coming, a red shipping container visible behind the horse. He called Igen.

'First one is here.'

'Yip. See him. Nicely on time.'

*   *   *

08:52

Tau pulled into the Caltex service station in Calvinia. Chrissie dismounted.

Tau kicked out the motorbike stand, got off, removed his helmet.

'It's Ishan Babbar,' he said. '*Fokken* Babbar, in the shotgun *bakkie*.' He took out his cell phone to call Igen. 'How are your hands?' he asked Chrissie.

'Cold,' she said.

'To the toilets. Get them under warm water . . . Shit.'

'What?'

He jerked his head, and looked up the street.

She followed his gaze.

The second truck with the red shipping container was pulled over at the side of the main street, the double-cab Toyota just behind it.

Tau rang Igen.

*   *   *

09:02

Tau saw two of the philistines running across the main street, towards the double-cab Toyota. Black uniforms, bulletproof vests, pistols on their hips. And shopping bags in their hands.

They signalled something to the truck, and jumped into the *bakkie*. Both vehicles began moving.

He called Igen, the strain apparent in his voice. 'Fucking philistines stopped to buy meat. Jeez. Meat. Number two is driving off now. It's going to be very tight.'

'Okay. Just stick to the plan.'

'Roger.'

Chrissie came back from the toilets.

'Hot water helped?' asked Tau.

She nodded. 'A lot.'

Tau snapped open the pannier on the right side, took out the sticky, snapped the box shut again. 'Helmet on, gloves off,' he said. 'Last truck will be here in five.'

He waited until she had the helmet on.

He gave her the magnetic bomb.

Suddenly it felt impossibly heavy.

103

09:06

Jericho Yon and the Basler were on the final approach, from the east.

He saw the narrow, tarred runway, one thousand two hundred and fifty metres long. And almost exactly aligned with it, the grey-black ribbon of the R27 which extended west-south-west out of the town. The dull stripes of Calvinia's golf course fairways to its right. At exactly one point seven three kilometres before the airfield gate the R355 veered off to the left, stretching away to the Tankwa horizon.

He saw the speck that was Igen's sheep lorry.

He saw a truck with a red shipping container driving past the golf course.

Hopefully that was gold truck number two.

★ ★ ★

09:07

The last gold truck, the one with the blue shipping container, passed Calvinia Caltex.

Tau waited for the *bakkie* to pass too, then started the BMW motorbike.

Chrissie sat behind him with the magnet bomb on her lap.

Tau looked around at her. His eyes were wild. 'Just like we practised,' he said. 'Slap me hard when you've done it.'

'Okay.'

'Hard. Or we're gone.'

Her heart began to pound.

★ ★ ★

09:09

The second truck drove past Themba, then past Igen and the airfield gate.

Igen heard the Basler. He looked out of the sheep lorry's window. He saw the plane come in, just a kilometre away.

All on schedule.

He switched on the lorry's diesel engine.

He felt the adrenaline start to surge.

* * *

09:11

Igen watched Jericho Yon turn the Basler, down at the western end of the runway, and begin taxiing back to the eastern end.

He reached for the AK-47, pressed the safety clip off. Cocked the rifle. Put it down where it would not interfere with him taking out and operating the RPG-30 'Kryuk' missile launcher.

The RPG was a last resort. He hoped it wouldn't be necessary.

He opened his window.

The wind was cold.

He hoped Chrissie's hands were warm.

* * *

09:13

Near Three Sisters, Griessel and Cupido talked about Basie Small. About his behaviour during Le-Lanie Leibrandt's death. How that, as always, was a pointer to previous, dishonest behaviour.

And then, just before the N12 joined the N1, Griessel was forced to a stop behind a long queue of stationary vehicles.

'*Jirre*, partner, I hope it's a stop-and-go,' said Cupido, and got out.

Griessel followed suit, to stretch his legs and get his circulation going.

They tried to see what was going on in front.

'Blue lights,' said Cupido. 'Looks like an accident.'

He opened the Suzuki's door. 'Come on, Benna, we're going to flash our cards, we don't have any time to spare.'

* * *

09:16

Chrissie saw the big green sign of the Ceres turn-off, five hundred metres ahead.

She felt Tau accelerate.

She looked down at the explosive device on her lap. She gripped the handle firmly in her left hand. She made sure the cord with the big ring wouldn't catch on anything.

Her heart was racing too fast: breathe, breathe.

Two hundred metres from the turn-off, ten metres from the black *bakkie*.

She saw her cold hand was shaking, she was going to fuck it up, her brain screamed at her, you practised this thing, damnit, breathe, breathe.

One hundred metres.

Tau rode even faster.

For a moment Chrissie thought his timing was off, he was too early, too hasty; he passed the van, the turn was right there, he was on the right side of the Toyota, she lifted the sticky, leaned over, let it clamp against the metal, grabbed the ring, missed, grabbed again, pulled it as hard as she could. The cord came free, she hit Tau on the shoulder with all her strength. He opened the throttle.

The driver jerked the *bakkie* to the right, the nose hit the BMW's left pannier.

She knew Tau was going to lose control, the bike wobbled. She forgot to bend down.

Boom.

A shock wave over her back.

The motorbike was out of control.

104

Igen saw the ore truck approaching from Calvinia's side, only three hundred metres in front of the last gold truck with the blue shipping container and he knew he would have to get this timing right.

He shoved the sheep lorry into gear, and revved up the engine. Don't release the clutch too fast, don't let the thing stall, don't look if Chrissie and Tau take out the shotguns, just focus on the ore truck.

The ore truck was here. He stepped on the accelerator, released the clutch, the sheep lorry juddered forwards, the ore truck blew its horn sharply, the driver waved his hand, then he was past. Igen pulled the sheep lorry across the road.

The gold truck was coming.

He saw Themba, in blue uniform, get out of the police van.

Themba stopped beside the road. He raised his arm to the gold truck, a gesture that said, slow down.

Igen pulled the RPG-30 launcher closer. Stuck it out the window.

He saw the explosion first: smoke and flames, the bomb on the black *bakkie*. Then the dull boom rushed past him. Behind the gold truck he saw the BMW motorcycle, careering wildly out of control: They're going to fall, fuck, they're going to fall.

The gold truck passed Themba. Themba ran to get two AKs from his police van.

The gold truck braked. Igen aimed the RPG at the cab.

* * *

Tau wrestled with the motorbike, the handlebars jerking in his hands. He kicked the brake: he should have turned off the ABS. Finally he got the bike under control and they stopped, just past Themba.

'Down, down, down,' Tau screamed at Chrissie.

She jumped down, ripped off her helmet, took off her jacket. Threw it down.

Whipped out the pistol from behind her back. Cocked it.

Tau dropped the bike, gloves off, his own helmet off. He grabbed an AK from Themba and they sprinted forward, towards the gold truck.

Tau to the right, Themba to the left.

Chrissie looked left, saw the little white building. Started running.

A man opened the passenger door of the gold truck's cab. Aimed an automatic weapon at Igen in the sheep lorry.

Themba shot him from behind. The man fell.

Chrissie kept running.

Tau shooting on the other side of the gold truck, short bursts: one, two, three.

She was close behind Themba when he reached the open passenger door of the gold truck, and fired.

She saw Igen hefting the RPG in the lorry, ready to launch. If there was no other choice.

She ran alongside the gold truck, then dodged left, towards the airfield gate.

More shots behind her.

She heard Themba shout: 'Clear!'

She didn't look back, she ran towards the building. Around the corner. The Basler was four hundred metres east of her, at the end of the runway, engines running. The forklifts were ready. The one with the AK in it was hers. She shoved the pistol behind her back. She jumped in, sat behind the forklift's steering. Hooked the AK's strap over her shoulder, the rifle behind her back. She was out of breath. She switched the vehicle on, disengaged the handbrake, put it in gear and drove around the corner, to the road.

Tau came from the front. He ran past her, to get the second forklift. Didn't look at her. A blank expression on his face, as if she wasn't there.

She saw the men who'd been in the truck, now lying in pools of blood. Igen was at the back of the shipping container with an angle grinder, Themba was almost at his police van, he had to pull it across the road. On the other side lay the black Toyota double-cab, a smoking wreck.

Lord, she thought, this is going to work. It was going to work.

She paused at the container doors. Igen cut the chain loose, the shrill whine of the angle grinder suddenly stopped.

'One of them was on the phone,' he said. 'We don't have much time.'

He jumped up, into the shipping container.

* * *

Griessel drove in the right-hand lane, past the long queue of cars, to just beyond the N12 junction, where an indignant traffic officer blocked their way.

Cupido got out, his identification card ready. 'Brother, we are SAPS, we have to pass, we have a very urgent case in Cape Town.'

'That's not gonna help you,' said the traffic officer. 'The road is closed.'

'Why?'

'Very high risk of fire and explosions. Petrol tanker and a gas tanker crashed into each other at the Three Sisters Ultra City entrance. One spark, and it's doomsday.'

'What are my alternatives?'

'Gravel road, sir. Your best bet is to take the N12 to Victoria West, then ten kilos out, you take Wagenaarskraal on the left. Twenty kilos, you *gooi* another left. Fourteen kilos, your last left, then you come back to N1.'

'Okay, cool, thanks.'

The traffic officer looked at the Suzuki sceptically. '*Ja*, take it easy with that little thing, Karoo gravel roads are not for sissies.'

105

09:36

Chrissie's final pallet loaded, she stood in the Basler's cargo hold and watched Jericho Yon unhook the winch hook from the third gold pallet. She took the hook from him, pulled it down to the loading door.

She looked through the square window on the starboard side. She saw Tau arriving in the forklift with the last crate. Themba and Igen hanging onto the back of the hoist, AKs over their shoulders.

And then, far behind them, she saw a movement.

Four hundred metres beyond the sheep lorry. A black Toyota double-cab burst through the boundary fence between the airfield and the R27. It bucked across the veld, on its way to the Basler.

She screamed for Jericho above the noise of the engines, grabbed her AK, ran to the loading door and jumped out.

She ran around the tail of the plane, signalling to Igen: Look.

He looked back, shouted something. Jumped off the forklift.

Themba did the same.

Igen and Themba each dropped to one knee, the AKs at the ready. Tau was coming past with the last gold pallet, around the tail, towards the hold door.

Chrissie went to kneel next to Igen, cocked the AK, aimed it at the Toyota.

'Chrissie, no,' shouted Igen. 'Get in.'

She settled into place. Themba fired off a volley of shots; single shots from Igen. She aimed. Fired.

The *bakkie* kept coming. She fired again, knew she'd hit the *bakkie*, but it didn't stop.

She realised what they wanted to do. They wanted to block the runway.

Themba's magazine was empty. He pulled it out, slid in a new one. She and Igen continued firing single shots. The *bakkie* kept coming.

Igen shouted something again.

The *bakkie* was on the runway, barely three hundred metres away. It stopped, the doors opened and they started returning fire.

Igen grabbed her by the shoulder. 'Come on.'

They ran. Themba fell. Stood up. Blood on his back, high, just under the right shoulder.

Around the tail. Lead smacked into the plane. Igen shoved her in first, then he got in, held his hand to the stumbling Themba. Pulled him up.

Tau was at the winch, the fourth gold crate was just in. Jericho Yon was in the cockpit. Igen began to close the three flaps of the cargo door.

Themba collapsed, his hand against his shoulder. Blood flooding through his fingers, shock in his eyes.

★   ★   ★

Jericho Yon had no time to strap himself in. He saw the *bakkie*, three hundred metres in front of the plane, in the middle of the runway. Saw the flashes of their weapons firing.

He did the calculations in his head. The Basler needed a runway of nine hundred and fifteen metres to be able to take off.

Calvinia's runway was one thousand two hundred and fifty metres long.

He would have to go around the *bakkie*.

He didn't know if it would work. They had more than four tons on board. Fuel tanks almost full.

He opened the throttles.

Bullets smacked into the windshield, the undercarriage, the wing. He instinctively ducked behind the instrument panel.

★   ★   ★

Chrissie pulled her bandana from her neck, sat down with Themba. She heard the deep rumble of the engines, she felt the Basler jerk forward. Themba rolled backwards.

She looked for the right place to press the bandana to stop the bleeding. Igen was beside her, large folding knife in hand. He deftly snapped it open, cut the buckles off Themba's bulletproof vest.

The Basler juddered across the field, lunging forward.

Chrissie saw the wound. The bullet had gone in just below the shoulder arch of the bulletproof vest. There was too much blood.

Themba's eyes were shut.

Igen grabbed her bandana, pressed it against the gunshot wound, took her hand, held it on the cloth. He crouched on his knees, pulled off his own jacket, then his T-shirt.

Suddenly, rough ground, they were tossed about, shaken.

The Basler swerved, right, left. Igen lost his balance, fell over Chrissie. Straightened up again. Back to Themba, now pressing his T-shirt against the wound, shouting: 'Themba! Themba!' The engines deafening as their speed increased, a window right next to her on the port side shattered, and she saw the Karoo flash by outside, faster and faster.

But they weren't getting airborne.

'Themba!' shouted Igen, his face distorted.

And then they were in the air.

106

A hundred metres above the ground. Jericho Yon began to bank to
the north, pressing the lever to retract the undercarriage to gain
altitude as fast as possible.

He heard the electric motor powering the hydraulic system, he felt
the vibration of the system working. He waited for that light bump,
the moment when the undercarriage was fully folded back into the
wing, and the acceleration that came with it.

He waited in vain. The red light, to show that the undercarriage
was safely retracted, did not come on.

The electric motor kept running.

That's when he first knew there was damage to the Basler.

* * *

Igen and Chrissie's hands were both pressed to Themba's wound.

His mouth at her ear, he shouted: 'Ask Jer if there's a medical kit
in the Dak.'

It was the first time she'd heard such stress in Igen Rousseau's
voice. She tried to get up, the plane banked, the G-force was strong.
She grabbed the gold pallet next to her for balance, waiting for the
Basler to stabilise.

The plane steadied after its turn and she tried to stand up.

She felt something scrape low against her back. She whipped
around. Tau Berger had grabbed her pistol: he raised it and struck a
blow to her head.

Chrissie staggered, searing pain above her ear, then fell back, trying to break the fall with her hands. She saw Igen, kneeling beside
Themba, looking up at Tau in surprise.

Chrissie, on her back on the deck, disoriented. Stunned.

She saw the pistol in Tau's hand buck, heard the report. She saw Igen fall backwards.

Tau fired again. At Igen.

Then at Themba.

He looked at her. A crazed look on his face.

She waited for him to shoot her too.

He shoved her pistol into the back of his trousers. Reached for a sheath on his belt, pulled out a long knife. 'Now I'm gonna screw you, bitch.'

Then he came for her.

★   ★   ★

Yon was unplugging the electric motor's circuit breaker, so that the motor wouldn't overheat and set the Basler on fire, his right hand on the yoke, his feet on the rudder pedals, his eyes on the instruments, when he heard the first shot. He let go of the pump, looked around.

He saw Tau with his back to him, down near the door. Arm outstretched.

Tau shooting. Again. And again.

Jissis.

Twisting, half rising from his seat, he saw Tau tuck the pistol into the back of his belt. Chrissie, lying on the deck, Tau moving towards her.

Jericho Yon did the only thing he could do in the circumstances. He slid back into the seat, stepped on the right rudder pedal, and turned the control stick to the right.

★   ★   ★

Chrissie felt the plane's floor tip, she saw Tau Berger staggering to the right.

She looked for her AK, saw it at the very back, sliding across the floor. Out of reach.

Igen's big folding knife. The closest weapon at hand. She stretched to grasp it. Tried to get up.

Tau regained his balance and stepped towards her.

The plane turned sharply to port.

Tau lurched against the gold pallet. He swore, stumbling over Igen's body, and fell to the floor.

Chrissie rolled with the Basler's motion, pressed against the wall, found her feet.

Tau struggled to get up.

She leaped forward and rammed the knife through his throat.

★ ★ ★

10:09

Chrissie slid into the seat beside Yon. He said something, but she couldn't hear him.

He took the headset off the port control stick and passed it to her.

She just sat holding it. Her hands were covered in blood.

He waited.

Finally she mustered up the strength to act. She put the headset on.

'Igen?' Yon asked.

She just shook her head.

'Themba too?'

She nodded.

'*Jirre*,' he said.

After a long silence, he told her: 'We're not going to make it. We have a fuel leak. And the landing gear's drag . . . And if we fly higher to save fuel, the radar will find us.'

She just stared out the window.

107

10:16

Emilia Streicher heard her front doorbell ring and went to open it. It was one of the female detectives sitting outside in the car.

'Ma'am, you may leave for the airport.'

Relief. 'So I can fly?'

'No, we are still waiting for that answer. But the director did let us know you can check in in the meantime. Otherwise you will definitely miss the flight.'

'Thank you.'

'And you can also turn on your cell phones.'

She closed the door, walked over to her handbag, switched the phones on.

She waited until both had reception.

There was no Telegram message from Tau.

Eleven minutes later she drove to the airport.

☆ ☆ ☆

10:58

In Beaufort West, Google Maps told Vaughn Cupido they would only arrive at Zorgvliet at ten past four.

'Benna, now you have to hold tight, because Uncle V is going to put pedal to the metal. Let's see what this little Suzie can do.'

They soon found that the Suzuki Swift's top speed was just this side of one hundred and sixty kilometres per hour. Downhill.

Google's estimated time of arrival updated regularly. Until it stopped at 15:32.

'Can you shower, shave and get dressed in half an hour, Benna?'

'This cute hairstyle takes a little more time,' said Griessel.

☆ ☆ ☆

12:07

Mbali Kaleni called Griessel. There was renewed enthusiasm in her voice, despite the long night. 'The ship, Benny. We think we've found it. A Russian cargo vessel called the *Lady R* docked at the naval base in Simon's Town earlier this morning. We were looking in the wrong place – ships en route to Cape Town harbour. The problem is, we're trying to get more information, but the Department of Defence is stonewalling us. Which sort of confirms our suspicions that this is the right ship. The fact is, Streicher's story is still holding up. We've allowed her to travel to the airport, but we can still prevent her from boarding.'

'Okay,' said Griessel. His mind was racing. He said: 'Colonel, there is only one road into Simon's Town. If we can set up a road block . . .'

'We're working on that. But we have to be careful about who we ask to do it.'

Griessel thought of his former colleagues at the Hawks unit against Serious and Violent Crimes. 'Call Frankie Fillander, Colonel. You know you can trust him and the gang.'

She considered it for a moment. 'Yes. That is a great idea.'

Griessel saw the road sign along the N1 announcing: *Laingsburg 20 km.*

* * *

12:25

Captains Frank Fillander and Vusumuzi Ndabeni were in the Hawks' white BMW X1, the siren wailing, blue light in the front windscreen, on the R300, on the way to Simon's Town.

Mooiwillem Liebenberg drove his own car from his home in Edgemead. He was on the phone, talking to the station commissioner at Fish Hoek, to ask for uniformed manpower for the roadblock.

* * *

12:29

A Scania truck with an orange shipping container on the load bed turned into the Simon's Town Naval Base entrance opposite Clarks Steps.

In the cab were the driver and four armed members of the South African Air Force.

In the shipping container on the back was a Gripen fighter plane, carefully disassembled and packed.

The gate sentry pulled the gate open.

★   ★   ★

12:32

Cupido behind the wheel, they were pulling out of the Shell Ultra City in Laingsburg, with a full tank of petrol, when Mbali Kaleni called again.

She spoke rapidly, with an excitement they had never heard from her before: 'There was a heist on a container truck, this morning at around nine o'clock, outside Calvinia. The police found thousands of dollars in the container. But the clincher is the fact that one of the bodies in what is assumed to be a support vehicle, was that of Mr Ishan Babbar.'

Griessel was going to say 'fuck', but he stopped himself just in time. 'Wow,' he said instead.

'The perpetrators apparently fled the scene from the airfield nearby, in an aircraft. We are now trying to trace it. And I've let Captain Fillander know we are looking at container trucks entering Simon's Town. Oh, and one other thing: we've decided that Emilia Streicher can board her flight. We believe she spoke the truth as she saw it.'

108

12:33

Emilia Streicher presented her passport and boarding pass at the Immigration desk in OR Tambo's International Departures hall.

She held her breath.

The man looked at her, scanned the passport. Paused. Then stamped her passport, handed it back and said: 'Safe travels.'

Relief flooded like a wave through her.

'You may go,' said the man. 'Next.'

Passport in hand, Emilia wheeled her case through border control. Then she stopped, took out the cell phones and looked at each of them in turn.

No message from Tau. Should she stay?

And then she made up her mind, and walked on, towards her plane's gate.

* * *

13:48

Just beyond the Scarborough turn-off, on Simon's Town's main street, stood Captains Frankie Fillander, Vusi Ndabeni and Mooiwillem Liebenberg, each with a Vektor LM5 semi-automatic assault rifle in their hands. With them were seven SAPS members in blue uniforms from Fish Hoek station.

They watched the truck with the red shipping container approach.

Fillander held his hand in the air and signalled for the truck to pull over.

* * *

14:03

Past Touwsrivier at a hundred and fifty kilometres an hour, Griessel played 'Bad, Bad Boy' by Nazareth to Cupido, at full volume.

Cupido said, 'I love it, I love it, *pappie*, that's my song,' and then the music stopped when Mbali called one last time, her voice coming over the Swift's sound system.

'Captain Fillander and the team got one truck at Simon's Town. Gold and dollars, we think the value is in the billions. But they might have warned the other truck, it is still missing.'

'Yes, baby,' said Cupido and pumped his fist in the air.

'That is great news, Colonel,' said Griessel.

'Indeed. I just wanted to tell you two that you have done wonderful, wonderful work. Thank you.'

'That's how we roll, Colonel,' said Cupido.

Kaleni said: 'Benny, where is the wedding venue?'

Why would she ask that? 'At Zorgvliet, Colonel. Near Stellenbosch.'

'Okay. I'm going to call the Stellenbosch station commissioner now. And ask him to send a vehicle to the Huguenot Tunnel. So they can escort you to Zorgvliet. We don't want you to be late.'

*   *   *

15:07

There were four police vehicles waiting for them, just beyond the toll gate.

Cupido flashed his lights and the sergeant in the leading vehicle gave a thumbs-up, motioning to them that they should fall into the middle of the convoy.

Sirens blaring, blue lights revolving, the N1 opened ahead of them like the Red Sea.

'Razamanaz' started playing over the sound system.

Jissis, thought Benny Griessel.

He was going to get married.

109

Seventy kilometres south of the border between Botswana and the
Caprivi Strip in Namibia, two hundred and fifty kilometres from
their destination, Jamba, Jericho Yon kept the Basler steady at five
thousand feet.

'Tsodilo, do you know Tsodilo?' asked Jericho Yon over the
headset.

Chrissie was still far away, staring at the misty African plain below.

'Chrissie.' Yon's voice was sharp. 'You worked in the Okavango.
Do you know Tsodilo?'

She looked at him. 'Yes.'

'There was an airstrip, I don't know what it looks like now. That's
our only chance. The fuel is finished.'

She just sat there.

'Chrissie!'

'Yes?'

'I need your help now – it's going to be a bad landing. We don't
have undercarriage. Do you hear me?'

'I hear you.'

'You have to check the pallets. The last one, it's not strapped
down. You must do that. Now. Make sure it's secure. I know you
don't want to be back there now, but if that pallet comes loose, we're
in the shit. Do you understand?'

'Yes.'

'Okay. Go strap it fast. Just here behind the cabin is a fire extinguisher and an axe. Look and see where they are. Just in case I'm not
with you after the landing. Do you hear?'

'I hear you.'

'When you come back, bring a duffel or something. Something
soft, that can act as a cushion.'

She nodded.

'Go. Now. Please.'

She stood up, much to his relief.

★   ★   ★

15:52

Chrissie came back to the cockpit, dragging Igen's duffel bag along with her. She sat down, put the headset back on her head.

'Pallet secure?' Yon asked.

'Yes.'

'You okay?'

She nodded.

'Buckle up, please,' said Jericho Yon. 'When we go in for the landing, hold that duffel bag in front of you. Like this. And you brace. Do you understand?'

She hesitated a moment. 'Yes.' Then she began to buckle herself into the seat.

Through the haze Yon saw the hills of Tsodilo, the only contours in this wide plain. He began his turn to port: he was landing from the west, so that the low winter sun was behind them.

'If I can put her down, and we're okay, we'll have to get away. There's a village, nearby. They will come and check us out. We will have to walk. Do you know where to head?'

'Yes.'

'Okay.'

He saw, far to the starboard side, the line of the run-down landing strip.

He checked through all the flight instruments, the condition of the engines, the fuel, again and again.

He bent down to test the hand pump for the undercarriage. If that worked, if he could get the wheels out and down, it would change everything.

He pumped and pumped.

There was no resistance. It was no good, all the hydraulic fluid was gone.

Yon completed the base leg, turned the Basler for the final approach.

He set the flaps to maximum and pulled the engines back: he had to bleed off as much airspeed as possible, to find that point just before the Basler stalled.

'The duffel,' he said.

She raised the bag, as though it was an immensely heavy burden, and hugged it in front of her, head bowed.

The rust-brown landscape was getting closer. A yellow ribbon of dirt road. Five hundred feet, three hundred, two hundred, one hundred. 'Brace!' he shouted, holding up the nose as long as he could, then bringing it down. The runway looked bad, too short.

The undercarriage gave way, the Basler landed on her belly and they slid, the noise deafening, too fast. The plane yawed askew, the port propeller hit the ground, the tail tipped up. They skidded over the eastern end of the runway, through the veld, and over the footpath twisting down the mountain.

And then everything was quiet.

★   ★   ★

Jericho Yon snapped off the master switch and the engine cut-off, closed the fuel tanks.

He left her in the cockpit, grabbed the axe and ran to the cargo door at the back, to see if it would open.

Igen and Themba and Tau lay there.

Yon tested the cargo door flaps. They opened.

He stumbled back through the cargo area, to fetch her. She was already on her way.

'Come,' he said.

She wasn't listening. She went to fetch her backpack, and Igen's. She threw out their contents. Then she walked over to the nearest gold pallet, and started packing gold bars into the backpacks.

'You're going to help carry,' she said.

110

16:11

Benny Griessel, in his wedding suit, stood facing Alexa. He looked at her. She looked impossibly beautiful to him.

He glanced down at the sheet of paper in his hand.

He read:

Alexa
I, Benny Griessel,
pledge you my loyalty, respect and devotion.
My love for you is as wide as the ocean.
I take you, Alexa, here today as my wife,
Be by my side for the rest of my life.
You're my small glass of sunlight, my goblet of rain,
I will stand by you, through the joy and the pain.
I give you my heart, I give you this ring
Forever together, Sweet Water we'll sing.

Acknowledgements

In the research, creation and production of *Leo*, I was privileged to have access to the advice, support, generousness, knowledge time, insight, patience, creativity, friendship and love of a group of exceptional people. The errors, deficiencies and poetic licences are all mine.

A huge thank you to:

- My wife Marianne for her limitless patience, understanding, love, care and support.
- My super-smart translator Laura Seegers. It remains a huge pleasure to work with you.
- My agent Isobel Dixon and South African editor Etienne Bloemhof. It's been almost thirty years of working with these two brilliant people.
- Nick Sayers, my British editor of many years to whom I owe so much, Executive Publisher Jo Dickinson, and the whole team at Hodder who are such a pleasure to work with.
- My polymath friend and ace pilot Dr Johan Steytler for all things aviation and medical, and the Cessna 210 flights to Doringbaai, Skoorstenberg and Calvinia.
- Coenie de Villiers for Diana Krall, and David Kramer for Sonny Terry and Brownie McGhee.
- Anna-Maree Uys of Sew Elegant, for Benny's wedding suit.
- Stellenbosch Municipality's Joan Felix, representing the Community and Protection Services.
- The National Prosecuting Authority's Sindisiwe Seboka.
- Stefano and Lida Masini for the Italian.
- George Supra, for his help in trying to find special forces soldiers involved in the 2011 Operation.
- Hannes Vorster, for Arabella's sixteenth, the fruit truck to Angola, and his astounding list of contacts to ensure that the gold trucks travelled at a credible pace.

- Mart-Marie Serfontein and Albert Marais for all things legal.
- Marette and Bekker Vorster, who made sure I had all the teen slang down pat.
- Special thanks to Max du Preez, Cliff Lotter, dr. Erwin Coetzee en Helen Turnbull of the Cape Leopard Trust.

Glossary of Afrikaans Words

ag – A filler word to express irritation or resignation.

ai – Meaning Ah, oh, ow, ouch, mostly used a little despairingly.

Aitsa – An exclamation that depends on the context: ouch, hey, yippee are all possibilities.

bafana – Doing a bafana – demanding more for being mediocre. (Township slang.)

bakkie – The word all South Africans use to refer to a pick-up truck.

bliksem – Mild profanity, used as an exclamation or adjective ('Damn!' or 'damned'), or a verb (I will 'bliksem' you = I will hit you hard).

bokkie – A term of endearment (a small deer).

bossies – Bush crazy, post-traumatic stress disorder, as in mentally battle scarred in the bush war.

boytjie – Guy, young guy.

braai – South Africa's national pastime, to barbecue meat over the coals, mostly outdoors.

dagga – Marijuana.

deurmekaar – All mixed up.

dhaltjies – Deep fried chili bites, Cape Malay cuisine.

djas – Teen-age slang for 'good' or 'great'.

dominee – Minister or priest.

fokkit – Fuck it.

fokkol – Fuck all.

gatvol – When you've had enough of something. Fed up.

gooi – Literally 'throw', also used as slang for 'pour', 'speak', or 'sing'.

hayi – IsiZulu for 'No!'. (South Africa has 11 official languages: Afrikaans, English, IsiNdebele, IsiXhosa, IsiZulu, Sepedi, Sesotho, Setswana, SiSwati, Tshivenda, Xitsonga. Township slang transcends all 11.)

heito – Expression of surprise or delight.

huppel – Gambol, frisk, hop or skip.

isitina – (From the Afrikaans word for brick) – A stack of money amounting to R1000. (Township slang.)

iyamangalisa – isiXhosa for 'stunning'.

ja – Yes.

jinne – My goodness.

Jirre – Cape Flats slang for God, approximated 'Gawd'.

Jissis – A harsh version of the exclamation Jesus!

jol – To have a fun time.

kêrel – Guy.

komvandaan – Someone's origin.

knuppel – Literally cudgel, batton or cosh, also slang for male gentital.

kwaai – Literally 'hot-tempered', but widely used in Afrikaans to denote superlative degree of comparison (she is *kwaai* competent), or awe.

laaitie – From the original South African English expression 'lighty', referring to a young man, still a lightweight.

laatlammetjie – A child born many years after its siblings.

lapa – Usually, a structure built adjacent to a dwelling to facilitate a gathering around a fire. The word comes from Sotho and Tswana and means 'home'. The word Lapa can be translated into English as 'yard' (referring to both the house and the land attached), or as 'family'.

lekker – Afrikaans word widely used for anything that is 'good', 'delicious', 'tasty'. ('Lekka' is Cape Flats vernacular, 'lekker' is formal Afrikaans.)

maaifoedie – Motherfucker.

manne – Men, or guys.

moerigheid – See 'Moer' below.

moer – 'Moer' is a wonderful, mildly vulgar Afrikaans expletive, and could be used in any conceivable way. Its origins lie in the Dutch word 'Moeder', meaning 'Mother'. Being the 'moer in' means 'to be very angry', but you can also 'moer someone' (to hit somebody), use it as an angry exclamation ('Moer!', which approximates 'Damn!'), call something or someone 'moerse' (approximates 'great' or 'cool'), or use it as an adjective: I have a 'moerse' headache – I have a huge headache. 'Moer toe' means 'fucked up', or even 'dead'. 'In its moer in' is used to indicate that something is, gone or destroyed.

moerse –See 'moer' above.

mokoro – A traditional canoe-like vessel commonly used in the Okavango Delta as a popular mode of transport.

mos – Surely/evidently.

nè – Hey.

oom – Respectful Afrikaans form of address to a male ten or more years older than yourself. Means 'uncle'.

orraait – All right.

ou – Literally means 'old' in Afrikaans, but often used as a substitute for 'guy'.

oupa – Grandpa.

pappie – Daddy.

se moer – Fuck that.

skarminkels – Bad people, crooks.

skelm – A Soundrel, sly wicked.

smaak – Literally 'taste', often used to indicate a suspicion: I smaaks me he's a bad person – I suspect he is a bad person.

snoek – A long, thin species of snake mackerel found in the seas of the Southern Hemisphere, and a popular food fish in South Africa.

takkies – Running shoes, trainers.

troep – The lowest rank in the army.

troepies – Soldiers of the lowest rank in the army.

umlungu – A white South African or the boss of the company. (Township slang.)

windgatte – A 'windgat' is a braggart, windbag, or show-off. 'Windgatte is the plural form.

yebo – Township slang for 'Yes'.